T0265923

Ogden

A Tale for the End of Time

Ben G. Price

Ogden

A Tale for the End of Time

Addison & Highsmith

Addison & Highsmith Publishers

Las Vegas ◊ Chicago ◊ Palm Beach

Published in the United States of America by
Histria Books
7181 N. Hualapai Way, Ste. 130-86
Las Vegas, NV 89166 USA
HistriaBooks.com

Addison & Highsmith is an imprint of Histria Books. Titles published under the imprints of Histria Books are distributed worldwide.

Library of Congress Control Number: 2023938039

ISBN 978-1-59211-313-2 (hardcover)
ISBN 978-1-59211-328-6 (eBook)

Prelude
A Spell of Words

Dreams are the language of world building and world ending. We live in a dream built on the magic power of words and numbers. We don't just believe them. We be-live in them.

Not one of us can remember all the combinations of words and numbers that conjure an airplane, a telephone, a city or an empire as big as a continent. The formulae for materializing those apparitions are stashed away in books and files, scribbled and printed, spelled out on the page, and in the form of numbers made static by magnets held suspended in time by copper and cadmium and rare earth metals in machines ironically called "servers." All that knowledge in the gossamer of symbols that we call information informs our every thought. Like us, the synthetic world we live in is as vulnerable to extinction as a snowflake collected in a box by a child heading indoors to warm up.

We don't remember how whole we felt when we felt ourselves in — all the way in — nature. We were children then. We had not learned "better."

Now informed by the spell of history, we divide nature into parcels, resources and property. We be-live in that fantasy world and believe that everything is "better" for the surrender of our true nature to the program of progress.

Seldom do we wonder who it is better for, and who it is not good for. But clearly, it's not better for the trees, the water, the air, the soil. It is not better for anything not under the spell.

Even the few people who want to don't know how to save the nature within and without us — without casting a counter-spell to the arrangement that is killing everything. The Spell of Words that creates in our minds false memories and perceptions keeps us separated from the world as it is. The Spell holds us mesmerized. It lets us experience the world as it is mediated to us, through images and half-attended whisperings. It censors our own eyes and ears and hearts, forbidding us to find community with the world beyond the manmade. Generation following generation, we betray our own children to this necromancy.

We need a counter-spell.

Chapter I
Nativity

Upon a time once real but now forgotten...

Final trills of thunder played gently on nearby rocks, then rumbled off into the darkness. The rain was done. A troll kept watch just inside the opening of his cave. His big misshapen ears twitched at every sound, every drop of water that hit the dank cavern floor. His chest reverberated with the blast of each thunderclap that rolled past him and then bounced off the inner cave walls, then echoed back over him where he stood in the outer gallery. His ears rang with the sound of gods speaking louder than his own inner voice.

These weren't the only sounds Huth could hear as he twitched and shivered. His mate, Tibbs, was in labor and old voices came barging into his right ear from the icons tucked within cavities chiseled into the rock walls. They commanded that he stand vigil until the little troglodyte was born.

Huth looked up at the cave ceiling where, over the years, he had painted images of animal spirits. He waited to glimpse the grandmothers who spoke in his ear from the world of the dead, but they weren't there among the bison, the single-horns, the great bears and the tree-heads he'd drawn. He could hear the ancient ones, but he couldn't see them.

The voices seemed to come from the unmoving stony mouths of crude statuary in a fire-lit alcove. Their words were muffled and seemed to come from far away, but their words were dancing in the space between Huth's ears, and he could not ignore them. He felt their presence as the past crashed into the future and created the present moment. He turned his back on them and tried to silence them, but they demanded his attention no matter which way he turned.

Huth's stomach grumbled, and he belched in answer to the voices in his head. He repeated that sentiment again, adding a throaty growl to the loud gust from his mouth. He had no patience for this whole birthing thing. It was going on for far too long.

The strong smell of musk and sweat mixed on a zephyr with the aroma of earth and dampness in his big flaring nostrils. It excited and agitated him. All this bother, just to produce an heir!

"An heir to what?!! Bah!" He bellowed all of a sudden, in answer to the unspoken thought. He had nothing and wanted nothing that could be inherited, having no respect for the idea of owning things.

Huth snorted and stared into the fire. Hot tongues lapped at the surrounding cool air. At their base, red embers glowed like living rubies and as he looked their cherry light swooned into visions. Huth's eyes widened and into their dark centers poured prophetic images.

Straight-walled buildings of rust-colored brick shimmered in the fluid light of the embers. From their uninspired linearity rose up tall tubes also of brick, and out of those tubes swirled thick smoke that spun around the tongues of flame and sent sparks tumbling up into the darkness of the cave's stone ceiling. Round about the man-factories that danced in Huth's eyes were forests on fire and withering things once alive. Either from staring too long at the hot glowing visions, or from grief, tears flooded and pooled and trembled on his lower lashes.

"Ruining, ruining, ruining," he said under his breath.

Then, the voices returned and spoke more plainly in his head.

Last is first and first is last.

The baby cannot stay with you.

The past is present; the present past.

With wisdom old we will imbue

A child of Troggles, a mouth to speak
To men bewitched by their own tongue
To either break the spell so bleak
Or let them dream and die among
The dung and dross their wills create.

We will him to grow fast and learn
The ways of men both good and ill
Into his mind each day will burn
More knowledge than a score of years
Would suffice for a child to learn.
And taller than a boy can grow
Your babe within a season
Shall gaze on men as small and low
Devoid of wisdom, love and reason.

This babe away this night will flee
But you did well to birth
A son of Troggles such as he
Who soon will prove his worth.

"For what?" Huth growled. "We're dead. That's that. The days when Troggles walked free on top the ground are done. I smell somethin' rotten in yer song, old uns. What's this mischief? Take my boy from me soon as he's born, will ya? Grow him fast ta let men folk chop him down like a chestnut tree — is that yer plan?"

The only answer that came back was silence, and he knew what that meant. There would be no more talk from the dead.

And then he caught a different scent…not the muskiness of pending child-birth but the minky smell of a deer just beyond the cave opening. It was just one pounce away from becoming dinner!

A branch snapped. Shaking his head from side to side, the big troll paced near the stone archway. He wanted to shout but spat instead. His lolling tongue cracked like a whip against cheek and chin. A large wad of spittle flew through the den's opening and landed on a bush just outside.

"Bah!"

His amber eyes, unblinking, spun wildly in deep sockets shielded by a heavy brow-ridge. His eyes watered as he paced.

Leaves rustled. Huth froze. He sniffed loudly, then heaved a heavy sigh. Something was out there. It was a buck, just beyond the trees that framed the cave's opening.

The troll's belly was empty and wanted meat. He'd eaten little more than mushrooms and dandelions. He was hungry for flesh. But he could not go.

Huth grumbled a curse under his breath and spat again. "By the stone on me pappy's grave! I hungers!" He kicked a makeshift bench lashed together with bear tendons, crashing the loose boards to bits. A pile of elongated yellow, orange and purple tubers gathered the day before tumbled about in the shadows like scurrying rats. He longed to shout to his mate "Enough! Squirt the Trogglet out! I hungers, and ye not done!" But he dared not. He wouldn't tempt the Old Ones to speak again. But hunger had a voice of its own.

Any hope of capturing that buck lay in the dim prospect that the whelp would be born soon, and without another bellowing shout from Tibbs. He could see a spindly rack of antlers darting at odd angles with the birch branches just a short leap from the cave's entrance. Unfrightened, the deer paced nearer. It marked the ground with urine. The wind was in Huth's favor. But still, he could not act.

Filled with frustration, the troll pulled at a sparse crop of wiry hair on his broad, bony head, then raised his mighty fist and pounded a crude oak table with a thunderous blow. It collapsed to the dirt floor in a heap.

Huth collected himself just in time to hear the buck scampering away deep into the forest. He bellowed just as Tibbs hollered out loudly in pain.

"Agggg!"

Crushed and defeated, Huth sank to the floor, glowering first at the cave's entrance, then toward the dwelling's innermost recess, back beyond where his mate lay panting. Then he turned his gaze to the carved stone figures that had spoken softly from the darting shadows of the fire. He knew what they wanted; what they demanded. But he could do nothing to appease their insistent whispers until the little troll was launched into the world. "I'll do it; I'll do it," he muttered to the shadows quietly enough, so Tibbs wouldn't hear.

Scratching his arse the troll spat again. "She-business!" And he pointed his bony chin toward the stone figures. "And ya've gotten me mixed up. All yer big plans. Don't mean nothin' to me. Tibbs'll box me ears fer leavin' our babe ta the chances."

He stared at the shadows and wiped his nose on his wrist. He heard Tibbs moan and then fall silent.

"By the stones of me grandpappy," he bellowed loudly, "Huth will not wait forever!"

Tibbs moaned from her nest. It consisted of little more than a pile of pine boughs and dry grass, but now it was wet and briny, since her water had broken. She panted before pushing again. It had been an arduous affair and the she-troll was nearly spent. The next contraction peaked as Tibbs bellowed, punched the stony chamber wall and grunted. She stood a moment, adjusted her stance, and crouched again.

Tibbs could faintly hear the commotion Huth was making but she had other things on her mind. She was in birth's final stages. The little one was at long last making ready for its entrance. She grabbed some fresh straw and put it beneath her on the floor.

From the outer gallery Huth heard another loud grunt, then for a moment there was silence. Huth took a breath. He strained to hear some sign. When none came, he stood and kicked the shattered table, making its top spin on the clay floor a full rotation. Then he ambled unsurely back into the cave where Tibbs sat, slumped with her back against the wall and her legs spread across the cold ground.

One final thrust and it was over. A bundle of squirming life appeared on the clay floor in front of her. Tibbs collected herself then leaned forward and gave breath to the newborn, holding it in her hands and shaking it slightly until it squawked for warmth. The baby was larger and more developed than human newborns. It was a boy child, dressed in a sticky red coat from the womb.

Eyes already opened, the newborn troll looked about and settled as best he could amid the mound of straw. He was exhausted and hungry and found comfort in the makeshift bed. Tibbs finished tending to the afterbirth, licked the newborn clean, then grabbed the babe with one arm, nursing him for the first time.

Tibbs ambled from the shadows toward Huth. She was as massive as her mate but shorter and squatter. Her body was covered by a sheen of perspiration. Desperate weariness roamed in her deep-set eyes. She cleared her throat and spat into an already well-saturated pit near the far wall.

Holding out her arm, the female nodded. "Sees you he?"

Dangling by his big toe from Tibbs' fingers, the newborn swung in space. He was content, his large eyes now fixed upon his poppa.

Huth stared at the ground and seemed not to notice. Tibbs stamped her foot then grunted. She was in no mood for Huth's stubborn nature. "Sees you he?" she demanded. "Sees you he…your son…your wielder?"

Huth straightened slowly. This was his son who would one day perform the Rite of the Stones when his last day came. But now, in this moment, he shared the troll-babe's first day. Huth's eyes filled with visions of distant days…forward and past…of stones in a circle, of more otherworldly voices, of things to come, some evil, some wondrous. He shivered and spat a name that bubbled out of his guts. "Go away, Ventego!"

Tibbs took another step toward her mate. She glared at him angrily. "Huth talks a foul name. This little 'un's got days on days comin'. Let 'im hear good sounds, not foul names his first un."

Huth wiped his nose with the back of his hand and dropped his arm to swing at his side. Tibbs shoved his chest hard with her free hand and shouted. "Sees you he, Huth's wielder?" She stood glaring defiantly, waiting for the customary response. Huth's empty belly went tense, and he couldn't breathe. The words of the Old Ones caused him to hesitate. Every move he made would bring him closer to giving the child away to fate.

"This!" she shook the newborn, "this, your son!" she barked then let go her grip. The baby tumbled to the floor, landed squarely on his head then rolled to one side, unphased.

Huth scratched his chest. "'Tis son of Huth. 'Tis Huth's wielder," he said reluctantly.

Satisfied that her task was through, at least for a little while, Tibbs plucked a tuber from the scattered pile on the floor. Biting it like an apple, she turned back toward the rear of the cave.

"Go. Tell the grandmothers," growled Huth, and Tibbs turned to glare at him over her shoulder. She stepped past the low-licking flames of the fire and into the shadows where open-mouthed figures with gouged stone eyes stared back and listened for word from the world of the living. Tibbs thought she heard one of them ask: "Has the Trogglet made the crossing to your world, Troggle?"

The little troll rolled on his side and looked after his mother, then rolled back the other way, got up on a knee, and scampered on strong legs toward Huth. He latched on, wrapping himself around his father's ankle, as troll babies are wont to do.

Huth spied the little one wrapped around his leg and swatted him away. "Don't hang on me. Yer gonna get lost," he grumbled. "That's what the old uns want. But Huth ain't so sure. Stay with momma. Poppa's gotta hunt. Huth ain't deliverin' a Troggle babe to the likes of men. Not even if the trees bark and flies fly and bees be."

Rebuked, the troll babe crawled over to the ruined table and began to bite things.

Huth was still hungry and there was no need to stay. His son was playing and would be fine. Tibbs would be sleeping soon, and she'd need meat when she woke. Tibbs would hear the baby if there was any trouble.

Just then a twig snapped outside the cave. The scent of fresh buck urine wafted through the entryway.

Huth moved toward the entrance. His son scurried back to his calf and latched on once more. This time Huth didn't brush him off. He shrugged as he crept out the cave thinking, "If it's what the old uns want, Huth's got no say."

His every sense was filled and focused on only one thing now: bringing that deer down. He turned back to the cave just to yell inside and grab a sharpened antler knife.

"Off to hunting, Tibbs!" Huth shouted as he reached for his club.

"Off to sleeping is Tibbs," the she-troll bellowed as she tumbled forward onto her fresh straw mat. She knew the baby would be fine. The babe was Huth's wielder. They had a life and death destiny together. Comforted in this last enveloping thought, Tibbs began to snore.

Moonlight found its way through the thick forest, accenting the haze in the humid air. Huth stood motionless at the cave's mouth. Scrunching leaves and the sound of hooves scurrying into the woods perked Huth's senses once more.

"I hears ye…"

Huth ambled outside and covered the entrance with brush and vines. Through all this, he was unperturbed by his precious stowaway. His mind and heart, spirit and blood spoke only of the hunt.

Chapter II
A Babe in the Woods

B ranches snapped nearby. Huth's nostrils flared as they filled with the animal's scent. A doe in season. Where had the buck gone? No matter. His mouth watered.

The troll babe tightened his grip as Huth scuttled down the slope, picking his steps quickly, but carefully. Moonlight shimmered on dew-wet leaves. Holly bristles scratched the newborn as his father plowed through the underbrush. The baby moaned but couldn't be heard above the din of blood lust that pounded in Huth's ears. Clinging on for his so-short life, the little one quickly learned to duck sapling branches and stinging briars.

Up and down the dark rocky hills of rolling forest they went, leaving home far behind. Periodically Huth stopped to listen. Then he doubled his pace. He darted behind outcroppings of boulders and made himself as still as one of the rocks until he finally spotted his prey. From then on, it was a matter of how much leeway to give, how much room he'd need for a broad jump, and how quickly he could strike.

Had his son been a few weeks older, the little troll might have appreciated Huth's finesse, but for the moment everything was too new, too fast. The unknown was full of confusing shadows, sharp poking things and wonderment.

Small night creatures froze when the old troll passed, but they had little to worry about. Venison was on the menu, on the mind and just ahead.

There was the doe. She was full grown and stood not ten feet away. Huth crouched completely motionless as the nimble beauty nibbled some leaves.

Suddenly she lifted her head; ears scissored and nose twitched. She felt a presence. Four eyes were watching her. The deer tensed then started to flee but Huth was upon her.

At the moment of impact, the troll babe lost hold and flew through the undergrowth. Hellebore, lobelia and fern fronds tumbled around in a vision of whirling subdued green that, to eyes less made for the night, would have been only a gray smear. The spinning ended with a thud. He landed with his feet in the air and head on the ground, nestled between roots at the base of a great chestnut.

He pulled away a damp leaf that formed a patch over his right eye and sat up blinking. Some distance away in the middle of a circle of ironwood trees he saw his father silhouetted by a slight brightening along the hills' horizon. Huth was stamping and kicking the earth in a rage. But before the troll babe could cry out, the big troll was gone again.

The doe had managed to escape, but Huth was a relentless hunter. He would not stop until that deer was properly stalked, felled and feasted upon. He knew he'd lost the little one, and his gut knotted at the thought of Tibbs's wrath. For the briefest moment he glanced around for his son and saw nothing. For the span of one inhale, he was torn between the hunt and retrieving the newborn Trogglet. But the Old Ones had commanded him to abandon the baby in the woods, and who was he to tell them 'No?' Now seemed as good a time as any.

Huth spat another curse as he sprinted four long gates of his gnarled legs in pursuit of his meal. Then he paused. Then he ran as hard as he could, until his chest ached.

The little troll scampered after his father and kept him in sight. Huth suddenly stopped. A dry stick snapped off in another direction. The young one stopped too, in imitation. Then the sound of more snapping branches, closer, much closer.

Huth sniffed the air to be sure. To the troll babe, his father seemed to grin.

The doe pranced through a clump of mountain laurel between the elder troll and his son, stopped, then sprang like a grasshopper over a fallen tree.

Huth was right behind, followed by the fevered footsteps of his son, each step taking them further and further away from home.

Huth was beginning to lose patience when the doe stopped again. She was tired and cautious, so he waited for her to relax her guard.

The deer started munching some nearby tall grasses, periodically sniffing the air. Ghosts of danger whispered through the branches. She stopped chewing.

The doe sprang from the ground in a panic, but a great weight fell upon her. Her spine buckled under it. And though she made a valiant effort, the struggle ended quickly with a snap of her neck.

From his hiding place in a depression left by a great wind's uprooting of an old hemlock, the baby watched as his father brought the deer down. In the aftermath the forest seemed to go silent, but for the sound of Huth gnawing and chomping at his hard-earned meal.

Morning light covered the forest by the time Huth was finished with his victory meal. The heart, a dessert of sorts, he saved for last and figured to take it back to Tibbs as a kind of peace offering for abandoning her baby in the forest. He didn't care that the little troll was lost somewhere in the understory. No matter what, he trusted the Old Ones. Content, he stretched out on the ground, belched loudly and scratched his well-fed belly.

When he woke up, sinew, pink and shining in the morning light, hung from his teeth and blood painted his chin and forearms.

The sun broke past the rocky ridge above as Huth got to his feet. He spat with gusto. Grunting, he swung the carcass over his right shoulder and turned homeward. He thought he heard the old ghosts talking in his ear. They chanted like a chorus at a solstice gathering.

For now, the child departs.

Let him go; no goodbyes.

Earth's soul to him imparts

Knowledge wise, the sacred arts.

Stars sing songs across the sky.

Moon and river, tree and rock

Teach him truth that by and by

Men are deaf to, or they mock.

So his destiny is tangled

In the honesty they lack.

Don't let your nerves be jangled.

Don't look back; don't look back.

Huth lay still while the voices sang, but then he jumped to his feet fast and dusted dirt and dry grass off his hide. A tear trickled down his cheek and left a clean trail through a thin cake of dry blood on his face. He shook his head and turned to mundane thoughts.

He knew Tibbs would be hungry by now. She would like chewing on some good meat, especially after he burned it in the fire a bit. He shook off the buzzing in his ear and shifted the carcass on his shoulders as he headed back along a trail he knew well, toward his cave. He stopped a short way down the path and looked up at the sky. He half turned to look back over his shoulder. "Huth…can't," he said quietly but out loud.

Then the buzzing voice returned. It scolded. It cursed. He had never heard the Old Ones so provoked. And then he saw a stirring in the ferns and knew it to be his son. The tiny boy had kept up with him. In pride he smiled to himself and bent forward to let the carcass slide off his shoulders, over his head and to the ground. But before he had leaned forward far enough for that to happen a shrill cry rang out, like a banshee in the night. A great owl swooped down from the trees with talons stretched out in front. It plunged into the dancing patch of fern and sprang back up into the air, its wings beating hard, with a bundle that kicked its feet and whined as it went aloft.

Huth cried out. "Curse ye old 'uns! Aww, ya'd give us life then rip it right from us, would ya?" Then he saw the owl's package tumble down through the branches of a nearby tree and land on a blanket of emerald moss. At that exact moment he also heard a voice speak plainly, calmly, in his ear, like someone was standing right beside him. "You will be reunited in days to come. Worry not. Now go!"

And so reluctantly Huth shifted the weight of the deer on his back and trudged ahead through the woods, away from his son and away from his own desire.

If only the infant troll had noticed his father's leaving, he might have cried out, but he saw nothing but a swirling forest spinning in a vortex of vertigo. By the time the trees rooted themselves to one place, the baby troll had lost interest in Huth's whereabouts. Soon he was busy playing with a box turtle, spinning it around as it lay upside down, giving it another whirl when it stopped. Each time it hissed and ducked inside its shell. This game went on for quite some time with the little one poking about the turtle's back-mounted house and giggling when the creature hissed in protest.

By now Huth was well on his way up and over the hill toward home, belching contentedly. If he worried even a little that he was abandoning his son, his wielder, in the deep woods for no good reason, it would have taken the shades of the dead to keep him from turning around, dropping the carcass, and looking for the little Troggle. No, he knew for certain that the Old Ones never speak frivolously. For him, the moment of doubt and crisis was yet to come. He had to face Tibbs.

Clouds frolicked past the sun; shadows and brightness played tag on the forest floor over lichen-spotted rocks. Crows caw-cawed overhead then swooped down to fill the top of a spindly spruce tree with cackling chatter.

The little troll rose to his feet, suddenly afraid. He stumbled to the place where he'd last seen Huth. He cried out. It was a plaintive, mournful sound, its meaning unmistakable. His father was nowhere to be found but his hand-iwork was everywhere. Flies were feasting on entrails. A swarm of them buzzed about his face when he stooped for a sniff.

The little troll ran, flailing arms all about his head to shoo them away. Then he stumbled into some huckleberry bushes. He shouted an incoherent protest then hung his head. He was alone. For the first time on this first morn-ing of his life there was an unwelcome emptiness that rivaled the grumbling in his belly. Whimpering, he picked a berry and put it in his mouth. It tasted good so he ate a few more.

Then something moved, off to the right. Remembering Huth, he froze.

A fawn stood only a few feet away, its black nose haunted by the stench of death scattered at her feet. Spooked, she bolted into the crazy quilt of trees and green.

The little troll exploded into action, instinct pumping hard through his veins as he ran; legs churning, feet slapping the ground, arms pushing the air and eyes fixed on the prize.

The fawn sprinted and nimbly changed directions while her hunter barreled through the forest. He began losing ground.

Rocks, boulders and hills got in the way. They broke his stride, almost made him fall several times, but he turned each stumble into added forward momentum and recovered into a strengthening charge. Young trolls are this way. Strong and agile at the beginning.

The animal was just ahead. For a while he was chasing only the sound of its clomping hooves, and of breaking branches.

Crunching leaves and twig snaps got louder then stopped then started again. Then there seemed to be nothing to follow. No sounds. Absolute quiet. The troll babe slowed his pace to a trot, then to a brisk walk, then to an arm-swinging saunter.

He was startled when, coming upon a sun-drenched clearing, he spied the fawn. She was surrounded by high rocks all around. Defiant, she faced him, ears snipping nervously.

The tiny hunter took half a step, but the deer didn't move. Muscles tensing, the troll scampered up the dipping side of a rock, mounted its summit and with a powerful kick leapt onto the animal's back. He wrapped his arms like grape vines around its neck.

The fawn took flight, trying to throw her jockey. He held fast, bouncing up and down and sliding from one side to the other. Through branches and brambles, up ravines and over fallen trees, they headed for high country, farther and farther from kith and kin.

On and on they went, brushing past birch and evergreen, splashing through mountain brooks swollen from the rains and across puddles that spat a spray of mud that mottled the troll babe's hide like the spotting on the doe he was riding. They galloped across a wide meadow where the bright sun momentarily dominated the sky. Then back into the wood and under the canopy of trees.

They were just beginning another ascent when the troll finally lost his grip. He was dizzy from the pitching forward and back, and side to side. With a sudden jolt to the left the little troll went flying backward as the baby deer, free at last, broke for safety.

Landing was a lesson in texture. Sharp stones bit at his buttocks and scratched at his knees and elbows. He sat hard on a thistle and then a multiflora rose bush and they made long red lines along his arms and legs. Finally, he rolled to a stop.

A baby troll deprived of its mother's loving comfort feels every injury. But no bones were broken, and the few scratches would mend quickly. His poor rump was another story. It was on fire from the spurs and thorns lodged in it.

What was worse than the bruises and bumps and scratches was the aloneness. There was no one to lick his little face or smudge the dirt away. No one in the forest seemed to care, not the birds, not the turtle, not the flying or crawling bugs. He didn't know that most troll babes aren't left out in the world to fend for themselves mere minutes after being born. But there he was, and the tears welling up in his eyes weren't helping.

He got up on one knee. Here the trees were sparse, with only a few sapling pines dotting the wind-owned summit. He could see a good distance down slope to where the forest thickened with huge trunks of oak and chestnut. There wasn't a fawn in sight.

Looking up, the babe noticed vultures circling above. They stretched their wings to catch an updraft, then seemed to fall as they tucked their wings close to their bodies, then rose again as they reached to embrace the sky with expanding wings.

He was a hungry troll. Smacking his lips, he picked up a stone and tasted it with his tongue. Not satisfied, he threw it. The quartz shard ricocheted of a large gray boulder and glanced off his big toe. Pain sent him dancing on his other foot. He fell back and landed on his bottom. He felt the rose thorns and thistle stubble still lodged there and yowled.

He whimpered for a while then, spotting a smooth carpet of rich green moss, he wandered to it like a sleepwalker, curled up and closed his eyes.

Dreams came to him: Momma and Poppa and the home he knew so briefly. Then suddenly a gnarled creature with moist red eyes and limbs like rotted wood emerged from nowhere and held out his hand. Immediately, the cave and Momma and Poppa disappeared. Another place filled his sleeping mind. It was strange and lonely. In the midst of a shadowy forest, he stood alone in a broad clearing with stars hanging so thickly above him they might have been a chandelier of hanging crystals that he could almost touch. Somewhere in that wilderness beyond the veil of dreams was home.

When he opened his eyes, he tried to hold onto the better images.... of Huth, the cave and Tibbs. He could just recall their general features. He had known them too briefly. Overwhelmed with sadness, the little troll tucked his knees up to his chin and wept silently.

When no more tears would come, he stood and faced the distant peak. His parents and their rocky shelter were out there, and it was either them or their absence that called to him. So, picking a direction, the little one climbed the next hill, little knowing he was heading away from Huth and Tibbs and all things trollish and toward the world of humans.

Higher and higher he climbed. More rocks, fewer trees. More sky, less shade. His path was growing steeper. The little fellow wanted food, sleep and home. The warming sun had disappeared from the sky, behind the rising hill. Clouds with deep gray swirling innards billowed up high and rolled low to touch the treetops. Eagles fled as light flashed and a cracking boom of thunder pounded against cloud, tree, boulder and troll alike. He heard something in that rolling, grumbling sky. A voice. But he could not know yet what it said.

Exhaustion gave way to panic as the wind picked up and the thunder continued. Then the sky sent down a torrent of cold wetness. The baby troll ran, his terrified whelps marking his retreat to the shelter of a half-fallen hemlock. It shed the rain and left the soft-needled ground beneath warm and dry. There the troll babe collapsed.

When the downpour at last subsided, the orphan continued his misguided journey. There was nothing else to do.

He found a stick with a spiral twist and dropped it on a bare patch of ground near his lumpy feet. Something magical tickled his mind. The vine-twirled branch seemed to offer advice, like it was helping him choose which way to go. Its long, twirled stem severed the woods in two. Its two ends pointed in opposite directions. The stick didn't decide which way he should go. But it narrowed the choices considerably.

He noticed a hard burl of bark on one end and clean bare wood on the other, where it came to a point. He leaned over and grasped it in his strong, small hand. As he made his weary way further up the hill, in the direction the guide stick seemed to point, he leaned on it for support. Approaching twilight greeted him in the shadow of cliffs of granite, but he climbed until he reached the top and then he found where the sun had fled. It was down in a valley, brushing the tops of distant trees. It made him squint.

Heartened by the sudden change in prospects from uphill to downhill travel, he forged forward more quickly. But in his recklessness and in the fleeing light he lost his footing. After toppling head over keister down the backs of round rocks decorated in-between by purple flowered thistles, the little troll whumped into a large boulder. He sniffed the breeze then spat, much as he'd seen Huth do.

A star poked through the darkening sky. Then one by one other stars appeared and glinted above, not quite so dramatically as in his dream. He thought he heard them humming in his ears and with each new star came a different strand of music. He felt a pleasant tickle in his chest.

He stopped to rest a while and looked up. A few more stars shimmered as blue turned purple around them, but they were intermittently hidden, then uncovered by fast tumbling clouds. He heard a tinkling like water over rocks, a sizzling like flame licking green branches, a rustling like leaves tasting the wind. When he lost sight of the stars as clouds moved in, everything became quiet. He stood up and started walking again.

At first it didn't matter which way his feet were leading, so long as it was downhill. But the descent seemed to last forever. Suddenly the little one's sinking heart filled with joy. He spotted a cave behind a twisted tree trunk with moss overhanging its opening. If he had known the words he might have cried out "Home! Home at last!"

It had been a harrowing first day of life and he imagined the sweet smell of straw, his father's booming voice and his mother's warm armpit making everything all right. The sight of the cave made him sigh contentedly.

The troll babe went inside. It was dark but comfortably warm. The impenetrable shadows were filled with snores and musty odors. The troll curled up beside a hulking, sleeping form. All the day's troubles melted as he drifted off to sleep.

Then the wind shifted. It swirled into the cave. A dark bulky creature bolted upright and sniffed. Something had invaded his home...and was still here.

The outraged creature let out a fierce roar that grabbed his uninvited guest from a dream and threw him back into the world. The little troll rolled twice over his elbows and knees to the downside of the cave and sat up blinking. This was definitely not home, and this strange bedfellow wasn't Huth or Tibbs.

Though he had never seen one, the sight of a full-grown cave bear struck terror in his heart. It snarled and swiped at him with long sharp claws but missed. Enraged, it tried again.

The little troll squirmed out of reach and broke for open spaces. He could see the entryway, but suddenly it was blocked. Without thinking, the little troll bolted between his captor's furry legs to freedom.

The bear started after him with a couple of bounding gallops but stopped abruptly, sending pebbles and scree clattering down the hill. Satisfied to be rid of that horrible stench, he turned and lumbered back up to the cave.

The young troll kept running. The bear claws and teeth seemed still to be after him. When he was too tired to continue running, he slowed his pace and walked and panted. He came upon other caves formed by boulders toppled and heaped on each other but stayed well clear.

The little troglodyte felt betrayed, alone again and discouraged. He didn't notice at first, but his path wasn't descending anymore. It was getting steeper. Though he fell again and again, the young troll didn't cry. Something terrible...beyond tears...kept him moving.

Eventually the land sloped down again, and he could see trees ahead. They were a welcome sight, yielding the high ground to the rock-strewn starkness interspersed only occasionally by scrub cedars. His brow-hooded eyes sagged with weariness and the little troll trotted toward the woods in search of concealment and rest.

The little troll sniffed as he approached the tree line. His eyes saw clearly despite the dark shade. Following a well-worn deer trail he came to an ancient hickory tree with a loose hide of bark and a trunk chewed out by bugs. There he took refuge. Tangled raspberry thickets formed a barrier around the old tree and gave him cover. Red-lobed berries offered a juicy treat. Crawling belly-down along a rabbit trail, he nibbled a little fruit and curled up inside the rotting trunk. He quickly gave in to sleep.

Owls kept watch. A black snake slid through the brambles, paused for a look, and moved on. A raccoon waddled confidently toward the hollow tree but hissed with surprise and turned away. Possums and polecats foraged, their eyes glinting like jewels in the darkness. All of this was lost on the troll babe who was off in a dream, following the child-like voice of a gnome who ran out ahead of him.

As dawn drew streaks of flat-bottomed clouds across the eastern sky, night creatures finished their rounds and then birds enlivened the brief silence with song. The troll-babe slept, unnoticed beneath his makeshift canopy.

Suddenly his dream was broken like an egg by a yowling pack of dogs, and he emerged back into the world fluttering and confused. A rowdy group of men followed the dogs into the clearing, yelling "Atta boy, Barkiller!" and "Git 'em Duke!"

The hunting party tromped about near the thorn-tangled tree trunk. A squirrel dropped a hickory nut from its hands and skittered up flaking bark and flicked its tail.

Closer and closer they came, dogs and men barking and howling to one another.

"Dath! Barkiller! Over here! See what Clyde's got."

"Yelp! Yelp!" The dogs all circled around, then Clyde got belly-down to the ground and tunneled into the thorny profusion of raspberry branches.

The little troll recoiled from a dog's probing wet nose giving a rude nudge to his arse. The hound sniffed and barked. Panic-stricken, the little troll could see no way out. A second dog appeared in front of him, head down and barking. Dogs and men moved in. Barkiller and Dath barked and yowled.

"What ya got there? Somthin' under th' brush?" Argis cried out.

"Yelp! Yelp!"

"Oh, aye! Git out o' the way boys! I canno' see nothin' wit ya jumpin' about. Here! Here now! Quieten down!"

Another man slapped the backs of the dogs with a leaf covered branch and when he could, he pulled the dogs back by the scruff of the neck until they heeded.

"Git o'er here. Good dog! Good Boy!" The stubborn ones that wouldn't listen got chased out of the way. "Git on now, Duke! Push off! Push off!" Barkiller stood near his master, obedient but ready to pounce.

"Now, let's see wha's causin' all the fuss." Argis crouched and peered through a tunnel of vines and brambles. Large black eyes stared back.

Clyde, the largest of the blue tick hounds and Jocko, a clay-colored blood hound with half a right ear, moved back in for a closer look. "Pull 'em back," shouted Argis with annoyance, ".... or I'll beat tar from their hides!"

The little troll sniffed, sticking his nose out from under cover of the shadows and, seeing that the dogs had backed away, he dared venture a right foot beyond the confines of the curling, brittle bark that was peeling away from the stump.

Barkiller, a golden long-haired mutt, launched himself back into the thicket. The troll whelp tumbled forward and out of the hickory trunk. He scampered through the berry brambles and straight at Argis. Out toward a flattened carpet of long grass he headed but tripped and sprawled flat out. He looked up at Argis' trousered legs.

"Well, I'll be! If that ain't a troll! I must be sleepin' wit me eyes open!" said Argis.

Several men swore under their breaths. Trolls hadn't been seen in these parts for four generations. Some claimed they still roamed the far hills. Old stories said they were nothing but trouble, so whenever there was unexplained mischief, trolls took the blame. Only three weeks past, a spate of attacks on livestock was attributed to a marauding band of trolls, even though it was most likely the work of wolves.

"Git outta th' way, ya damn mutt!" yelled Argis as Clyde moved in again. "Grab th' ropes an' have a sack ready! Be quick," he shouted over his shoulder to one of the men.

"Ya gonna take it alive?" puzzled the old quarry worker, Tom.

"Oh, aye! Master Drowden's gonna pee his pants!" cackled Argis.

In no time the men had their captive snared about the neck, waist and legs with hemp rope. The little troll cried out, but his protests only excited the men more.

"Little bugger, ain't eee?" Nith Piegel gasped. He'd feared trolls all his life, though he'd never seen one. What he really feared was what everyone said about trolls. He kept his distance, rubbing his bare bald head all the while.

The men dragged the roped troll along the forest floor a short distance, laughing and imagining as loudly and wildly as imagination can conjure, what people would say when they brought home a live babe o' the woods — a troll babe.

The little being was roundly mocked as the men pulled a burlap bag over its head and tied it closed. "Cinch it tight!" Nith ordered.

"Do ya think we'll get a reward fer it, Argis?" Bill Macatee beamed.

"Won't matter if we don't get us some rabbits and quail. A deer would be even better," answered Argis.

Bill nodded then called out to the other men, "Check them traps we set! We need somethin' ta show that ol' kitchen witch! And get those arrows flyin'!"

Over what was left of a brightening morning and an afternoon full of diligent hunting and trapping they made up for lost time, bagging several rabbits and two deer that traveled unluckily together and died the same way. Master Drowden Erebus would be pleased, and so would Odelia, the congenial queen of the kitchen, who swore there'd be an end to what she called "bone stew" when after the last hunt they'd come back with just a pheasant and a few squirrels.

As afternoon fizzled into evening, the troll babe began squirming violently within his confines and almost broke free. "Oh no ye don't!" Argis threw himself on the sack. "Fred! Bill! More rope!"

Small, gnarled brown hands shot out from everywhere, poking holes in the twisted burlap, but with Argis pressing his whole weight down and three men busy wrapping rope around both ends and a hoop of twine around the middle, there was no room for their prisoner to move.

Argis told the Bigworth brothers, Bobbin and Harry, to carry the sack between them, and then he pushed his way past the others to the head of the procession through the forest. "Keep them dogs in check!" he called over his shoulder.

They picked through the undergrowth, talking excitedly, with Fred and Bill carrying one deer lashed to a pole, and Nith and Tom carrying the other the same way.

"Hurry on, lads!" shouted Bobbin, his squeaky voice crackling through the words. "Master Erebus'll be havin' guests at his table in the mornin' an' if we don't get there soon, we'll be up all night dressing out the venison!"

"Don't be a turd, Bobbin Bigworth!" Argis chided, "The Master'll forget about breakfast an' guests once he sees what we got. Now, git yer back into it. I'll knock the teeth out of ya wi' me knuckles if ya let our troll escape!"

It was a three-mile trudge down out of the hills and across a boggy creek-bottom toward a grove of small trees. The Bigworth boys wrestled their booty through a sun-drenched stand of short dogwoods to the clearing where the buckboard and horses stood waiting. Once their bagged treasure and the slain game were secured in the wagon, the men and the dogs piled onboard. With a triumphant hoot they rolled along a pitted and rocky road through the forest.

In three hours, the hunting party was in sight of Hapstead Manor. The sun had dipped behind the hills in the west, but the sky was still bright. Argis reined the horses for a moment and then gave them a husky "Ya!" as they neared the gates. Once inside the yard, he drove the cart rightward toward the barn and jumped back into the wagon.

"Nith! Bill! Tend the horses! Harry! Run in an' fetch Master Drowden! Don't say nothin' 'bout what we found! Just tell 'im he's gotta come see somethin' wondrous. Don't ferget the wondrous part."

He shoved the sack of rabbits toward the rear of the cart. The dangling deer carcasses lolled off the back end, dripping blood that the dogs lapped up eagerly.

Argis hollered to Bobbin as he scurried across the yard toward the summer kitchen. "Bobbin! Git back here an' help git these deer ta Odelia. She'll want 'em butchered right away!" He pointed with his eyes to Willbee. "Grab the rabbits an' take 'em too."

In ten minutes Argis watched Harry trot back from the Manor House, out of breath. "The Master is busy, he says."

The troll babe was struggling within his bindings, rolling about the wagon-bed, kicking and thrashing. Argis swore, "Go back an' tell 'im it's important. Tell 'im it's of peculiar interest!"

Harry shook his head. "You know the Mistress don't like me. She said to come back later. She said he's too busy."

Argis threw himself on top of the rambling gunny sack. "You git in there and tell 'im we got us a troll! Make 'im hear, got that? Don't tell the Mistress. You've gotta talk ta Master Erebus. Tell 'im we got us a troll…! Just tell 'im! Now!"

Chapter III
A Guest of the Manor

Argis leaned back to catch his breath, grateful that the burlap sack had stopped jigging across the wagon bed. Drowden Erebus never came. Harry couldn't get past Dorina Erebus, so he came back, listened to Argis cuss a while, and then curled up in the back of the wagon with the burlap bag between him and Argis.

Argis did his best to sleep through the night right there in the buckboard, next to the whimpering and flailing bundle. Whatever kept Drowden Erebus from coming down to the yard yesterday must have been very important, he thought. Or else that no-good idiot Harry hadn't tried hard enough to get past Mistress Dorina.

"Never mind," he thought. "Master Drowden is gonna like his prize Aye. He won't mind interruptin' his breakfast fer this!"

He pulled an old and chipped bulldog pipe out of his pocket and thumbed a plug of dark tobacco into the bowl. He was just about to light it with a wooden match when the little troll started struggling again. The sack rolled about like it was filled with snakes.

"Be still! Damn thing!" Argis shouted testily.

It had been twenty minutes since Argis planted a foot in the small of Harry's back to wake him and chase him back to the house to again try to get Master Erebus to come see what they'd brought him. He gave Harry orders not to come back without him.

Argis climbed up to the driver's bench and glanced over his left shoulder. The bag rolled from one side of the wagon to the other and Argis landed a heel hard on the footboard. "Be still! Respect a man's smokin' time. Set quiet!"

He thought about Harry's habit of dawdling in the scullery, then he cursed. The troll moaned and kicked hard, sending a toe through the fraying burlap. Argis called to a stable hand he saw crossing the yard. He figured it was Willbee by his lanky gait. "Willbee! Git ta the Manor House an' find out what's keepin' Harry an' th' Master, before this thing breaks loose!"

"What!" Willbee yelled, trotting over and peeking into the buckboard. "You still got that troll baby in a bag? You ever gonna let it out?"

"Yer gonna see 'em soon enough…" Argis chided. "Providin' Master Erebus an' slowpoke Harry git back before our prisoner 'scapes on us! Grab me a snare!"

Willbee grabbed the only thing he could find, a rope from around his waist, and tossed it to Argis, who looped it around the writhing bundle and cinched it tight. "Go an' git Harry!"

Willbee gave the sack another look. "I need my belt!"

"Since when did ya begin carin' if yer pants're on or off?" growled Argis. "Cinch 'em over yer belly and run! Jus' don't trip up when they furl about yer ankles."

Gathering his pants about him and clenching the too-big waistband in his fist, Willbee looked down at his skinny middle. "I ain't got a belly, Argis."

Argis just nodded with one eye pinched and Willbee scampered toward the house. Halfway up the packed clay path he lost his grip and his drawers dropped flat to his ankles.

"I didn't trip!" he hollered, looking backward across his shoulder to make sure he caught Argis' eye. Then he bent over and wiggled his butt at Argis, who shouted a profanity. He hoisted up his trousers and ran double-time to the house.

The troll lay motionless. As milky bursts of smoke ballooned up from his pipe, Argis stole a few minutes to think what he liked to call "big thoughts" about his life, the people in it, and his place in theirs. That pretty much meant Hapstead Manor and everyone there. That and some friends at the pub in Irongate.

It was going to prove a very interesting morning, he told himself. But then again, working at Hapstead Manor was usually interesting one way or the other, especially since Drowden Erebus had come to wed the mistress however many years back. Must be going on twenty, he realized.

Drowden Erebus swung the door open that Harry had let swing shut as he ran out ahead. "Harry, tell Argis I've got people to meet on business over at the bullpen. I'll see what he wants as soon as I'm through!" He couldn't tell if Harry had heard him.

Drowden was the son of a scrivener, an ink squeezer, Argis would call him, and he inherited his father's love of books. Drowden had the sense to marry into wealth. Though lowborn, he was well read and put what he learned to practical use. His keen understanding of crops and animal husbandry, along with a shrewd business sense that seemed to come naturally, gave him an edge over the competition when he was courting Fligard and Hesprina Mofely's only child.

The beautiful rolling hills of Hapstead Manor and the fine gabled Manor House were a source of family pride. The Manor's rich soil yielded never-failing crops of wheat and corn and barley. A respectable herd of oxen, plus a yard full of penned hogs, a chicken coop to rival any in the district, and even a small flock of prize angora goats were just enough to keep the covetous neighbors a little in awe.

Few men would be given the opportunity to pursue both the hand of Dorina Mofely and the inheritance of Hapstead Manor. And the bookish commoner who came to work for Fligard Mofely, Drowden Erebus, did not promise to be the exception, at first. But when, after only two years as assistant foreman on the farm, he was entrusted with its overall management, it became clear that there was something special about him. Though lacking a pedigree, he was eminently suited to administer a prosperous estate.

The Mofely's had no son, and they came to like no man better than Drowden Erebus for his comfortable mastery of all farming skills and his honest accounting of everything. Besides, in two years' time it was also very clear that Dorina loved him and would take no other for a husband.

Erebus seemed in no hurry to wed, wanting to prove his worth first. He won over the master of the house by doubling the assets of Hapstead Manor within a handful of seasons. When the way seemed clear, Erebus lost no time courting Dorina and winning her hand.

When Fligard Mofely fell ill in the seventh winter after Dorina became Drowden's bride, Drowden was given full reign over its operations. The years as Master of the Manor brought Drowden Erebus a share of respectability in social circles that once would have shunned him.

He still made time for a weekly card game in the field hands' bunkhouse. Dorina didn't understand his continuing attachment to the coarser things and only barely tolerated the fraternization. As for the men in the bunkhouse, they thought it a great treat to have his company.

Off sitting in the buckboard Argis smiled when he thought about the Master of Hapstead Manor and the jokes he shared on card night. That was a rare privilege for a callous-handed plow pusher.

Drowden Erebus' other favorite pastime was the study of trolls. As a young boy, Drowden heard the stories, as everyone had. But after he saw one with his own eyes the stories became animated in his mind — no longer flat and lifeless fables. It was from a distance to be sure, but he knew instantly that the shadowy figure lurching across the field against a purple twilight sky was a troll. And he'd tell anyone who'd listen, even to this day, how he had tried to follow it into the wood.

Last night's dream was still running around in the daylight of Drowden's wakefulness. Through the years he had collected books, parchments and anything else that helped him understand trolls as living, breathing creatures. He sensed that there was more to them than the stories of their hiding under bridges and turning to stone. From what he'd been able to gather, Drowden suspected that trolls might have a rich culture and things worth learning.

He hoped one day to devote more time to his avocation, but for now he contented himself by cataloguing everything he could. He secretly prized his collection of troll lore more than his respectable achievements. And every now and then he'd dream, as he did last night, about meeting a troll. But this one was a very odd dream. It felt different, and it left him with a sense of premonition.

Argis smiled to himself as he spotted Drowden coming down the stone path from the house. "Wait 'til he sees what I've got," he said excitedly under his breath. But then Drowden turned toward the front of the house and peeked inside a carriage that had arrived only moments before. Argis yelled out "Master Drowden!! I gotta show ya somethin' important!"

Drowden waved backward and called over his shoulder "In a while, Argis."

Drowden had business with Nathan Bladic and Ospin Tapple, wealthy businessmen from Irongate. They'd brokered the manor's purchase of a prize bull and were there to deliver it. From the library window he had seen them roll up the lane, and he dashed down the hall, and out the door past Harry. They were already out of their carriage and the bull had been penned by his men, so he quickened his steps toward the barnyard to greet his guests.

Argis tamped his pipe with an ash-blackened thumb then checked on the sack in the cart bed behind him. He sputtered a profanity and blew a big cloud of smoke out his nose and mouth.

Suddenly, the ruckus began again. The bag rolled across the floorboards from side to side, bumped up against the tailgate, then rumbled back to its original station. Springs squeaked and splinters flew. "They best git here soon," the foreman huffed, "lest that critter break fer th' hills!"

Up at the Manor House kitchen breakfast was in the works. Odelia stood at the stove, turning griddle cakes with a spatula as hickory cured bacon snapped and sizzled in a big iron pan. Wafts of steam carried the aroma into the house.

Upstairs, Drowden's maiden daughter, Miranda Erebus, yawned and stretched. Her bare feet hit the cool wood planks of the floor, casting any remnants of sleep free from their moorings. The sun shone bright through lace curtains. They'd been her mother's as a young girl, and until recently were Miranda's favorite.

She'd grown to be quite the contrarian of late, finding fault with everything and everyone...most of all, herself. Mother called it growing pains and assured her it would pass. For days a dark cloud of melancholy had loomed overhead, but this morning the storm seemed to have passed and she felt light as a feather.

She dressed and lilted down the hallway, whistling a lilting tune until she got to the staircase. Mother would not approve, she said to herself. "Ladies don't whistle," she could hear her saying sternly. With a giggle she reached for the banister. Ian slid down the long handrail just last week, and she was half tempted to give it a try. But Mother wouldn't hear of it. So she looked over her shoulder and smiled playfully, descending two steps at a time. Then she jumped the final three to the landing that turned the stairway to the right.

Triumphant, Miranda pivoted on the ball of her foot and jumped again, clear to the parlor floor just as Willbee crossed her path. They landed in a crumpled heap on the ornate carpet.

"Whuuuuuh!"

"Willbee!" the young girl blushed. "What are you doing here?" Miranda righted herself against the stair post.

"Lookin' fer Master Erebus," Willbee stammered. He was flustered and, to tell the truth, infatuated. He could barely stand to be in the same room with Miranda. He held his britches up despite the collision, much to his amazement and relief. "Is he about? Harry came lookin' an' I came lookin' for Harry so I guess I'm mostly lookin' for Master Erebus, Miss Miranda!"

The young girl pursed her lips then smiled flirtatiously, just as Dorina shuffled into the foyer. She frowned at her daughter for being so familiar with the servants.

"Willbee!" she called sharply. "You're getting mud on the carpet!"

"Sorry, ma'am," the shaken young man bowed. "I need ta find the master."

Dorina sighed as she pulled on the servant's bell cord. "Well then, can't you come in through the kitchen?" She glanced at the fist that held the gathered waist of his pants and blanched a moment. But she held her tongue.

Jada the housekeeper scurried to her mistress' side. "Yes, ma'am?" Without further comment, she curtsied then stooped and brushed at the soiled rug with a whisk. Miranda rolled her eyes and thought of going back up to her room but decided that would only create more problems. Better to say she stumbled on the stairs and get on with breakfast than spend the whole day at odds with her mother.

"My husband is tending to business, as you should be, Willbee," Dorina said, turning away from her daughter a bit pointedly. "He's with Masters Bladic and Tapple, out by the bull pens I should think."

"Oh, aye." Willbee looked to the floor. "Best I find him then." Bowing to both women with one hand firmly on his trouser waist band, he left.... adding more dirty footprints to the rug. Mother and daughter went in for their morning meal with only a halting explanation from Miranda. Jada stooped and stepped forward as she swept along Willbee's path out the door.

Willbee raced out the door, down the porch steps and back over to the wagon. "Can't find Harry! He's naught inside. Neither's Master Erebus! They say he's gone to buy a bull!"

Argis jumped up. "I know. I just seen 'im not a minute ago. And worthless Harry. And now you. Can't deliver a simple message."

"Over there." Willbee pointed to the other end of the yard, "Over to the bull pen with Master Tapple and Master Bladic. That's where Master Drowden's gone."

Argis rubbed his eyes. "I know an' I'm done waitin'," he said. He sat forward on the seat and grabbed the horses' reigns. Then he snapped them to action with a hearty "Hayahh!"

The wagon jolted forward then stopped. Hard. He'd forgotten to release the brake. A yowl came from the burlap bundle in the back as it slid hard against the front board. Argis just barely managed to stay on the wagon. He spat and swore under his breath, "Bile, black an' fragrant!"

Grabbing the brake handle, he released it and called to the horses again. "Ye Ahh. Hayahhhh!" The horses exploded into a gallop across the yard. Will-bee darted out of the way as the wagon rumbled past. "Woah! Woah!" Argis cried, pulling the tethers tight to his chest.

"Woah, ye turkey offal! Woah!" The horses didn't respond to Argis' commands until they had run past the bull pen. Argis knew he'd hear an earful from Nathan Bladic, who found fault in everything a working man did.

The Master and his guests were discussing the lineage of the new bull. Erebus looked up as Argis regained control of the wagon. Ospin Tapple glanced wicked brows his way. "Seems to be something wrong with that man."

Drowden rubbed his chin. "...let's see what's the ruckus."

Argis reined the horses to a halt, and just to show who was in charge, tried to make them back up to the gate, rather than turning the wagon around. But the horses had other ideas and lurched forward again. The burlap bag with its squirming contents rolled backward, clean over the tailgate and to the ground with a thud and a grunt.

Yard dogs flew from their kennels, hoping to get a good sniff of what was in the squirming bag, but Argis was standing over it in seconds with a raised stick. "Back now, ya buggers! Back, an' I mean it!"

Old Piscote trotted out from his tool-sharpening chores. He thought it must have been a bag full of snakes wriggling at Argis' feet. His handy way with vipers was legend. When the local boys cornered a coiler, he'd let them have their fun for a while, but it was always his job to finally capture the creature.

As he eyed the moving bag on the ground behind the wagon, he was certain the hunters had dragged in a nest of wigglers. But it only took a minute for him to realize the day's catch wasn't a knot of nice clean snakes. The stench was awful!

Argis jumped down and herded the sack with his stick so the left back wagon wheel and a fence post cornered it. "Stay still, ya bugger!"

Piscote offered to get some more rope. Willbee came trundling up, a fresh cinch round his trousers and an apple in his mouth. Just then a fierce cry came from the burlap bag. The little creature lunged and smashed repeatedly into the post. Argis dove on top to stop the troll from dashing its life out before meeting the Master.

"Git more rope!" Piscote cried as he helped steady the parcel. The stench nearly took his breath away. "Whatever ya have in this satchel is a champion farter!"

"Oh, aye!" Argis agreed, "that ain't the half of it!"

Willbee shook his head and pulled the rope from about his waist and tossed it toward the huddle of men. It was just barely enough to secure the bag to the fence post. The captive inside began struggling again. Argis raised his cudgel for a silencing blow but was stopped mid-stroke.

"What have you there?" Drowden Erebus held the stick fast in his raised hand. "And what smells so bad?" Argis released his grip and stood up straight. He was smeared with mud, sweat, straw and feces from head to toe. Nathan Bladic and Ospin Tapple stayed a safe distance, listening intently.

Tapple gasped at the stench and reached for the tin of snuff in his waistcoat pocket. He pinched some to his nose. "Whatever died should be buried!" he shouted in his high-pitched voice.

Argis bowed slightly to the guests and accepted a rag from Piscote. Wiping his forehead, he spoke to Drowden. "Fergive th' fuss, Master Erebus. May I speak wid ya?" Drowden nodded to pardon himself and then moved off a little with his foreman.

"We caught somethin' special yesterday mornin', sir," he said once they were free to speak without being overheard.

"Special, how? A wild boar? We haven't had a wild tusker in months, but this one's rather small. Maybe we should give it a chance to fatten up, eh Argis? Why don't you take it to the high meadow and let it go free."

Drowden turned to go but Argis stopped him. "No sir. Nothin' like that. You wouldn't want ta eat what's in that bag."

Drowden Erebus shook his head impatiently. "I have unfinished business. What is in the bag, Argis? Out with it."

"Well sir, it's a...."

Just then they heard Ospin Tapple shriek "It's loose! It's loose! Eeeeeeee!" as he ran toward the house.

Suddenly the bull let out a tremendous roar. He began stomping and getting ready to charge. The bull shook his great horned head menacingly. Reeling around in a full circle he bellowed again.

Argis paled under the layer of filth and took off in the direction of the bullpen.

"It's in there!" Willbee pointed to the far end. The bull was turning to face its hapless guest, poising to charge. Willbee ran to the barn and scampered up a ladder and into the hay loft.

Drowden was at Argis' heels. "Back that bull off!" he called to the assembled ranch hands who scrambled into action with ropes and prods. As the dust settled, Nathan Bladic made his way over to the yard. Ospin Tapple came back down the hill he'd run up for safety and surveyed the scene.

"See? Over there?" Argis pointed. Drowden looked to the furthermost corner.

Drowden gasped. "Argis, it's a...."

"Aye, sir. It's a troll! A little fighter if ever there was!"

Drowden Erebus' heart skipped a beat. "A troll!"

"That's ridiculous!" Tapple hissed. "There are no more trolls in these parts. We ...that is, they are all dead."

Bladic rubbed his chin as if remembering one of the old tales he'd heard. "Maybe it's turned to stone! Just like in the stories!"

"Oh! Aye!" Old Piscote recalled the same tales. "That's the way I heard it! Safe in that sack against the curse but goes to stone in the morning light."

Drowden shook his head at their ignorance. He ran to the outside far corner of the coral, with his men following behind. He stepped up to the corner fence post for a closer look, but as he looked down over it, he could only see the creature's back.

The bull protested madly at being tied on a short lead to the opposite end of the yard. Undaunted, Drowden leaned over the crossbeam for a better view. The troll was hunched in a ball, trembling.

Looking up at this new stranger, the little one let out a shriek. Tears splashed down his face.

"Why, it's just a baby!" Drowden Erebus called over a shoulder. "Frightened half to death, but alive and I think unhurt."

The bull let out an angry snarl. Ropes snapped and twanged. Hands burned and bled. Breaking free his restraints, it charged. Harry leap-frogged over the animal's back to get out of its way and tumbled into a bale of hay. Piscote was on his back in the dirt. Argis was pinned under Piscote. Drowden looked up as he heard the steer thundering across the pen. He didn't have time to climb over the fence to grab the little troll.

Just then a storm of straw swirled down from the hayloft overlooking the bullpen and Willbee flew out, arms flailing and mouth caterwauling like a hill yodeler. He flapped down like a goose making an ungraceful landing, spun away from the charging bull, bent low as he ran and scooped the little troll into his arms, then tossed him over the fence and into the arms of Drowden Erebus, just in time to get a foot up on the fence rail and launch himself back into the air from where he'd come, and over the topmost rail.

The cross rail that had a moment before supported Willbee's foot snapped as the rampaging bull pounded the fence with his head. Drowden wrapped

his arms tightly around the little troll and recoiled back from the fence. Willbee tumbled head over heels and bounced back to his feet. Somewhere in the
tumble he had lost his trousers. His bare rump seemed to gleam in the sun.
But only for the moment it took him to bolt off behind the barn and out of
sight, leaving a baffled Ospin Tapple to wonder what he'd just seen, and an
astonished Nathan Bladic with the raw material for a sensational story to tell
at the gentlemen's club.

Harry, Argis and Piscote lassoed the steer and confined him to a smaller
pen. Erebus made a quick check of himself and the little troll. No abrasions,
no broken bones, but both needed a bath.

From a distance up the hill toward the house, Ospin Tapple squealed over
his shoulder, "That bull was brought to you unharmed! A deal is a deal; troll
mischief be damned!"

"Yes, of course." Drowden replied in an impatient shout. Then he turned
to Bladic, and to his workers. He nodded. "Perhaps you will excuse me. As
you can see, I have my hands a bit full with new business."

He wanted the world to vanish, for everyone to just go away so he could
have time to get acquainted with his woodland guest. The little troll struggled
forcefully against his tight grip, but Drowden held on.

"Well," snorted Nathan Bladic, "my business here is done, and I have no
interest in breathing another breath near that slop-coated monstrosity. Tapple
apparently agrees. We will be leaving without delay."

Ospin Tapple was scrambling across a grassy hill to the hooded wagon he'd
arrived in. The driver stood nearby and jumped up behind the still hitched
horses. Tapple leapt into the carriage and waited for Nathan Bladic to join
him.

"We are leaving," he muttered nervously to no one. "A troll. By all that's
right, what's a troll doing at Hapstead Manor?"

"I insist you stay to freshen up," Drowden cried out, finally remembering
his manners. Nathan Bladic kept walking away from him and waved the back
of his hand.

"I insist you stay! Go to the Manor House. Have Jada show you to the library for a morning eye-opener. I'll join you before you reach bottom. Then we'll have breakfast. Dorina is expecting you. Let's not disappoint her."

Bladic climbed into the carriage, and then both men leaned their foreheads together to talk. Tapple popped his head out the window and tipped his hat. He whispered in a high, squeaky voice to Bladic, "I want to get out of here, now!"

"Well, I'm famished," Bladic laughed. "So let's forget about the Trog and settle up with Erebus. I want to get paid, and I want to eat."

He reached out the window and tapped the carriage below the driver's foot. "We're staying," he said. "Ride to the big house and park out front." He turned to Tapple and smiled. "I'd like to clear the dust from my throat before we make for Irongate." Then he cried out as the carriage lurched forward, "Drowden! We expect not to be kept waiting!"

The horses sped up the hill with the men inside yelling at each other. Ospin Tapple bellowed profanities that a gentleman wouldn't allow to be heard in polite company.

"Argis! Be quick!" yelled Drowden. "We need to wash up and confine that little troll. I'll get rid of our guests as quickly and gently as I can."

Argis called to Odelia who stood fists on hips at the kitchen door. He yelled for several pails of water and some fresh clothes. She ducked inside and grabbed two boys by the shoulder and sent hold of both bucket handles and sent the boys back to Odelia. He walked along with Erebus a few paces toward the barn. The little troll, to both their amazement, was breathing deep gulps of sleep and snoring gently in Drowden's arms.

"Sorry 'bout the mess an' the ruckus," said Argis.

"Nonsense, man," Drowden chuckled. "You've brought me a troll. A real, live troll." He nodded for Argis to put the bucket down and leave his fresh clothes by the barn door.

"Help me stall for time while I find a place for this sweet creature where he'll be safe and can't escape. Then I'll wash quickly, change and meet those dandies at the house. Go on up ahead of me and pour them a tumbler of clover mead. Tell Dorina I sent you and don't be turned away. Give them both a hemp stick to smoke. I'll be along directly."

Drowden trudged off toward an empty wire kennel in the far corner of the barn where last winter he had nursed an old wolf back to health that he'd found near death along his favorite hiking trail. That's where he deposited the little troll, on a thick mound of straw. "I'll be back soon," he promised the sleeping troll babe.

Drowden bathed with the cool well water and a brick of lye soap. He stripped and dressed as fast as he could and checked on the little troll one more time.

Bladic and Tapple were already enjoying their second tankards of mead when Drowden bound up the front stairs and entered by the main foyer. Breakfast had been served in the dining room, and the plates were just being cleared. Lady Dorina skittered about, trying to keep her husband's guests entertained with empty gossip.

"Ahh, Drowden!" Nathan set his cup on an ornate side table. "Your wife has been entertaining us with her stories of domestic comedy. All is well with your new acquisition, I trust?"

Drowden half nodded conspiratorially. It seemed Bladic had not mentioned the troll to Dorina. It was an unexpected friendly gesture. Tapple seemed unusually closed-lipped. His receding forehead rippled with the tide of some inner gravity. Drowden nodded approvingly toward his Dorina and smiled.

"Thank you love," he said to her. And to his guests: "She has a gift. Yes Nathan, I'm quite pleased. The bull is a fine specimen. Thank you kindly for your part in its purchase. I'll have your commission sent to you through my man in Irongate."

He poured a tall cup of mead for himself, glad for the biscuit and bacon sent to him from the kitchen by Jeda. Dorina curtsied and left with no more comment.

"Are you gentlemen ready for a refill?"

Tapple drained his glass and held it out with a flat "Much obliged!" Bladic brought his over for a refill with feigned reluctance.

"Gentlemen," Drowden raised his cup, "today we toast to luck and to fortune! I have a new bull. But more importantly, I have a troll." He raised his cup. "Here's to luck and fortune!"

Ospin Tapple reluctantly raised his drink and touched cups with him, saying "This is no luck. It's an ill omen. A troll can only bring curses and disaster. I raise a glass to you and your family but with a friendly warning. That troll cub is going to become a big, brawling Trog the likes of which haven't been seen since...since the last time. Some of us won't tolerate a troll."

Nathan Bladic shook his head. "No," he said. "That's a horrible toast!"

"Why so sharp about this, Tapple?" Drowden lowered his drink. "Ill omen you say. Won't tolerate it? Why is that?"

Tapple replied, smiling insincerely. "Trogs, excuse my vulgarity, trolls are shadow-men, immune to being civilized and utterly dangerous around women. They are tricksters, despite being mentally slow. They can never be trusted. I doubt they can even speak, but only grunt and howl at the moon."

Drowden frowned disapprovingly. "That's all? Just rumors and hearsay? And . . . we don't use that word in this house," he said.

"Let's stop this unpleasantness," Bladic piped in. Then he cleared his throat. "Allow me to say a few words to make this right!"

Tapple shook his head doubtfully, but Drowden picked up the pitcher of mead and filled all three glasses to the brim.

"Very well. We are ready. So hear me," said Bladic. "I propose to wager fate and fortune. Let chance show me to be a fool or a wise man."

"What a queer toast," Drowden interrupted.

"Well let me continue," said Bladic. "Tapple says a troll is no good omen. I've heard him say letting them live puts nature out of balance . . ."

Tapple shot a glance at Bladic and tried to kick his foot surreptitiously, but nicked Drowden's ankle instead.

Drowden winced slightly but laughed and raised his glass all the higher. "Take heart, Ospin! It sounds like a friendly wager in the making. Name the challenge, Bladic! Name the challenge and the stakes!"

Bladic paused to catch Drowden's gaze with his own. "Very well; here it is. Do you think you can tame that troll?"

Drowden considered, swirling the suds in his cup idly. "I do. Yes. If what I know of them is true, trolls are intelligent. Say they are uncouth, but dull brutes they are not. They live beneath the illuminating sphere of mind as surely as do men."

"Hmmm...." Nathan rubbed his chin. "That seems unlikely. Can you teach it to speak?"

Drowden pondered this for a moment. But he blurted out, "I believe it can be done."

"Well," Bladic laughed, "are you willing to place a wager on it?"

Again, Drowden paused. He didn't know what overcame him at the moment, but heard himself say, "I mean to do it."

"Wonderful!" Bladic cheered. "Now, let's toast!"

"Not so fast!" Ospin Tapple chided. "If you want me to be a witness to this gamble, then we need a time frame, else the wager would be held forever in a sea of excuses."

All three men laughed.

"But seriously. You can't teach a brute animal to speak!" said Ospin Tapple. "Bladic wants you to try. You should refuse such an impossible challenge!"

Drowden studied his guests. He felt sure that they knew very little about trolls. And he thought himself rightly the expert among them. He had a moment's trepidation, but it passed and was forgotten.

"I may very well succeed, Ospin. Trolls are not mutes by nature."

"I'll grant you that," Bladic replied. "I've heard they mutter under their breaths constantly. But they're beasts just the same. Might as well try to teach your new bull to recite poetry!"

Tapple was tired of waiting for the formal toast, so he took a long swallow. The mead went down sweet and smoothly to his toes and then rebounded toward his noggin.

"No need to be silly," scolded Tapple. "A bull reciting poetry or a troll able to talk. Both equally absurd. Can we forget this nonsense?"

"Ospin, I know my books! What are the terms of this wager, Nathan?" Erebus drank then brought the pitcher up for another pour.

"Splendid. Let's sit and talk of terms over another cup," Nathan Bladic slurred a little. Once reseated away from the main table, the three men leaned in from their high-backed upholstered chairs over a low serving table. Drowden took them into confidence.

"I hesitate to tell you this, but I've been having portentous dreams about trolls. I had a dream about a young troll who turned into a caterpillar and then morphed into a butterfly, right in front of my eyes. Laugh if you like, but having this young whelp show up here today gives me reason to think anything is possible."

"And now you think it reasonable to believe in your dreams!" laughed Bladic. "Look, there's no history of trolls growing that fast. It's just a fairy tale. But if you want to base a wager on pipe dreams and nonsense, then I'm feeling particularly lucky."

Drowden held up a hand and fluttered his eyes. "I don't know why I believe it's true but here's what I know. The troll will grow faster than a puppy grows into a dog, from a troll babe into a full-sized troll. So fast, in fact, that I'm certain he should be able to speak intellig….able…..intelligibly," he stammered, "before a stalk of this year's corn grows as tall as his brow!"

"That's absurd!" Bladic chortled.

"Such silliness. Such foolishness." Tapple unwrapped a finger from his mug and pointed it at his host, "But the corn is well grown knee high already."

"Nonetheless Ospin," Drowden swaggered. "I have faith in my instincts and can't help believing my dreams mean something. They aren't nonsense."

"Aye," cried Nathan, "and I know a sucker when I see one. You can't possibly do it! Plain as the mole on the nose on my face, you've lost already! So for the sake of satisfying your pride of intellect ...oh, and your belief in dreams as prophesy, give up this wager or name your stakes!"

Erebus looked keenly into Bladic's eyes but wobbled slightly. "You name them, sir. You are my guest, and I bow to your decision."

"Very well..." Bladic thought for a minute. "Here's what I propoh-hhhse..." and he drew out that last word like it was a trombone. "Since we're comparing how fast your troll grows and speaks next to how fast your corn grows, I say we set the stakes as this year's crop. I've got about the same acreage planted as you have here at Hapstead Manor. So, that's it! Mine against yours! What do you say? Do we have a bet?"

Drowden filled their cups again to the brim then raised his high. "We have a bet, friend! Before the corn is as tall as the troll's thick brow, I'll have him talking. Your harvest is as good as mine."

Drowden winked at Ospin Tapple. "And what about you? Care to weigh in?"

Tapple sputtered. "Leave me out of this silliness," he squealed. "Trolls aren't for wagers. They're good for one thing..." His voice tapered off.

"And what's that?" Drowden raised an eyebrow and gave a glassy look.

"You never mind what. Get on with it. Seal your bet." Tapple picked up his drink and held it out. The three men clinked cups and drank them empty then sat back in their chairs to savor the moment.

Bladic leaned forward and waved a finger under Drowden's nose. He laughed with alcohol's borrowed glee. "You'll never get that Trog to say hello or goodbye. Not for at least two years, if ever. I thought you were a business-man, but it turns out you're just a dreamer."

Drowden stretched out his hand to shake on the deal. When Bladic ex-tended his hand, he squeezed it fiercely. "You have yourself a bet!" Then he filled their glasses one last time and they raised them high.

"To the corn wager!" Bladic almost yelled. "To the corn wager!" they cried in unison.

"You know…" Ospin slurred, "mead is a fine bev'rage, but shouldn't we seal such a wager like this one with corn whiskey?"

Drowden and Nathan laughed. "Splendid idea!" said Nathan. "But only if our host can part with his already fermented crops. He won't have any corn this coming season to make more."

"Don't count my corn as yours just yet," laughed Drowden. "I'll have plenty to spare when I take yours from you."

With that, they moved to the drawing room, and each poured a generous glass of the Manor's best sour mash. For the next three hours they traded stories, told jokes and talked of the wager until gradually first Tapple then Bladic fell asleep in their chairs.

Drowden managed to stumble to the servant's cottage nearby and sent Piscote to get some food and a pail of water into the troll's kennel. When he got back to the house, he poured another glass of mash and then put the decanter back in the cabinet. He intended to sit just a few more minutes to say good night to his guests before climbing the stairs to bed but was soon snoring with them in a chair with his half-drunk drink on a simple table nearby.

When he woke, Erebus was capped and gowned in his own bed and it was morning. Dorina was standing over him with a damp cloth, pressing it to his face and looking put out.

"Your gentlemen friends made it to bed after I spilled some water on their laps. Rude men. Mouths capable of shaping air into unlikeable conjurations. I do not care for them! And you! Oh, Drowden Erebus, before I treat you as I did our unwanted guests, repeat what you just said. Something about corn and trolls?"

His head throbbed and his tongue felt like a carp lodged in his mouth. When he spoke, his voice crackled. Dorina handed him a cup of water. "Well?"

The water gave him more of a voice. "Please, dearest. Some willow bark tea, then we can talk. I beg you!" Dorina pulled the servants cord and sat by him on the bed.

"You drank quite a bit!" She looked at her husband, pitying his headache but very annoyed.

Erebus rubbed his throbbing temples. He took another sip of water. "Yes dear. We were celebrating!"

"Celebrating what…?" but her voice fell off as Drowden raised a hand in supplication. "A moment please," he whispered. Dorina fell silent and sat staring out the window until she heard the servant at the chamber door. Dorina left the room quietly, and when she returned, she brought the steaming cup to his side.

After the tea he felt not much better, but he told Dorina he did, and about the troll, the wager, and his intention to teach the little being to speak.

"You can't be serious." She gasped. "I can't believe you would do such a thing! Keep a troll at Hapstead Manor? One year's crop! Once you're good and sober, you'll think better of all this and change your mind!" Dorina's voice turned shrill. "You *will* change your mind!"

Drowden held his head. "Please, I beg you. My brain is about to explode." His stomach churned. "Besides, dear wife. I can't back out of a wager without losing it. And more to the point, I'm going to win. I swear it!"

Dorina turned on her heel to leave the room. Drowden called after her. "Please don't slam the…." Too late, the deed was done, bringing on new waves of nausea. He grabbed for the nearest thing, the water pitcher, and vomited into it.

One word escaped his lips between upheavals "…door."

When he finally came up for air, there was a crooked smile on his face. He pushed matted hair out of his eyes and lay back on the pillow, looking at the ceiling but seeing much more. "A troll," he whispered to the room, "I have a troll!"

Chapter IV

The Road to Irongate

Nathan Bladic's carriage rumbled steadily down the dirt road sending billows of red dust spinning in its wake. An early start had .them miles from Hapstead Manor. Ospin and Nathan squinted against the warm sun spilling into the coach's open right side.

Tapple was in a foul mood. Though he had been in a hurry to leave when yesterday's business was done, the astonishing arrival of the infant troll persuaded him not to leave until he learned Drowden Erebus' plans for the creature. Now that he knew, he was seething inside.

Sweat prickled on his back-sloped forehead and he wiped it with a clean blue kerchief. His small eyes were irritated, and they watered. At least he hadn't slept in his clothing, he thought, though he couldn't remember getting ready for bed.

Ospin pulled himself up from a slouch so his feet no longer touched the floor. Dabbing his face again, Tapple sat back and watched the sun flicker through fast passing branches.

Nathan leaned toward his traveling companion. "You made a nice profit from Drowden Erebus on the sale of that bull."

"I made a bundle!" Ospin smirked with self-satisfaction. "It's amazing what a few boasts and a good brushing can add up to in cold profits! But, all in all, Drowden Erebus got himself a good bull." He paused to watch a blue jay fly by. "Mind you, he bargained me down from my original price considerably."

Tapple groped for his snuff box and held a pinch under his flat nose. "He's a bit of a dreamer, eh?"

"True. But there's more to him than that. You've got to admire how he's pulled himself up from nothing and made something out of himself. Imagine. A Scrivener's son!" Nathan shuddered with indignation.

"He's either ruthless or lucky," Tapple suggested.

"It takes more than luck, my friend." Nathan sighed and thought of smoking his pipe. He fished around and finally found his pouch in a jacket pocket. "A successful man is a keen observer of human nature. But for all Drowden's shrewdness, I have the clear advantage!"

"What advantage this time?" Ospin queried. "This competition you have with him...will it ever end?"

"He's a farmer, Tapple. Just a farmer and it's all he'll ever be. The only future he sees is the turning of the seasons in a big circle. He can't imagine the endless road to bigger and better things stretched out in front of us the way I can."

"Indeed. You think he's small-minded. With no imagination. No higher aspirations." Tapple's voice was measured, coiling like a snake, slowly getting ready to spring.

"He's got nothing *but* imagination!" Nathan's voice lurched out loudly, beating Tapple to the punch. "His head lives in legends. He loves trolls!"

Ospin Tapple screeched like he'd been pronged with a stick. "Damn him! Damn his stupid fascination with filthy, maggoty, pustulent grime of the world miscreants! And damn you for reminding me. I thought I had only dreamed it!"

"Well! No mistaking where to find your tender spot!" Bladic guffawed.

Tapple squinted and leaned forward, hatefully eyeing Bladic. "Think you've got the better of me, do you? Did you know that, aside from studying Troggle lore, Drowden Erebus has a new hobby? It's true! He's reading everything he can get his hands on about steam power and turning lignite into money. Watch out, Bladic! Can you hear him sneaking up behind you, getting ready to replace you as the top mogul in the land?"

"You're a sniveling liar!" Bladic bellowed.

Tapple spat angrily and grazed Bladic's cheek. "It just might be true!" he shouted.

The ruckus startled the coachman. "Everything all right down there?" They heard him yell.

Bladic waved him off with a hand out the window. He pulled his arm back in and pointed at Tapple. "I can stop poking your sore spot at any time, and you can stop irritating mine. But how would we know we're friends if we did that?" They both laughed cryptically and looked out opposite windows.

Nathan Bladic sighed and looked at his hands. "Successful men are usually sworn enemies on some level. Whether they like it or not. The same fuel that fires our ambition burns in our veins and boils our blood." He reached under the seat, found his satchel, and produced a flask. "Hair of the dog?"

Tapple agreed to a nip.

Nathan took a swallow and passed it. "Hot-blooded men, Ospin." He continued. "Put them together, there's bound to be a bonfire of competition."

"Very poetic," Tapple yawned, handing the flask back to its owner. "My preference is for economy of words. There's more than a passion for business flowing through your veins, if you ask me."

Bladic took another swallow then closed the lid. "Pray tell."

"You, good sir, are jealous of Drowden Erebus!" What he'd been thinking for quite some time was now in the open. Nathan's face reddened, but otherwise betrayed no hint that Tapple had struck a nerve.

There was silence between the men for a time. Ospin peeked out from under his hat brim and watched an assortment of expressions cross Bladic's face.

"It doesn't matter, Nathan," he finally said. "You have what you want." Bladic gave no comment, so he continued. "I am a jealous man and I admit it. I am jealous of anyone who has more than I do. That's why I spent a life-time accumulating what I can…land, money; it makes me happy, and I'm not ashamed to admit it!"

Arms crossed over his chest; Nathan Bladic could think of nothing to say.

"You are even greedier than I," said Tapple. "You want everything and don't care who you step on to get it. But you don't really like having enemies. Too much work. Me? I don't mind enemies. When they become too irritat-ing, I get rid of them."

Bladic's jaw tightened at this last comment. "Careful, sir," Bladic scolded harshly. "It might irritate you quite a lot if I stop this carriage and put you out. It's a long walk from here to Irongate!"

Tapple raised a hand in defense. "Hear me! In your heart of hearts, you see Drowden Erebus as a blood enemy. But you don't let anyone know, most of all, him. I only see it because I know you so well. You'd have to give up his respect if you showed some teeth. His respect is worth more to you than you'd admit."

Nathan slapped his knee hard and bolted forward, grabbing Ospin by the lapels so they were nose to nose.

"Don't tell me what I think, who I like or how to manage my affairs. I'll cut you down so fast even you'll know what a sawed-off package of flatulence you are! You'll need a ladder to put on your shoes!"

Tapple stared deeply into Bladic's bloodshot eyes. When at last he spoke, his voice was high pitched as ever, but even and cool. "I wish you wouldn't take such pleasure in ridiculing my height. It's the one thing I can do little about. However, I can do a great deal about loosening your grip on my collar."

Nathan suddenly felt a sharp prick through his jacket and between his ribs. "Yes, friend Bladic, it is a knife. This blade and a few gold coins in the driver's pocket would end your story here along the road in a shallow ditch. Now. Let go!"

Nathan's fists unclenched, and both men pulled apart. "Apology ac-cepted!" Ospin sneered as he put away the blade.

They fell to silence again for several miles, eyeing one another coyly. Then Ospin spoke up. "I have big plans for Drowden Erebus. Plans where he is the victim and I the victor. Let there be no question of my intentions!" He shifted in his seat. "He thinks he can shelter a troll. He has a lot to learn," he said more to himself than to Bladic. "But all the same, I'll have a little sport, make a little fun and enjoy the spoils. You can bet against the troll and hope you win. I intend to bet against the troll and make sure it loses."

Tapple patted his friend's knee and winked. Gradually the tension between them evaporated. "Will you be going to the society tea at Hapstead Manor? A good chance to see what's going on with the troll. You can keep me informed. I won't be attending. Much too busy for such fluffery."

Tapple jerked his chin toward Bladic. "When will that be?" he asked.

"In a fortnight. You should go."

"No," Tapple shook his head. "Better I don't. I'll send someone. For my purposes, it will be better to seem uninterested."

"We're two of a kind," laughed Nathan. "I smell the makings of intrigue. Tapple, I don't know who's the bigger sneak!"

"You are!" Ospin cried out as both men dissolved into peals of laughter. Bladic quietly slipped his own knife back into its sheath, which was strapped under his pants cuff.

Bladic rolled his head against the leather upholstery. He kept his eyes shut, but he felt the light and shadow on his eyelids as the carriage rattled on through a dappling of tree shade.

"What did we have for supper last night?" Ospin asked rhetorically. Nathan raised a brow. "I don't remember. Did we dine?"

Tapple took a breath. "My head may be muddled from all the mead and mash, but my stomach can still think clearly, and it says definitely not! We had no supper!"

Nathan nodded, his memory coming back. "A remarkable oversight for a woman of Dorina's standing, and with a well-known reputation as a first-rate hostess."

Ospin laughed at his friend. "It was no oversight. She was livid."

"Livid?" Bladic's eyes popped wide open on that. "She was the embodiment of all that pleases! She spoke nothing but soothing words!"

"Tsk…. tsk…" Ospin shook his head. "She was courteous, nothing more and just barely that. We had fallen far too deeply into our cups to notice but take my word for it. She was livid. She let us make stew of our brains and figured that was all the nourishment we deserved!"

Bladic nodded, understanding. "I think that Dorina agrees with you."

"What are you talking about?" Tapple asked incredulously.

"Think man!" Bladic pointed to his own head. "Now I think of it, it was bloody obvious. Dorina wasn't so miffed with us last night as she was with her husband. He welcomed that little barbarian into the Manor. He upset her orderly and comfortable world. Put simply my dear Tapple, she loathes that ugly smelly little thing, that troll, almost as much as you do!"

Tapple shrugged and made out that he didn't know at all what Bladic was talking about, but he wouldn't quit.

"It's you who hates trolls. That troll threatens your neat little world more than it threatens Dorina's! Observe!" Bladic pointed a finger. "Number one: You thought trolls had been eradicated in the wilds. You thought it certain they'd all been hunted to extinction by the Secret Brotherhood."

"Careful," said Ospin Tapple.

"Two," another finger shot up, "you are sure that good breeding is what made you the man you are. Three, " the middle finger rose for the count, "you see the likes of Drowden Erebus, a success in spite of his low-born station, and you think you'd do anything to stop it from happening again…"

A strange look came over Ospin's face. He shook his head vigorously and whined his response. "Everything you attribute to me I can as easily say about you. You want to bring down Drowden Erebus. He's too much competition for you."

"You think that's why I made the wager with Erebus?"

Ospin's brows relaxed. The furrows smoothed and he pulled back in his seat with a shrug. "You're risking a whole crop on it. You know nothing about trolls and yet you're willing to risk a great deal on your convictions." Tapple took a breath. "You may be a good businessman, Nathan, but in this I think your judgment is clouded."

After a thoughtful stare into space, Bladic smiled appreciatively. "I like to win my wagers, Ospin. And you have a stake in this too, so you want me to win as well, and the thing is this: I do have an ace up my sleeve. Well, at least I wish she were up my sleeve. That ace is Dorina."

Ospin leaned forward, his interest heightened. "Dorina? Have I missed something?"

Nathan laughed. "No. Not really. Only the obvious. You see, if she is as opposed to the troll and her husband's plans for it as I think she is, then perhaps with a little cajoling she can sway her husband to give up the delusion he can tame the ugly thing." He rubbed his chin, a sudden thought crossing his mind. "Isn't her annual charity tea only a few days away? Imagine if that troll somehow makes a mess of it. That would bring an end to Drowden's experiment. I'd be at no risk. In the end, Dorina would be working for me without even knowing it." Bladic's lips curled into a self-contented smile. "I have an idea."

Tapple thought a moment. "Then you don't think Drowden will tell her about the wager?"

Nathan laughed. "A drunken wager? A foolish wager? A wager which guarantees that a troll will stay at Hapstead Manor indefinitely? Would you tell your wife that you've been such a dolt?"

"No, I wouldn't," Tapple replied. "But Drowden is another case entirely. He's honest. That's the difference between your relationship with Hattie, mine with Matilda and the likes of Drowden with Dorina. Those two are, for all their bickering, in love. Good friends, even. And I'm not at all sure your ace up the sleeve isn't a joker in disguise. You may have a wild card but playing it at the right moment is everything."

"No friend, it's the only thing!" said Bladic. "And I will!"

By now they were descending Fallsbend Hill toward Irongate. Nathan Bladic's mind turned to Alliahe. She was a surer bet. He pictured her in lace, waiting faithfully for him in town; the lantern light flickering across her doll-like face. It filled his mind and made his body stir to life. But then, from the shadows of his conscience, Hattie materialized, waiting to scold. He slouched back and told himself she'd have to wait another night. Tonight, he belonged to Alliahe.

Evening crept around the carriage as its passengers prattled on about business and contracts, bribes to placate the cooper's guild, the new merchant ship in which they had invested, and the uppity dock workers at Deepwater harbor.

Ospin shuddered in the damp night air and pulled his coat tighter about him. Nathan pointed beneath his companion's seat and produced a blanket from under his own. Both smelled a bit horsy.

"Trolls can't talk. Can they, Tapple?" Bladic asked.

"I don't know," Tapple answered. "I wouldn't let one have the chance."

The carriage groaned and creaked under them for several more miles. There was no moon, only the noise of their progress.

From a rise in the road they spotted the lights of Irongate. This was a critical point in their journey. Bandits had been known to terrorize late travelers in the wooded hills west of town. Such incidents were frequent enough to keep all eyes darting and imagination active.

Tapple swung a foot out and caught Bladic's knee, startling him out of a shallow doze. "They've been calling that shanty town down by the river 'Bladicville.' Catchy, don't you think?"

Bladic grumbled something about ungrateful vermin and turned sideways to rest his head against a pillow.

The carriage ambled down the well-worn road. Finally, cobblestones rattled the wheels and the hoof beats turned to a rhythmic click-clack.

Bladic snorted awake from another short doze. At a familiar intersection, he whistled to the coachman. "That way!" he shouted. The driver signaled the horses and after a sharp turn and a short gallop the carriage came to a stop.

Tapple pulled himself from the cramped cab, descended to the stone curb and turned to the driver.

"You know where the stable is, lad. Tend the animals then find lodgings for the night. Be back for us by dawn."

Chapter V
Baptism by Water

Drowden Erebus stood in front of the kennel and stared through the meshed wire at the troll. "No mistaking it for a girl," he muttered under his breath.

Polished obsidian eyes flicked chips of light toward Drowden from the shade of a pronounced brow. The young troll crouched in the corner, palms on the floor in front of him, looking forlorn but also ready to bolt.

Drowden reached into a gray wolfskin pouch slung around his neck. He'd managed to purloin a few scraps of venison from Odelia's cutting board and a chunk of bread.

There was a slight whimper from the pen as Drowden tugged a fatty string of meat from the bag. He held it up at arm's length and dangled the dripping flesh so the troll could see. "Want some?" the Master asked. Reaching with the other hand, he unlatched the gate and opened it. The food mesmerized his little guest, whose eyes followed only the meat.

Before he could think what to do, the babe snatched the deer flesh from his hands, fell on top of it and began to eat noisily.

Drowden stood back and hooted: "This isn't at all what I had in mind!" He laughed at the spectacle before him. "Little beasty, you have all the manners of a raccoon at the compost dump! Let's see if we can't improve this a bit."

Bending over the troll, Drowden reached for the pink slab of meat. He wanted to show the babe a thing about proper eating etiquette. The troll saw something coming toward his food and reacted on instinct. Erebus recoiled with a painful shout, holding his hand under his armpit and wincing. "You little bastard!" he laughed. "You bit me!" But the troll paid no heed and was back at work on the venison.

Drowden shook his hand at the wrist and examined the damage. No doubt about it, he thought, trolls are born with a full set of teeth. Luckily it had only been a warning bite that left a welt, not a gash. He would make a note of it in his ledger tonight and keep a record of all his observations. One day, he told himself, he might even write a book about his personal experiences in troll tutelage. He meant to stay up tonight and make a start.

"Well my little friend. You've taught me a lesson today," Erebus said while he plopped down on a mound of straw next to his pupil. "Never try to take food from a hungry troll; even a baby one. But let's see if you can learn something from me in exchange. It's called sharing."

Drowden put a hand on the troll's elbow. The babe glanced at him warily but never stopped chewing. Soon Erebus had his arm gently placed around the little beast's right shoulder. With his left hand he grasped the other end of the meat. He picked this up and brought it slowly toward his own mouth. The troll watched as Drowden opened up and shoved the raw meat between his lips.

The creature's eyes widened perceptibly, and his own chewing slowed, but then an expression of amusement flooded his face. He made a low purring sound, then started rocking back and forth gently.

Drowden was filled with awe. To have the little one accepting him in such close proximity was humbling, and certainly more than what he had hoped for in one day. In fact, passing the time together seemed to have a calming effect on both of them. Drowden enjoyed the warm glow of acceptance, of growing trust. He pretended to eat a crude meal with his woodland charge. But soon he began chewing in earnest.

Master Erebus was used to oven-crisped meat, juicy and brown. But as he chewed, his jaws felt overworked and ready to split from their hinges. The gamy taste was overwhelming. The taste and texture shocked his palate and twisted a knot in his stomach. Still, he chewed, grimacing.

Jessa, second in command of the kitchen after Odelia, wandered by the pen on her way from the servant's quarters to the Manor House. For a moment she paused at the gate that had been left ajar. She lifted a hand over her small mouth. A cry of startled surprise was held in check. There sat her master, haunch to haunch and arm around the uncouth naked beast, ravenously attacking a horrid-looking chunk of bloody flesh.

Drying flakes of blood covered both their faces and white knots of fatty gristle hung from their teeth. As she stood gazing and uncomprehending, terrible images played out in the poor woman's mind; images of her master and that barbaric heathen stalking some innocent wild animal, or maybe a child, together, slaughtering it on the spot. She shuddered, gagged in disgust, and thanked the Secret Brotherhood silently for their vigilance.

Both man and troll looked up from their meal with questioning eyes. "Jessa?" Drowden hooted. "Isn't it wonderful? Look how fast he learns!" Jessa couldn't bear the sight another minute. She turned her head away and started off at a trot to the Manor House.

"Jessa!" Drowden called after her, concern in his voice. She stopped and cautiously went back to the kennel.

"Master, forgive me," she cried mid-curtsey. "You seem to be learning his habits more quickly than he yours!" Then she turned on her heels and continued at half a trot along the flagstones leading to the kitchen's side entrance.

Drowden rolled backward onto the ground, convulsing with seismic belly laughs. He pounded the earth hard with a balled-up hand and grabbed his sides. The troll bounced back and away from Drowden Erebus, his toothy mouth gaping to expose a tongue as wide as three fingers. His brow-hooded eyes and smooth cheeked face suddenly bloomed into a flower of delightful astonishment. Finally, the man sighed deeply and lay still. The little troll waited a while, making sure the fit was over, then sidled up to his companion and bent over to see if he was still alive. Examining the clean-shaven face, long lashed eyes, and strange body coverings, the little troll pushed and poked coat buttons, probed pockets and twirled his tutor's long hair between a fistful of stubby fingers.

Suddenly, Drowden opened his eyes. The little troll jumped back and tipped over the bucket of drinking water. He landed on his bottom in a puddle.

"Well lad!" Drowden hollered cheerfully. "This is going to be... no, it already is...a most splendid day!"

The troll was watching every move, his head bobbed with each gesture made by the man-thing. Still, he kept his distance.

"Oh now, don't be so skeptical. I know what I'm talking about!" Drowden Erebus laughed and sat up, rounding his arms about his knees and leaning toward the troll babe, who'd gotten interested in squishing clumps of mud between his fingers and smacking great gobs of it on his chest.

"That's going to dry and make you very uncomfortable, I can assure you. But...." Drowden poked an index finger at his temple, "you'll learn. You've everything to learn, and experience is the best way. So! Mud pies today; trifles tomorrow!"

He sat there for a long time, watching the little troll make a mud encrusted lump of himself.

Drowden finally got up and dusted his shoulders, knees and buttocks with a quick swipe of a hand. Dried dirt billowed off in clouds. He leaned down again to retrieve the gnawed remnants of a shank of meat. It was already covered with flies, and he shooed them away. Picking up the foul remnant at arm's length, he straightened up and turned to the troll.

"You won't be wanting this, I suppose. And even if you do, I won't hear of it!" Then he chuckled to himself. "I'm surprised I put it in my own mouth."

He held the meat and examined it again. "Maybe Duke and the other dogs would like to quarrel over it." Leaning into the kennel, the Master made sure his guest could see his face. "I'll be back," he winked. "Have fun for now."

Backing out of the pen and carrying the dogs' treat, he latched the gate. Flies buzzed and tormented him until he tossed the scrap over the fence. The dogs yelped and jumped to their feet. Grisswold reached the prize first, but when Old Duke bound forward and pounced, the other dogs yielded their claim and retreated, circling in hopes of finding something left when Duke was done feasting.

Meanwhile, Master Erebus met Odelia at the water pump. He snatched up a wooden bucket with a rope handle and waited his turn. Odelia was unusually silent as she worked the pump handle. She stepped back to let Drowden get at it and finally huffed a clear grunt of disapproval by way of a comment.

"What is it, Odelia? You've got something to say?" Drowden asked without looking up from the spout.

"Me? Master Erebus? No! Not a thing!" There was only the squeak of the pump handle and the intermittent swoosh of water into the bucket for a moment. Then Odelia laughed, unable to hold back.

"You've sure got Miss Dorina in a tizzy this mornin'!" she whispered.

"Oh?" Drowden looked up, wiping sweat from his forehead with the back of his hand.

Odelia shrugged. "Not my place to say so, but I think she might even be, well, peeved at your dalliance with that thing over there." The maid jerked her head toward the troll pen.

Drowden smirked and gave the handle half a pump. "Did Jessa say anything?"

Odelia rolled her eyes. "Plenty! But she wouldn't with the Mistress in earshot. Imagine what Miss Dorina would think! Jessa said at first how she thought you'd gone mad!"

"And what do you think?" he invited her frankness.

"Humph!" she sputtered. "I'm not one to judge." She picked up the bucket and set it near the already filled one, and hooked a yoke to the handles of each, preparing to carry them to the kitchen.

"Still," the maid turned to face him completely, "If you ask me, I think it's just dandy, you takin' it in and wanting to make it civil. But mark me, sir. You've got children of your own, needin' the same kind of attention. Without somebody to guide us, we're all just nature's animals. I wouldn't forget Miranda and Ian, were I you."

Master Erebus smiled indulgently. "Point well taken, Odelia. I assure you they come first. But they've got a head start. And this…." He waved a hand toward the troll "…this is new to me, and exciting and…"

The well-padded kitchen maid held up a hand. "I understand, sir." She paused. "But Mistress Dorina…? Maybe not."

"Yes. I know," he said, though in truth he knew he hadn't given her much thought in the matter. "She comes from a fine family that understands character and breeding. I'll try hard not to disrupt her routine."

Odelia smiled and turned to her work, lifting the buckets onto the yoke and shouldering it up to the kitchen without further comment.

Drowden finished filling his bucket. He watched farm hands off in the distant fields moving slowly under the warm sun, bent to pick ripe vegetables and drop them into wicker baskets harnessed to their backs. It was a perfect day. Or almost perfect, he thought as he heard an upstairs window open and saw Dorina lean her head out. Her long golden tresses fell forward off her shoulders and billowed in the wind.

"Drowden Erebus!" she called. "What are you up to now?"

He looked at his wife and smiled with a shrug then lifted the bucket for her to see. "The troll needs a bath, love. I'm going to give him a much-needed bath!"

"Well, just look at you!" she said, scolding him gently. "You're an absolute mess. Supper will be set in an hour. Will you bathe yourself, too?"

Drowden chuckled, his heart full of love. "Of course, my dear." Then with a flirtatious wink, "It's good to see you wear your hair down, the way I like it."

"I'm up here making myself presentable. As for you…"

"But you are perfect even now!" he shouted back. And she was; sun gleaming on her fair locks, her creamy complexion and her pebble blue eyes: Drowden Erebus was still in love with her after nearly twenty years.

Dorina looked around playfully, a little flirtatiously and called back under her breath: "You don't want me cavorting about like those women Nathan Bladic keeps, do you?"

Drowden opened his mouth to answer, but she continued before he became witty.

"I thought you liked me to present a reserved side in front of the servants," she hushed herself from shouting to him from the window.

"I love you dear, no matter what side you present!" he teased and ducked as she threw a bath sponge at him. He caught it before it hit the ground.

"Thank you love. This will do just fine. See you at dinner."

"Ooooohhh!" she growled. "Just like a man. Your hobbies always come first!"

"My lovely Dorina," her husband cooed. "You are my favorite hobby!"

She forced a mocking laugh and pulled her head inside, closing the window with a sharp clatter.

Drowden shook his head, feeling warm and content. He crossed the yard toward the pen, carrying his bucket and sponge and making a detour to the shed where the caldrons were stored. The soap-making vat was lined with residue. He scraped some of it with a fingernail until he had a handful of fluff that he compressed into a fair-sized ball. Then he closed the shed and continued to the pen.

He heard light footfalls behind him and knew them to be Miranda's.

"Father! Father! May I watch?" she called to him. He stopped and waited for her to catch up. She skipped to his side, long braids twirling in the air behind her.

"Certainly angel, please join me. But don't get that dress of yours soiled. Your mother will have us both drawn and quartered!"

Miranda rolled her eyes. "Oh Father, I'm not a child. Don't you think I can take care of myself?"

He smiled and hugged her shoulders. "Of course I do. There isn't anything you can't do."

They walked quickly to the pen and Drowden leaned forward to open it. The little troll was covered top to bottom with globs of mud. Suddenly Drowden wheeled on his feet and stood like a wall between the troll and his daughter.

"Oooooohhh! Whoops!" he said with embarrassment. "I forgot! He's not clothed. Maybe you'd better go back into the house!"

Miranda huffed in disappointment, hiking her hands to her hips with a stubborn expression on her face. "I am not a child!" she said curtly. It was almost a perfect imitation of her mother, and he couldn't help but laugh.

"Oh, all right. I suppose there's no harm. But first, go get a smock and put that dress somewhere where it won't get soiled. I'll wait."

In a twinkling, Miranda was back, dressed in an oversized workman's smock. "Will this do?"

"Yes. But let's hurry, now. Here. Take the sponge and soap while I rinse him down."

Miranda smiled broadly and took the sponge and wad of soap from him. She watched silently as Erebus doused the young troll with one bucket, then another of cold water. After that she chimed in to say: "Honestly Father, did you think you were going to bathe him without help? Look at how he prances and runs from the water!"

Drowden fiddled with the bucket a moment and looked up. They exchanged an amused glance. "I'd forgotten how much you've matured, my love," he said. "You're not just my little girl anymore. You're becoming a woman. And a smart one at that!"

She smirked coyly. "Well! I'm glad somebody's noticed!"

Drowden doused the troll again and wiped off as much mud as possible with his hand. Then he doused him again and took the acrid-smelling soap to his tough hide and worked up a lather that darkened quickly with dirt. Another dousing and the sponge was employed. Seeing how inept her father was, Miranda stepped in and took over.

"You said I could help, Father! Else why should I be wearing this musty smelling coverlet? All I've done so far is hold the bucket and watch. It's my turn now."

Drowden wiped his brow, holding the troll babe firmly by the wrist. "I'll hold him, you sponge. It'll be all for nothing if he gets loose and slops through the mud again!"

The troll didn't much like the ordeal of being bathed. Nothing at all like what his mother's warm sticky tongue could've done. The water was cold. The suds smelled unnatural. And he was just getting to like being covered in gook.

But when Miranda approached and gently dabbed him over with the sponge, the troll relaxed and no longer strained against Drowden's grip.

"I think you've got the touch I lack," her father noted with mild amusement. "It's the woman's touch."

Miranda answered, not looking up from her work. "Ah yes," she agreed. "It's the woman's touch!"

When they finished drying him off, they heard the familiar clanging of the dinner bell. Miranda stopped suddenly and looked at her father. "You're a mess! Mother will be furious!"

Drowden agreed. "You go on ahead. Throw a brush through your hair. I'll get changed and be down for supper shortly." Miranda went quickly to the shed and exchanged the coveralls she'd donned for the dress she'd left there, then ran on to the house.

Drowden went to the shed and changed. The only thing he could find other than the mud-crusted coverlet used by Miranda was a pair of old blacksmith aprons. These he applied, one front ways, one back ways to help preserve his dignity for the short trip to the Manor House mudroom, then up the back staircase for a quick scrub and fresh wardrobe.

Supper was quieter than usual. Forks and knives clattered delicately; Odelia circled the table spooning out portions of fresh cooked greens, fluffed potatoes, sauces and relish while Master Erebus gingerly sharpened the carving knife and went to work on the lamb. Dorina looked up at him quizzically when he turned down his customary large helping of meat.

"Aren't you feeling well?" she asked.

He looked up from a spoonful of lima beans, paused, then put it in his mouth. After a chew and swallow he replied, "Never better, dear."

Little Ian ate at eye level with his plate, pushing food to the edge of it and sticking out his lower lip, pretending it was a drawbridge and his mouth the castle. From plate to mouth with a spoon shove, a heap of potatoes disappeared.

"Ian!" Dorina scolded. "Sit up straight. Don't play with your food!" Mother was not in the mood for barbarism at the dinner table and shot a look of annoyance at her husband as if blaming him for their son's bad form.

After a few mouthfuls were daintily put away, Dorina dabbed her lips with an embroidered napkin. "So," she said, placing the cloth on her lap, "I expect you'll have Argis return that thing to the forest tomorrow."

She didn't blink. She didn't resume eating. She sat, wide-eyed, expecting immediate confirmation of her expectations.

Drowden flushed and didn't look up from his plate. As though suddenly famished, he began churning his supper into his mouth, almost filling it beyond capacity.

"Drowden Erebus!" his wife pronounced the name like a profanity.

Ian broke in, "Mommy, are you and Daddy going to have a fight?"

Dorina looked to her child. His face was smeared with gravy. "Finish your supper, then you and Miranda go out and play."

Drowden gulped his food and raised his water glass to wash everything down.

"Drowden?" Dorina spoke again, trying for a little less edge to her voice.

"Yes, dear?" he asked, pretending he hadn't heard anything.

"Speak to Argis tonight! No point in delaying it until morning. That thing must be returned to the forest!"

"But Dorina!" Drowden suddenly stood, pushing his chair back with his legs. "I have no intention of abandoning that little troll in the wilds. He's only a baby, dearest love! Would you take our little Ian out into the forest and leave him for the wolves?"

Ian hooted. "Oh boy!" and twirled his spoon between his chubby fingers like a baton. "Let's do it!"

"Would you even maroon one of our sheep that way?" Drowden continued, ignoring his son's antics. "Of course not! You have a kind heart, and that's why I love you. You would never do such a thing."

Dorina half closed her eyes. She felt suddenly weary. "I don't intend to spar with you on the fine points of valor, husband. That creature is a beast from the wild. It is an untamed part of nature, it's uncivilized.... crude....not akin to our ways or natural to our home. Argis found it; Argis can return it." Dorina lowered her eyes empathetically, "I wouldn't be surprised if some heartbroken mother troll is looking for the wretched little monster, even as we speak."

Miranda dropped her fork on her plate with a loud clatter. "He's not a monster! He's not a wretch at all! He's a baby! He needs someone to care for him!"

Dorina turned angrily to her daughter. "Young lady...."

"She's right, Dorina." Drowden winced. "He's harmless. And he needs the same care any youngster needs."

"Goody!" Little Ian clapped his hands. "Can we keep him?"

"No!"

"Yes!"

Master and Mistress spoke in unison.

The room's air grew thick with a heavy silence that lasted several minutes. Suddenly Dorina got up from the table and threw her napkin onto her plate. "We'll talk about this later, good sir," she said while brushing past her husband toward the stairs.

They did not talk about it later. They did not talk about anything.

Chapter VI
Nocturne

A single candle lit one corner of the room, extending a dim aura over the table where it rested in a pewter base. The light poured over the high-backed leather chair where Master Erebus sat, book in hand and reading spectacles balanced at the very tip of his nose.

The rest of the room was full of shadows, which seemed to breathe in rhythmic cadence with the candle's flickering. Drowden looked up from his studies and let his gaze fall on the bed where his wife lay, sleeping somewhat restlessly.

Drowden was having difficulty concentrating on his studies. "The Maleficence of Trolls" by Jacob Jerkins, a so-called 'learned scholar' from Folkscience Academy was disturbing in its assertions. According to Jerkins, trolls were "an incorrigible and disagreeable fringe-race, the likes of which would not be missed if extinguished from earth."

It made Drowden shudder. While he had to admit that his love of troll lore was irrational and indefensible against his harshest of learned critics, he could defend not even one argument in favor of the genocide already visited upon this "fringe-race."

For any number of reasons, he'd acquiesce to the opinions of the woman who owned his heart, and she was adamantly opposed to anything that would support, promote, make way for or give the impression of alliance with the interests of a captured troll. Dorina's pillow talk was all about preparations for the fancy social not more than a week away. Nothing must spoil it and nothing should divert Drowden's attention from making the grounds ready. And yet one little troll had utterly possessed his mind.

"Mind the day," Dorina had scolded him. "There's so much to be done, yet all you do is fuss over the troll. I am jealous for your time and getting anxious about loose ends. The party is in a week!"

Drowden Erebus reluctantly confined the little troll to its pen and devoted hours to managing the workers, until Dorina seemed comfortable with the pace of preparations. It helped that the troll slept most of the day, but in the evening and well into the night Drowden shared the company of the troll babe and endured the complaints of his wife.

On this one thing Erebus found he was unable to yield. On this one single idea he thought he must stand immobile. Though he worried that he might come to an unsettled and irreconcilable dispute with Dorina, he refused to hear her pleas to return the troll to the deep forest.

The little troll would not be turned out. Of that he was determined. Not tomorrow, nor the day after. That sparkle in the little one's eyes hinted at intellect. Drowden suspected and desired that trolls and humans had very much in common and may in fact be kin. He vowed to himself to uncover the truth, no matter the hardship. Those he found along the way.

This night, Drowden stepped cautiously into his bedroom after long hours of observing the troll and recording endless speculations in his notebook. Dorina pushed him away and wept bitterly into her pillow when he attempted to lie down next to her. She knew he'd decided to keep the troll, no matter what she said or didn't say. He tried to hold her, tried to explain the countless perils the troll babe would face all alone in the woods if he were returned to the wild. If she heard him, she seemed not to hear. The night was long on silence and short on sleep for both of them.

For a troll, thought Erebus as he tossed in his pillow, human beings must be the worst danger of all. Even though the Secret Brotherhood was believed to have hunted them out of existence generations ago and become little more than a gentleman's drinking club, Drowden Erebus shuddered.

Out of simple loathing, the great-grandfathers of those men making up today's Brotherhood collected troll heads, scalps, hands and feet to be stuffed, mounted, then sold from a canopied pavilion at the annual fair, only then to be hung by stupidly grinning collectors above fireplaces in civilized drawing rooms. Drowden found it easier not to believe the badly preserved limbs and heads he'd seen mounted in one or another parlor belonged to real trolls, even when his hosts had identified them as such. He had always presumed they were secret trophies from old wars, not mere relics of planned murder. He had even come to think that a subculture of deceit had grown up among his business associates, and that they had a winking understanding among themselves to refer to their mercenary war trophies as "troll parts." It was a personal belief that helped him cope. But now, with a young troll to protect against an ignorant world, he was sure he had been far too naïve.

Jacob Jerkins, author and scholar from Folkscience Academy, was no longer an expert in the eyes of Drowden Erebus. According to Master Erebus' newly formulated estimation he was a dangerous crank who must be proven wrong.

Dorina rolled over and in the flickering candlelight for a brief second looked deep into her husband's eyes. Between sleep and waking she knew that he would not be moved, so she let him kiss her, then kissed him back and lay back down on the pillow without a word.

Drowden smiled triumphantly. He wanted to dance. There was no trace of sleep in his body. He knew Dorina would sigh in protest if he kept fidgeting, so he leaned up to a sitting position, turned to sit and fiddle with his toes for a pair of slippers, then stood up and headed for the chair nearby.

It bothered him to no end that Jerkins' work was entirely speculative, based on old wives' tales. And based on ignorance, the lionized fool had encouraged nothing short of genocide. Drowden Erebus did something unusual. He pounded a fist into a palm and vowed to the shadows to make a difference with facts.

The thought pushed any trace of sleep from his mind, so he sat in his chair and made notes in the margins of Jerkins' book.

The book was awful. Jerkins' style was singularly condescending to his reader, and he had a penchant for explanations that took the long way around to make their point.

On the night air Erebus heard the troll howling mournfully. It may have been going on for hours at a quieter pitch, but now it was getting louder and louder.

Drowden threw Jerkins' book aside and picked up another. It was his opinion that Jerkins lacked objectivity and relied too much on hearsay for his research. Drowden preferred reports of first-hand meetings between trolls and men.

Alouisius Deepay, for instance:

"It is significant to make mention of the fact that such occasion on which I was lucky enough to encounter a troll in the wild country, the chance crossing of paths occurred at night. I have made the early conclusion, rightly or wrongly, that trolls in all probability are by and large nocturnal creatures."

As Drowden read this passage from Deepay's "Trolls of the Blackrock Mountains," he sat up straight in his chair and cocked an ear. The little troll was still howling.

In another room Dorina stirred under the covers and muttered something incoherent.

He read on.

Alouisius Deepay was a keen observer, and Drowden found he was easily swept away by this author's concise and keen insight, even though the language was mildly archaic. Deepay's expressive style gave Drowden the impression of an ongoing study with imminent promise for new and better understanding and discoveries. What really captured his interest was the sense that Deepay's words were reverberating across the years of silence and ignorance, and that somehow, he, Drowden Erebus, was reviving the study, as if uninterrupted from where Deepay left off.

There were obvious differences of approach, of course. Until yesterday, Drowden had merely entertained an uninvolved fascination for trolls. They were a little less mysterious and mythical to him than to the common man, owing only to his familiarity with nearly everything ever written about them. He had never been so bold as Alouisius Deepay, who spent years of his extraordinary life hiking on the frontiers of little-known lands and seeking with single-minded dedication all sorts of living things that avoided plough and plunder.

Drowden read with awe the single account recorded by Deepay, of cooperation between a man and a troll. It was an extraordinary story of a night stroll that might have turned into disaster for the old scholar, but instead influenced him to devote the rest of his life to broadening his understanding of the wild race known as trolls.

Deepay had set camp in a ravine some miles removed from familiar territory. What was familiar to him was deemed enchanted by others, so that it was all but a new world. Thinking he heard someone cry out in terror, he grabbed a flaming bough from his campfire and plunged into the dark woods, tracking the sound. He saw only shadows, glow-worms and the eerie green eyes of owls reflecting back the shimmering flame. But he was careless with his makeshift torch. Red embers fell on a place carpeted with dry grass. In only moments fire leapt up all around him. The forest was suddenly bright and menacing in all directions.

Horrified at his stupidity, as Deepay recounted the incident, he ran with all speed back to his encampment to grab his blanket. He returned just as quickly to the site of the blaze to see if he could smother the fast-spreading flames.

The surrounding forest was illuminated by the approaching torrent. Suddenly the scholar took note of a giant form at the periphery of the fire. It looked to be a man, but it was not. The thing grasped its arms about the tree, squatted, and then suddenly stood straight up with a lurch, uprooting the tree in one motion. Then the mighty creature dropped the leafy end upon the burning grass, lifted it high then dropped it again repeatedly, tamping out the fire. The flames subsided.

Deepay ended his story, telling how he stamped and stomped on blazing mounds of grass to help contain the fire, but it was the troll who truly saved the day. Finally, all that was left was a black smudge of smoldering ash. Alouisius Deepay wrote that he fell to the ground, exhausted and covered with soot. The uprooted tree lay smoking nearby, but there was no sign of the troll.

Drowden looked up from his book. He yawned; his jaw cracked. A cool night draft chilled his feet and he sat for a while rubbing them together. Scrunching down in the high winged chair for warmth and comfort under the twisted confines of his robe was practically impossible. It wasn't long enough, or his legs were too long. The draft got through and the shadows became patches of cool air. Reading was useless. It was time for sleep. But he forced himself to read on.

Getting up to a squat, he shifted the chair to try for better lighting, and finally succeeded. An hour of diligent reading passed, then he took up his leather-bound notebook to capture a tribe of his desultory thoughts within the boundaries of inked words before they wandered off into the thickets of his brain and got lost.

Suddenly he slapped the quill down on the parchment and slapped his forehead. The troll had been caterwauling all night.

"I'm the worst researcher," he swore under his breath. "Here I sit, devouring the words of dead men, taking them to be experts…when I have the real thing right under my nose." With that he bound out of the chair and flung off his robe. He stripped his nightclothes off in a heap.

Drowden grabbed for work trousers, shirt, and waistcoat from his wardrobe near the door. After buttoning his garments, he sat to put on socks and boots. He paused to blow out the candle, leaving a tiny red spark glowing at the wick. Dorina rolled over without waking as his shadow filled the doorway.

"Good night, dear lady." He blew a kiss off the tips of his fingers and fled down the dark hall to the top of the stairs. He paused a second to grab another idea by the shoulder and shove it into an alcove of memory before it wandered off, then clomped down the wooden back staircase two at a time.

It was a spectacular starlit night; trees bristled in the balmy breezes. On the far horizon, gold-licked clouds hid the rising gibbous moon. Its light cast shadows as gentle as the finest cobweb, turning the short-cropped grass to a carpet of gossamer.

The yowling was far worse at the steps to the Manor House. It reminded the Master of a wild cat's snarling in one of Argis' leg traps. Loud snarls, hisses and grizzled throaty moans rang out across the empty yard. He began to wonder if the little troll had hurt himself and he quickened his pace.

The moonlight was enough to show the ribbed shadows that fell on the pen's interior. Drowden's eyes widened in horror as he made out the form and contorted face of the baby troll, hunched over with his hands raised up to the sky. In that moment, Erebus felt the hair on the back of his neck stand on end and he knew, or thought he knew, that it had been a gigantic mistake to bring this creature of the wild to his home.

"No more than an animal! Akin to the wolves!" he thought. "Intelligent, yes, but untamed and untamable."

He stopped himself short. "No!" he said aloud. "I can't have been that wrong. Certainly this creature doesn't know how to act in a civilized way; all this is new to him."

The babe must have heard Drowden speaking, because suddenly he fell silent. Only the rustling trees and the Master's footfalls could be heard. Drowden welcomed the silence. The little troll turned attentive and dropped his odd stance that seemed to help project his keening howl into the night as the man came closer to the pen.

"Good evening, sir. I do hope I've not disturbed you with my late serenade!" he imagined the troll saying. Drowden bowed low. The troll looked up with an angelic smile, eyes glistening warmly.

The latch clacked as Drowden threw open the gate. "Well, good evening to yourself!" he proclaimed in high spirits. "You're too young for love songs, so I suppose it's a lullaby you've been singing. A bit flat, I'm afraid." Drowden smiled. "Come on then, let's have a look at you!"

He reached over the fence and pulled a lantern from where it hung on a nail of an adjoining shed. Lifting the chimney, he lit a match on the weathered fence post and touched it to the wick. "Ah!"

The troll jumped back but then relaxed. "I bet I know what this racket is all about! You're hungry, aren't you? No doubt you're always hungry, being a growing boy and all. I should have remembered! It hasn't been that long ago since Ian had the house in an uproar, squealing and yowling. I guess I just don't have the innate instincts that a mother does. Now Dorina! Sweet Dorina, if she'd condescend to take an interest in you, she'd know your every mood."

Drowden balanced the lantern on one of the fence posts and scooped the troll babe into his arms. "Ugh! You're an armful! Now, let's see what's been abandoned in the kitchen."

He marched off toward the house with the lantern swinging at his side and the troll babe in his other arm, listening to its belly growl. The kitchen's pitch darkness melted away as they entered. He set the lantern on the massive oak table, then propped the troll on a small chair that had been only recently given up by Ian in favor of a place on the bench next to Miranda. And it was she who was the first to join the midnight raid on the pantry.

"Miranda! What are you doing up at this hour?" Drowden said defensively as she stumbled out of the darkness of the next room.

"I'm coming to see what all the fuss is about." She came up to her father. "Actually, what all the quiet is about. Is the little troll alright?"

Erebus smiled and patted her head. "Yes. Quite. Only mildly famished, I think." He turned quickly when he heard the outer door creak open and gasped surprise. "Odelia! What are you doing up?"

"I heard a commotion then saw you in the yard and, well, now here you are in my pantry!" she huffed.

"All's well! Maybe you can help." Drowden grinned. "What late night fare can we offer our poor, starving guest?"

Odelia laughed. "So that's it! Stand aside and I'll see what can be scraped together." Then in a lower voice she said: "Oughta put a diaper on the little one, sir. Fer the sake of us ladies."

Erebus nodded gravely. Just then the door creaked again and in popped Argis, his wife Petrina, and close behind came Jessa and Hector. Both men with hatchets gripped tightly in their hands. Petrina sported a rusty old carving knife.

"Whoa!" Drowden started. "What is this? An invasion?"

Argis blustered. "No sir. Thought there might be trouble. We heard strange noises, and then saw the light. Didn't want ta take no chances."

"Everything is fine. No need for alarm. Only an attack of hunger. But come on in anyway. You may as well join us. And leave those hatchets on the sideboard. Odelia, you've got your work cut out for you now."

"So I see, " she mumbled.

"Well, come in and sit yourselves down. For my sake keep your voices low," the Master entreated. "Dorina and Ian at least are still sleeping."

"No I'm not, Daddy!" a little voice crept around the doorjamb and Ian peeked his head in from the shadows. Drowden threw up his hands.

Ian cackled gleefully as he climbed up on the bench next to Jessa, who gave him a warm hug. "You sit by me, darlin'. Stay away from that smelly thing!" she said, hoping the Master wouldn't overhear.

Odelia grumbled as she threw an apron over her head and tied it behind. "It'll be warmed milk, some bread, butter and jam, and what's left of the spicy sausage…cold. I dare not start the fires. The mistress'll know something's up."

"I'll pass on the sausage," Drowden protested.

"Sounds most invitin' ta me," Hector chimed in. "I was jest about ta dig into my rucksack for a hunk o' jerky when I saws ye up 'ere."

Drowden set himself on the floor in front of his troll and watched the babe's changing expressions in response to the clamor and clatter of people. There was an undeniable intelligence in his eyes; something that either comprehended the friendly nature of the gathering, or at least had the patience and serenity to wait and discover what was going on.

The food was set on the table and hands shot out from all directions. Drowden raised a hand to halt the undignified food orgy.

"Please! A little decorum! We have a young guest! What kind of manners are we showing him?"

Hector smirked and dropped a crust of bread back onto the serving plate. "Pardon us, sir." Then pointing to the troll. "'He does seem a likable little feller, though."

"Yeah." Argis laughed. "Even if he keeps us awake half o' the night wi' his damnable howlin'. Go on! Give 'im the first share."

Master Erebus presented a piece of bread to the troll and winced a little as the babe o' the woods snatched it fast and shoved the whole slice into his mouth at once. "Ah! He likes it!" Drowden cried out. Then the rest of the company cheered as quietly as they could.

"He eats like one o' us!" Hector cackled.

"True!" the Master agreed. "Maybe we can teach him better! But who wouldn't forget their manners under the spell of Odelia's oven magic?"

They all laughed raucously, happy to be at once on equal terms with one another. The night's darkness and the homey feel of the pantry blurred the distinctions between rank and caste.

Odelia stood back in the paucity of light beside the dry sink. "Day old bread! Master Erebus is trying to get on my good side again!" Jessa choked with laughter, a mouthful of milk in her throat.

All the while, Drowden, his children and servants, bantered back and forth, trying in vain to keep their voices down. The little troll munched and studied each face in wide-eyed wonderment.

As Argis reached the height of silliness, imitating an old codger by distorting and tugging his face, the little troll began barking staccato sounds from deep in his chest. Spontaneously, everyone stopped what they were doing and looked at the little creature rocking in his seat.

"Is he alright?" cried Odelia.

"Ah ha! Of course!" chortled Drowden. "He's laughing! He's laughing! I think."

"A troll, wi' a sense o' humor!" Argis gave Hector's shoulder a slap. "Wha' next?"

"It's so cute," chirped Miranda. "The way he rocks and giggles when he's happy."

But with all the attention suddenly landing on him, the little troll turned shy and sat passively, watching the others and sometimes accepting a morsel from Drowden's hand.

Finally, there was no more to be eaten and Odelia could not be persuaded to dig into the larder any deeper than she already had.

"Tomorrow is another day. What ye eats now, ye misses then."

Drowden backed her up and bid the servants good night, accompanying them to the door and then shutting it gently behind.

"Don't worry about this," Odelia smiled. "I'll clean up. You go 'head and take care o' the little one."

The Master smiled warmly. "You know, I think everyone has come around to liking him." Drowden stooped and picked the troll from the floor then stopped and rolled his eyes upward. "Well…almost everyone. But believe me," his eyes fell on the little troll, "the two of us will be working on it."

"Now, Miranda and Ian, it's off to bed! I'll be back upstairs soon as I can. So be quick. I'll peek in on you and tuck you in."

"Yes Father." Miranda yawned.

"Ya!!!!" Ian bobbed his head with a big half-toothless smile. He was still bright-eyed and full of energy.

"I mean it, young man! No detours to the playroom. Straight to bed!"

Both children scurried off and Odelia finished wiping the table. Then Drowden took the lamp and accompanied her back to her quarters. Afterwards he continued across the yard to the pen with the troll babe in his arms.

He felt guilty, leaving the troll exposed to the night air with no roof and no proper clothing. He'd attempted a diaper from some old sheets in the pantry. He knew it would only last so long. The little thing kept tugging at the makeshift britches. But somehow everything seemed different now that the troll had been inside. It was as though he'd been through a rite of passage.

Drowden resolved to find him more suitable lodgings, but it would have to wait 'til morning. He got some straw from the barn and spread it about the pen, then set the troll inside. This time, the baby laid down, stuck his thumb in his mouth, and fell instantly to sleep.

Drowden bounded lightheartedly into the house and up the stairs toward Ian's room. Peeking inside, he saw that Ian was peeking back at him from under a tent of covers.

"Hi, Daddy!" he laughed giddily then squealed as he plopped on his back and pulled the blankets up over him.

Drowden sat on the edge of the bed as Ian tugged the blanket from his head. "Did you see me?"

"Just a lump! A big lump on the bed. Could have been anything!"

"Like what?" Ian giggled.

"Oh, like maybe a bear, or a piglet from the barn…"

Ian giggled uncontrollably. "Or maybe a troll!"

"A troll?" Drowden asked. "And what would have happened if you'd been a troll, hiding under there?"

Ian jumped up with a growl and threw his arms about his father's shoulders. "I'd grab you and hug you real hard!"

Drowden laughed and held Ian close. "Then I wish it had been a big troll! But for now, I have you!" He kissed the boy and tucked him in. "I love you. Good night. Now try to get some sleep."

Drowden yawned and scratched his belly. The bedchamber door creaked quietly as he gave it a nudge. In the candlelight, Dorina dreamed. Her golden hair seemed fluid, spilling over the pillow.

Erebus tiptoed to his side of the bed, desperate for sleep. He pulled back the quilt, exposing his wife's arm and leg to the night air. The candle showed goose bumps on her forearm. Dorina had taken up a good majority of the bed and he calculated his way into the covers.

He maneuvered himself onto the feather mattress and pulled the quilt back over them both. Dorina stirred but thankfully didn't wake. Drowden was too exhausted for the myriad complaints his good wife might raise about the lateness of the hour. "Yes, the tables are all in place. The gazebo is scrubbed and freshly painted," he thought, as if answering those complaints. Everything she had asked him to see to had been seen to in preparation for the formal social tea.

It was hard to get comfortable, hanging off the edge of the bed as he did. Dorina was petite, but her legs and arms were stretched out in all directions. It left very little room for Drowden's lanky body.

After a while, he slipped his toes onto the floor, grabbed his pillow and slid out from under the bed covers. He lifted an extra quilt from a low table at the foot of the bed and stretched out on the floor. In no time at all he was snoring.

Chapter VII
Baptism by Fire

A slice of sunlight knifed through the slit of slightly parted curtains. It shafted across the room and spilled onto Drowden's eyelids. They fluttered as he came to wakefulness, eyes watering.

To his horror, Dorina's foot dangled above him and before he could get a word out, down it came on his chest.

Dorina shrieked and stumbled over him, then crashed to the floor; her nightgown flying up and twisting around her arms. Drowden gasped and choked, but even in his misery he managed to scramble to his wife's side to offer help.

"Dorina…" he gasped, "…. are you alright?"

She twisted and squirmed to pull her dressing gown down while untangling herself from the robe, but only managed to pull both garments completely off. She lay panting and naked upon the carpeted floor.

Drowden could not help himself. Regardless of his own pains, he wrapped his arms around her slender waist and pulled her to him, stroking the small of her back and wiping her tears with his fingertip.

"Oh love, forgive me." She was a tempest of feelings, trembling between outrage, fear and hunger for her husband's nearness. Suddenly she wept openly and gave herself to Drowden's kisses. Soon they coupled in passion, both full of renewed longing for one another.

Below, the house was awake with servants bustling in and out, scurrying about doing their chores. Scuffling feet and voices were muffled, but nothing could mask the scent of sweet rolls coming to life and browning in the oven.

The Mistress fell back to sleep after their lovemaking. Her husband lay there with her on the floor, listening to the world outside and feeling grateful for life's fullness.

Crisp summer air fluttered through the bedroom curtains, reviving him. Dorina slumbered on. He lifted her gently from the floor to the canopied bed, pulling a sheet up to her shoulders. Then he slid into his slippers, working them on with squirming toes.

Finding his robe, Drowden tossed it over his shoulders then worked his arms into his sleeves and fastened the belt about his waist. Everything was done very quickly, very quietly. He grabbed his clothes and balled them under his arm then crept out to the hallway and ducked into Ian's room to dress.

He used the pitcher and bowl on the nightstand, splashing cold water over his face. Ian had not bothered to bathe, that was obvious. In the mirror, Drowden could see that the blankets on his son's bed were lumped and knotted in profusion.

The next room over, Ian's playroom, reverberated with the boy's rambunctious laughter. The rocking horse was gently creaking floorboards, carrying Ian's imagination on some adventure far beyond the hills of Hapstead. Ian made clopping sounds with his tongue like horses' hooves, then gave his best effort at a horse's whinny.

His father's dripping head poked into the playroom. Drowden gave his son a wink. "Morning, lad! An early start at your busy day speaks well of your industriousness. But do keep the racket down! Your mother is still asleep, and your father wants it that way!"

"Yes Daddy!" Ian gave a sharp chop at the air with his chin.

Drowden returned to his morning ritual, patted himself dry with a towel hanging at the side of the highboy chest, then smacked himself squarely on the cheeks to finish, blushing slightly under the blow.

He dressed in a hurry, but carefully, referring to the looking glass for verification that his collar was straight and shoulders square.

Drowden grinned broadly at himself in the glass then trounced light-footed down the hall and grasped the banister for support and skipped down the steps, two at a time to the world below.

He stopped at his desk alcove to flip through his ledger and make a mental note to dedicate some time there before ordering supplies. Then he breezed through the main house and went out the side door to the kitchen.

Odelia was so absorbed with breakfast preparations, she didn't notice Master Erebus until he was directly behind her, and then only after he cleared his throat. "Oh!" the maid jumped. Crepe batter splattered across the hot iron topped stove. The droplets sputtered and smoked in the heat then burned to black dots of ash.

"Don't do that!" she turned to face the culprit. "Master! Pardon my tongue sir but you frightened me!"

Drowden laughed like a schoolboy. "Forgive me dear lady," he said bowing deeply, "I didn't want to break the spell you were weaving over that porridge. Smells delicious!"

Odelia grinned, showing the spaces between her teeth. "The makings of a mediocre apology. Food's not quite ready but there's coffee in the pot. Will the Mistress be down soon?"

Drowden dabbed his finger in the mush and shoved it in his mouth with a wink. Currants, nutmeg and a touch of honey. "Mmmmm! No. She's sleeping in. She was a bit restless last night. But the children are up."

Odelia strained her ears then shrugged. "I don't hear anything."

"I told them to be extra quiet."

"It seems to have worked," Odelia said. "What did you use for a bribe?"

Drowden chuckled at the maid. "I promised them a breakfast surprise." His smile was sincere.

Odelia stopped stirring and spun about. "A surprise? I wish you'd let me know when yer expectin' me to prepare something special. Sir, a bit of notice…."

Drowden raised his hand. "Fear not. I will be in charge of the surprise." Drowden was being cryptic. His face revealed nothing. "Is there enough for an extra serving?" he asked while spooning sugar into his coffee.

Odelia made a quick survey, but it was all for show. There was always plenty. "I think we can squeeze more milk from the cow, if she don't mind. Plenty of eggs....and I made some extra biscuits." She walked to the window and poked out her head. "Jessa!" she called.

"Very good, then." Master Erebus put the spoon in the dish pail.

"I'm going to give the little troll another try at table manners...."

Odelia whirled around, crossed her arms over her chest and huffed. "No! Do you dare?"

".... while she sleeps!" he said to cut her off. "Do we still have that old flatware set with the big wooden handles?"

"Yes, sir. It's in the hutch. Just a couple pieces left. I...."

"Good!" Drowden placed his cup on the counter and made way for the door. "I'll need a place setting and a wooden bowl or two. And a wooden mug. Nothing fancy.

"Of course, sir." Odelia curtsied.

"I'll be right back. Tell the children I want to see their best table etiquette! Everything smells delicious, Odelia." With a rub to the tummy, he was gone.

Odelia shook her head and checked the rolls. "Really! Our best behavior, for a troll!" She closed the oven as Jessa came in. "We need more milk, quick! And a few more eggs! Master Erebus is having a guest for breakfast."

Jessa flustered. "So little warning! I can't imagine visitors this early!" She raced out the door and ran right past Drowden, calling "Good morning, sir!" over her shoulder. Jessa thought it odd that the master would be heading for the troll's pen when guests were arriving at any minute!

Chuckling at the commotion he'd caused, Drowden reached for the gate and opened it. "Good morning, lad! Hope you slept well!" The troll was sitting on his haunches, the makeshift diaper soiled and drooping low. He'd been watching a bee in flight until he saw the master coming.

Without changing position, the little troll greeted Drowden with a pleasant grunt and grin.

"Time to get cleaned up, boy! See? Bucket and sponge already laid out. And this?" Drowden pointed to a bundle of cloth. "This is your new outfit. Around here we tend to dress for table."

He set the bucket down so the troll could see it. The little one backed away, moaning and hissing warily as Drowden approached.

"It's alright," he whispered. "Let's have that diaper off you!"

Drowden's calm, even tones seemed to allay the troll babe's fears. He stood motionless and patiently as his soiled diaper was stripped from his bottom.

Bathing and re-diapering went smoothly. The troll seemed to know what was expected. But when it came to rigging the drawstring trousers, the troll wanted none of it. He hissed, barked and snarled as Drowden struggled with each leg. He'd get one in its proper place, then start on the other only to have to do the first again. This went on until the master's patience ended. And he cried "Enough!" The troll froze.

"That's better. Now, just stay still a little longer." He reached for the tunic and tried to put it over the babe's head, succeeding only after holding the babe's body down with his legs. Arms found their sleeves with no less a battle, but it was done.

"Now I'm a mess!" Drowden sighed as he got up and started pounding the dust from his clothes. Then he stood back and looked at the troll. "This will have to do. At least you're clean and covered. Now, come with me!" Taking the troll's small hand in his, Drowden led him out of the pen.

"Today you will honor us with your company at breakfast!" The little troll pulled and tugged at his garments. "You'll get used to it, lad. All part of growing up, I'm afraid. Take my word for it. I was born naked too!" Drowden patted his chest. "Now look at me."

They trudged up the stone footpath to the kitchen steps. The troll's nostrils fluttered at the aromas coming from the window. "Smells good, doesn't it? Well, we better get in there! Keep your fingers crossed that my wife is still sleeping!"

Drowden led the agile infant through the door. "Here we are, Odelia! You may serve!" The kitchen maid's mouth fell open in a quiet gasp.

"Good morning, Miranda, Ian. Hope you slept well, what little there was to be had!" Ian started to say something, but Miranda shushed him. Odelia had secretly hoped the Master wouldn't follow through with his plan. She felt a deep foreboding but shoved it aside.

Suddenly Ian couldn't contain himself. The troll was rolling his eyes and sniffing the air like one of the dogs begging for a juicy tidbit. Ian burst into giggles. Miranda fell into peals of laughter too.

Master Erebus grabbed a stool with his free hand and slid it over to the table. "Odelia, I'll seat our guest then you may serve anytime." And to the troll "You are about to experience one of life's pleasures. Odelia's porridge is a gastronomic delight!"

The kitchen maid looked over her shoulder. "But the mistress. Sir. She's bound to…"

Drowden waved her to silence. "Then I suggest we get this over with before she finds out." He set the troll on the stool and drew up his own chair. "Ian, stop laughing! We're going to teach our friend here how to use a fork and spoon!" The boy covered his mouth with his hand but continued to smile toothily behind his palm.

"Do you think we can?" Miranda asked. She wrinkled her brow with worry.

"If we really work at it! Ahh! Here's the porridge! Well, Mr. Troll, this is a spoon." The little creature stuck his head into the bowl, ignoring the spoon. He immediately drew out his face, moaning like a scalded cat.

"Hot!" Drowden cried, then grabbed his napkin and wiped the gruel away. "That's why we use these things!" He wrapped the troll's fingers around the spoon and watched as the little bugger slapped the table with it. Ian burst out laughing, exposing a mouth full of mush.

Garbled by the lump of porridge, Ian tried to say, "I don't think he wants to learn right now, Father!' He giggled after a swallow of milk.

"Perhaps you're right, son. That doesn't mean he won't." Taking the spoon with the little troll's hand still attached, Drowden guided the troll through the basic motions.

"I remember not too long ago, when you were doing the same thing as our little friend here," said Drowden. "See how well you do now? It's a skill that can even be learned by a barbarian like you."

Ian laughed out loud. "Ha! I'm a barbarian!"

He repeated it joyfully until Miranda placed a hand over his mouth and hissed "Shhhhhhhh!"

By the time the course was ended, the little troll was wearing more mush than he'd eaten, but spoon manipulation was almost mastered.

"Eggs get managed with a fork, lad," Drowden said very seriously, "and so does the sausage. I'll cut it for you. Knives can wait for a while."

Miranda offered her clean napkin to remove the latest layer of food from the troll's face. "Here." She dabbed the cloth along his lips and swiped his cheeks. "We like to put our food in our faces, not on them!"

Ian clapped his hands and giggled. "See Daddy? I'm a big boy! I know how to eat!" Then he picked up his spoon and shoved a huge portion of gruel into his mouth. His cheeks puffed out under the load.

"Ian Erebus!" the boy's father scolded, "We are trying to teach our friend how to be civilized, not piggish! Now, smaller portions and chew your food."

The lad swallowed and took a sip of milk. "I'm sorry, Father." Then he scooped a more modest spoonful to his lips. "See? I know how to do it. I *am* a big boy!"

"Very good." Drowden smiled. "You certainly are a big boy. And getting bigger every day!"

Miranda signaled Odelia for another napkin or two as she picked bits of currant jelly from behind the troll's ears and out of his hair. "You seem to have gotten it everywhere but where it's supposed to go!" she smiled, keeping her voice lilting and soft. She turned to her father. "Why don't you eat something and let me try for a while?"

Drowden nodded. He was hungry. "Sounds like a good idea, but don't you forget to eat."

Miranda had no taste for mush, even with honey and she had already eaten her fill of eggs, bacon and rolls. "Please Father," she sighed, "you need nourishment, too."

With that, he picked up a fork and made quick work of his eggs and meat. Odelia offered to fill his plate again but was waved away. "Your cooking is good, but more's not better." Drowden licked his lips and reached for a sweet roll anyway.

Ian meanwhile had gotten into the spirit of things. He moved his chair, cup of milk and place setting nearer the troll, then climbed back up and grabbed his fork.

Miranda looked to her father. "But I...."

Drowden sighed. "Both of you could show him some of the finer points. After all, I taught you. Now both of you can teach our little troll."

"See?" Ian began. "It's easy! You put the fork into your hand, pick up some food, then put it in your...."

The troll plucked the piece of sausage from Ian's plate.

"Hey!" the boy cried out. "That's mine!"

Drowden looked up to see his son grabbing at the troll's wrist. "No, Ian!" he cried, unheard.

"Give me back my meat!" Ian shouted, pulling at the troll's fist. "No, Ian!" Drowden slapped the table with his hand. "Don't."

Suddenly chairs toppled. Boy and troll were wrestling on the kitchen floor, kicking, punching, nipping, grabbing and howling.

"Ian! Stop it!" Drowden jumped out of his seat. Miranda, who'd gone to get an apron, rushed to the fray, dropped to her knees and tried to pry the troll's arm, which was wrapped around Ian's waist. Drowden held Ian and

Miranda yanked at the troll's shoulders, both trying to pull the fighters apart when Mistress Dorina swung open the door and burst in.

"What?" she shouted. Her voice was shrill and indignant. Everything stopped, including the troll. "What is happening? I won't believe it. This can't be real!" Dorina looked around the room. Bits of breakfast had made their way onto the walls and floorboards.

"Who let that…that thing into my kitchen." Her eyes fell upon her battle worn and bloody-nosed child. "Ian! Oh, my poor baby!" Dorina waited until he moved away from the troll then went to him. "Look at you, poor thing!" and to her husband, "How could you?"

She snapped a finger and Miranda brought a warm damp cloth to her mother, who wiped her son's face and checked for bites and bruises.

Drowden looked sheepishly at his wife. "I tried to tell him not to take food from the troll, but not soon enough." He paused, knowing the words fell on deaf ears. "It all happened so fast!"

Just then, Odelia came up from the root cellar. Her eyes widened at the tumbled chairs and spray of food. "What the…." The maid's heart skipped a beat when she spotted Dorina. "Oh! Mistress!" She scanned the room, noting food flung everywhere, chairs overturned, the porridge bowl upturned on the floor and milk spilled in a wide white swath under the table. "Oh…my," is all she said.

Odelia turned to get a bucket and filled it with warm water from the stove.

"Fetch the medicine powders used for animal bites, Miranda!" Lady Erebus snapped. "Ian, keep your head up or that nose will never stop bleeding!" While his wife shouted orders, Drowden picked up his troll and made for the door. "A moment, husband," Dorina called out. "I want a word with you!"

"I'll be right back, dear," he replied. "I just want to put the troll back in his pen, then…"

Dorina righted a chair and lifted her son into it. "I don't want that creature on display in my yards!" she cried over her shoulder. "I don't want any of our party guests to see it or hear it or have the slightest inkling that it exists! Drowden, do you hear me?"

"Yes, love." Drowden called backward and darted out of the kitchen, troll in arms.

Outside, servants were milling about, whispering and wagging their heads. Argis stepped forward. "Sir?"

Drowden shifted the troll to his other arm and closed the door.

"Everybody's alright," he assured the gathering. "Argis, Willbee, all of you, get back to work!"

Drowden asked Harry to fetch a bucket, then he carried the troll back to its pen. He checked for injuries and wiped the surface muck from his face, hair, fingers and legs. "That will have to do for now, lad," Drowden said with an air of impatience. "We'll sort this out later."

Once he was sure the troll was calmed and comfortable, Drowden washed his own face and went back to the house to face Dorina.

Chapter VIII
A Maddening Tea

The invitations were sent out weeks ago. Dorina was pleasantly surprised to receive positive responses from nearly everyone she wanted to attend; though it perturbed her to think the busybodies who originally sent their regrets wrote back to say they would make every effort to attend. "If I have to move mountains," Lady Ubal's note read. "I will be there!" In each of the belated responses there was some mention of the troll.

On instructions, her courier inquired after accommodations for his mistress' twin terriers Buffy and Button. He needn't have asked. Hapstead Manor had an excellent dog run at the lower end of the informal garden where the affair was being held. There would be plenty of soup bones and scraps for all canine guests.

A large awning billowed lightly over the seating area set up to the left and down a small path from the kitchen. Pendants waved from the tents' masts, most of them long slips of brightly colored fabric.

Hapstead Manor's coat of arms waved above them all from atop a twenty-foot-tall flagpole. This was the more formal banner, hung for special occasions.

The motto, drawn on a fluttering banner above the new emblem, read "Honor Leads. All Else Follows." Fligard Mofely had it designed shortly before his death and gave it to his son-in-law with as much ceremony as a dying man could offer.

Of the countless other chores in preparation for the party, Jessa had the daunting task of making sure the ceremonial flag was cleaned and in good repair. The everyday standard was also cleaned and stitched, then set in a cedar chest. After the gathering it would be returned to a daily routine of being raised at sunrise and lowered at sunset. It had no tassel or trim but was nevertheless impressive.

Dorina checked her list of party preparations several times a day, and as the time drew near, she grew more and more obsessed.

"I know why they're coming," she muttered to Odelia while they reviewed the menu for the hundredth time. "Tongues have been wagging for weeks, I just know it. 'Hapstead Manor is housing a troll!' That's all they care about. We've become a social oddity."

The kitchen maid said little as she folded napkins into fanciful floral shapes.

"They're expecting to find the Manor in ruins over this troll business," the mistress thought to herself. "Well, we'll just see about that."

Her husband's opinion of these society women was less kind, more cutting. His imitations of them sent Argis and the other men, and even some of the women, into fits of laughter.

Tea party eve found Dorina unable to sleep. She lay beside Drowden until he snored, then got up and sat at the writing desk with last-minute menu additions and more suggestions for lawn games. She scribbled notes and then put them in the household memo box stationed on the table outside their bedchamber door. Assured it would be collected very early in the morning and delivered to the appropriate hands, Dorina went back to bed and at long last drifted off as the clock chimed four bells.

She woke with a start two hours later, full of worry. "They are just hoping for something to go wrong," Dorina cried gently as her husband held her. "Please tell me everything will be fine."

"All will be perfect, love." Drowden stroked her cheek. "You are the perfect hostess. You've planned everything to the last detail. What could possibly go wrong?"

Dorina let flow a fresh flood of worries, envisioning the countless ways things could go terribly, terribly wrong — and they all had the little troll at the center of them.

"As professional gossips," Drowden continued, "they feel it is their duty to investigate and report back to the community-at-large." This didn't help Dorina's nerves one bit. Flustered, Drowden tried for a bit of humor.

"Besides," he pointed out, "it's a free meal! Most of those old biddies live from trough to trough!" Dorina forced a grin but only half-heard him as she re-thought her idea of what to wear. She sat straight up, swung her feet to the side and got out of bed.

"You will keep that thing...I mean to say 'your troll' out of sight!" she scolded while rummaging through her closets. The blue striped frock selected days before lay in a heap, rejected on the dressing room floor. She considered a more formal dress, but rejected that too, and with that choice, she also set aside a momentary temptation to retrieve from their secure hiding place the large ruby pendant and matching earrings her grandmother had left to her.

"Too much ostentation," she said to herself as she let the thought pass and picked up the blue striped frock from the floor. Looking it over again, she thought that Miranda would look good in it by next season. Holding it once more, close to her body as she stood before the long mirror, she made a mental note to have Becky rework the garment for her daughter, then set it aside.

Suddenly an image of the little troll came to mind and she blanched. She wanted to insist Drowden release the crude beast back into the wild, but she knew he was adamant in his decision to keep it. Still, she couldn't stop herself from trying one more time.

She called into the bedroom from her dressing room. "There's still time to have Bobbin and Nith take that troll up into the hills and set it free. They're both useless to me today. Bobbin will linger near the pantry and steal sweets. Nith will hide somewhere anyway, until the work is done. Won't you do that for me, sweetheart? Just have them load that beastie thing into a wagon and come back without it?"

"We spoke of this, dearest," he said, putting on his work clothes. "He will be kept in the barn, up in the loft. And anyway, Nith is afraid of trolls. And Bobbin is helping Odelia set up tables. I'm going to put the finishing touches on the latch and lock and try to make it passably comfortable for him."

Drowden Erebus kissed his wife's forehead. "You and your guests won't even know he's around!" With that he walked with a gangly gait out of the room and through the hallway and then down the back staircase.

"Gossips or not," Dorina sighed into the looking glass, determined, "this will be the best tea of the season!" She examined a pale pink gown that had been made for last year, but not yet worn. Pink wasn't her favorite color, but this one was subtle enough and would work well with her lace petticoat and ivory slippers. Dorina wanted her party preparations, not some barbaric troll, to be the center of attention and comment.

Drowden meanwhile worked in the barn, turning part of the loft into a comfortable billet for the forest creature. He observed that the troll was growing inches taller every day. "Well lad," he smiled, "at least you'll be out of the wind and weather."

The troll grunted, as if agreeing. "Someday," Drowden predicted while stuffing straw into an old, discarded mattress, "someday those sounds will be words!" He whip-stitched the bedding closed, covered it with an old blanket, and then looked through the open shutters to the scene below.

From the work yards to the manor house itself, everything glistened and gleamed. Compost piles had been moved to far fields, hedges trimmed to within an inch of their lives, according to Hector, and grass close clipped with a long-handled scythe.

Drowden was pleased to think that his troll's arrival hadn't impeded preparations. Dorina's long list of chores was punctuated with check marks and notes. He'd never hear the end of it if anything were left undone. But there was nothing to fear.

Tom had weeded and scrubbed the flagstone path from the carriage house to the main house and the gravel path from the parlor to the garden as well.

Bill Macatee made sure there was plenty of feed and straw for all the horses and extra tethers should any of the guests' animals prove skittish.

Thanks to Hector and Fred, the road up from the main gate was manicured, weeds pulled and pits in the lane filled with a fresh layer of stone. The gate had a new coat of paint. All in all, Hapstead Manor was a welcoming showcase.

Odelia scampered about the kitchen, driven mad by menu changes, overseeing breakfast preparations and early arrivals. Much of the silver still needed polishing and guest linens still blew in the wind on the line out back.

The kitchen maid drafted every available hand and sent them running in different directions to perform various deeds. Bad enough feeding half the population of Irongate and Deepwater but housing a handful of them overnight mocked patience.

Hector trudged innocently through the kitchen door and was ambushed. "Here!" Odelia cried. "Wash those grubby hands and get over here!"

Dumbfounded, the poor man was scrubbed, aproned and stationed in front of the stove before he could utter a sound. "Just stir that until it boils, then remove it from the heat. You'll find two more needin' the same attention on the counter….and by all means," Odelia paused, "don't burn anything! And don't set anything on fire."

"But…" Hector complained, "I'm no cook. The wife! I'll go an' git…."

Odelia looked up harshly from her kneading. "Your wife's in there, helpin' get th' rooms sorted for our high-flootin' guests. So watch what you're doin'! I just cleaned those walls yesterday mornin'!"

Hector was mortified. "What if Argis or one o' the other fellers see me like this? Wimen's work! I'd never live it down!"

"Never you mind!" Odelia scolded. "Argis an' them are doin' their share o' unseemly work today." She pointed in the direction of the informal garden where Picote and Harry were helping spread great cloths over long low planks set on top of barrels.

Dorina dashed into the kitchen, poured a cup of coffee and put two sweet rolls on a small plate. She looked wonderful in the pale yellow gown and straw hat that had been her original choice weeks before.

"Thank you, Odelia!" she called while heading through the door to the service path. "Everything looks wonderful!" The kitchen maid giggled when she realized Dorina was talking to Hector's back, mistaking him for her.

"You're awful cute in that apron, you are," Odelia cackled under her breath.

Dorina sat on a bench, ate half a roll and sipped some coffee, then got up and placed baskets of wildflowers at each end of the long tables. On the shorter, round tables she placed bud vases with sprigs of mint and more wildflowers. She clasped her hands together and looked to the sky, "Please, weather! Be kind."

Miranda rushed out the door to help her mother, looking lovely in her lace blouse, pink skirt and petticoat trimmed in pink satin silk ribbons. She wore a bow in her hair, though she had protested that it made her look immature. But Dorina was not to be moved. She said it was fitting for her age and left no room for comment.

She looked up as her daughter drew near. Miranda would need a whole new wardrobe, from hats to undergarments, she mused. Her daughter was growing into a beautiful young woman, complete with a cute upward turn to her nose that she inherited from her grandmother Erebus.

"The dishes are coming out right behind me!" Miranda reported. "The silver's done and Finn is helping with the water pitchers!"

"Good, very good." Mistress Erebus smiled. "I just hope we have enough of everything!"

Mother and daughter walked the length and breadth of the garden, making sure place cards were set so that none of the guests would be uncomfortable with their tablemates.

Dorina was pleased to note the number of high-born families with eligible sons who would be attending. Some of them hadn't even been invited but sent word that they would be able to visit nonetheless. Perhaps there was some good to come of having a troll as guest of the manor after all, for surely that is what they hoped to see.

Dorina had hired the best string quartet and madrigal singers in the region. They arrived early and were now fed and setting up music stands and chairs and applying resin to their fiddle sticks.

Drowden was expected to entertain the men who would accompany their wives, daughters and mistresses. "Your father will show off that monster of his," Dorina whispered to her daughter while they supervised place settings. "I'll be happy to have some of them out of our hair a while."

Just then the word came down that Lady Ubal was already in her rooms, primping and pruning what little remained of her beauty. Buffy and Button could be heard barking noisily from an open window. Her presence at the party assured all eyes would be upon Hapstead Manor.

Lady Gretchen was the wife of prominent goldsmith Quetal Bas Ubal, and self-proclaimed mother of the twin terriers. They were her pride and joy and part of her entourage. Lady Ubal only went where the best people went, and her yapping little mutts enjoyed all the benefits of living within the corona of her prestige.

The dogs had a reputation for yammering and yawling at the smallest thing, although it was said they had been trained to take commands by a genius named Blaxton Piel. It was assumed that Lady Ubal simply didn't care what her 'babies' did in other people's homes, but this time Piel had accompanied her to Hapstead. It was also said of most society dogs that they were apt to replicate the personalities of their masters, but maybe, Dorina thought, their behavior would be better than that this time.

She recalled with dismay the R.S.V.P. list included five inked notations stating: "Princess will accompany, of course," "Please have those lovely little snacks dear William loves," and "Tinky will be bringing along her new little brother Tommy, so please have a blanket ready."

"So much for the flower beds," Dorina sighed. Then, "Quick!" she yelled after Harry. "Send Rachel or Jessa up to Lady Ubal with a glass of red wine before she has time to call for it!"

After a final look at the tables and tents, Mistress Dorina set out for the kitchen to oversee final touches on finger cakes, fruit salads and savories on their silver serving trays.

Jessa and Petrina scuffled through the service door. Both grabbed trays laden with food and were heading back for the door when Petrina stopped dead in her tracks.

"Husband!" she cried, noticing Hector tending the stove. She couldn't hold back laughing.

"Hector!" Dorina cried between chuckles. "Is that you?!"

The poor laborer's face puckered with embarrassment.

"Now, enough!" Odelia stood to his side, "Don't tease! I think he's bein' rather gallant, dropping his manly chores to help me." With parting giggles, Petrina and Jessa took up their trays once more and raced out the door.

The clatter of more coaches sent Lady Erebus through the house, mopping a sweaty brow. Guests were arriving in earnest now, even though they weren't scheduled for another hour.

Morbid curiosity, she mused, but smiled brightly for each guest...invited or otherwise. No matter, there was plenty of food and the garden lawn was large enough. Lots of chairs and side tables, lots of room, plenty of every-thing...she kept telling herself.

Drowden was still busy with his troll. Dorina made the excuse that he was finishing some business in the lower field and would join the welcoming line shortly.

Meanwhile, Odelia grabbed every available hand to work on some tasks. Those who cleaned up well were put in their Sunday best and sent to serve sherry and trays of tidbits to the guests, some of whom were assembling in the main parlor. The rest of the servants were sent to tend after horses, luggage, carriages, pets and anything else which needed attention.

More and more guests arrived. Dorina flitted from group to group, making sure everyone was comfortable and generally showing all in attendance that sanity and civility reigned supreme at Hapstead Manor, no matter what anybody had heard about a wild woodland troll in their midst.

Lady Erebus sent word for the musicians to commence, and soon the air was filled with their lilting refrains.

Well met are we plain folk.
Come see a fair sight.
Warm greetings and tidings.
Now be our delight.

"Come!" Dorina called to the assemblage in the house, "Let's go outside. It's a beautiful day." With that, she opened the door and led her guests down the main path to the garden.

And what a fine setting met their eyes! The canopies, flower baskets, carved wooden cherubs and tilt-wicked candles were entirely festive and evoked ooohhs and ahhhs from the lips of many.

Pure white bone china and tall crystal goblets sparkled in the sun; each tablecloth boasted a highly starched crispness and every piece of flatware displayed a polished brilliance. Everything was perfect, down to the dogs' bowls. Butterflies tinkered with gentle breezes, birds harmonized with the string quartet; everything was, as Dorina overheard more than once, absolutely enchanting.

She smiled broadly in the glow of success and even responded cheerily to questions about Hapstead Manor's woodland guest. "Oh that!" she tittered to Mildred Boxlie-Dwyer of the Deepwater Boxlie-Dwyers. "Why, I hardly know it's here!"

Daphne Keldridge and her mother fanned themselves in feigned horror. "Mrs. Keldridge, I can assure you that my husband has taken great pains to keep the creature from disturbing our household!"

Lady Ubal looked up from her gaily decorated place-setting. "My babies! What if they wander within reach of that beast? What would become of them?"

Dorina waved a hand. "Please madam, upon my word, all is well. Button and Buffy are free to enjoy the hospitality of Hapstead Manor without fear or concern." Then to the group at large, "Please! You are all safe. Your pets and horses are safe!" And she added for her own satisfaction, "And of course you know this, or you would not have come!"

Soon all the dogs were gnawing soup bones under a wind-rippled canopy. All but Button and Buffy, anyway.

Men's laughter spilled from the barn, where Drowden was recounting the story of his troll's arrival. Gentlemen escorts, coachmen, grown sons and groaning husbands assembled around a keg of ale, the great equalizer, and listened to the so-far eventful tale of the troll-babe's brief stay at Hapstead Manner. They sat on bales of hay in a circle about the barrel, mugs filled to the brim with the manor's own frothy brew.

The troll lad was restless with all the commotion outside. He had managed to open the barn window and was intently watching the guests move about the property. The sweet smell of Odelia's cooking had the troll's stomach grumbling louder than Ian at bath time.

Soon the sights, sounds and smells got the best of the young troll. He leaned out the window to see for a way out and down. Parked below was a wagon of hay. It had been left outside the barn to make room for the gentlemen guests who could be heard below laughing and carrying on.

The troll turned and went backwards out of the window. With deceivingly strong arms and hands, he grabbed each side of the sill and lowered himself down. Thinking he could lower himself enough to gently drop down into the wagon, he looked back to aim his drop. Suddenly, from around the back of the barn, two dogs came running up barking maddeningly. Startled, he lost his grip and tumbled uncontrollably the remaining ten feet into the wagon.

Shaken, but not hurt, he poked his head out of the pile of hay. Button and Buffy had come running from the shade of a tulip tree and they raised a howl at the sight of the troll's head peeking over the side of the wagon. Blaxton Piel turned on his heels and walked quickly from the barnyard and ducked inside where the men were gathered.

Not knowing what to do, the troll put a finger to his lips as he had seen Master Erebus do and loudly sounded, "Shhhh!" To his amazement, the dogs went silent.

Jessa strode by carrying trays of cheese and fruit, bread and sausages to the barn where the men were drinking. She didn't notice the troll peeking over the edge of the wagon but kicked her feet toward the two spaniels that were jumping and barking. They fled a short distance but returned when she stepped inside the barn. By now, the keg was flowing freely, as was the conversation.

"Nathan Bladic says he's cornered you into a wager!" Jake Resh, a tall coachman in formal attire and a reedy voice said as he wiped foam from his upper lip.

"Did you really bet him you'd have the imp talking before the corn grew taller than its brow?" a second chauffeur inquired, slapping his knee and laughing.

"Good sir!" one of the women's escorts chided. "Have respect for your host. He has been kind enough to set this spread before you and extend his hospitality!"

"I mean no harm," the man protested.

"I wouldn't have wagered a whole year's crop on that!" Biddy Alderot's somber manservant bellowed in his deep, bassoon of a voice. "The corn grows well this season, an' 'tis already knee high! It'll outstrip yer little heathen in a week!"

"A whole year's crop?" gasped a leather-vested man with mutton chop sideburns, who no one seemed to know. "You don't know what you're in for!

Nathan Bladic would never wager so much if he had a fart's chance in a gale of losing!"

A rolling rumble of laughter put life in the vibrating rafters. Drowden Erebus took a long swallow and set his tankard on the barn's dirt floor. When he raised his head, he was smiling. "But," he pointed to the man, "Nathan Bladic doesn't know trolls like I do!"

"Ha! A few good books and a fluke capture of a baby troll, and suddenly he's an expert!" Gabel Witson chided, the oldest man present and a died-in-the-wool know-it-all. Witson had accompanied his wife Leelah to the gathering. The troll was all they talked about all the way from Irongate.

Gabel stroked his fading red beard and held his mug out at arm's length. "I'm grateful for your hospitality." He reached over and pulled the stopper. "Still in all, you're not my master so I'll speak plainly. You're a fool, sir. And you're going to lose your shirt to Nathan Bladic if you try to beat him at gambling. He's a man o' the Brotherhood, and he knows all anybody needs to know about trolls." A wicked grin crossed his face and he winked a shared confidence at Kit and Resh. "Bladic doesn't part with money easily, and I'll put up a month's salary says he'll be sending his wagons to Hapstead Manor this fall to collect his winnings!"

There was general laughter and cheer at his boldness.

"So, you'd drink my ale and call me a fool!" Drowden mumbled just loud enough to be heard. "You're wrong, Gabel. I accept your friendly wager, and yes, I propose to think of it as friendly. Either way, I'll be glad to take your wages if you can afford to part with them."

Resh guffawed. "He can afford it! He's a regular miser, isn't that right, Kit?" The man with the brass voice nodded cheerlessly. "I've never known him to gamble or buy the drinks when it's his turn either!"

Gabel glared. "Humph! Not the way you drink! But I ain't afraid to put my money on a sure thing."

"So!" Kit's voice rang out, "Let's see the little bastard! I'd have not sent the mistress' young sprite Harley to drive her out this way if it weren't for a chance to see the troll."

Jake nearly choked on his beer with laughter. "You mean old Queetal lets Harley ride off with Lady Ubal all alone? I hear she's got an eye for the young ones."

The others joined in the laughter. "Why'd she let you come? Is it your turn, Kit?!!" Gabel slapped Kit's back and nearly choked on his ale.

Drowden felt it his duty to change the subject. Master and Mistress Ubal were pillars of the community and he didn't want to be accused of being party to defaming their characters, even in jest.

"You said you wanted to see my troll!" he spoke above the din. "Well, here's your chance! He's right here in the barn! In the loft above your very heads!" A few of the men looked up and fell silent.

"Well!" Kit perked up. "Let's have a look!"

Drowden led the way up the ladder and soon the group stood behind him on the straw-covered boards. He looked around, squinting into the shadows, but saw nothing. He stood silently, hands on hips, and whispered just audibly, "He's gone!"

The shuttered loft window hung open, the boards creaking in the afternoon breeze. Drowden spotted Hector in the yard below and cried out to him.

"Quick! Get some help! The troll's gotten out! Hurry!"

Hector ran for the bunk house, shouting as he shoved the door open, "All 'ands! Now!" Men grabbed for ropes and nets and spilled into the yard, some still hopping into their boots.

A million horrific visions streaked through Drowden's mind. He shook his head. "My wife will never forgive me if…" He refused to entertain it. "No. Everything will all be all right. It's got to be."

Forcing upon himself a calm that caged mental chaos, he climbed down the ladder, briskly but without showing urgency. He told the merry makers to wait in the barn and help themselves to the ale while he fetched the little troll for them to see. He hoped it would be that simple.

Drowden could hear the strains of music from the party and breathed easier, taking it as a positive sign. The scent of roasted beef poured out of the kitchen and filled his nostrils as he got closer. He imagined the little creature being mesmerized by the aroma and lurking near the back door to get a scrap. Trying to think like a troll, Master Erebus stationed himself near the door hoping to bag him before any of Dorina's guests spotted the young troll.

Trying to appear as inconspicuous as possible, he sat on the steps and pulled his pipe from a vest pocket, tamped a good portion of tobacco into it and lit a match on a stone. The smoke billowed around him and joined the heady ale to calm him, almost to lethargy. He saw Argis and Hector scurrying about the yard, searching under bushes and wagons, inside empty barrels and up in the trees for the little imp.

The quartet took a short break then began to play an original composition. Odelia managed a brief appearance, overseeing the carrying of a huge, elaborately decorated castle cake. She was greeted with enthusiastic applause, curtsied and blushed then quickly retreated to the familiar world of her kitchen where she finally sat down.

Suddenly Odelia heard a series of screams and shouts. Her heart stopped. Harsh cries wrenched Drowden to his feet. "It's the monster! Help! Run for your lives!"

"Oh no!" Odelia raced from the kitchen to the garden, arriving just in time to see the troll dodge a flying castle cake.

Mistress Dorina was running five directions at once, shrieking, her arms flailing about in a combination of rage and horror. "Stop! Oh stop! Stay! Please! Everyone be calm. All will be well!"

No one paid any heed to Dorina's pleas. She stood watching in horrified wonder as the most splendid party of the season transformed into a nightmare of flying centerpieces, toppled tables, and upended chairs. Her wondrous soirée was tossed into shambles by a mob of madly fleeing women and unrestrained lap dogs.

The last tray of hors d'oeuvres came to a crashing end as Buffy and Button rounded the corner, their leashes trailing behind them.

Lady Erebus took a deep breath and raised her custard-spattered arms above her fruit encrusted head and shrieked at the top of her lungs, "Drowden Erebus, you bastard!" Great sobs shook her as she cried out once more, "Husband!"

The guests scattered about the yard, knocking over garden ornaments, flowerpots and one another as dogs and farm hands sprang from bushes and out of buildings in pursuit of the troll. Gretchen Ubal's pups were now leading the remaining pets on a mad dash through valleys of bunched up tablecloths and bowls of overturned salad greens, barking and baying, the troll close behind, not ahead of them.

Howls and growls, shouts and screams now filled the afternoon air. A bowl of punch toppled from a filigreed pedestal, its contents splashed and spilled, soaking Mimby Darean as she struggled with a hem in her dress that was caught under the leg of her chair. The more she struggled, the worse things got, 'til at long last she managed to break free, losing her skirt in the process.

Dorina tried to reach her but was knocked over by the young troll as he chased the yapping pair of Buffy and Button Ubal. He plowed into her full force, planting his thick-skulled head into her chest and forcing the breath out of her. She fell to a faint, uninjured but in shock.

Drowden Erebus ran into the garden. "All of you! Stop shouting! You're only making matters worse!" One of the guest's bulldogs lowered his head and growled, barring Master Erebus' progress, so he pushed it forcefully out of the way with the side of his foot. Rebuked, the animal whined and backed down.

He reached the center of the storm, grabbed for the cake-covered troll, but had to pry another dog away that had tangled its teeth in the scraggly hair on the back of the troll's right arm. He lifted the giggling woodling into his arms. Everything fell silent.

"Forgive us, ladies," he said with tightened lips. "I know it will be easy to blame this little creature for what's happened, but it is not his fault." He looked around at the bedraggled and besmeared party guests. "It is my fault, and yours. This is the damage that blind fear created."

There was a general hoot of outrage.

Kaylin Wanvers came up to him in red-faced rage. "And what of that beast? It has no regard for our comfort or safety. I dare say you'll pay dearly, Erebus, for all damages! My husband is in league with the law, in case you had forgotten!"

Drowden spotted his wife, lying prone in a pile of food. He brushed Lady Wanvers aside with a nod. "Yes, yes, of course. Have your solicitor contact mine. Excuse me."

He ran to his wife's side. "My darling!" he cried out, pained. Dorina was not bleeding but lay very still and very pale. Button and Buffy were licking bits of cake and food from the mistress' shoes.

"Git!" Drowden yelled at the dogs. "Git!" he swatted one of the dogs on the arse. It glowered back at him, showing its teeth and threatening to rend flesh. "Piels! Contain these dogs," he yelled.

"Argis!" he called to his foreman who trotted over. "Take our troll here back to his quarters and padlock the door and window. Don't delay."

"Oh, aye, sir!" Argis replied. "So, the party's ended then? Eh?"

Master Erebus was too worried for levity. "And get Miranda! Her mother needs help!"

Lady Ubal approached. She opened her mouth to say something, but Drowden glared at her. "You!" he accused. "Get those mutts off my wife!"

Button and Buffy ran to Gretchen Ubal when she called to them. "My poor babies! What have they done to you?"

Drowden knelt and scooped up his wife. "Somebody get Odelia! Is Doctor Meigelson here? I believe the Meigelsons were on the list!"

Lady Darean ran up and stood in Drowden's path. "Look at me!" she screamed. "I shan't go home like this! My dress is ruined!"

Dorina was beginning to come around. She mumbled something incoherent into her husband's ear but kept her eyes closed.

"My dear Lady Darean!" Drowden glared impatiently. "You look lovelier than ever," he said sarcastically.

"Well!" Mimby shouted in indignation. "I never!"

"Probably not!" Drowden replied over his shoulder as he took his leave, "But should you ever, please do so in the privacy of your own garden! In the meantime, I am sure you can find something to wear in that steamer trunk you brought!" And with that, he was off to the house, Dorina still limp in his arms.

Odelia met him at the door, with a cold damp cloth for her mistress' forehead. Then she scurried to the yard to organize a quick clean-up.

"Please, everyone!" Miranda stood where the musicians had been playing. "Come! See? Everything's being made right. Please!" She signaled to have more sherry poured and called for the juggler to entertain while one of the musicians restrung his fiddle. Some of the guests refused to stay a moment longer; Gretchen Ubal among them.

Once the musicians regained their composure, they played again, casting wary eyes in the direction of the barn where they were told the troll was housed under lock and key.

Meanwhile, Dorina stirred from her swoon slowly. She lay on the bed in her husband's arms. She listened intently to the world outside but heard no terrified screams or crashing tables. Instead, it seemed as if nothing at all had happened, with the exception of the occasional clop clopping of horse hooves and carriages wending their way back down to the gate.

"Husband," she sighed. "I…." Then it all flooded back, in horrid and horrifying detail. "That troll!" she cried out. "You and that thing have ruined me!" Dorina's hands became fists. She beat them against Drowden's chest. "That beast is out to kill someone! Do you hear me?" Her voice grew shrill. "Today we were lucky! What about next time?"

Doctor Ambris arrived, out of breath from the neighboring Borigan Estate. "You host an unusual garden party!" he said ironically as he came into the room. "Mistress Borigan has finally delivered their long-awaited firstborn. They send their regrets for not attending the Hapstead...ah, er... affair."

"I thought Claude Meigelson was here," said Drowden while Dr. Ambris opened his bag.

"Oh he was here, Father," Miranda replied, "but he decided to leave with the Ubal entourage."

Ambris nodded. "I'm not surprised. Meigelson's her nephew, you know."

Drowden rubbed his chin. "And Bladic's grandson," he said. "He's a coward to run off when his medical services were needed. But I'm glad you're here."

George Ambris had been doctor to the Manor for what seemed like a lifetime. When Lady Erebus had trouble with Ian's birth, he had been there with herbs, powders and experience at the ready to be sure both mother and child came through the delivery alive and intact.

Even now, he was mixing chamomile, valerian and honey into a tea for Dorina. "Drink this, my dear." He bowed his head slightly to look at her eyes. "You'll feel instantly better." And she did.

After a short while, Drowden rose. "I must go see after our guests." His wife said nothing but nodded in agreement. "I'll be back soon." He turned at the door. "I love you."

"I love you, too," she whispered, then lay back on her pillow and surrendered to sleep. Jessa came to the room and asked after her mistress.

"She'll sleep for a few hours," Doctor Ambris speculated. "No bones broken, no abrasions. She'll be fine." He closed his bag.

"Would you be interested in a cup of sherry and something to eat?" the housemaid offered. "Odelia has both ready for you below in the library."

"I'd prefer something more spirited if you have it," the doctor laughed. "I think I have some catching up to do."

Jessa laughed behind her cupped hand as she escorted the physician down the back stairs, through the kitchen, down the hall and into Drowden's book-lined lair.

By dusk, most of the guests had departed. Exhausted, Odelia grabbed a piece of leftover pastry and popped it into her mouth. "Best stuff I ever made!" she mused. "Plenty of time for clean-up now that we've already cleaned up." Everything that should have been brought indoors had been, and all that remained was the laundry and tons of dishes.

One by one the other servants came and joined her at the kitchen table. Odelia pulled an unopened bottle of grog from under her skirts. "Master Erebus told me we should share what's left, and there's more where this came from!" Everyone grabbed for wooden mugs and tumblers and they filled them to the brim.

"Here's to an unforgettable party!" Petrina toasted. All raised glasses high above their heads.

"And to our troll-friend," Argis added, "who made all this possible!" Everyone touched vessels then drained them. A warm, merry glow settled over them like a halo.

The grog was poured again as women took pots of boiling water from the stove and poured them into huge tubs for washing and rinsing dishes. The men reached for pipes and pouches. "Not in here, you don't!" Odelia scolded. "I'll never get that smell outa my curtains!"

Argis and Harry led the other hands to the knoll outside the kitchen shed. "Thar troll was certainly a busy feller ta-day!" Old Piscote laughed as he pulled a plug of chewing tobacco and popped it into his mouth.

"Aye!" Argis grinned. "D'ya think the master'll be allowed ta keep 'im?"

"Don't know...don't know." The old snake charmer mused. "But t'would make an' int'restin' bet, eh? Wanna lay odds?"

Just then, Hector came running up from the garden, Mimby Darean's torn skirt wrapped about his waist. "Looks better 'n a apron on ye!" Harry laughed.

Behind him Drowden came striding down the path from the barn, wiping his brow. Everyone fell silent. Bottles were snatched up and tucked under chairs and behind counter clutter. "How's the mistress?" Argis inquired.

"The mistress will be fine. Everyone and everything is, for the most part, unharmed," he replied.

"Thar were some party, sir!" Piscote smiled, wiping the tobacco juice from his chin.

"Yes, it was! And you've all worked very hard. I see you're enjoying the spirits I had Odelia set aside for you. No cause to hide those bottles. Come on now. I'm a little parched." Everyone cheered.

"I'll send me missus ta look in on yers," Argis offered.

"Good idea!" Drowden agreed. Then he looked around the kitchen. "Seems I lost sight of Ian and Miranda shortly after the excitement began. Has anyone seen them?"

"Here Father!" a tiny voice spilled through the open door out of the darkness. Miranda came up the path, herding her brother who stumbled about. "I'm afraid Ian's been sampling the leftover sherry. He got sick all over my dress!"

Drowden spun around and knelt in front of his children. "Looks bad." He sighed, shaking his head. "Well, no use scolding him…he'll feel it well enough in the morning. Could you get him to bed for me?"

"Yes Father, certainly." Miranda smiled sweetly.

"Good. Then get changed, check on your mother and come back here."

The girl grabbed her brother's hand. "I'll be back soon," she called from the stairway. "Save a small bit of that for me!"

"Just like her mother," Drowden thought as she guided Ian up the steps.

The young troll sat in his loft in the barn, perplexed. Today's excitement had exhilarated him, but everyone around him showed nothing but annoyance. Feeling the pangs of boredom, he let out a long sigh and lay down. He lay there for a while until dreams overtook him. As he turned on the bed, he heard young Ian's voice come to him out of the fog of sleep. He tried to imitate a sound that Ian made and uttered quite audibly to the darkening room something that sounded quite like the word "Fun."

Chapter IX
Name Day

The next morning was clear and breezy. Memories were all that remained of the previous day's chaos. Dorina had not stirred from bed. After socializing with the workers, Drowden lay with her a while, stroking her forehead and speaking softly. Though he wanted to stay with her, he took linen and a pillow from a closet to the barn to sleep near the young troll's pen.

The troll was awake most of the night, growling and howling. The moon peeked through the spaces between barn roof and eaves, and Drowden wondered if he was calling to that celestial sphere. At long last, with the moon set and the night rolling toward morning, the troll grew calm and quiet. Drowden dozed off with thoughts seeping into his dreams like water into sand. But sleep was all too brief.

The sun was just risen when Drowden woke in his makeshift bed. He stretched and yawned; remembering where he was. He yawned once again. He heard someone approaching. Gravel crunched on the walkway leading from the summer kitchen to the barn.

"Good morning, Father!" Miranda whispered as she peeped inside. Seeing that he was not sleeping she pushed the door open with her hip and set a tray on a wooden bench. "I've brought you some tea and sweet rolls. Odelia said it would be all right."

Drowden smiled and wrapped the blanket tightly about him and got up to join his daughter. "You are the soul of kindness, child," he said, greedily swallowing a huge mouthful.

"Did you sleep here all night?" Miranda asked, looking around. "This is no place for you. You should be in the house."

"I was comfortable enough here," Drowden smiled. "I talked with your mother last night. She's upset, and I don't blame her. But things will get back to normal."

Miranda nodded knowingly. "She puts on a brave front around Ian and me, but I know she's been crying."

A pang of guilt stabbed through his heart. "Yes, I know." Drowden sipped the tea. "I feel terrible about everything. Your mother is so disappointed."

"Mortified," corrected Miranda.

Drowden nodded and blushed. "Yes. I'll do my best to make it right with our guests. The troll — well it wasn't really his fault. Those horrible dogs…but no. It's all my fault. And I know your mother very much wants me to set our young friend free out in the wild, as far from Hapstead as I can. It's just that…." There were no words to come after that; the living part of him seemed to rise up out of his body, leaving an empty feeling that he wanted desperately to escape.

You think this is something you have to do?" Miranda completed.

"Let's just say I am…compelled to explore the possibilities here. So many years of reading, dreaming, wondering about trolls and how they lived and what they were like and whether they were much like us; then to have this opportunity to study a real live troll in my own home, with my family sharing the adventure. I want to teach him, to talk with him, to learn from him. I sense we are connected in time to a shared destiny. You understand, don't you?" He looked to his daughter hopefully.

"Of course, Father!" the girl replied. "And I believe Mother does, too, on some level. Underneath all the confusion over yesterday's fiasco…" Miranda sat back down. "Her pride was hurt, more than anything else."

"Everything would have been fine if Lady Ubal's mutts had just left the poor creature alone!" Drowden sighed. "It's like they intended to provoke him."

"Yes! And they tore Grandmother Moffit's lace tablecloth to shreds, too!" His daughter sighed, remembering. "Mother is probably just as upset at that as anything else."

"I'm sure it didn't help matters." Drowden smiled wryly. "In truth, the whole ordeal would have been quite funny if it had happened as part of a skit — or to someone else."

The smile faded from his face. "Nonetheless, your mother has every right to be upset. I was not careful about how the troll was housed. It wasn't secure. I take full responsibility."

He imagined how the gossip surrounding Dorina's party would be embellished as the story made its way through various scandal mills in Irongate and Deepwater. And for every mouth that spun the yarn and every ear that listened with glee, he knew Dorina was imagining worse, and more than his imagination could conjure.

Drowden felt horrible about that. His wife's reputation as premier hostess and mistress of the finest estate this side of Deepwater was probably being dragged through the mud even as they spoke. Drowden's social reputation didn't matter so much to him. But on behalf of his wife, he took umbrage. "I'll prove them wrong," he muttered.

Just then the young troll hooted through the chicken wire mesh of his pen. Drowden climbed up two steps of the short ladder leading to the pen door and opened it. The troll leaped out past him without using the ladder and scampered around the barn. He came back after sniffing out every corner and stood at his side. There was something different about him, it seemed to Drowden. But just what that was, he could not say.

The troll crouched just out of reach and made a low, purring sound. Miranda smiled and pointed toward the woodling. "Do you think he'd like one of Odelia's biscuits?"

"If he doesn't, he's no friend of mine!" her father replied. "Let's see what happens!" Drowden got up and cinched his blanket with a bit of rope. "Stay seated," he directed Miranda, "but give me those biscuits!

His daughter tossed the buns to him one at a time. The troll stayed where he was, watching. His head bobbed as each roll arched through the air. Drowden caught them easily, then moved until he was sitting on the barn's dirt floor, facing his pupil.

Miranda sat, fascinated. She hardly breathed, for fear of startling the creature.

"Alright. First things first!" Drowden smiled broadly. "Good morning, lad!" The troll sniffed, his purring was even and pleasing.

"I'll take that as a 'how do you do.'" Drowden kept his voice soothing and musical. "Here is something we call 'bread!'" He held a bit of the muffin in his outstretched hand.

"Thraaaawwww!" the troll responded, reaching for the morsel. Drowden let the woodling swipe it from his palm. The motion was swift; he barely felt the troll's touch.

"Tastes good, eh?" Drowden sat back on his heels and studied his pupil, who plopped the bit of biscuit into his mouth and chewed ravenously, smacking his lips.

The little woodling inched closer to his teacher, sniffing for another piece. "So, you're pretty hungry, eh?" Drowden smiled. "Well, around here we don't just grab things that are offered." He broke off a smaller scrap and leaned toward the troll, who managed to steal this bit, too.

"Well!" Drowden laughed. "You're quick! But that's not what I had in mind. Here, watch!" Then he turned to his daughter, "Care to help?"

"What can I do?" Miranda leaned forward eagerly.

"Come over here and sit down. Bring your stool, just don't make any fast movements. Oh! And the buns, too!"

While the girl made her way nearer, Drowden kept the troll engaged with his remaining biscuit. He pulled it from a fold in the blanket but raised it over his head. This was just barely out of the troll's reach.

"Well! It seems you've grown a few inches since yesterday!" Drowden remarked. "I'll have to get a proper measurement, lad. But I swear you're taller than even last evening!" The little imp was on his feet, reaching with his long arms toward Drowden' upraised fists. He finally had to stand to keep from surrendering the treat.

"Ready, Father!" Miranda said, just in time. The troll moved slightly away. "He remembers the bath!" she giggled.

"He'll warm up to you again. Let's see now, how can we do this?" Erebus got another stool from a few paces off and sat down. "Alright now, lad. We're going to learn more about eating together."

"I'm glad we're not using raw meat!" Miranda giggled as she handed her father a sweet roll. The troll moved closer again, his eyes flashing in the dim morning light.

"Yes. Poor Jessa thinks I've gone feral for sure!" Drowden muttered. "Good. We have his attention. Now, act like you're very interested in having a treat. Let me correct you, then praise you when you do well. Got it?"

"I think so." Miranda nodded. She followed her father's lead, acting just as the little troll had done, jumping up, trying to reach and pull at Drowden's arms.

"No!" Drowden shouted, stomping his foot on the hard-packed floor. The girl froze, startled. Drowden winked at his daughter then looked over at the troll. The poor creature was sitting very still, eyes wide and fearful.

"Now then, let's try this the right way!" He motioned Miranda to sit down, then sat as well and held out the now slightly mangled bun.

The troll moved closer again, cautiously but interested.

"Come over here, lad!" Drowden encouraged, though for the life of him, he didn't know why. And for whatever reason things happen, the troll did go over and stood very near Drowden and Miranda.

"Good! Close enough! Now, Miranda…. ask me for some food."

The girl did her father's bidding, holding out her hand. The troll watched this interplay, unimpressed with all but the passing of the biscuit. "Thank you!" Miranda smiled when the transaction was complete. She even took a bite out of it, making a big show of how tasty it was. "Mmmmmmmmm!"

"Very good! Now lad, it's your turn!" Drowden turned to the troll, sweet roll in hand. "Eeeeeeeeeemm!" the troll cried out. He started to leap up to grab it, then stopped and stood, perplexed. Drowden kept his biscuit-laden hand outstretched, not sure what to expect. Suddenly the troll held out his hand, palm up much as Miranda had done.

A thrill went up Drowden's spine as he gave the woodling his well- deserved treat. "Good! Very, very good!" Drowden beamed. "Did you see, Miranda? He so much as asked me for that!"

"Yes Father!" she shared her father's joy. "He's a very quick study!"

Drowden broke up the last of the sweet rolls and, one at a time gave a piece to the troll when he held out his hand, then wolfed them down.

Ian came into the barn and started to speak, but Miranda and Drowden shushed him quietly and turned their attention back to the troll.

"Let's try something else. Can you fetch me that pitcher over there and that mug? There's probably just enough water left." Miranda went and got the items then filled the cup.

"Thirsty lad?" Drowden asked as the troll swallowed a mouthful. "Ooooooooooooaaah!" the troll sighed. He started to lunge forward but caught himself, stood firm and put his hand out once more.

"Good!" Drowden smiled. "This is 'water, ' we serve it in a 'cup.'" He took a mock sip to show how it was done, then gave it to his student who sniffed the mug, turning it over in his hands and spilling its contents in the process.

"That's right, lad. It's a 'cup.'" Patting the woodling's hand lightly, Drowden repositioned it so he could pour a refill. "Let's try that again. I'll help this time." Together they went through the motions of offering, asking and passing the cup. This time, the troll took the cup and sipped a little from its lip.

Miranda congratulated the troll and her father, then got up. "I'd better go back to the house; Mother is probably looking for me." She brushed the dust from her skirts. "I have a few chores to do but will be back as soon as possible."

But as she headed for the door she stopped sharply. Dorina stood in the doorway, an impassive expression on her face, but a folded stack of clothing for Drowden in her hands. Drowden jumped to his feet. "Dorina, my love!" She shook his words off like a splash of water.

"Go on with what you were doing," she sighed. "I didn't mean to interrupt."

"Not at all! Not at all," Drowden stammered, but Dorina shook her head again.

"Proceed, husband, as though I were not here. I've brought you clothes, and you can change when you are finished with your lessons. Goodness knows, some manners are long overdue."

Drowden gave a half smile as he looked from Dorina to Miranda, to Ian, and then to the young troll.

"Well, alright. I have something else in mind. You see, my little friend has never been properly introduced to our family. And so..." He took a slow, cautious step toward Dorina and gently placed his hand on the shoulder of her calico dress. "This is Dorina!" he said to the troll, patting her shoulder for emphasis. "Do-reen-ah!"

Then he stooped to place a hand on Ian's shoulder and said "This is Ian! Eeeee-annn." The troll watched curiously, tilting his head to one side.

Drowden patted his own chest and said "Drowden! That's my name. Drowwww-dennnn."

Finally, he stood and placed a hand on Miranda's shoulder, repeating the routine. "Miranda! This is Mmmm-ahhh-rannn-dahhhh!"

The young troll perked up and smiled. He comprehended that some game was afoot, looked first to Dorina, then to Ian, then Drowden, and at last he stood up off of his stool and patting his chest as he had seen Drowden do, he looked from one to the other and sputtered "Ogggggg.... Ogggggggggg........" He paused and tried again. "Ogggggg.... Ogggggggggg....." and with a head shake he finished "dennnnnn! Oggggggg.... dennnnn!"

Dorina let out an audible gasp. Miranda shrieked with excitement, and Ian clapped his hands rapidly.

Drowden stood upright, slapped a hand on his knee and exclaimed loudly "What magic is this?"

He looked to Dorina, his eyes filling with moisture. She looked at him and her heart melted. The disaster of yesterday evaporated in the sunlight of seeing her children and the man she loved so singly unified in joy over so simple a thing as a little troll seeming to give itself a name. Her eyes too filled with tears, and she reached out to grab his outstretched hand. They pulled each other into a close embrace and laughed joyously. Miranda and Ian laughed too, and the troll plopped back down on his stool and cackled most peculiarly.

Drowden held onto Dorina's left hand and grabbed Miranda's right hand and he knelt to look Ian in the eye. "I don't know if he knows it or understands it, but we're going to start from here. His name is Ogden!"

Drowden's gaze migrated from wife to daughter to son, and then to the deep obsidian black eyes of the young troll. He said proudly and loudly:

"Your name is Ogden!"

Chapter X
Thunderstorm

T he wind swirled loose leaves and dandelion wisps round and round, scooping them up to the brilliant blue sky where they scattered and fell, to be scooped up again. Drowden took a deep breath, expanding his chest to its fullest, and then exhaling long and hard. "Ahhhhhh! That smells good!"

He stretched, cracking his back and neck, then pulled his notebook out of his satchel and sat on a limestone boulder. Drowden and Ogden were on a hillock at the eastern end of the estate; below them stretched the pond, fields, pens, corrals, main well, barn, outbuildings and worker's lodgings of Hapstead proper. Behind those, Northemberly Creek and the rest of the manor rambled on, with grain storage barns, a large equipment shed, a carriage barn, the blacksmith's shop, a second well, a large fenced-in horse pasture, a second spring-fed pond and more of the small, tidy cottages for the workers and their families tucked within a little valley where the creek meandered before pooling in a wide pond.

The wind gusted suddenly, and shadows fled across the hilly meadows below. Drowden Erebus paid no attention. He dipped his quill pen in an ink bottle that was nestled in a depression in the boulder. Ogden was busy playing with Ian's long gray-haired dog, Hal; they were sniffing one another with great curiosity. Drowden described this scene in humorous yet scholarly detail.

"Troll and dog are rolling about. These moments reveal subject's natural instincts; strangely human, though primitive. His curiosity and playfulness are not unlike those of my own children. My son Ian in particular romps with the dog in remarkable similar fashion...but for the troll's unsavory habit of sniffing! I must

here note the unusual rate at which this creature is growing — nearly a foot in only a week and almost as much the week before."

Drowden looked up from his book in time to see Hal leap on the troll's back. The pair then tumbled to the ground, yelping and snarling in frolicsome delight. He let them play a moment longer while he trimmed the tip of his quill. Then he got up and went over to the wrestling duo.

"Come here, Ogden!" Drowden said, pushing Hal to one side. "Go over there, boy! There's a good dog!" He tossed Hal a bone he'd carried up from the summer kitchen and gave the young troll a crust of bread.

Ogden grunted appreciatively and took the morsel in his left hand, then popped it into his mouth. "Look here!" Master Drowden began, squatting next to him. "This is my arm!" he flexed his arm, pointing with his other hand. "See? Arm! You have one, too! In fact, you have two of them." He reached down and took the young imp's arm. "See? Arm! It has a name!"

"'Hrrrrrrrrm" his student purred, then touched his right arm with his left hand. "Oooooggggg!"

"Very good, lad! I don't know if you made the connection or are just imitating me, but…very good, either way!"

Drowden pulled a piece of cheese from his sack. "Now, we'll try something else. You should remember this one." He placed the chunk in his student's hand. "It's Cheese! Ch-eeze!"

Ogden popped it into his mouth with a satisfied smile. "Greeeee!"

"You like that, eh lad? Try again!" He found another bit of cheddar and held it out. "Cheese!" Drowden said brightly. "Ch-eese!"

"Grrrreeeeeeezzzz!" The troll growled, trying to grab the cheese from his teacher's hand.

"No!" Drowden chastised. "Mustn't grab!" He pushed the troll's arms away. "No, no, not that way! Sit down. I'll give you some!"

He plied the woodling into a seated position, then gave him the treat. "Sit!" He continued the lesson, making himself comfortable next to the troll. "It has a name! The name means this!" His student chewed noisily, smacking his lips and licking his fingers. Then suddenly he spattered the air and Drowden's sleeve with flying masticated cheese. He was bubbling with uncontrolled laughter while his eyes teared-up and he rolled over on his side bellowing "Means!!! Means!!!" as clearly as an elocutionist.

Drowden's heart was beating fast. His mouth went dry, and he could feel the hair on his neck prickle under his collar. He didn't know what to make of it. There was nothing solid to point to and relate to the word "means." How could he explain its meaning to the troll? He knew how to connect sounds to real things but not how to make words relate to insubstantial things.

Drowden decided it was just a case of mimicking. He continued making word sounds and showing the little troll the things he wanted to attach to the sound.

"Fingers!" Drowden clasped the troll's right hand and splayed it wide, "Fingers!" he repeated, "they're called 'fingers!' and 'hand' and 'arm!' and…. oh, so much more!" His student looked on, bemused, making strange noises and smacking his lips.

"There's a whole world of things, lad!" Drowden smiled. "Every one of them has a name, and with a name a thing can have a purpose and a meaning." He became pensive and sat down on a limestone boulder. Despite the whole family's elation at the young troll seemingly having named himself, he wasn't at all confident that Ogden understood just what power is in the act of naming a thing.

Drowden retrieved a chunk of bread, a skin of water and some fruit from his satchel. He divided these, and handed half the bread, cheese, and fruit to Ogden. "Here! Eat this while I write!"

They'd been up in the hills for the better part of the morning. It was a nice break from the barn for both of them. Drowden watched as the young troll delicately fingered his bread. The man took a few mouthfuls of nourishment then returned to his work.

Drowden noted the day's progress, recording his observations and indicating that the troll might be making an effort to communicate. But he wasn't sure.

"The troll makes sounds that are not at all the words I am trying to teach him. Initial consonant sounds of words come out of his mouth following my demonstrations, but it all seems to be mere mimicry. This is disappointing, after initial hopes that he would begin to understand. Perhaps trolls are just not able to learn meanings the way we use language. Even so, I am constantly amazed at subject's patience and determination to please me. He seems to understand commands."

He paused to look up at the troll, to be certain of what he wanted to write.

"I have previously noted his rapid growth. There is another thing: the troll is also becoming quite muscular. His arms have thickened with toughening sinews. His once quite tender hands have enlarged a little out of proportion to the rest of his body. They are now as big as my own and somewhat knotted at the joints. And there is another thing that is as troubling as it is unexpected. He has sprouted hair in places indicating oncoming maturity. It is dark and wiry and begins to sprout a little on his forearms and shoulders as well."

Just then, Ian appeared out a sea of wildflowers that grew as far as the eye could see on the hills to the east of Hapstead Manor. "Daddy! Daddy!" he called. "Is Hal with you?" The dog ran toward his young master, barking merrily and wagging his tail. Ogden scurried over to Ian as well, cooing and purring while he sniffed the boy's head, face, butt and crotch.

"Daddy!" Ian laughed. "He's acting like a dog!"

"Yes," Erebus rubbed his chin. "It's a habit I hope will be broken. Ian, I'd like your help."

"Okay! I can help!" The boy was excited to be asked.

"Good! Good!" Drowden smiled. "Will you take Hal back down to the yard and keep him there for just a little while? It would really help me a great deal!"

Ian frowned. "Can't I stay and help?" he sighed.

"No, son. See those clouds?" He pointed up at a darkening tumble of shadows in the sky. "It looks like we'll be having rain soon and I want you near the house." The young boy shrugged his disappointment.

Drowden thought a moment. "There is one other, very important thing you can do…. if you're able."

Ian raised his head and puffed his chest. "I'm not a baby! I can do anything!"

"Yes, you certainly are a big boy! And only big boys can do this job!" Drowden patted his son's head. "You can carry my satchel down to the barn before my ledger gets wet. Hang it on the hook on the back of the tool shed door next to the barn. Can you do that? No dawdling?"

"I can do that, but it's not that much fun," Ian pouted.

"It's not supposed to be fun! It's just important. Do this for me right away! I'm going to stay up here just a few more minutes with Ogden." He put the notebook, pen and ink and a bundle containing a stone, a feather and a leaf inside the satchel and cinched it closed. "Now hurry, Ian! The sky is darkening. Just look at those clouds!"

Without looking up, Ian took the bag, slung it over his shoulder and called to his dog. "Come, Hal!"

Hal joined him, barking and prancing about, and they went down the hill through a meadow of wildflowers that concealed all but the top of Ian's head.

"Thank you, Ian!" Drowden called after him and laughed. He watched for several moments as the youngster made his way down the hill toward the barn. When he turned, Ogden was standing very still, eyes closed, nose raised to the air, sniffing. The wind had suddenly picked up and great, dark clouds were gathering overhead as they crested the eastern hills.

"Looks like we won't have any more time for lessons. That storm's not going to wait!" Drowden exclaimed. "Come, lad! We'd better get indoors as well!" He grabbed a hold of Ogden's hand and started trotting toward home. The troll kept pace easily. They were halfway down the hill when suddenly a huge bolt of lightning flashed across the sky, followed by a deafening blast of thunder.

Ogden froze in his tracks, stopping so fast it sent Drowden flying forward. He landed in a heap on the ground a few feet downhill of where Ogden stood, transfixed.

The rain began; first with large flat sounding drips, then fine sprays, 'til at last the full storm was upon them. Lightning flickered and sliced through the heavily laden storm clouds, and then thunder boomed and rolled away over the eastern hills.

"Come on, lad!" Drowden shouted above the din. Ogden didn't move so he picked him up and threw him over his shoulder. "You're getting too big for this!" he said with a groan. "Next time, you carry me!"

Drowden sped down through the nodding asters, lace flower and milk-weed once more, but as the hill met level ground, he lost his footing on a wet patch of lamb's ear.

His foot went forward; his head went back, and he flopped with a soggy splash into a mossy puddle as Ogden flew into the air and landed uphill onto a tall, purple-flowered thistle. He stood instantly with the sharp sting of thistle thorn in his rear and looked to the sky. Drowden struggled onto his elbows and finally righted himself.

Ogden began howling long and low. "Oooowwwwwwwww! Ooooowwwwwww!" Then he bolted back up the hill away from Drowden and disappeared over the crest. The man stood to chase him but slid and fell flat on his face on a soggy mud-coated carpet of velvety lamb's ear. It took him three tries to get his feet under him, and then he paused, transfixed by what he saw.

Ogden stood at the crest of the hill, arms stretched out to the sky, palms up, as ball lightning danced from one hand to the other. Rain and tears flowed down Drowden's face. He saw imminent death dancing like a hedgehog of fire in the hands of his troll.

At the same moment, Ogden felt lifted out of himself, freed from the substance of his body as he joined the pivot and pirouette of light and heat that leapt like a comet from one hand to the other. The sky roared and rumbled in his chest. It was a voice amplified by having no bounds and it spoke wordlessly to his heart. It imparted the essence, not the definition, of what "means" means, showing him the way sound shaped into words paints pictures in the mind of listeners. When someone paints pictures inside your head with words, the fiery apparition showed him — that's what it is to "mean" something.

Although he didn't yet have control of his mouth and tongue to say the words out loud, Ogden could hear sounds that he conjured in his head say: "is — mean!"

Drowden was on the ground again and momentarily lost sight of Ogden. He shoved his fingers into the mushy soil and forced himself to his knees, to his feet again. Regaining his balance, Drowden wondered what to do next, but he didn't wonder long. Suddenly Ogden bolted past him at break-neck speed.

"To the barn, damn it!" Drowden found himself shouting as his legs began churning beneath him. He made it to the work yard road before falling again and saw Ogden dash into the barn before he could get back up and fight his way against the storm to the barn.

A lantern burned cheerily off to one side. Perhaps Miranda had come out to warm the place for her father. There was a kettle of tea and two mugs on a workbench, and a small brazier with coal, matches and a striker at the ready. Drowden smiled, then glanced about the barn and spotted Ogden standing in the shadows, dazed and drenched but otherwise unharmed.

"Sorry about that, lad!" Drowden walked over to him. He looked at him curiously and touched his hands. Not a mark on them. At a loss for what else to say, he said, "Let's get out of these soaked clothes and have a nice warm cup of tea!"

The troll followed him round to the workbench. Drowden grabbed an old milking stool and gestured for Ogden to sit. For a moment, Ogden stood there, not seeming to understand. "Sit!" Drowden encouraged, placing a hand on the troll's shoulders and pushing lightly until he sat. "You understand commands. I meant for you to sit, and you did. Very good!"

"Is mean," Ogden said quite clearly.

Drowden did a double-take and stared at the troll silently, wondering "how did you do that? 'Mean, means, meant!' It's an irregular verb. How did you do that?"

"Something about commands," Drowden said out loud. "You're not so fast with descriptive words, but you do respond to the imperative."

Drowden got a flame in the brazier and put the kettle on to boil. "I don't know if that's all to the good, but you know what I mean when I command you to do things," he said with his back to the troll.

"Stay here!" he instructed, then began rummaging about for something warm for them to wear.

He found some old work clothes, horse blankets and even a pair of faded wool socks in a trunk to the left of the door and brought them back.

Soon they were toweled and dressed, blanketed and cozy before the small fire.

The rain pummeled the roof. Thunder and lightning toyed with one another in the sky and Ogden's big dark eyes darted up and around as he listened intently to the voice of the sky. He quivered with anxious desire to bolt outside again and stand beneath the storm and hear its revelations. But here within the barn he was dry. Soon his eyelids curtained his sight and he breathed with a gentle snort.

Drowden sat awake long after Ogden fell asleep. He found the satchel Ian had carried earlier and reached for his journal. Chilled and sleepy, he kept this entry short:

"Thunder and lightning caused subject to behave unusually, freezing as it were in his tracks. Then he..."

The quill froze in place. Drowden hesitated. How could he write what he saw? A baby troll toying with sky fire? He doubted his own eyes, and who could blame anyone reading his notes if they doubted everything else he had written, if he recorded this unbelievable observation? He began writing again.

"The troll reacted strongly to the loud thunder and bright flashing lightening. He outstretched his arms and seemed to embrace the sky. A particularly loud peal and blinding flash left him dazzled — something uncanny about the storm touched him, and he seemed absorbed by it, but soon he recovered. As I watch him sleep, he seems to have suffered no injury. Much to learn about, much to ponder. It's been, all in all, a good day."

Chapter XI
Ogden Speaks

Drowden Erebus studied the notes in his journal while Ogden napped in his loft bed. The weeks were rolling by, and summer was now at its peak. He took up his quill and began to write.

"In only two weeks Ogden has grown taller by as many feet. Physically, he is no child. This raises some concerns in my mind, with the women and a young daughter about and the troll having free rein to wander."

Drowden looked up from the page and paused. He shook the thought from his mind and resumed writing.

"Fingers and hands much more dexterous. This troll might understand what certain tones of voice mean, judged by consistent reactions. But I begin to doubt he will ever connect words to things and derive meaning. In fact, he seems intentionally resistant, as though acknowledging the connection between things and words is offensive."

He rubbed his chin, reminding himself to shave. Then the pen scratched afresh.

"Examples: When asked 'hungry?' subject responds with grunting sound and puts fingers in mouth. The word 'hello' causes the semblance of a smile for lack of better term. Most attention shown him seems to bring a cheery light to those dark eyes. But try to name an object; he balks, shakes, nods his head in a clear message of rejection, and predictably turns attention to something else, as if changing the subject in annoyance."

Drowden grinned, not wondering if Ogden understood a smile for what it was. The answer was "yes; he understands a smile," and already had written his observations in this regard. He dabbed his pen for more ink and wrote on.

"'The word 'quiet' seems to be understood, as the troll sits perfectly still and makes not one noise when that word is uttered, especially accompanied by a finger crossing the lips. This suggests a depth of comprehension with regard to certain gestures. This raises the question of whether or not some of these gestures could be universally understood by…people?"

Goose flesh rose on his forearm. "Is Ogden a person?" he asked himself quietly. And then the secret observations that he declined to record in his notes paraded before his eyes. Juggling lightening in his hands was the most impressive, but in recent weeks other uncanny behavior left Drowden lacking words, quite literally. Aside from withdrawing attention when Drowden tried to teach Ogden terms for simple objects, the troll sometimes stared intently into his eyes and seemed to steal the breath from his throat, so that he could not physically articulate the word.

Drowden noticed that he had unconsciously written these thoughts into his ledger. He was poised to scratch them out but stopped himself. He paused to re-read what he had written, taking time to fill a pipe and light it as he read. A billow of pale gray smoke surrounded his head. He continued writing.

"Still in all, the scamp is becoming renowned throughout Hapstead for creating mischief. It's been mostly harmless antics, but sometimes they upset the servants. He sleeps during the day, and he roams actively at night, ever since I freed him from his locked pen. Peeping into windows and frightening the animals and children has resulted in more than one alarm being raised. It's not clear whether this sleep pattern indicates that he prefers solitude and not the company of people, or perhaps he is exhibiting the purported nocturnal habits natural to trolls. Regardless. Much practice in the social graces is needed!"

The barn door creaked, and Miranda stepped inside. "Father?" she called out. "Mother wants to know if you'll be joining her for lunch." She saw him, back hunched to his work at a make-shift table. "I brought you a snack, in case you said 'no.' And there's something here for Ogden too."

Drowden thought a moment, then turned toward Miranda. "Thank you, dear. I plan to work through lunch but I'm happy to have the broth. Tell your mother to expect me for dinner."

Gnats buzzed in the cool shadows. Miranda shooed them away with her free hand. Drowden seemed unphased. "Are you comfortable working here?" she winced.

"Call it a compromise," Drowden sighed, "but it will suffice."

The gnats returned, swarming about Miranda's head and tickling her nose. She sneezed, "Kaaasoophhh!" and the tray of food rattled and tipped. But before the bowl and mugs could topple to the floor Drowden caught the tray and set it on the table.

There was a loud plunk and scamper overhead. Miranda and her father looked up to see Ogden clattering excitedly down the ladder to join them.

"Well hello!" Miranda greeted him cheerily as the sprouting young troll nuzzled close to her. He was now much taller than Miranda and he sniffed her perfumed hair. Then he sniffed the air and stood over the tray, eyeing the tea and broth.

"I've brought a late breakfast for you too, Ogden," Miranda said cheerily. "Father and I were almost wearing it!"

Ogden stepped out of the way as Drowden and Miranda shoved his journal, notepads and books to the side and emptied the tray. Then all three sat on time-scuffed ladder back chairs that had been salvaged from the Manor House attic.

Drowden broke off a chunk of bread and gave it to Ogden, then pulled off another piece and stuffed it in his mouth. Chewing briskly, he grabbed a mug and took a swallow. "Don't worry, girl. I'm not in the doghouse," he said at long last. "Your mother and I are fine. But she prefers I work with Ogden here rather than in the main house. Sometimes I think he'd progress faster if he lived as we live, with us. But we have to adjust our preferences so they aren't out of rhyme with each other's cares."

Miranda rolled her eyes and gulped milk. "It's a nice enough doghouse," she smiled with a milk mustache above her upper lip. "But it would be nicer if Ogden had his own room in the house with us."

Drowden breathed deeply and waved his arms expansively. "Well, home is where you hang your hat. And look! There's my hat!" He pointed to his old straw field hat.

Miranda laughed. "I think Ogden likes it, Father. It's an improvement on that old kennel."

"It's very comfortable up in the loft," Drowden agreed. "And I bring the books I need with me from the house in the morning. I can oversee the workers from up in Ogden's loft. In fact, there's been a lot more work getting done since I've been spending more time here."

"I know!" the girl laughed. "You should hear them complain! They can't get away with anything anymore!"

"Oh, they're all good workers, don't get me wrong," her father said firmly, "or I wouldn't have them. I hope they know that I'm not trying to spy on them."

"I think they know that, Father." Miranda took a dainty portion of bread to her lips. "But no matter. When it comes to Ogden, they're on your side. They've told me!"

Drowden's brows narrowed and formed furrows over his nose. "It won't do to have them or you taking sides with me and your mother at opposite ends. I won't have it. Your mother is quite reconciled to having Ogden stay with us. I want you to understand that and help me make everyone at Hapstead understand it too."

Miranda reached out and patted her father's forearm. "Yes Father," she said with a soft smile. Drowden sipped his soup in silence.

After a while he shook his head. "It's time to get back to work. What shall I do today to teach our friend some new trick of civilization?"

"I know!" Miranda said excitedly. "I've been thinking about it all night and I came up with an idea. That's why I brought this along!" She picked up a cloth sack that she had dropped by the door when she arrived and reached into it. An assortment of odds and ends spilled to the floor: articles of clothing, brushes, brooches, and belts, and even Ian's toy bugle.

"Oggggg!" the troll sighed as he watched the items drop.

"If we teach him the names of lots of things, he may learn faster," Miranda suggested.

"Hmmm. I've tried repetition and it has failed me. Maybe your idea will work." Drowden nodded approvingly at his daughter's ingenuity. "I'll add to your collection, and we'll see what kinds of things interest him."

He went to an old tool tote in the corner of the barn and came back with an armful of wrenches, hammers, bolts, nails, a short piece of barbed wire, a filthy oil-stained rag and a crowbar. Now there was a nice assortment of paraphernalia to work with.

"You start," Drowden said.

Miranda plucked a scarf from in front of her, stretching its embroidery between her hands and rolling it up. "Scarf!" she said plainly, presenting it to the troll for inspection. "It's called 'scarf!'"

The young troll looked up at it and rolled his eyes. "Oooooo-aaaaggggg!" he grumbled unappreciatively.

"Scarf! Scarf!" Miranda cried out.

"Oaaaggg!" Ogden seemed to disagree. He began imitating Miranda's motions, holding his hands up as if displaying an object that was there only in his imagination. But he made no attempt to imitate the sound of the word.

"Try another. How about…this?" Drowden grabbed the first thing he could — a foot-long length of barbed wire and dangled it near the troll's nose. "Wire!" he said brightly. "This is barbed *wire*!" He accented the word "wire."

Ogden's mouth shaped and changed, like he was trying to sculpt the word out of thin air, but he made no sound as he glanced from Miranda to Drowden. His eyes pierced theirs sharply. Miranda's face showed alarm and she felt her throat tighten. Drowden wagged his hand in front of her, trying to convey reassurance. He had experienced aphasia before while working with the troll. Both father and daughter felt their breaths blocked and they lost control of their voices; neither could speak the word "wire." It went unsaid, though both Miranda and Drowden were trying mightily to get the word out.

As they watched helplessly, Ogden seemed to wink at them. He smiled. Then he formed an imitation of the sound they were trying to make. "Wrrrrrrrr. Rrrrrrrr! Aye! Wriye! rrrr!"

Drowden exhaled explosively. "That's right, lad! 'Wire!'" Drowden exclaimed triumphantly, "Wire!"

"What just happened?" Miranda cried out. "I don't understand!"

Drowden clasped her arm and looked piercingly into her eyes. He didn't say anything aloud, but she knew what he was saying. There are things about this troll neither of them understood.

"How about this!" Miranda chimed, grabbing at a frayed pair of suspenders. "I'll bet he can say 'suspenders!'"

Ogden gazed at her a moment and she averted her eyes to avoid the spell of speechlessness that had come over her before.

"Sssspppppp. Sssssppppp." Was all they got out of him after a dozen tries.

"I'm afraid that 'suspenders' is going to hold him up a bit." Drowden smiled.

Miranda groaned at the attempted pun. "Father!"

He grinned with satisfaction. Suddenly Ogden exclaimed "suspenders" with perfect diction.

Miranda laughed and clapped her hands. Drowden slapped the tabletop. "Ha!! Let's try…. this!" Drowden held up an old skirt that Dorina had discarded. "Skirt!" he instructed. "Try saying 'skirt!'"

Suddenly the little troll wiggled his feet nervously, itched and scratched, then cringed and hid his head in his hands.

Drowden dropped the cloth in his lap and leaned toward Ogden. He placed a hand on his shoulder and asked with concern, "What's the matter, Ogden? Don't be silly, now. What are you afraid of?"

Shaking her head with a knowing smile Miranda said. "He's not being silly, Father. He's just scared. He knows that's Mother's and he's afraid of offending her. She's not very nice to him, you know."

Miranda was right, but her crude analysis of the situation didn't make Drowden any happier. He folded up the skirt and handed it to Miranda. "Put that one away," he said flatly. "I'll have to speak to your mother. I know she wouldn't want Ogden to fear her."

The troll calmed once the garment was no longer in sight. With fallen spirits, Drowden continued. "All right. Let's try another word." He picked up a tool. "For example, 'wrench.'"

Ogden held his hand in the air in imitation, again holding an imaginary wrench in his hand. "Rrrrrrrrrr...." he tried. Then he paused and again silenced Miranda and Drowden with a pointed gaze as they tried unsuccessfully to mouth the word.

"Wrench," Ogden said perfectly. Then he smiled. There were two audible gasps for breath, and Ogden picked up another item from the pile. It was a candlestick.

"Candle," said Drowden.

"Candle," said Ogden, and he reached for a spoon from the pile.

"Spoon," said Drowden.

"Spoon," said Ogden.

This procedure went on with a dozen other items until bellies grumbled for another meal and the afternoon sun was a piddling remnant of its noon glory. After so much success, for three hours all they got from the troll were grunts, grumbles and groans, a few sputters and haws, and initial consonant sounds for the words they presented in their lesson. There were no more speechless interruptions, but Ogden was clearly not interested in learning more words.

Drowden was drained. And Miranda knew that her mother would have words with her for spending so much time in the barn. She'd left her room a mess and had completely abandoned Ian. She stayed, nonetheless, but remained quiet, leaving Drowden Erebus to his thoughts and to the task of scribbling notes in his ledger.

A demon of doubt toyed with his innards. Although Ogden was growing rapidly and maturing at an incredible rate, he couldn't be sure Ogden was attaching words to the objects they corresponded to. Drowden scribbled in his log.

"Teaching a toad to play the harp might be easier. I have the growing impression the young troll dislikes words. I mean, actually has an aversion to them, like they taste horrible in his mouth. It feels like he is mocking my attempts to teach him language, and that he's only imitating sounds."

But he scratched that out with five bold lines and tossed the quill to the side. Drowden was thinking about Dorina and how he had promised her he would tame the troll, teach it to talk, dress and bathe, and that soon everything would be back to normal. But now Ogden was getting much bigger. And he was growing strong. But he could only communicate rudimentary ideas.

Drowden put the last teaching tool away and turned toward Miranda. He sighed resolutely. "Any other suggestions?"

"Ogggg…" said the troll, as if to answer.

"How about grooming?" Miranda suggested. "We might get him to brush his hair. It's always matted you know. He'd look much prettier if his hair were tidy."

Drowden pounded the bench top with his fist, rattling the boards. "He'd look prettier if his nose didn't lie on his face like a blob of candle wax and if his eyes were set further apart, with two eyebrows instead of one extending across his bony forehead! I'm not interested in what he looks like! I'm interested in what he can learn!"

Instantly, he felt foolish for his outburst. He was frustrated and the unsettling feeling of being loved less by Dorina added to the pain. "How can I be so selfish?" he said out loud to the rafters.

His neck was stiff from craning over his notes while sitting on a hard wood chair. His clothing smelled of horses, and not the best parts.

"I'm sorry," Drowden said at last. "Let's have a go at grooming."

Miranda smiled. She wasn't ready to face the drudgery of chores or her mother's ire. She reached into her bag and pulled up a brush and hand-held mirror. "Ah ha!" she cried out.

"What have you now?" Drowden asked.

Miranda didn't reply. Instead, she flipped the mirror over in her hand and at the same time, a sun beam shown through a crack in the barn wall and fell on to the glass surface. The reflection bounced from the dirt floor, rolled up the wall and deftly traversed along a rafter then plummeted downward.

Ogden stood transfixed. His head and eyes followed the ball of reflected light as Miranda wiggled it around. Suddenly, he smiled so broadly that his teeth stood out on his face like piano keys. Even his eyes smiled.

"Oggggggg!" he growled with pleasure. Miranda showed him the mirror, letting him see his own reflection. "Oggggggggggg!" he growled again. "Ogg…. Oggggg…. Oggggggggg!"

Drowden bolted forward in his chair and came to his feet. "Miranda, my dear!" he fell to one knee next to Ogden, gazing in wonder as the troll changed expressions, as if to amuse the face in the mirror.

"Ogggggggldddddddd!" he continued to grumble, sometimes under his breath, sometimes in loud snarls. He was obviously overcome with joy at seeing himself for the first time.

Miranda covered her open mouth to stifle a cry of joy but held the mirror firmly in front of the young troll. "Oh Father!" she sighed, and two tears fell down her cheeks.

The troll's fascination grew. His dark eyes shimmered in the rebounding glow, and though his attention was riveted by what he saw in the glass, he cast cherubic glances at Drowden then Miranda and shared his joy with them. "Ogggg…. Ogggg…. Deggga….. deggaaa!!!!" he kept uttering all the while.

"He's trying to say his name," Drowden gasped. Suddenly the troll jumped up off his feet, consumed with elation. He came down, catching his balance with the knuckles of his left hand, then he bounced back up to the tips of his toes. He waved his hands up over his head then down to his sides, then back up again, shouting. "Oggggdaaaaa! Ogggdeeh! Oggdahr! Oggddenh!"

Then, just as suddenly, he stopped jumping and stood, mesmerized before the mirror with Miranda and Drowden watching his every move breathlessly. For an eternity of seconds, no one spoke or moved. Then the young woodling reached out very gently and took the mirror from Miranda's outstretched hand.

"Og-den!" he said, plainly and evenly. "Ogden." And he pointed to his reflection, then to his chest. "Ogden." He breathed it reverently, as a prayer.

"There!" Drowden whispered to his daughter. "He knows his name! And he knows it means *him*. Ogden!" He said it with admiration, and as he did, the troll turned to him and wrapped his strong arms around Drowden's neck, hugging him tightly.

Then Ogden stood back and stretched out his arm so that his hand rested gently on Drowden's chest. He said plainly, "Father!"

Drowden Erebus gasped, wiping his cheek and beaming a broad smile at his daughter. "This is a day to celebrate," he said with wonder in his voice.

Miranda rose from her chair and joined them, hugging her father and the troll with both arms. "Ogden!" she laughed and cried. "You are wonderful!"

Drowden smiled at both of them, his eyes still welling with tears. "He is a wonder."

Just then Ian scampered into the barn, panting. "Hey! What's everybody doin'?" he yelled loudly.

"Hugging," said Miranda. She broke away and Ian descended on Ogden with playfulness in his eyes. "Hi, Ogden," Ian shouted very loudly.

Ogden patted Ian on the head and said, "Hi Eeeaaann!"

Ian stood back, hands on his hips. "You mean, you could talk all this time?"

Drowden laughed. "When he named himself weeks ago, we thought that was a good start. After all, if you can name yourself, you've got half the world in a box. The other half is out there to pick over at your leisure, as soon as you learn all the words. Looks like he's already learned a few and saved them up."

Ian laughed as Ogden mimicked the boy's actions, first hands on hips then mouth hanging in wide amazement. Then Ian looked back at his father. "Are you going to be famous, Daddy?"

"Famous? Not me, Ian. Ogden's the one who everyone's going to notice. But there's work to do. I've got to prove to Nathan Bladic and Ospin Tapple that Ogden not only knows names, but that he can talk."

"Well!" Miranda jerked her head. "What should we do?"

Drowden answered, "For now, I think you'd better go. I've kept you far too long."

"Oh!" Miranda flushed, ready to object but then remembering her chores.

"Thank you for the snack and the lessons. May we borrow this?" he indicated the mirror, which Ogden had taken up again.

Ian watched the troll for a moment. "Can I stay?" he asked.

"No, you run along too. Help your sister with her chores and be extra-special good." Drowden reached for his son and gave him a bear hug, then looked him in the eye. "Please, be extra good."

"At least I'll have fun watching Miranda get yelled at!" Ian mumbled un-happily. "I'd rather stay here!"

Miranda moaned then turned to her father. "I can't wait to tell everyone! Ogden knows his name and he's starting to talk."

"Shhhh!" Drowden implored. "Don't tell anybody! It'll be our secret. You too, Ian! It'll be a surprise! There are too many blabbermouths around. I want to work a little more with Ogden before we go spreading the news. Promise? Don't tell anyone! Not even each other!"

Miranda sagged a little, disappointed. "That's just silly, Father. But don't worry. I won't tell anyone."

"Me neither!" Ian added. "I won't tell, too!"

Miranda and Ian hurried out of the barn and ran across the yard. A piglet squealed, caught off guard by their rushing past. It clomped for cover into a bed of day lilies.

Once the children had gone, Drowden turned to his notes again, occasionally glancing up at Ogden over a pair of reading spectacles.

After writing a detailed account of how Ogden had recognized his own image and how he attached names to people, he pulled a measuring string from his left pocket and had the troll stand up straight. The string was marked where Drowden had taken weekly measurements of Ogden's height.

He measured him again from floor to crown and jotted down the information. He had another string in his right pocket and it too was marked at various intervals. He held them in one hand with their ends together. "It's a good crop of corn," he said to no one. "But it'll never keep up with Ogden."

Drowden tried to pry the mirror from Ogden's hand and was rebuffed. "Very well, you keep it…. Ogden." He patted the troll's head. "You called me 'father.' I know it's what the children call me, and you were copying them, but even so…" He broke off and looked to the papers spread out on the plank table. "Occupy yourself while I write a letter…then maybe we'll learn more words!"

He handed Ogden a bit more bread and a bowl of milk. "You've earned this." Then he went back to his notes.

Drowden smiled with satisfaction, thinking about the message he was planning to send Nathan Bladic and Ospin Tapple. Speaking to himself out loud, he said, "I won't mention anything specific about the troll…nothing specific. Just enough to tease. I'll mention how tall the corn has grown, but nothing about the troll."

Just then, he heard another word erupt from Ogden's lips. It came as a question. "Troll?"

The hair on Drowden's neck stood up. His eyes widened. He bolted upright in his chair. "Yes!" he cried. "Troll! Do you know what 'troll' means?"

Ogden reacted similarly to Drowden's elation. He jumped excitedly, crooning "Troll! Troll! Troll!"

"Troll!" Drowden repeated. Ogden repeated it back, "Troll!" They hollered the word back and forth to one another. "Yes lad," Drowden Erebus laughed, "you are a troll!"

"Troll! Troll! Ogden! Troll!" Ogden hooted and laughed. Drowden Erebus jumped to his feet, grabbed the troll's hand and danced him around the barn, singing "Ogden the troll! Ogden the troll!"

Ogden reciprocated by imitating his teacher, "Ogden the troll! Ogden the troll!" Together they pranced and shouted until both were hoarse and dizzy.

They finally stopped when Argis burst in. "Master Erebus, are ya aright?"

Drowden spun around on his heel one last time and stood panting and sweating. "I'm absolutely wonderful!"

"Won-da-ful!" Ogden jerked his head with the word bursting forth.

"We're all wonderful!" Drowden cried out. Argis stood speechless, until his master calmed. "Well! What is it, man?" Drowden asked at last.

"I were just comin' in ta git somethin, sir," Argis mumbled. "Did Ogden learn somethin' today?"

"A bit… Quite a bit." Then Drowden told Argis all that had happened, swearing him to secrecy. "All in all, it's been a good morning!" he concluded, glowing.

"Ye done good, sir." Argis smiled. "Ye said ye could do it, an' ye did! I'll be hanged if ye didn't do it!"

"Bladic and Tapple will be chewing fingernails all the way from Irongate!" Drowden laughed. "I've got to finish this note. We'll need a courier ready to ride shortly."

"I'll see to it. Willbee is a fast rider," the foreman assured, hurrying toward the barn door. "Oh! Almost forgot!" he grabbed a rake from the wall rack.

Drowden picked up the letter and shoved it in an envelope. "We're going to drive those two dandy gentlemen out of their minds, lad!" he said to Ogden, while affixing his seal.

Chapter XII
Wager Won

Nathan Bladic received Drowden's invitation to visit Hapstead Manor with annoyance. The note said:

> "Something big has happened concerning our troll, Ogden. Please come with all speed and bring Ospin Tapple with you. Truly yours, Drowden Erebus."

With Willbee standing on his porch, Bladic paced and flicked the sheet of paper with his finger. He wanted to leave as soon as he read the note, but he wanted to inspect a new machine being built for him. It was driven by steam and the burning of coal, not wood, and it held the promise of replacing ten men. That would free up funds that he'd otherwise have spent for their up-keep. In just a few years he could keep all the profits with none of the over-head.

As much as he wanted to find out what new trick Drowden had taught his troll, he could not send word back with Drowden's messenger to expect him on such short notice. It was just impossible.

Finally, he stuck his head out the front door and barked rudely at Willbee. "Tell your master it's not convenient. Tell him…let the corn grow. Got that?"

Willbee stood silently, his face one big question mark.

"Do you understand?" Bladic shouted.

"Yes sir," stammered Willbee and he wheeled around to depart.

For the next three days Bladic attended to business details. Then after delay followed by delay in the preparation of his machinery, a full week went by unproductively. He soothed his curiosity with the thought that it was just as well to wait a little longer. If Drowden had managed to teach the troll to speak — but that was not likely — then why not give the corn as much time to grow as possible. Surely that little bugger hadn't sprouted up to the height of the tallest stalk in a fully-grown field of corn, he thought. So, while he tended to ledgers and correspondences, he satisfied himself picturing the little troll getting lost in a forest of stalks and tassels.

When at last Bladic was confident the new contraption would be shipped carefully in wooden crates that would protect the disassembled parts, he made ready for the ride to Hapstead Manor. There was some further delay because his wife, Hattie, was in bad humor. When he heard from Ospin Tapple about riding out to Hapstead Manor with him, he replied that he had to wrap up some final business. That delayed the trip another two days.

By the time Tapple arrived at Ironwood Manor Bladic was in a gray spirit. Finally, he watched as Tapple's carriage descended the high hill toward the main gate and came to a stop in front of the Manor House.

When Nathan Bladic opened the carriage door and leaned in, he watched as Ospin Tapple fidgeted with his cuffs. "Get in," he said. "We'll take my rig."

"No," said Bladic, "we're taking mine. I'm packed and loaded. Have your man transfer your things and tend your horse. And he can stay with my workers while we're gone."

Tapple's bags were stored and secured by a large servant with a severe look about him. "Ready to go, sir," he said in a deep, gravelly voice.

"Good," said Bladic, leaning forward and poking his head out the window. "Keep the workers in line, Traunton. And give Tapple's man something to do. I'll be back as quickly as I can."

The carriage rumbled away on the hard surface of the lane. Neither man spoke at first. Then Tapple looked at Bladic firmly and said, "You don't think he has that animal speaking, do you?" His high whiny voice filtered through the clopping of horse hooves on the last cobblestones before the road turned dusty and rutty.

"Hardly thinkable," Bladic sighed impatiently. "Whatever it is, we will find out soon. Sooner had you not tarried."

Ospin Tapple smiled ironically. He had kept Bladic waiting for the better part of a day, fussing with his wardrobe. And he had a last-minute argument with his wife that lasted longer than a minute.

A late summer wind whistled in the trees and the clopping of hooves filled the silence between the two men. Ospin felt ill at ease. He tried a stab at conversation. "What do you suppose he wants to show us? It has to be something important, summoning us so urgently!"

Nathan squinted at his traveling companion. He wanted so very much to stop the carriage and leave Tapple by the wayside for making him wait. But for all his faults, Ospin Tapple was at least a willing witness, should there be any need for one.

Instead, he pulled a pouch from his coat and reached for his pipe. "Maybe he's taught the little bastard to wipe his arse!" he joked. "I don't know. But I've got a whole crop of corn on the line if that troll of his can talk" A cloud of sweet smoke wafted between the men. "Besides, I'm just doing you a favor, asking you to come along." He paused for a long drag on the pipe, and then added, "I hope you brought some money. Horses don't feed themselves, you know."

Tapple stiffened in his seat. "Naturally, I expect Drowden Erebus to feed his guest's horses." Ospin searched his pockets then his satchel for a pipe. "I.... must have...left it in my other jacket," he said to himself, and Bladic rolled his eyes, assuming he was pretending to look for his money.

Bladic held his tongue and changed the subject. "Why do you think Erebus didn't explain what we're supposed to see?"

"That's easy, friend!" Tapple grinned. "Drowden Erebus is toying with you. He did it to agitate. And he's done a beautiful job!"

"Seriously," Bladic hesitated. "What if he has gotten the bugger to say something?"

"Nathan, I'm going to tell you something. I didn't come along just to be a witness to Drowden Erebus running away with your corn. I came because I've got to know how clever a troll can be. And unless Erebus has a stunted crop, it worries me that a troll could grow as tall in a season as the corn has already done. Think what that would mean. I wasn't too concerned that the troll seemed incapable of anything but destroying a tea party." Tapple lowered his high-pitched voice. "You did hear about that, didn't you?"

"Yes, yes!" Bladic laughed. "In fact, I have it on good authority that Erebus released the troll to the woods at his wife's insistence. Erebus is going to concede that he's lost the wager. That's why he summoned us, if you ask me."

Tapple laughed, recalling with glee Lady Ubal's account of the party. He'd gone to visit Master Ubal on some pretense and heard firsthand how the doglettes, Buffy and Button, were almost killed by what Lady Gretchen described as a vicious, beastly monster.

"I'll admit his message unnerved me at first," Bladic exhaled a bit of smoke, "but upon thinking, it seemed more as a ploy to catch me off balance. So, I'm playing along with this cat-and-mouse game; knowing all the while I shall win in the end."

Tapple shivered, despite the warm morning air. "Your confidence is reassuring," he sighed. "But it still worries me." He sneezed into his scarf, swore as he pulled it away from his nose and rolled it into a ball and set it aside. "That goldenrod will be the death of me," he whined.

"Roll down the dust curtain," Bladic suggested. "Don't want to be dying of allergic shock before we get there."

Tapple did so and the smoke from Bladic's pipe bundled around him. He sneezed again and rolled the curtain back up, securing it with a single knot. "Have you thought about what that troll represents?" he asked after wiping his nose again.

Bladic pulled a clean kerchief from his pocket and tossed it to his companion and answered, "I don't know what you mean, Ospin. It's a young troll. We thought they were gone from the world, so I suppose it means we were wrong."

"Yes, it means that." Tapple put his head back and closed his eyes. "And it means there are others out there. Big ones. Baby trolls don't spring out of the ground; they're born because a big he- and she-troll had time to find each other in a wilderness we thought was free of trolls for generations."

Bladic leaned forward and touched Tapple on the knee. The other man opened his eyes and returned Bladic's gaze. "I know," said Bladic. "And you know I am a lifelong member of the Secret Brotherhood. And I know that you're in it up to your fuzzy eyebrows. And I know this troll business has you losing sleep. But to me it's just a social club. I've got no interest in traipsing through the forest to slaughter Trogs."

Tapple shot a warning finger at Bladic. "Not another word, Nathan. That's business you shunned, and you can't just sit idly while real men do what must be done. But not one more word from you, or there'll be a knock at your door one night, and I won't be able to help you."

Bladic sat back in his seat. He spoke quietly, evenly. "Real men indeed. Don't threaten me, Tapple. You talk big for a very little man who's afraid a baby troll might be taller than you. For a man who can't do what comes natural to your average wild troll in the woods."

Tapple reached for his knife as he had done once before in this carriage, but Bladic motioned a cautionary wave of his hand. "The coachman knows what to do if I don't call him off," was all he said, and there was a tap from above on the carriage roof. A small bell had rung at the coachman's knee, prompting him to check below. When he received the second signal that all was well, he drove on. Bladic let the rope in his hand swing free.

"I'm a reasonable man," Bladic continued. "I pay some of my workmen well, so they do my bidding. And I don't hate trolls the way you do. Maybe your reasons are sound. But they aren't mine. I have only one interest in Drowden's troll, and that's a wager we made. So, I'll have none of your shenanigans while I'm on business at Hapstead Manor. Am I being clear?"

Ospin Tapple was quiet for a moment, and then changed his expression with a shrug. "It's all the same to me, Nathan. Stay ignorant. Let the trolls overrun us like they did our ancestors. I wouldn't let Drowden Erebus best me in a wager where a troll decides things. You can think what you want of me. I think you're a sucker and although you might let Erebus play parlor tricks and take your property, I'm not going to let that little demon best me on any terms."

Bladic winked at him. "I'm no fool. I won't accept just any dribble as real talking. It has to be something identifiable and human. Something with meaning...and I need proof the troll understands what he's saying and what I'm saying."

"Yes!" Tapple wheezed. "Anyone can teach a raven to speak, but to understand words and use the words correctly is another thing" The carriage hit a hole and lurched sharply, sending Tapple into Bladic's lap, face first. The carriage quivered to a stop.

"You aright in there, Master Bladic? Mister Tapple?" Jasper hooted, gaping at them from the trap door above. "The road's bad these parts!"

"I'm fine, I think," Bladic called up to the driver. Jasper jumped down and inspected the wheels, then climbed back up top. Resuming the journey with extra care, Jasper thought about the comforts ahead at Hapstead Manor. There was always plenty of mead and a good card game going on. The coachman smiled then reined the horses more tightly to keep their speed in check. The hilly road ahead was thick with shadows.

"You were saying?" Tapple looked up at Bladic.

"I was saying, I'll take no baby-talk, no woodland chatter as proof the troll can talk. There must be real comprehension and proper responses!" Bladic folded his arms across his chest. "That is, if he hasn't already given up and set the gremlin loose in the wilderness."

"Then you are.... not worried?" Tapple asked, choosing his words carefully. "Or do you foresee some progress?"

"No, I think Erebus will simply concede that he made a foolish wager and be done with it. He's an honest man, though he's also an impractical dreamer. I'm more curious than anything else. According to my sources, as of last month the troll was making noises; nothing more..."

Tapple gasped, but Bladic shook his head. "Fear not, my friend! There was nothing intelligible in it."

"Are your sources reliable?" Tapple's voice was small.

Bladic shot him a glance that made Tapple smirk appreciatively. "They are my own men, sir! Erebus pays them for field work; I pay them for other things."

Tapple held an empty hand in the air. "What makes you think the servants at Hapstead Manor won't just take your money and tell you what you want to hear?"

Bladic's prominent nose wrinkled. "Not for what I pay them. I think they'd be afraid to be so bold."

Tapple chuckled like dry grain shaken in a bottle. "Deception is a tangled web. Once you get started, it's hard to know when you're looking straight at the truth and when it's looking at you."

"You're the expert at lies and trickery," Bladic yawned. "I'll take your word for it."

Ospin decided to change the subject. "These treks are tedious!" he said, fussing with his collar. "It doesn't seem like it should take this long. Only twenty miles from Irongate and just fifteen from Ironwood Manor, but these foothills and craggy passages spread the distance further."

"And tire my horses!" Bladic added.

The two men fell silent once more and remained so for the rest of the trip.

The carriage creaked and skittled as it slowed for the turnoff to Hapstead Manor's private lane. The torches had not yet been lit, but one of the hands was scurrying to uncap them and light them for the night.

Jasper pulled the carriage up to the manor's ornamented entry where Willbee was waiting to raise the latch and bid him enter. Inside the carriage, Ospin's breath quickened as he fussed and adjusted his collar. "Am I presentable? I always get so rumpled on these cross-country excursions!"

"Stop acting like a ninny!" Nathan chided. "Accept the facts. You look like a vagabond! That's how people look when they've been bounced around on a dusty road."

Ospin fumbled with his hat. His companion did likewise, but with calm efficiency. If Bladic was anxious, his cool demeanor betrayed nothing.

They dismounted, shaking the wrinkles from their coats. Nathan spied Dorina's silhouette in the upper window of the manor house. Ospin noticed too, and made a soft, lowing noise.

"You sound like a bull in heat, Tapple! Quit drooling before Erebus hears you!"

Tapple took exception. "You're looking, too!"

"Yes," Bladic replied, "but looking only. Keep your noisy thoughts to yourself."

Ospin started to answer, but Nathan held him up with a finger in the air. "Lower your voice."

Both fell silent as Drowden Erebus approached in the fading light. They shook hands and inquired after each other's health. "Well, you've come a distance! Are you up to a little chat before retiring? Would you like to freshen up first?" Drowden asked.

"We're fine!" Nathan answered, a bit quicker than he'd intended. "Perhaps a cup of sweet tea would do the trick...." he added sociably.

"Very good, very good! And you, Ospin? Tea for you, too? Come!" He led his guests to a warm, fire-lit parlor. The day's warmth had given way to evening, which ushered in a little briskness. "What am I saying? There's sherry if you prefer." Drowden pointed at the table in front of a long ornate sofa. Tapple brightened.

"Just the thing," he said. "To cut the chill is what I mean."

"Of course!" Drowden smiled. "Autumn is on the way. The nights are getting cooler."

Pouring them each a glass of sherry, Drowden exchanged more small talk. "The weather's been good, most days. Plenty of sun. Rain when we need it. We're in for a bumper crop this season!"

Tapple sipped and looked over the edge of his glass. Bladic drained his drink and set it down. "Shall we get right to it then? What news?" he asked. "The corn is tall. Is that what you're going to say? What of it?"

"I'll show you soon enough!" Drowden grinned. "But first, here comes your tea, and it seems Odelia has sent us a few scones as well!" Jessa curtsied and placed the serving tray on a low table, then left.

Bladic nodded. "I'd appreciate a bit more sherry, if you please."

Ospin raised his now empty glass. "If you please," he repeated.

Drowden got the decanter and a glass for himself. "This is a particularly good batch. Aged long enough, clear.... I am quite happy to have it."

Ospin sipped. "Sweet. Smoky. Woody." He swallowed. "It really is quite good."

Drowden sipped his portion slowly. "Perhaps we should wait until you've rested from your journey before we enjoy too much of the spirits," he suggested.

"Nonetheless!" Tapple whined, louder than intended. "I'm sure we'll rest much easier once we've found out what is going on!"

Bladic nodded in agreement.

"It's nothing, really," Drowden baited them. "I shouldn't have bothered summoning you like this; it's nothing which couldn't have waited a few days."

"What do you mean?" Nathan Bladic grumbled. "Tell us, man! We didn't ride all this way for nothing! No more suspense. Tell us why you asked us to come. Do you even have a troll anymore?"

Drowden hung his head in mock chastisement. "I just wanted you to know that my troll has a name."

Bladic and Tapple caught one another's eye. "I feel cheated!" Tapple sighed, draining his snifter. "I thought there would be something bigger to report. You could have just sent the news with your messenger."

Bladic swirled his sherry, watching the liquid play against the glass. "I think there is more to this, Tapple," said Bladic. "But I'll play along." Then to his host, "What is the little bastard's name that we might drink to it?"

Ospin sat back and allowed his embers to cool. "Yes…. What would one name a troll of such distinction? Mortimer? Henry? Or is it Junior?"

Drowden laughed at the merchant's remark, unaffected by the intended sting. "His name is Ogden."

"Ogden, is it? Where did you get that moniker?" Tapple asked. "Some dead relative? Or perhaps one of your favorite troll writers? I'll bet that's it. One of those pseudo-scholars who claimed to have lived among trolls in the wildwood for years."

"Five'll get you ten, he's right!" Nathan Bladic chimed in.

"Don't throw your money around like that, Bladic. You've lost enough already!" said Drowden. He set his empty snifter down and poured three cups of tea.

"You don't mean…." Bladic paled slightly.

"Let's have a scone and tea first," Drowden suggested. "And there's no hurry. The light will be much better in the morning. Then you can see for yourself. Who knows? Maybe the corn will grow another inch or two over-night."

"No more delays," cautioned Bladic. "I want to know where my assets lie: in your hands or in mine. Can you rouse the troll at this hour?"

Drowden shook his head. "Ogden is up and awake most nights, but I'm about ready for my bed. Besides, it's too dark to be roaming around in the cornfield looking for the tallest stalk, don't you agree?"

"Yes," agreed Tapple. "Too dark for that. Never know what other wild beast you might meet out there."

"Morning is soon enough for this business," Drowden assured him. "Neither I nor Ogden nor the corn are going anywhere. Rest well, friends. Tomorrow will be a new day for all of us."

Resigned, Bladic shook Drowden's hand and bid him good night. Ospin took a scone from the tray and carried his tea with him to his room. Drowden turned down lanterns, blew out candles and left the shadows in charge of the Manor for the rest of the night.

In the morning Tapple and Bladic were anxious to get out into the cornfield with Drowden and Ogden. They agreed to postpone breakfast and get right to the business at hand.

"Very well, then," Drowden said. "Come with me, gentlemen." They followed him in silence toward the door.

"Don't forget your jackets," Drowden called behind him, reaching for his own cloak from a hook on the closet door. "There's still a nip in the air."

Outside it was chilly and full of brisk morning dampness. Their feet crunched across the gravel path to the road. The barn lay ahead and to the left. Inside, all was still and in darkness. Drowden pushed the door open and reached for a lantern, which hung by a nail just inside. It soon gave off a yellowish tint, revealing workbenches, tools, and saddles.

One area was arranged with a table, desk and chairs. Drowden lit candles and offered his guests seats. He pointed above them. "Ogden is asleep right now."

"I don't care!" Ospin spit. "I want to hear it speak! I didn't come all this way for a tour of your barn!"

"Hush!" Bladic chided. "Let Erebus gather his beast and let's get on with business."

"Ogden isn't an animal, Nathan." Drowden turned to his guests with a stern look. "That's a fact that I will prove to you directly. Now, if you'll please be seated, I'll be right back."

Drowden climbed the ladder to the loft. They heard him above, walking across the floorboards, then speaking in a low voice.

"Do you really think….?" Tapple started to ask his companion, but he left the often-asked question unfinished.

In a few minutes their host returned. "He'll be right down. Has to get dressed." Drowden stood at the foot of the ladder, hands on hips.

Bladic looked to his manicured fingernails. "There'd better be no trickery here, sir!" he warned. "Do not think me easily handled!"

"To the contrary, Bladic," Drowden retorted. "You will see only the truth. A forest troll, grown tall since last you met but the same troll nonetheless."

The three men turned as they heard Ogden stepping heavily down the ladder. No longer a small wild thing, the troll stood before them in the pale light. He was at least three feet taller than Ospin Tapple and head and shoulders above Nathan Bladic. Next to all of them, including tall and sturdy Drowden, he was burly. He wore a tunic and work pants, and it looked like he'd need a bigger size before long.

"How do we know it dressed itself?" Tapple asked, eyeing Ogden with trepidation. The troll was muscular, barrel-chested, and those pitch-dark eyes hooded by a thick, bony brow gave him an ominous demeanor that set Ospin Tapple on edge.

Drowden reached under his desk and pulled out a bundle. "Here Ogden, put these on instead. Those things are getting too small for you! Let's show our friends what you can do!"

Deft fingers rode across buttons and fabric, until the troll stood naked before them. He was shockingly well developed, no longer on the verge of maturity, but fully arrived. Bladic rubbed his chin but said nothing. Tapple gasped, and then bit his lip. The troll got dressed with skill, and even a degree of delicacy.

"Here Ogden." Drowden held out a pair of sandals. "These go on now." And to his guests, "We're still working on the sandals part. He prefers going barefooted, but see? He knows how to work the straps." The sandals were a good fit, having been made special for Ogden by Heath, the Manor's cobbler.

"Very good, lad!" Drowden patted his troll's shoulder. "Now, let's go for a little walk. Get your sheepskin cloak; it's chilly outside!"

Tapple made no comment as the troll strapped on sandals and pulled on his cloak, but Bladic was a constant chatterbox. "How did you get him to do that? It's like training a monkey, isn't it? Do you have secret hand signals? I know circus performers and they train their bears with food and gestures."

Tapple turned to Bladic. "Will you stop yammering?" Then to Drowden, "All this is immaterial. You've housebroken the troglodyte, but…" he raised a pointed finger that showed signs of brittle stiffening, "he hasn't spoken yet! And I don't think he will."

"I haven't asked him anything yet, Ospin. If it's one thing I've learned about trolls it's that they're sparing with their words. A little patience, I beg you."

"Sparing to the point of muteness," Bladic chuckled. He looked Ogden up and down and the troll stared at him quizzically.

"Besides," continued Drowden unperturbed, "it's a lovely morning for a walk in the cornfield. Let's just enjoy it in silence for a moment, shall we?"

"Well, if you ask me…" Tapple started to say.

"No one's asking you!" Bladic retorted, cutting Ospin short. With that, there was an end to conversation until they were well on their way.

They set off on a rutted road in the morning light. "See how the dew shimmers on the grass?" Drowden pointed to the side of the gravel and clay road. "I imagine that living in the city affords you little time to enjoy such simple pleasures, Tapple."

"I have seen more than enough dew in the grass, fog in the trees, and other quaint mockeries of normal life in my line of work," Tapple replied. He spoke nervously, ever mindful of the tall and robust troll walking to his left and casting a shadow across the ground in front of them. He changed the subject. "And how is that bull you bought from me faring?"

"Very well! Very well, indeed!" Drowden smiled. "I believe we'll have a new calf or two, at least. He's an eager stud. Some days I think I may have underpaid you, Ospin."

Tapple seethed as he walked and, tired of the troll's proximity, dropped back a pace behind the rest of the group. From that vantage point he observed how the troll carried himself, and he shuddered at the tableau of Bladic, a businessman; Drowden, a gentleman farmer; and Ogden, an uncouth but clothed and shod woodling taking a stroll down a country lane.

Drowden was saying something to Nathan Bladic as Tapple slowed his gait to almost a stop and then slipped into the cornfield on the west side of the road, seemingly unnoticed. Soon he had disappeared amid tassels, stalks, ears and wide waving leaves. Nathan Bladic and Drowden Erebus walked on, talking animatedly about training Ogden to eat at table, show gentleness with the farm animals, and also, at long last and after many trials, to speak. Drowden explained that the one thing he had so far failed to do is break Ogden of his night-prowling habits.

The troll followed close behind, appearing to listen intently, but he watched corn stalks jostling unnaturally up on the hill in his peripheral vision.

The three stopped by the roadside in front of a wall of corn. "Where'd Ospin go?" asked Drowden. He looked back toward the direction of the barn, but the road had descended a small hill and if Tapple was behind them he was still on the other side of the crest.

"He's an idiot," Bladic explained. "If I didn't depend on him to ship me certain supplies and specially made machine parts, I'd want nothing to do with him."

"I'm sure he'll catch up. Why don't you find the tallest stalk that you can? We'll use that to compare with Ogden's height. Then we'll have a little chat with Ogden."

Bladic looked at the troll, then at the corn. "If he can talk, it won't matter what stalk we stand him next to," he said dejectedly. "Your troll is clearly taller than any stalk in sight."

Drowden placed a hand on Ogden's shoulder. "What do you say to that, Ogden?" The troll stepped forward and looked Bladic in the eye. He opened his mouth, ready to say something, but a jostling in the field stopped him short.

With a sudden storm of waving green leaves and shaking corn stalks, Ospin Tapple emerged from the orderly jungle that towered over him. "Not so fast!" he said, winded and whiney. "Up there on the hill. The corn is taller there."

Drowden looked up the hill and shrugged. "Alright. Let's go up there," he said, and with no further word Bladic followed behind him and Tapple between rows of corn. They followed the terraced row up the hill to a spot where Tapple indicated the corn stalks reached their greatest height.

"Here," he said. "Look around. Much taller than down there by the road."

Drowden nodded. "You're right," he said, and looked around him. The stalks were indeed taller. Nothing could be seen but columns of corn in every direction.

Bladic let out a defeated sigh. "Yes. Taller. But have a look at Ogden."

Ogden stood between two towering plants, the most robust on the hill, and he blew at the tassels that reached up to his chin.

"Still, not as tall as the troll," moaned Bladic. "I'm afraid that part of the wager is lost."

Drowden turned to Tapple. "Are you satisfied that the corn's growth has not outstripped Ogden's?"

Tapple was staring into some distant place in his mind and didn't immediately answer, so Drowden spoke again. "Tapple? Are you satisfied?"

Tapple's attention bolted back to the moment. "Sorry. You were saying?"

Drowden laughed. "Oh, I was just saying how interesting it is to have a troll about the house!" There was a lilt of whimsy in his voice.

"So I've heard!" Bladic laughed. "Have you thought of bringing him to the Cotillion? I understand he was quite…. entertaining…. at your wife's party."

Drowden laughed heartily. "Yes, I dare say he made quite an entrance on to the social scene." He stopped and turned to Bladic. "Just so you know, the dogs actually started it. Ogden was hiding in the bushes when Buffy and Button lunged for him. Ogden was caught off guard. And he hadn't yet learned the niceties of social interaction."

"My sympathies then to Mr. Troll!" Bladic mocked. "But enough of this. Tapple! Are you satisfied that the troll is taller than all the corn? You are my witness in this wager."

Tapple blustered and reached into his vest for his pocket watch and pretended to look at it. "Yes, proceed. I heard you the first time. Will this take long?"

Drowden laughed gently while Bladic crossed his arms impatiently.

"For the sake of brevity, Drowden, there's only one question to answer. Just one!" Ospin spat. "Can it or can it not talk?"

"Yes." Drowden nodded. "That does seem to be the question of the hour." And Drowden smiled. "Why don't you ask him? Ask Ogden something! Ask him his name. Let him speak."

"Very well! I shall!" Ospin walked toward the troll but stopped just short of what he imagined was the troll's reach. Bladic took a step from behind Drowden for a better look.

"Mister Troll!" Tapple stated, his reedy voice sounding shrill as a flute crossed by a strong wind. "What is your name?"

The troll stood for a moment, perplexed.

"Go ahead, lad. Tell them!" his teacher, Drowden, encouraged.

"Og-den," the young troll replied. "Ogden."

Tapple smirked. Bladic tssked in disgust. He mocked the troll's utterance saying, "Anyone can teach a magpie! This proves nothing! Mere syllables! No comprehension!"

"Wait!" Drowden raised his hand. "Pardon, lad? I didn't hear you. Could you please…?"

Ogden nodded slightly, eager to satisfy Drowden. "Og-den," the troll responded. "Ogden. They call this troll, Ogden."

His great wide teeth and massive tongue gave the troll a funny accent, but the words were unmistakable. It was all true.

Bladic's knees went weak. He felt them crumbling so he leaned on Tapple's shoulder as a crutch. But Tapple seemed just as unsteady and with the weight of Bladic pressed against him he stumbled forward but caught himself before actually falling.

Bladic grabbed Tapple's jacket and pulled him upright like a pillow being stuffed with a clean case. "Beaten!" he thought. It was a thought he couldn't believe possible.

"Well!" He was at a loss for words and torn between conceding gracefully and making some protest.

"I'm impressed!" Bladic heard Ospin saying. "You've actually done it! You've taught a wild troll to mimic speech."

"But wait just one minute!" Tapple's voice grew shrill with anger. He moved to the next row of corn and pointed at the ground. "What kind of chicanery is this?" he squealed. "Would you really stoop so low, Drowden Erebus?"

"What are you blabbering about?" Bladic blustered with annoyance.

"Tapple, what are you getting at?" Drowden asked defensively, but with some ire. Ogden stepped aside as Drowden and Bladic came to Tapple's side to see what he was looking at.

"I mean those cut stalks! Look!" He was pointing at the ground at two cut cornstalks, jabbing his finger toward them. He stooped to wave a hand over them and looked up at the other men. "Here; look. There's no mistaking it. There are two missing stalks of corn. And notice the breadth of what remains. They must have been giants before someone cut them down."

"Do you mean to accuse me…?" Drowden's face was red. And he had a hard time keeping his words in order.

"Tapple, that's absurd." Bladic stepped between the two men and leaned over, facing Ospin Tapple and wagging a finger in his face. "I know Drowden Erebus and he's as honest a man as you'll ever know. I won't hear any more of this."

"Then it was one of his field hands!" Tapple yelled. "Maybe not Drowden Erebus, but someone is trying to cheat."

Drowden pushed Bladic aside and stooped to look Tapple in the eye. "Not one of my men would betray me," he said. "And no guest at Hapstead Manor is going to accuse me or my people of double-dealing. So, what is it, Master Tapple? Have you simply made a big mistake?" Drowden's brow was furrowed. His lips were tight. His eyes didn't move.

Tapple's face was white. Drowden straightened up and hitched his hands on his hips. Glancing from Drowden to Ogden and back, Tapple reached for his belt and retrieved a seven-inch dagger that Nathan Bladic remembered well. Tapple took a step back and began shouting in a terrified voice.

"You keep that monster away from me. Don't let him set a hand on me. You just get back; leave me alone. Get back. I mean it!"

"Whoa! Whoa! Put that thing away. Tapple, you've gone too far! Calm down. No one is going to touch you, isn't that right, Drowden?" Bladic stood between them and held out his hand. "Give me the knife Tapple."

Tapple held it with white knuckles. "He'll turn that troll on me; I know it..."

"Tapple, you insulted the man. You called him a cheat. You've got no proof of that. Take it back. Make it right. Drowden, tell him your troll won't do him any harm!"

Drowden looked to Ogden. The troll had hunched down on one knee. He looked at Ospin Tapple curiously, but not angrily. Drowden winked at Ogden and jerked his chin at Tapple.

"Ospin, put that thing away before you cut yourself. Ogden has no intention of bothering you. And I'm done talking with you. So sheath your knife and let's end this business."

Bladic reached out his hand to Tapple. "Give it here. Show Drowden you've got no plans to use it. Hand it over to me. I'll give it back later."

Reluctantly, Tapple surrendered the knife, handing it, blade-first, to Nathan Bladic. As he took the knife in his palm, Bladic looked down at Ospin Tapple and sneered sharply. He stopped himself from exploding in anger when he felt the sticky sap on the sharp iron blade. Corn sap, he thought. Without a doubt, corn sap.

"That's better," he said to Tapple with a forced smile, but kept his suspicions to himself. "Why don't you apologize to Drowden Erebus? Let's make this right. I know you know it's the right thing to do!" He wiped the blade with obvious flare on his pant leg and repeated, "I know you know it's the right thing to do!"

Tapple blanched and stammered. He understood Bladic's veiled message. "Yes, of course," he said nervously. "I'm sure I was mistaken. Drowden, I hope you'll forget what I said. It was intemperate and wrong of me to make such an accusation."

Drowden Erebus took three long strides and stood at Tapple's side. He draped an arm over his shoulder. "Forgiveness is a gift I give gladly, friend. But are you truly satisfied that I've fulfilled the terms of the wager and that I, or rather, that Ogden, has won the day?"

Ospin Tapple felt squeamish and wanted to shed Drowden's arm but wouldn't dare. He looked up at him sideways and put on a fake smile that hid much more than it revealed. He shrugged under cover of the smile and Drowden lightened his hold and then took a step back. Tapple spoke cheerily then.

"I was just wondering," he pretended real interest. "What else can the beast....er, I mean, can Ogden say?"

"Oh, many things and more things every day!" Drowden said brightly. "Ogden!" Drowden called to his troll. "Are you hungry? Want breakfast?"

Breakfast had become one of the troll's favorite words. He smiled broadly. "Breakfast, yes!" he said, and he patted his belly.

"Gentlemen," said Drowden, "I think it's time we all had a bite to eat. Let's get back to the house. We can talk at greater length with Ogden on the way down."

As they left the cornfield Ogden led the way. They walked back toward the barn in silence and the troll broke off from the others, heading for his loft to lie down, out of the bright sunlight.

Ospin Tapple had been searching his mind for something to ask, a trick question to leave some doubt about Ogden's skill at conversation. At last he said, "So, Mister Ogden. Do you like it here at Hapstead Manor? I mean, is it better than your home in the forest?"

Ogden looked to Drowden, who said "Go ahead, Ogden. Say whatever is on your mind."

The troll stopped and looked around. "This…. home for Ogden," he said simply.

Drowden flushed with pride and patted Ogden's shoulder. "Very good, lad! Your breakfast will be in the barn, go eat. We'll join you later!"

The troll nodded then made his way inside the barn. Drowden turned to his guests. "Come, gentlemen! No doubt you're famished by now. Odelia has prepared a breakfast for us! Go freshen up and join me and mine at table!"

Nathan Bladic muttered something agreeable and smiled. Ospin Tapple nodded as he entered the Manor House. Then Bladic added, "Over breakfast we can settle the terms of the wager and method of payment," he said. "I think we must then ride for Ironwood."

"Yes," Drowden smiled. "We'll settle this matter on full stomachs."

Chapter XIII
Of Tools and Trolls

D rowden Erebus woke to the aroma of buckwheat griddle cakes, rich dark coffee and hickory cured bacon. Yawning, he stretched one last time then fumbled to pull his robe up over his shoulders. It wasn't until he really started moving about the room that Drowden felt the effects of the previous night's celebration.

He smiled, remembering how Argis, Willbee and even old Piscote had howled at the moon, standing arm-in-arm with Ogden, who led the braying chorus. Even Dorina reluctantly joined in the hullabaloo after a great deal of cajoling. The sherry helped put her in the mood, but when she finally let her hair down, she had scant competition. He delighted in the mental picture he knew he would long cherish of his lovely wife hugging Ogden with real affection.

The party last night was in celebration of the harvest to come. He had won the wager with Nathan Bladic, and today he would gather his tools, wagons, and field hands to journey to Ironwood Manor, Bladic's sprawling estate that was burgeoning into a brick and smokestack fortress of industry. Drowden, Ogden and the men of Hapstead Manor would journey to Ironwood Manor to take the corn crop that was theirs. Bladic refused to harvest and deliver the corn he'd lost in the wager. "I won't pay my men to cut your corn," he told Drowden on the morning they settled the corn wager.

Ogden had done more than prove him right. Trolls could not only speak; they were people like anyone else. Without a doubt, Ogden had matured with incredible speed, and he learned new words, new thoughts, and new skills almost immediately. In the few weeks since Bladic and Tapple visited

Hapstead Manor, Ogden had all but mastered the art of conversation. He and Argis were becoming fast friends, and he constantly showed he had a sense of humor. Drowden pictured him laughing with self-deprecation while Willbee and Hector imitated the brutish misrepresentation of trolls caricatured by the likes of Ospin Tapple.

Drowden stirred from his reverie and watched Dorina, still sleeping under a disheveled pile of blankets. He sighed at her gentle breaths, her sweet face and her halo of yellow hair. After sliding his feet into slippers, he went to his wardrobe and picked out a set of work clothes appropriate to the day ahead. He was dressed and lacing up his boots when Dorina finally stirred and stretched with a yawn as she opened her eyes and smiled at him.

"Good morning my love. I hope you got some rest," he said gently.

"Yes," she said in a still sleepy voice, "no thanks to you." And she smiled broadly. A quiet laugh washed over Drowden and Dorina joined in as she rose up on her elbows and he leaned in to kiss her.

"Go get your breakfast," she said, pushing him away gently. "I know you've got lots of work to do. I'll be down shortly." As he got up and headed for the door, she called after him, "Good luck getting the workers up and on the road this morning. I'm afraid not all of them are going to be as happy to see you as I am."

Drowden smiled to himself as he descended the stairs and turned down the hall to the dining room. Odelia called over her shoulder as she was exiting into the kitchen. "Help yourself sir. It's all there. Miranda and Ian have already eaten."

"Thank you, Odelia. Good morning. I'm going to be quick; then I'm off to the Bladic farm with the field hands."

Through the door he heard her laugh loudly. He smiled and shook his head. He pulled a covered tray toward his place setting, slapped four griddle cakes onto his plate, trapped a bundle of bacon between his fork and forefinger, and then dabbed a knife tip of butter on top of the stack. He made short work of all of it and was quickly out the door with a weather-beaten straw hat pushed down on his head. He thought again about the day that went before.

The memory of it all made him feel giddy and grateful, vindicated and humbled all at once.

The barn door was closed. Drowden entered, lit the lantern and called up to the loft. "Ogden! Rise and shine, lazy bones!" There was no reply. "Ogden!" he called again. "Time to get up! We've got lots to do. Time to go!"

Drowden raced up the ladder to the loft. The troll's billet was neatly arranged and his bed cold to the touch. "Where in blazes did you go, Ogden?" he said aloud. With his nocturnal habits, it was unusual for the troll not to sleep-in until mid-morning. Drowden left the barn and trotted down the manor's main road, gravel crunching with every footfall.

At the furrowed road that turned into the hay field he paused long enough to catch a few breaths. He could hear the swish-swishing of a sickle in use somewhere off to the right but couldn't see over the meadow's sea of fronds and flowers.

"Ho there! Argis!" Drowden called, expecting his worker's husky voice to respond. Instead he heard Ogden's rough baritone call out, "Ho, Father!"

Drowden pushed through the wildflowers and encountered the young troll with a broad grin.

"Well I'll be!" he said. The troll was standing aside a row of felled hay. Ogden looked up from his work and smiled.

"I've been looking all over for you, lad. What's going on?" Drowden asked looking around.

Suddenly Argis pushed through the high brush and stood before them with a swarm of gnats flying around his ears. "He's been helpin' wi' th' hay, eee has. No worries, though, Master Erebus. Th' wagons er loaded. Got all th' tools up in th' buckboard except I wanna be sure ta bring along a bolt o' twine. Th' horses er all hitched ta th' panel wagons an' all's set fer the ride ta Ironwood."

"Then let's get to it, men," said Drowden. He winked at Ogden and slapped Argis' back. "Come on. We'll drop off those scythes and grab the twine. Daylight is not to be wasted. Let's be on our way."

The shed was stuffy. Drowden opened the door and then turned back to Ogden, outstretching his arm to point at the tools hanging from hooks on the wall.

"Those are for working in the earth," he said. "That's a hoe. We use it to turn the soil and do away with weeds! See this steel piece?"

Argis coughed again. "He already knows all them names, sir. I taught 'im myself."

Drowden laughed and slapped Argis on the back as all three left the tool shed and headed for the carriage house. On the road in front sat four wagons — the buckboard was in the lead and three paneled flat boards were lined up behind. The teams were harnessed and prancing. Willbee sat on the third wagon as driver. He was looking down, talking with Harry and Hector. They broke off when they saw Drowden, Argis and Ogden coming their way. Harry climbed up on the second wagon in line and Hector got up on the driver's seat of the fourth.

"All set?" asked Drowden.

"All ready ta go," answered Willbee.

"You climb up with Willbee," Drowden said to Ogden. "I'll ride with Argis. What do you say?"

Ogden looked to each of the men and smiled, then climbed up to sit next to Willbee and tower over him. As the wagons turned around a curve past the Manor House, Miranda stood on the front stoop and waved. Ogden suddenly cried out to her, "Off to get Master Bladic's corn!" The men all laughed and cheered as the horses jerked into serious action and the wagon wheels started turning more quickly.

The miles passed in a blur of green and pink maple trees. Autumn looked to be settling early over the valley, and cicadas chirped a thousand conversations throughout the surrounding forest. Hector seemed affected by the woodland incantation. He began to sing, at first quietly to himself, but soon the others heard his sonorous voice rise in syncopation with the clopping of hooves.

The bright silver buttons on Jillian's coat
Shine like the light in her eyes.
Her smile is as sweet as the berries of spring,
Still her promises are nothing but lies.
The suppers she feeds me are tasty, it's true.
And she kisses me better, I'm sure that I'm right.
And she tells me she loves me more often, I bet,
Than the others she deigns to delight.

The song went on for many verses, and the gist of it was clear in the first, but it got coarser and bawdier the longer it went on. But the miles went by too, and the coolish morning became a warm sun-lit afternoon, then a quiet chill evening. The small column of wagons came to a stop in a clearing at the top of a cedar-crowned hill. Drowden instructed the men to tend to the horses and to build a fire. They passed around bread and cheese and wine after camp had been set. In the morning they would rise early and proceed down the Near Valley Road that forked off to the east just a mile further on and would arrive at Ironwood Manor before Nathan Bladic would have finished his breakfast.

They settled in for the night with the fire burning low. Hector, Willbee and Harry were all snoring before long. But Harry only pretended to sleep. He lay on his side, away from Ogden and Drowden, listening. Ogden lay on his back, propping his head up on his crossed palms, which were cushioned in a soft bed of trimmed cedar branches. Drowden sat on a log looking up at the stars in a moonless sky. He kept looking up as he spoke.

"Ogden, I wanted to talk with you about taking another trip with me. Next time, to Irongate. It will be in about two weeks. I have some new equipment to have shipped from the warehouses in Deepwater, and I think it's time for you to see how other men and women live. And for them to see that a troll is nothing to be afraid of."

Ogden looked over at Drowden. "The memory is fading…clouded, Father, but some say this troll made some scared and angry Hapstead Manor visitors. Another thing; are you saying me the truth? Will you make so many changes to Hapstead, to home, that before long it will not be Hapstead; will not be home?"

Drowden chuckled quietly and left off his stargazing. "That transgression was when you were young, Ogden. Many things are forgiven youth. But as we age, we learn. When I was younger, I thought the world was friendly and I could always find an agreeable way to make tomorrow livable. I haven't seen it that way for a long time."

"Not so very long ago," Ogden sighed.

"No, but look how civilized you've become since then. That might help them, maybe even me, forget, even if you don't."

Ogden said, "Remember, and forgive. That way seems better." Then his face drew tighter and his lip quivered imperceptibly. His eyes glistened. "This troll has a hard thing to do. In me, many voices whisper. They cry out at night. They drown out the song of the stars sometimes. I call you 'father,' but the Old Ones, they are all our fathers and mothers. They cry-out from the caverns of time. Father, seeing you join Nathan Bladic in making fire and Earth and wind and water do all the work of 'facturing so many things — it makes what I must decide echo with a deep hurt inside my heart."

Drowden whisper-whistled. "That sounds serious!" he said quietly. "We manufacture things to make everyone's lives easier. What do you have to decide about that?"

Ogden's eyes narrowed and a tear rolled out and down his cheek. "How it will end. How life will end. How it will all end," Ogden said a bit too loudly. Then he sighed quietly. "Life is not easier, at all."

Harry secretly rolled his eyes and disguised a sigh of disgust with a feigned snore and snort. Drowden shook his head.

"That's far too much worrying for such a young troll."

Ogden had noticed another light just over the hill and turned toward Drowden, who puffed gently on a bent wooden pipe that reflected its own delicate glow on the palm of his cradling hand.

"See that fire, behind yon hill, Father?" he asked. His black eyes shone red against the shadows all around him.

"That's Bladic's machines," answered Drowden quietly. "I don't fully understand them myself, Ogden, but I'm studying them. There are big cauldrons and chimneys and wheels turning and smoke everywhere." He shook his head and tapped the pipe on the log. A few embers danced out across the ground and Drowden stepped them out with the heel of his boot. "We'll see them soon enough. And maybe someday we won't have to visit Bladic's Ironwood estate to see their likes. They have a way of making it cheap to get rich. That idea keeps me awake at night. I can't pretend I'm not curious. Let's sleep now. All this is just a lot of words that could change everything, or it could be just gas past the lips. We have work to do tomorrow. Let's sleep."

Ogden's eyes grew distant, with starlight sparkling in them as he spoke. "Men won't stop what they are just beginning, even when they've robbed all the tombs of our ancestors. For years to come, they'll steal their corpses — the soft black stones of their bodies and the slippery black goo of their guts — and they'll burn them to turn their wheels. They'll stoke the fires and their hunger for more of everything, will turn the remains of every being who ever lived before into useless, wasteful things. The graves where the Old Ones rest will be opened, their contents shoveled and siphoned into foul-smelling cauldrons. Empires will grow in the glow of your forges. But time is only a dream, and the land won't forget that you unleashed death from the deep pits where it was buried with the cadavers of the Elders. It is a grave trespass and won't be forgotten."

"You're young, Ogden. Some things are hard to understand," Drowden grumbled and shifted his shoulder off a sharp rock and wriggled his head on a makeshift pillow.

Ogden whispered, "Even the Old Ones do not understand."

Stars sparkled like hoar frost on the window of time. Ogden's eyes gathered all the many filaments of time on which they sent their light and braided them into a single tapestry, no longer separate stars glimmering in the night, but now a single moment with no past or future history.

Drowden turned away grumbling. "Get some sleep," and fell silent.

Ogden wasn't sleepy, but he lay down without closing his eyes. As Drowden pulled a blanket up over his shoulders and turned onto his other side, Ogden lay on his back and watched stars twinkle high above. He had been watching one bright red dot every night for weeks, and noticed that it was moving slowly, slowly, but noticeably eastward against the constant background of the other unmoving stars. And its song was strangely metallic, like a metal can being whacked with a stick, while all the other stars sang like strummed harp strings and lutes and oboes, except here and there some odd ones accented the sky symphony with a 'dud-dud-dud' sound. He didn't know why, but he never mentioned the sky songs he heard to anyone. Maybe he would someday.

He listened to the night sounds of the forest too. A horned owl called out intermittently 'hooo—hoot-----huuh—hooo--hooooooooewww.' Off to his right, Ogden listened to a large centipede crinkling a leaf. And he listened as the four men snored, stretched and shifted.

The fire gradually curled into its own smoky folds and coiled up to repose in its gem-like coals. Ogden watched them shimmer and lick the air with vagrant tongues of light. He thought he saw small salamanders made of fire jumping out of the base of glowing ash. His dark eyes gaped, and he lay motionless as images of unfamiliar faces jelled in the bright shadows and rich dark flames that occasionally shot out of the fire's bed. A homely woman whose gloomy eyes made him shiver with baffling fright. A big man with kind eyes who was unbearably consumed by sporadic flames that jumped up to devour him. He stared wide-eyed and watched in horror. The fire's phantoms enslaved his attention. He heard only its soft, hot breathing within the ring of stones the men had built.

Ogden blinked and looked away. Gradually those disturbing images evaporated from his eyes and again he watched the forest come to life with peering eyes, sniffing snouts and startled scampering. The orange glow of Bladic's machines beyond the horizon never lessened.

Morning was hardly established when the men pulled themselves out of their slumbers and harnessed the horses to the wagons. Drowden passed around the water jug and unwrapped a loaf of sourdough bread. Ogden was up and about before any of them, and he called out when he heard them stir, to let them know he was nearby. Harry went looking and found him just beyond the clearing, squatting near a patch of velvet-textured pale green lamb's ear.

"Finish up an' git in the wagon, troll. Off to work fer us. Let's go!"

"Yes. Will be there!" Ogden hopped to pull up his trousers. When he returned to the camp clearing, he was greeted by quiet 'good mornings' and a large tear of bread from Drowden. Soon the wagons were rolling to the crest of the hill and turned left at the fork, then downhill on the Near Valley Road.

Three long switchbacks stretched out their descent into the valley but kept the grade manageable. From the top of the road, they saw dark clouds of smoke spreading into a wide-spanning layer of black that concealed most of the valley. At the second sharp turn, the source of that cloud was revealed to be three sooty columns of rising smoke, and at the lower turn they could see the tall stone chimneys that spewed that murky miasma.

Ogden squinted and puckered at the sight. "There's the sin," he said quietly, under his breath. His shoulders waggled as the cart clattered over a rocky patch in the road. Then he yelled out loud: "It's wrong to free the sunlight trapped long ago inside those black rocks. The waters will rise against you. The air will stifle your breath. This must be stopped before it is too late."

Willbee looked at him sideways with his mouth hanging open. Drowden looked around, turned back forward, and shook his head without comment. No one said a word. They didn't know what to say.

On the hills surrounding the large stone and metal buildings attached to the high flung brick chimneys they could see a pasture dotted by brown and white cattle, and another field teeming with a flock of sheep that seemed to flow in a choreographed dance across the ground like a swarm of doves in the sky. It was the remains of what was once the pastoral look of Ironwood Manor, before the machines came.

The four wagons, their horses and their human and troll riders rolled down the hill clattering on the hard, dry surface. They passed a horseless and driverless wagon loaded down with chunks of coal. The spokes of its right front wheel were cracked, and the rim hung away from them at a sharp angle. It had been pulled aside onto a gravelly patch of ground, so the road was not blocked.

"That explains the black trail of coal dust we've been following all the way down." Drowden turned on his wagon bench to call back to the others. "They must bring in whole caravans of the stuff to feed these belchers." He coughed and pulled a kerchief from his pocket. When he blew his nose, he deposited a dark wad of grime onto the white linen.

The air all around was like cotton in their lungs. It pulled the moisture out of them and left each one breathing in shallow gasps. They coughed in a chorus until the wagons descended under the hovering brown cloud and then they spat heartily to clear their throats.

When the road leveled Argis saw a yellow painted single-spired gate dropped across the way and secured to a post at its narrow end. He pulled up on the reins to halt Elmore, the horse pulling his cart. Drowden held a hand up to signal the wagons behind to slow and stop.

A man with a dented and rusted helmet and a pike with a brass tip covered with a green patina approached. He came up from an embankment that dropped off to the right of the road. The paunchy man puffed as he mounted the hill. His yellow hair blew like dead seaweed spilling out of his head gear. Nothing about him said 'welcome.'

A clear voice rang out. "Drowden Erebus here. Master Bladic expects us."

The ridiculous guard eyed them wordlessly. Without indicating approval, disapproval, challenge or greeting, he lifted the end of the spire from its mooring and swung the gate open to let them pass. The hinged stretch of cedar creaked and pivoted on an ironwood peg and vacillated over the wildflowers growing down the hill on the left of the road. The wagons rolled past it, past the guard, and into the jurisdiction of Ironwood Manor.

The manufactories belched black smoke that went skyward and then came back down, settling on anything out of doors and depositing a fine dusty itch on the skin. The air vibrated with noises imperceptible to the ear. They filled the innards of everyone with a strange uneasiness. Gray plank fences eight feet tall surrounded the gloomy buildings with the tall smokestacks. Nathan Bladic called them "money belchers."

Sentries stood at the manufactory entrances, which were blocked by gates made of sinuous twists of peculiarly strong wood that was impervious to the best axes, except those made here at Ironwood Manor. Next to the ironworks stood the slaughterhouse, where steam-powered blades cut cattle into meat that was stored in the icehouse, an adjacent cylindrical building. Next to the slaughterhouse stood another manufactory. No one was supposed to know what enterprise went on inside that structure. The workers, when asked, simply referred to it as "the mill."

The column of wagons rumbled down the road to a cluster of more homely buildings that stood below the spired Manor House. A stable and a carriage house seemed the right place to pause.

Argis inquired inside about water and hay for their animals and waved to steer the others toward a field next to the carriage house. The wagons were soon lined up beside each other. The drivers stepped down and stretched.

Drowden looked over his shoulder saying, "I'll be back soon," and disappeared between two outbuildings, walking in the direction of the Manor House. Ogden stood by the chocolate mare that had pulled his wagon.

The men and women of Ironwood seemed unreceptive to social chat. A few friendly attempts to start conversations were rebuffed with silent stares. Willbee's smile faded quickly after he was "hrumphed!" by a woman dragging a heavy burlap sack who refused his offer of help. Hector shrugged when a man with a leather cap precariously perched on his head waved him away when he asked him if he knew the time.

After about a quarter of an hour, Traunton, Nathan Bladic's foreman, showed up and asked their business. As Argis explained, Traunton stared with an air of disinterest.

A burly man with a bony brow, flat nose, forward-leaning gait and the smell of too many working days without bathing, Traunton seemed unhappy to have to talk with any of them. He weaved his way between the wagons and horses, stooped to look under the bed boards, and when he found nothing of interest, he turned to leave.

Suddenly Ogden stood between Traunton and the wagons. "You troll?" he asked. He gazed directly and unblinkingly into the foreman's cold, dark eyes. "You troll?" Ogden repeated.

Without a word, Traunton grabbed Ogden by the collar of his shirt and the waist of his pants. Lifting him like a bag of air, the foreman tossed Ogden with a loud groan. Ogden flailed his arms in the air with nothing to grab. He slammed hard into the side of Chelsie, the old paint still harnessed to the third of Drowden's wagons. Chelsie stumbled at the blow and fell on her right side. The wagon tilted onto two wheels but didn't topple completely.

"Did you call me a troll?" Traunton grumbled. "You got no room to talk."

Ogden scrambled to get up and turned to pull Chelsie to her feet. He righted the horse and the wagon with a single pull,   but   Traunton ran up from behind him and shoved him hard again, causing Ogden to topple over Chelsie's back and against a stone block that was the base of a large water trough. Chelsie panicked and scrambled to her feet. With one smooth movement she both came to an upright position and kicked Ogden squarely in the forehead, stunning him so that his knees buckled, and he fell face down in the dust.

Traunton moved in to finish the job, but Argis saw what was happening and, jumping down from the buckboard where he had been sorting the cutting tools, he ran to intervene. As he came off the wagon, he grabbed a coil of rope and on the run tied a slip knot to form a coil. He caught up just as Traunton reached down to grab Ogden. With the loop in the rope stretched wide in both hands and the end wrapped tightly around his right hand, he threw it over Traunton from behind and just as quickly ran the other way until he felt the chord zing tight and then go loose again as Traunton was pulled back on his heels and dropped flat on his back.

Willbee was there in a minute, with a scythe in his hand, standing over Traunton and hollering "Stay put, ya filthy back-biter! Leave poor Ogden be!"

Argis was there with the other end of the rope and twisted it around Traunton's neck, not tightly, but menacingly. "Do it, I suggest!" he bellowed, but Traunton tried to squirm free of the rope that pinned both his arms to his side. "Harry! Go see about Ogden, if he's alright!"

But Harry just stood there, unmoving and yelling at Argis. "Leave th' Trogs ta kill each otter! Leave 'em go!" he yelled.

Now Argis was screaming at Harry, Willbee was menacing Traunton with the scythe, Traunton was squirming to get free of the rope, and Ogden was stumbling to his feet, dazed. His eyes seemed to have disappeared in his head from swelling and his head seemed bigger than it used to be. But though he stumbled, he made his way forward and leaned over Traunton. He put a hand on Willbee's forearm and pushed the scythe down. He pointed to the rope in Argis' hand and said "For Ogden, let this man free. Unrope him, please Argis."

Ogden leaned down and pulled the loop around Traunton until it was loose, saying "You are a man with muscle. A strong man whose muscles don't like the naming of 'troll.' It's good that you name you and not someone else. This troll is sorry." He held out his hand to help Traunton get to his feet but was rebuffed.

"Just stay your distance, trog," he barked as he got up. "Else I'll shuffle the rest of you." He dusted himself off and made to leave. Willbee and Argis braced Ogden's uneasy stance and noticed the large growing lump on his forehead.

Harry winked at Argis and said to the side as he followed after Traunton, "I'll set stuff right. No need to worry. Le'me have a word wif him."

Harry caught up to the foreman and then walked backward in front of him for a moment. Argis couldn't hear what he was saying, but he watched as

Traunton shook his head, seeming to agree with whatever Harry was telling him. Just then, Drowden Erebus rounded the side of the stables, but before he could ask what was happening, Traunton yelled at him, "I told you Nathan Bladic ain't around to talk to you! Now, collect your forest dog and your cheat corn and get your smelly company off of Ironwood land."

Drowden tried to say something, but Traunton stormed off in the direction of the Manor House without another word. Argis and Willbee yammered together, trying to tell Drowden what had happened. Harry kept saying, "I smoothed stuff over wid the big ugly guy."

Drowden held up a hand. "Everyone, slow down! I can't understand what you're saying. One at a time." Then they each took turns telling what had happened as Drowden examined Chelsie, the wagon, and the troll.

"Ogden, are you hurt badly?" He put his arm around Ogden's shoulder and looked closely at his swelling forehead. The flesh under his eyes and above his thick cheek bones was beginning to turn purple and red. His eyes seemed small and retreated into the inflamed bumps that were his eyelids.

"This noggin hurts, Father. But it's time to work, not time to worry."

Drowden shook his head silently and bit his lower lip. Finally, he slapped Ogden lightly on the back and said, "Alright gentlemen. Let's collect Ogden's corn and leave this unfriendly place."

They boarded the wagons and moved them a little way closer to the cornfield, which was adjacent to the stables. Soon they were busy cutting and piling and loading Nathan Bladic's corn crop for the ride back to Hapstead.

Inside Ironwood Manor the curtains were drawn closed. A fire within the ornate marble hearth warmed the shadowy coolness where the sun could not. Nathan Bladic stood behind his elaborately carved chestnut desk with the curtain pulled back slightly. He was peeking out the window and watching as Drowden Erebus, his workers and that troll drove their wagons into his cornfield.

Across the desk from Bladic another man sat on a cushioned chair with needlepoint floral embellishments. In front of him was a lightweight serving table with a pot of hot tea and a small tray of sweet blueberry biscuits. He was talking to Bladic's back.

"You don't have to do a thing but stay out of it. All I need from you is that you do not interfere. Can I count on that?"

Bladic said, "They're taking my corn. I made a foolish bet, and now I'm paying for it. But I've had a revelation of sorts. It makes no sense for me to grow the stuff, to feed and shelter workers to plow and sow and weed and harvest. Why should I waste my wealth on the dregs of the earth when I can take from them a share of what *they* labor to produce? I've had a stroke of genius, Tapple."

Ospin Tapple pursed his lips with irritation. "Did you hear me, Nathan? I need your reassurance that you'll stay out of it. If necessary, I'll buy your cooperation and silence."

Bladic let go the curtain and turned away from the window. He crossed his arms and looked sternly at Tapple. "I've ordered the machinery already. I'm going to build a coal-driven steam mill and let the dirt farmers from miles around pay me to grind their grain and corn. Then I can turn out a dozen field workers and knock down one of the bunk houses to make way for my next project."

Tapple tried to interrupt. "Really, Nathan. I want your word..."

"Think of the genius," Bladic kept talking, "think of the generations of hoarded knowledge it's taken to yoke nature to do the work of a gaggle of field hands. Steam that's made from plain water and fire that's freed from wood and coal — that's what pushes the gears and wheels of my mill into action."

"Yes, yes, all very impressive." Tapple nodded as he sipped his tea. His upper lip quivered with agitation, and he tapped his foot impatiently, waving away the rest of Bladic's long-winded rhapsody on machines. "Yes, yes. It's all quite remarkable, but have you heard a word I said?"

Bladic's expression of enthusiasm dropped away. He looked expression-lessly at Tapple. "I heard every word. You plan to take the Brotherhood out into the wild for some troll hunting. It's nothing to me. I don't care a jot. You can count on my silence because it will come naturally. I don't give a whit what you and your drunken band of bored idiots do in the forest."

"That's all I wanted to hear," said Ospin Tapple, returning to his chewing. "Leave the Trogs to me. Where there's one young one, there are at least two sweaty mongrels that found some attraction in each other."

"Then you've set the date? You have a plan?" asked Bladic.

"Yes," Tapple answered while pouring another cup of steaming tea. "Everything is in place."

"And where would you say is their place, those sweaty trolls?" asked Bladic. "I know! Under a heap of rock and earth, hidden from memory?"

"Aye," said Tapple. "Deep and forgotten."

Suddenly the door to the study flew open and Traunton burst in yelling "The corn thieves are here, and they brought a Trog. Still want me to just let 'em take it?"

Ospin Tapple bolted up from his chair, knocking the small wooden table forward. It landed on the tapestried rug with a crash, sending cup and pot and tea and biscuits splashing and clattering and rolling. His chair wobbled behind him as he recoiled in horror at sight of Traunton. Bladic laughed and called after Tapple as he retreated through an archway separating the study from the sitting room, stumbling past two potted ferns on either side of the portal. He fell to his knees and crawled behind a couch to hide.

Bladic yelled for a servant to clean up the mess, and then called to Tapple. "I can see your miserable self hiding back there. Don't be a coward. Come meet my man Traunton. Really, he's not a bad Trog."

Traunton approached Bladic. "That troll's a troublemaker. I almost killt him. Mighta been best if I did. Should me and the boys go after 'em?"

"No," said Bladic. "I don't want any harm to come to them or the troll while they're here. Just make sure they stay away from the bunkhouse, the mill, the sick house and the jail."

Traunton nodded, then stepped closer and lowered his voice. "I got news," he said quietly, almost a whisper. Bladic raised his chin and turned an ear toward him. Traunton leaned in. "Drowden Erebus' man Harry tells me that his troll is goin' to Irongate with his keeper in a fortnight. I want a second try at that troll. I might get it in Irongate if you let me go."

Bladic rubbed his chin and shook his head 'no.' "I've got another idea," he said. "Now get out of here. My guest seems unlikely to come out of hiding with you in the room."

Traunton grumbled something obscene and went out the door and down the steps with heavy feet. When he was convinced the mixed-breed foreman was gone, Tapple pulled himself up to his feet and re-entered the study. Bladic's servant was just finishing cleaning up the toppled tea and biscuits and exited behind him as he stood toe-to-toe with his host.

"When did you start hiring his likes?" he squealed, looking up to meet Bladic's eyes.

"None of your concern. You've got your secrets; I've got mine." Bladic returned to his desk chair and, sitting, indicated that Tapple should take a seat on the upholstered armchair in front of the desk. "Now, about your business with the trolls..."

Tapple raised his thick right eyebrow and pointed with his left hand. "I thought we had settled that."

"It's done. Not a peep from me, Ospin. But if I know you, slaughtering a couple of wild trolls in the forest won't be the end of it. You want Drowden's troll. 'Ogden,' is it?"

Ospin Tapple leaned forward, interested. "Today? Here?"

"Don't be a fool. I'm not going to let harm come to that brute while it's here at Ironwood, under my protection. I need the goodwill of Drowden Erebus in this community. But there might be a way for you to..."

"What is it? What have you got in mind?" Tapple interrupted.

Nathan Bladic stood up and bent over his desk, leaning on his spider-splayed fingers. "I have some information you might find useful."

The corn harvesting was done. Three wagons were loaded to the top; the horses were freshly harnessed, and Drowden was down by the road talking with Bladic's foreman, who seemed less confrontational, if not exactly friendly.

Willbee was up on the tool wagon taking scythes and machetes from Argis, Hector and Ogden as they handed them up. Harry seemed to be shadowing Ogden, eyeing him peculiarly. Finally, he piped up, pointing at the young troll. "That head tater makes ya almost look yooman," he said. "No horns fer brows. Maybe a good chuck ta the head now an' then would be good fer ya."

Willbee spit in a long arc that landed on Harry's shoe. "Ogden's me friend. Let 'im be."

Harry tried to reach up to grab Willbee's leg and drag him down off the wagon, but Argis grabbed his arm and held it firmly. "Haven't we had enough fisticuffs fer one day? Wise up, Harry."

Harry yanked away, freeing himself from Argis' grasp. "Yer always stickin' up for the damned troll!' he yelled. "If it was me, I'd string him up, or drag him from a horse."

Argis stuck his pointing finger under Harry's nose and eyeballed him directly. "Hurt tha' troll an' I'll see ya livin' wi' th' roofless ones in Bladicville; hear me? Ya won't even git a shanty shack. He's done nothin' to ya, an' you'll do nothin' ta him. Hear me?"

Hector was more eloquent. He walked to Argis side and took another step forward, shoving Harry's shoulder. He pointed to Ogden, then glared a long moment right into Harry's eyes. When Harry blinked, Hector turned his gaze and went about gathering tools.

None of them ever spoke of it again.

By the time Drowden returned, the loading was done. The wagon drivers took their seats and Ogden jumped up behind Drowden and Argis in the tool wagon. Argis looked back and winked at the troll. "He's a good worker, Master Erebus," he said as he gave Chelsie a tap with the reins and the wagon lurched forward.

"It's true," Drowden responded with a broad smile. Then off the four wagons rolled, out of Ironwood and up the Near Valley Road and onward toward Hapstead Manor.

Chapter XIV
Keepers of Time and Place

Ogden lay on his back looking at the stars from a mown grassy hill. He smelled the fresh cut green field that to our eyes is but gray in the darkness. And yet his pitch eyes were wide and receptive to everything that is visible to us in the light of day.

He looked up at the sky, motionless for a long time, until he heard something approach and he rolled to a stooping stance, glancing about. It was Miranda. He saw her move from hiding behind a red-painted outhouse into the open. She stood with hands on hips and cocked her head to one side.

"How did you know it was me and not some roving wolf ready to pounce on you?" she asked with half a laugh.

"Ogden heard you. Smelled you first. Then knew your walk."

"Smelled me, is it? And do I smell like something? What is it I smell like, Mister Troll?" She feigned insult, but truly wondered how she must smell to a troll.

"Like Miranda," was all Ogden said.

Miranda approached and sat down next to Ogden on the hill. The grass was soft and comfortable. They were both quiet for a while, so Ogden lay down on his back and resumed his skyward gaze.

Finally, Miranda spoke. "What are you looking at?"

Ogden didn't answer immediately. She nudged him with a slippered foot. "Did you hear me?"

"Listening to the stars," Ogden said quietly.

"You mean 'looking at the stars,' don't you?" she corrected.

"No. Listening to the stars. Hear them? They know so many things."

Miranda looked at him, puzzled. "What does that mean?" she asked. "I look at them. They're beautiful. But..."

"You can't hear them?" Ogden rolled toward her and propped his head on the palm of his hand, his elbow planted in the grass. "Every night when there are no clouds, and especially when there is no moon, the stars sing."

Miranda shook her head slowly. "That doesn't make sense."

"They don't try to make sense," he explained. "They don't sing like that. They sing in living notes, not dead words. It's hard to tell you what they say, because they don't say things that can be said."

"Well, now I am completely confused, Ogden. Are you learning to play jokes on people? Or are you learning to talk in riddles? Which is it?"

He sat up and shrugged. "Words don't say what is. They say what sayers want hearers to see. Sometimes this troll has no words to tell it with and borrows other words."

"They call that poetry, Ogden," said Miranda diffidently.

"Ogden knows the night," he said. "The whole world speaks without words then. These eyes can see best then. The world glares these eyes when the sun is high. Light shouts all around. You say 'stop squinting, Ogden.' But the sun squints my eyes. Only at night: then things are easy to see, and the stars are easy to hear."

"Yes, and apparently you can hear the stars singing too. Well, if you say so then it must be so. Who am I, but someone older and wiser than you?"

Ogden's broad lips stretched into a wide grin. "Wiser than Ogden?" he laughed. "Maybe Miranda can say what is real with borrowed words. That is poetry?"

"Yes," she answered haltingly, "I mean, no. Poetry uses words to say the truth in a way that helps you see things more beautifully. Some things are hard to say, but there is always a way to say them. So, what do you mean, really, when you say that the stars sing?"

Ogden pursed his lips and scratched his head. "Some things are real even if you can't say them. Without a name, there are places. Without a name, there are things to know. The stars really sing. It's not words making it seem like they sing. Ogden isn't saying poetry. The stars sing. Listen! They sing!"

"Ugh!! You're infuriating!" Miranda stood up and walked toward the house. "Good night, Ogden. I hope the stars sing you a lullaby and let you sleep."

Ogden bubbled with laughter and called after her. "No! They sing this troll awake! Awake! In the dream of the night, where words don't make things live that can't be lived. The stars help this troll walk awake and alive. The words make be-live of everything."

"It's not be-live, Ogden. The word is 'believe,'" she called back to him. "Words can't make you be alive."

"Stars can," said Ogden. "Words make you be-live things that aren't."

Miranda didn't answer. She was gone inside the big mansion, where candlelight shone through windows like mute stars. The stars that shimmered above Hapstead Manor filled Ogden's senses with a music that seemed to peek out from around the corners of awareness. Upon the light that fell to earth, of blue-white crystalline light, and sapphire brilliance, the orange of a flame's outer spirit, the prismatic white sparkling of a latticed snowflake — these and other incandescent points in the eternal darkness filled the night and sang of things strange, uncaptured by thought, unknown in books, unsaid in words. Their notes crisscrossed and played a fugue on the pipes of time. Their light vibrated intricately, carrying infinitudes of form compacted to information.

Ogden walked slowly down the grassy hill toward the pen where Drowden kept Briggs, the mighty bull. As he walked the sound of the stars' music changed in pitch and seemed to reveal a different story. Images of his first day at Hapstead Manor poured in and filled his senses: the smell of the big animal; of the hay, of the mint and burdock growing around the fence periphery, of the dirt that showed the marks of Briggs' heavy footfall. Here his story among men and women had its start. He heard the sound of panicked voices, of yelling and scuffling feet.

As he approached the stable where the bull stood quietly in the cool shadows, he heard it snort with recognition and greeting. They shared history together. They both had come to Hapstead on the same day, and in the span of a season each had learned that it is a friendly place in most respects. Ogden stroked Briggs' neck and looked into his left eye, a large globe that strained to look back at him, showing its white vein-lined sclera. The singing of the sky continued, for he could still see the constellations hanging above the coral like the ornate chandelier suspended over the table in the Manor's formal dining room. He had seen those crystals, but they were no match for the stellar enormity that drooped down from the sky above.

Place and premonition: these themes seemed to dominate tonight's celestial symphony. For there was something about being here, in this place, that carried with it a sense of memory, but also a sense of foreboding.

Ogden left Briggs and the bull pen. He wandered through the yard that was surrounded by small cottages and the summer kitchen. The lights in every one of them had been doused for the night. On the broken bough of a yellowing elm tree an owl as big as a kit fox moved its head jerkily left-forward-right-forward-left. It watched warily as the tall troll below watched him with brow-hooded eyes, and it waited.

Ogden's nocturnal wanderings led from yard to field to fern-covered hill near the trail that led into the wooded wilderness beyond Hapstead. Amid the scent of rich autumn fronds, he spied the glowing eyes of a polecat. A toad took its time loping from damp stone to wet earth.

Ogden's eyes saw more by star and moonlight than men see by the light of the sun. He looked to the source of a spring and there saw a mist hovering above it. He watched as the diaphanous veil of vapor curled into the shape of a water elemental spirit, an undine. She danced above the gurgling spout of water as it bubbled and folded into a trenched pool a few inches deep, and then spilled over and flowed down a small gully toward the pond behind the carriage keep. Ogden nodded to the nymph, and she bowed in return and made him an offering of visions.

"What thing may I bestow, friend troll?" asked the water nymph. "Is there some small thing we can do?"

Ogden thought a moment, then he ceased thinking and an answer came to him. "Yes," he said. "Is it in your power to change one word in all the worlds that men inhabit?"

He heard a splishy tittering of laughter, then, "Yes, this we can do. What word do you wish to change?" she asked.

"When men say 'believe,' let them now say instead 'be-live.' That is the wish you can fulfill."

A happy bubbling of laughter filled his ears and then, "This we have done. Do you be-live what we say?" she asked.

Ogden simply nodded, and he smiled to thank her.

The eastern sky glowed with a brightening silver luminosity for two hours. The music of the stars was gradually subdued by this increasing fog of light, as if in hushed anticipation and deference. Then rose the moon, full and large against the horizon of tree spires on the hill. Ogden watched as it slowly ascended the vault of the heavens.

The ringing voice of the moon filled Ogden's mind. New images arose from the incantation of light. While staring long at the bright globe of the night sky, he felt a growing presence invade his heart. It was his mother, the oldest memory in his life. The moment felt eternal, but the image was gone in an instant.

Ogden shook from his core to his elbows, as if chilled. A pool of tears welled in the corners of his eyes. He felt tugged by the vision conjured by the song of the moon. It was always changing from night to night. Its visions came quickly, stayed what seemed forever, but immediately disappeared.

For Ogden, the songs of the stars were more constant and fixed. They held time and place together. They defined the permanency of each moment in eternity. The intersection of all the beams of starlight far and near form an intricate knot of luminous being. That's the world. That's the everything.

But the moon and the wanderers gliding among the stars create the motion and change we experience as the life of lived moments. These are the dream shadows we live in. The life of the eons is remembered in the song of the stars. Ogden understood all of this. The stars had explained it to him.

And that is why tears trickled down his cheeks. He worried about the coming changes and wondered if he could stop them from happening. What if he refused to leave Hapstead? Maybe things would stay unchanged.

Ogden was overwhelmed with the prospect of leaving this sheltering place. He knew that even here the earth suffered. The undine at the spring had showed him in the blink of an eye how many trees were felled to make room for crops and pastures and the pond her waters filled. He listened to the sylphs, the elemental spirits of the air, as they whispered past his ears about the intentional burning of fields, the scent of animal flesh being torn asunder and the smell of their fear preceding that horror. A gnome scampered madly up and down the side of a willow tree whose hanging branches had been chopped back where they once hung across the path of riders and wagons on the back road. For Ogden, Hapstead Manor was alive with more than the people and farm animals occupying its space. The place itself was alive with the presence of life and time locked into memories in all its forms. Ogden was alive to all of it.

Now the idea of going away, of traveling with Drowden Erebus to Irongate and maybe beyond, gripped Ogden's imagination more viscerally than the singing of the stars and the prattle of the elementals. He worried that his part in the story of Hapstead might be coming to a close. And he wondered if the stars would remember, if the rocks would recall, if the brook would speak of and the gnomes recount to others that he had once been part of their lore.

Chapter XV
The Brotherhood of Troll Gutters

A babble of men's voices filled the back storeroom of Ospin Tapple's sundry warehouse. Bottle-lightened laughter sometimes drifted like balloons above the rumbled din of twenty conversations. Men's words clattered like dry beans in a tin can among the big beam rafters and the high-pitched slate ceiling. Two men dressed in long robes with their faces hidden in the shadow of floppy cowls stood guard at the entrance and opened it a crack when they heard the signal of three short, four long, and two short knuckle knocks on the heavy oaken door. The rest of the men scattered about the room and clumped in small groups were dressed the same, but most had dropped their cowls off their heads and back over their shoulders. They each knew the face of the other here in the meeting hall, but outside the gathering of the Secret Brotherhood of Troll Gutters, they kept their membership hidden from neighbors, relatives and children. Outsiders knew only whispered rumors about a group that was simply known as "The Secret Brotherhood."

"The bugger is a wild beast and Erebus needs to put it down with an axe," Cornelius Baldegger shouted in a voice that could just be heard above the general din by the two men closest to him. Thad Krebbermoting stood to his left and grabbed his shoulder and pulled at him for attention. He shouted back:

"Axe, carving knife or rope from a tree: it doesn't matter a fart in the night pan to me how he does it. That cursed and twisted mockery of a man-thing has got to be cut out of tomorrow. No room for it in this life."

The man to Cornelius Baldegger's right was Pip Skleverly. He yanked at Baldegger's right shoulder with his left hand and drew him closer, and with his right hand yanked at Thad Krebbermoting's robe. "Awwye, sure. But Drowden Erebus won't do the deed, gentlemen. He loves the stories, the old lore, and doesn't understand like we do that there's no place for trolls among men."

Across the room in a circle of five one could hear a similar conversation. "What've we been wasting our time on, if Drowden Erebus can bring one of the wankers right out of the wildwood and into civilized company?" That was Chetter Flaxton talking. "If it's true that it talks — and Bladic wouldn't have paid up if it wasn't true — then what? May as well have talking wolves, or rats that sing."

Milky Prupe laughed and shoved Chetter with a palm to his chest. Half a pint of ale jumped from Chetter's mug and splashed on the plank floor. "We already have men like you who talk out of their bloomers," said Milky. "I don't be-live a word of it. Trolls are just mangy bears. Take for example the party Dorina Erebus invited our wives to. That twisted little monster tore up the place, scared everyone half to death, and what came of it? The critter got spelling lessons! Now, I don't care if it learned to recite the whole Land of the Heroes legend. We should just ride out there to Hapstead and rope up the troll thing snug and secure and drag it from there to Irongate behind a horse. That'll shut its flapping chops for good and all."

"But we can't!" Lester Lint cried out and was heard by the others in his circle. "First of all, you can't just ride into Hapstead Manor to kill a troll."

"I meant we'd ride in disguise!" Milky complained.

"Oh sure!" said Shadri Triboli. "Expose the Secret Brotherhood as troll killers! And ride against Drowden Erebus, one of the most respected men in the region? What do ya think that would do to our reputation??"

By the time the entrance to the storeroom was barred shut with a red-stained four by four-inch cut oak rail that was slid into its iron braces, fifty men had stolen away from wives and children and parents and masters and bosses to be here together. The noisy babble of voices rose to a crescendo that was deafening, until a loud banging of the flat side of a hatchet on a hard block of wood let a familiar voice break through all the others in a nasally constrained tone of complaint.

"Quiet, men. Shut up! It's time for serious talk and planning."

Some straggling conversations chased their own tails, but gradually petered out. Ospin Tapple stood up from a chair behind an ornate dark-stained table that looked out of place amid racks of store goods, some shoved to the side to make room for the gathering. Chair, table and Tapple were raised above the rest of the room on a wooden platform.

Tapple waited for the chatter to end, then raised his chin and looked down over his wire spectacles. Derrick Deneb raised a fist in the air and shouted, "When do we go get that monster Erebus is keeping for a pet?" A murmur of assent wound through the crowd.

Howe Bistrep slapped him on the back a little hard and yelled, "It's a crime against all of us to let it live! I say we ride out to Hapstead at daybreak and skin that troll scourge and salt it down, so it barks for death."

Shadri Triboli felt the blood rise to his cheeks and a charged bolt of fire shot up his spine. When it reached his throat, it burst out of his mouth in a blast of words that made the men around him step back in surprise. "Is it a war among neighbors you want? Do you think Drowden Erebus won't fight to stop us? Do you be-live the dream that he'll just let us ride into Hapstead in force, take his property, bloody his land with the gore of that afflicted creature, and go home unharassed? Do you think Drowden Erebus has no friends to avenge him? Won't our children despise us? Won't our own neighbors shun us? Are you mad?"

Kreg Jutribackle jumped with a spring of his legs to see over the heads of the men around him and find out who was talking. His toothy face was twisted in a grimace of rage. Bloodshot eyes popped wide and an accusing finger extended over the others' heads. He screamed, "You coward! You pustule! I'll gut you for practice, Triboli!"

Ospin Tapple banged his axe gavel and yelled a high-pitched order. "Jutribackle, shut up! Triboli, close your jaws!" There was some shoving that made the crowd of milling men undulate with energy, but no one spoke. Tapple waited for an end to the jostling, and then said in a more subdued voice, "Listen to me, and no more wasting time. We have serious work to do."

He took a gulp from a flagon that rested on a shelf next to his makeshift dais and wiped foam off his upper lip. "Before you make plans to kill that damned troll child, you might ask yourself why we have this problem."

Someone shouted, "It's the fault of Drowden Erebus!"

"Oh, is it?" Tapple yelled back over their heads. "Did Erebus spawn it? Did Erebus make it out of mud or wood or a misshapen child he found in the woods?"

"What's the difference?" bellowed Bos Fudlow. "He's keeping the cretin alive."

"The difference is this, my fine friend," Tapple answered. "Our forerunners thought they'd wiped out the last of the plague of trolls in this region. That thing Erebus keeps came from somewhere, and that somewhere is the loins of breeding trolls. We kill it, and we're doomed to see its kith roaming the woods, killing our goats, terrorizing our dreams. Unless we hunt down the kin of Drowden's pet and finish the job, we're wasting our time gutting the young one."

A mumbling broke out, and more shoving and squabbling. Fudlow hollered out, "We're with you, Tapple! At least the ones of us with guts. We're ready for the hunt."

"Alright then," said Tapple. "Who's with us? Come forward. Give me your mark on this paper."

The body of men heaved and swirled. A large group surged one way. A smaller group moved forward toward the table where a scroll was rolled out and a quill stood ready for inking.

The oak door at the entrance was flung open. Hoods went up over heads as a steady stream of men not inclined to join the hunt walked through and into the main warehouse, then out the side doors and into the night.

Back inside, the new True Brotherhood of Troll Gutters made their marks and sealed their oaths. Bos Fudlow was first, and he was named commander of the troop. Cornelius Baldegger and Thad Krebbermoting signed. So did Derrick Deneb and Howe Bistrep. Pip Skleverly, Milky Prupe and Chetter Flaxton had their turns, followed by Burl Oonep, Hopskel Dwil and Lathon Urobandis.

Someone remarked that Kreg Jutribackle was missing, and Fudlow snorted a deep sarcastic laugh. "That blowhard has to ask his nag Shully first. Maybe he'll join us. Maybe he won't. All depends on Shully."

Ospin Tapple spied the exodus of cowled men at the back of the store-room, and counted the men lined up to sign the parchment. There were eleven, not counting him. "Just as well," he said out loud, as much to himself as to the others. "I don't want any doubters and non-be-livers on a death hunt."

Then he said, louder to the men in line, "We meet two days hence, in the back of the slaughterhouse next to the rubbish dump. Bring your favorite skull splitter or hog gutter. We've got butcher's work to do."

Chapter XVI
Voices and Visions

Tibbs lifted a carved stone image of a corpulent woman from its altar nook and spat on it, then rubbed the spittle into a coating of fly ash from the fire pit that had come to rest on the sacred idol. The dry, cold embers dissolved, and she smeared a coating of gray cinder paste across the entire surface of the feminine form. Its proportionally huge breasts drooped down and rested on a granite torso.

It may as well have been an image of Tibbs, so like the she-troll in form it was. When she replaced the idol into its chiseled alcove, Tibbs covered her forehead with an ash-smudged hand and closed her eyes, resting the lower edge of her hand on the shelf of her brow. The lids of her eyes fluttered, concealing agitation underneath. From above and a little behind her right brow she heard the voice of the grandmothers, speaking. It was clear and present and loud. Tibbs held her eyes closed and listened intently.

"Daughter.

Keeper of the old way.

Leader of Trogglemen.

Knower of the three roads.

Moon tracker.

Attend to our voice."

Tibbs groaned. Inside her belly something leapt and pranced. "Tibbs hears you," she said. "Say your sayings now. No tricks. No spell weaving."

The voices wailed like a wind high up in the crowning branches of straight-trunked hemlocks. The words were sharp like ice cracking at a stress point where two great rivers converge at winter's end. They breathed into Tibbs' mind not the way words enchant men with thoughts, but as light livens the mind to creation. Tibbs departed the confinement of her cave at the invitation of the voice and walked among the ancestors.

In a fairy grove of great white oaks, she ambled with a forward-leaning gait and cried out to them who she could not see: "Huth took the baby Troggle of my warm belly. Huth stole him for a snack. Went out with little Troggle. Came back with blood and muscle in his teeth. Three moons past. Tibbs spat him. Tibbs bruised him with flying fists. Huth ran from this rock house. Big fat Troggle ate the one you sent across from dreams to me. Every sun of day is sad. Every dark of night is haunted. Tibbs weeps. Tibbs won't laugh."

A voice grew — a sound that branched out and rattled wood and emerged out of the deep grainy bark where the trunk of the largest tree in the forest split into two huge outstretched oaken arms. The beginning and the end of all that is and was and will be wrapped round its braided being and, touching everything and everywhere at once, reached up from the earth through the roots to talk to Tibbs.

The young one lives.

Eats with flat-faced Troggle killers.

Hears their shadow magic

Voices like this one

But full of deception;

Sees the dead bark of things

The Spell of Words conjures,

Not We. Not what lives inside.

Words conjure lies

And bind the law-makers,

And blind the life-takers.

They be-live all their days
In the spell of their words.
Will the Troggle babe become
Possessed like those men?
We don't say yet
But maybe dead is better.

Tibbs felt her chest lighten. The wiry wisp of gray hair on her head felt charged with sparkling energy. "Lives?" she gasped. "Troggle kid lives? This is what I know. This is what you grandmothers show. This is what my knowing knows."

The wizened voice of the great white oak gave way to confused babbling that came from all directions. The guttural voices of Trogglemen, not the crotchety rhythm of the grandmothers' nasal intonations, filled her mind. They spoke against and atop and around each other and made a jumbling muddled clutter of sounds. But the message came clear, through words that were inchoate and unintelligible.

Troggle, comes danger.
Troggle, comes darkness and fire.

The grandfathers had broken through. The grandmothers had allowed them to speak a grave warning. But they were silenced quickly and spoke no more.

Tibbs whispered through clenched teeth. "What secret do grandfathers tell me? What saying of things coming do they tell?"

The wind again blew voices out of the high branches, like leaves being dislodged and twirled through the air.

We cannot say the whole of it.
We dare not say the fullness.
We see the living Troggle child.

But down another path we see one falling

Away to the land beneath,

The place where Troggles long-gone live.

"You say," said Tibbs haltingly, hoping the ancestors would say more, "my Troggle baby Huth didn't eat? He, the big fat Troggle, isn't fat on little Troggle from my warm belly?" The wind in Tibbs' mind blew like any wind, without a word, without answer.

"Say now!" she bellowed suddenly aloud, filling the cavernous surrounding rock with echoes. But no more words from the ancestors came.

Tibbs held her breath as the sound of dripping water *splish-splashing* on the cave floor replaced the immediacy and presence of the voices that had emerged from the roots of her being. She opened her eyes and looked around, blinking.

"Come, old Troggle," she said to the shadows in the far end of the cave. From out of the darkness emerged a vision of a forest canopy, and underneath she could just discern the form of a troll resting by a clear running stream. "Find your Tibbs," she said to the shade. "Tibbs wants Huth."

Chapter XVII
The Place of Memories

In a glade with springs bubbling to the surface Huth sat on a mushroom-laden tree trunk that bridged across a gully traversed by a shallow stream. The bright yellow fungus growing on the sides of the barkless hulk was slowly digesting the felled elm tree, turning it to loam. Huth rolled his big shoulders to loosen the tightness in his back. The sunlight making its way through the trees made him squint. He preferred moonlight traveling in the wood, but he was unable to sleep even in a comfortable dry cavern he'd found nearby. He picked at the bright fleshy mushroom caps, chewing them into an orange paste that coated his teeth and lips.

The pupils of his amber eyes widened despite the unaccustomed sunlight and the forest came alive with the colors of orange-red spice bush berries, pale blue cowslip flowers, pink blossoms of milkweed on an exposed hillside touched by sunlight, and the sound of crows high in the trees, the loamy smell of rotting vegetation, the musky scent of a bull elk who had marked his territory, and the satisfying earthy rich flavor of the mushrooms that he continued to chew and swallow in great gulps, interspersed with cool clear water that he cupped in his big hand from the brook that ran under his dangling feet.

He could sense the multitude of living things that had once and still did count on the rejuvenating waters that here gurgled from the earth.

A sudden tugging in his chest made his heart race. He placed both hands on the log and turned to one side then the other, sniffing the air and sensing something reaching out from far off to touch and squeeze his arm. There was no sound, only that feeling that grabbed his attention and prompted him to slide down from the log and stand in the gently flowing water. Without wonder or doubt, Huth stepped up onto the mossy stream bank and walked northward at a forward-leaning trudge through the thick fern, out of the wet hemlock glade and into the hardwood covered hills.

He faced more than a day's walk before he would reach the hidden entrance to the cave where Tibbs impatiently awaited his arrival. Before the sun had shoved a hand's breadth above the horizon he found and followed a wide path through a forest dominated by maple and hickory, his bare calloused feet glad for the soft grass growing damp with dew down the middle of the course.

The broad trail led into a gorge with severe ledges and cliffs of hard slate jutting out into open space. Green lichen stained the sheer rock face where the valley wall was smooth. The trunks of fallen trees grown too large for the shallow soil to hold them stood upside down all along the sides and foot of the cliffs.

Huth trudged fast into the ravine. He felt the sun on his back and a rising dew of sweat rolled across his brow and down both sides of his face. He spied a tall brown hawk perched on the uppermost bough of a scaly barked hickory and eyed a dozen juncos as they fled his approach from one clump of shrubbery to the next.

As his feet carried him further into the gorge his pace slowed and the muscles in his torso tightened. He breathed roughly, and his lungs rattled. In his head he felt a rushing of blood. The sound of a raptor screeching overhead blended with the voice of the wind in the leaves and branches. He was overtaken by vertigo. Images of a great slaughter of trolls rushed in and filled his mind. From above, all along the cliffs, descended huge rocks and spears, arrows and lances, and from each end of the gorge charged a phalanx of horsemen wielding swords and battle axes, maces and clubs.

The gorge remembers the carnage in a dream-awakening way. Infinite in duration, it haunts the rocks and waters, the crags and trees.

Huth staggered and almost crumbled to a heap on the brittle shale-covered ground, but he caught his weight with an outstretched left hand, gouging his palm on a shard of sharp fallen rock. Shoving himself upright with a mighty

thrust, he stumbled rightward. Then, with two unsteady steps forward he regained his balance and focused his eyes on the land in front of his feet. Hurrying blindly through a stupor of visions and a dissonant cacophony of shrieks,
screams and wailing cries of pain that came from all directions, Huth willed
himself forward to be free of the stony gorge and its apparitions.

The path out of the slate valley remained wide and then disappeared into
the sameness of rock-strewn level ground. Huth's head gradually cleared of
the horrific place-memory that his presence had summoned. A clearing ahead
stretched for a quarter mile below the forested hills to the north and he quickened his pace in that direction.

Huth pushed on, but turned a little west, avoiding the upward trek into
the woods. He kept the rising ground to the north on his right and clung to
sparser terrain populated by rocks of granite and chips of mica in the sandy
ground that sparkled in the warm sunshine.

Some hours into the day the land north changed from mixed hardwood
forest to woodland dominated by ever larger chestnut trees whose tops still
held the clouds of lingering morning fog in their crowns. Hours later, with
the sun high overhead and the fog at last lifted from the highest reaches, Huth
skirted the base of a boulder festooned crag that rose to support a small plateau. Here was the grand lith quarry. For time out of memory, trolls had mined
the great monuments and dragged them off in all directions. They erected
standing stones to encircle dozens of crater-like depressions in the surrounding
country. Men called them henges, and in their fear and wonder of how such
grave structures could come to be, they conjured fables that terrorized children's dreams.

The sinews of Huth's neck strained to look up at the gray rock behemoths
that lay exposed by oft-pounded chisels and oft-swung picks. He felt the
ground underneath him utter a rumble of recognition with his arrival. Arrows
of sunlight ricocheted off the boulders in all directions. He knew the place
and knew that the unfolding of its story was imminent and that it would en-
velop him as did the visions in the slate gorge.

Disjointed from common time but integral to the quarry's true nature, this moment when a lone troll appeared at the cross section of all things past and all things future worked to summon an important part of the dream that is the sum of the land's existence. A long age of troll industry had marked the eternal form of this place, and through Huth's eyes, the place-memory arose with new life.

Huth quickened his pace as soon as his head exploded with sounds and visions. He remembered an old shaman related to his father telling him he could not stop the flood of images nor escape full immersion into the soul of a place steeped in power until he physically left it behind. He felt that rapt fascination overcoming his every sense and taking him into a world invisible to men but into which his own feet had carried him. The involuntary summoning of the memory of rocks and soil, of wind and sky would stalk him until he was gone from the place.

Some troll initiates learned to sing ancient songs to summon the land's dreaming, but Huth's soul had been opened like a door that would blow wide just by walking onto hallowed ground.

He saw and heard a hillside full of toiling trolls digging the dirt away to free a great monolith and pry it loose with long poles. Some poured large buckets of water from above to wash the soil down in muddy gullies, undermining the earthen foundation that held the boulders in place. Then, with a mighty crash and a rising of dust in the air, the gray giant rolled and fell to the base of the hill onto waiting stone-stripped logs.

A procession of burly trolls strapped thick ropes all around a lith. Some pulled from the front; others lodged the ends of wooden poles under the back end and lifted with straining backs, rolling the great stone forward on the logs. Still others retrieved the smooth trunks from the rear and placed them forward of the rocky giant, making a constantly renewed track for it to move along. More trolls lay buckets of small stones and gravel ahead of these, to firm up the ground and make the way smoother for the passage of the monument.

Accompanying the procession were she-trolls, some of them young girls freshly painted and tattooed. The shaman led the way garbed in cave bear hide, a headdress festooned with hawk feathers and brightened by cardinal and blue jay feathers. In his left hand he gripped a six-foot-tall sassafras cane, entwisted with a vine of honeysuckle fashioned into the form of a snake, painted with ochre pigment.

Huth hurried his pace. The sound of clattering logs, crunching gravel, groaning trolls and singing girls faded and ended when he turned away from the broad path and trudged upward into the tree line above and to the west of the quarry.

He found a path that was little more than a deer trail. It was canopied by great chestnut trees, some with the girth of twelve barrel-chested trolls standing side by side in a row. The forest was broad and open, with trees reaching hundreds of feet into the sky and a canopy of leaves that eventually blocked the sunlight from reaching the ground as he ventured deeper into the woods. A constant twilight cooled the air. Big clumps of mushrooms, some red and spotted white, some yellow and also mottled, popped through the mossy forest carpet that covered the rolling ground all around the giant trees.

Two handfuls of bright red mushrooms made a quick meal, spiced with a few ginger roots that Huth pulled from the loose ground near a tree root as thick as his forearm. He set off north through the forest where there was no path and alternately stooped under fallen trees spanning mossy hillocks or climbed over them where they rested on flatter ground.

An hour into the chestnut wood the sky broke through momentarily as the forest paused and stood back from a solitary behemoth of a tree even larger than the other giants. The chestnut multitude seemed to break and encircle it, standing off at a respectful distance. To one side a rock outcropping made of stacked boulders, with sheltering caverns, drew Huth inward. There he paused and from a hiding place among the rocks he spied upon the colossal tree. Smooth brown chestnuts littered the mossy ground all around. Two thick roots rose up from the loamy soil like bended knees clenched in the front by entwined fingers of wood.

Gradually, Huth saw the colors change in the rich green moss, the spotted leaves, and the dark brown trunk of the river-wide tree. The sun was lost above a jungle of leaves held at their tips by tier after tier of branches as big as mature trees that ascended several hundred feet into the air. Huth's eyes watered in the light that did reach through, and the colors all around deepened and quivered and transformed into different hues. His hearing became more acute and from the shadows of the rocky fissures below where he stood he heard a whispered voice, high in pitch and accented with lyrical notes of mirth.

"She comes. She is here. Listen, Troggle. See with opened eyes and heart."

The roots of the mammoth chestnut pulsed, and the folds of the great tree's bark seemed to move and breathe like gills. When he looked up past midway between the ground and the first spreading branches, a knotty burl as wide as his arm span seemed to move and twist with expression. Across the burl, a deep crack in the wood formed a mouth that suddenly puckered and pouted. Instead of speaking, it let loose a deep sigh.

The air vibrated with life. A small flying creature that Huth had mistaken for a dragonfly exposed its true faerie nature, flew up into the leafy forest ceiling, and returned with a swarm of delicate, winged maidens who followed her and alighted with a bobbing of leaves on the deep brown branches of a nearby sapling. The turtle ceased its lumbering across the ground. It froze and became rigid, taking on the form of a rounded half-exposed lump of limestone.

Huth rested his chin on the boulder he'd been hiding behind, no longer trying to stay concealed. He watched with wide amber eyes, breathing with panted rhythms through his parted lips. Suddenly a rough, broken tree stump that was half buried in a jade mound of soft moss shook off the tuft and leaves and soil, rolled forward in front of the rock outcrop and sat up in a crouch. It turned out to be a wood gnome with a long, crooked nose that had a pink earthworm hanging and jigging from its tip. The gnome leaned forward and rested its chin in its splintery fingers as if mocking Huth.

Pointing with one of those fingers, the gnome said, "Welcome friend. Have you come to ask a question? She's very busy, so be quick." The voice sounded exactly like the one Huth had heard come from within the rock fissures. It was high-pitched and lyrically mirthful, and this time it did not whisper but spoke plainly.

Huth turned to the faerie queen and her consorts. He blinked by way of nodding respect and said, "Huth's son gone lost. Gawd, Gawd. My Tibbs chased out Huth. Wandering in wide sunlight, Huth can't find Huth."

A hardly audible titter could be heard. Then the wood gnome grumbled, "Stupid Troggle. Not her that flies. Don't ask faerie folk your askings. Ask her that reaches deep down in the ground with roots that touch the beginning and way far up in the sky with branches that tangle star song into leaves. She's the mouth of our Mother Earth. Talk to her, you idiot."

This time Huth bowed his head before he spoke. His thick hairy brows hid his large amber eyes, which scanned the ground between him and the gargantuan chestnut tree. Both hands he held out, palms up. "Pardon. Pardon Huth. Through places near home Huth wanders, not to go far and be gone always until all the ends have ended. Huth wants Tibbs. Tibbs beat Huth with rocks and fists. Little Troggle, Huth's son, is gone and lost and dead most chancy. At night Huth hunts him. All day Huth hunts him. The wood keeps hidden the place Huth's son must be. Why won't ground and sky and trees tell Huth's heart that story in place of all the others that haunt and taunt? Tibbs, Huth's mate, is lost to Huth and Huth is lost to Huth." He broke off, looked at the tree gnome, then the faerie queen. Then he nodded to the great chestnut and pointed to the barky mouth with the fourth finger of his left hand.

"Answer this: why did you send my Wieldier away from me? Will you give him back to Tibbs and me? Now Huth will listen. He's tired of talk."

The large burl on the side of the great tree moved and the split that ran from side to side opened to again reveal a mouth that spoke with the sound of dry sticks clicking together, a woody xylophone out of which words seemed to find their way like clacking notes brushed by a broom into the air. They swept up on a curling gust and into Huth's ears.

You know already the answer, Troggle.

Why ask you what the winds have told?

Why walk you toward home?

Why bother all creation to tell your head

What your heart knows?

Huth's lips curled at the corners into what seemed a secret grin. He thought he knew the answer, but now he was sure. But the clacking voice returned.

The She-Troggle called you through us.

We whispered in your heart her call.

To her you go, and yet you pause for further telling.

And this we tell which you did not know,

Nor thought to ask:

Old Troggle, your story is near its end.

The world will change in every way.

Men hunt Troggles, and soon they will hunt us,

To uproot us,

To spill venom into our blood-waters

And vaporous poison upon our breath.

What matters it to us if Tibbs wants Huth?

What matters it to time if your babe is safe?

Only this: what has a beginning will have an end,

For time is a circle with neither beginning nor end.

Huth grimaced. He was confused again. "Enough riddles. Where is the little Troggle? Dead or living?"

A cacophony of wooden tones filled the air. The wind made the leaves chatter, and it blew the faerie assembly from the sapling's branches into a cloud of tumbling forms. The wood gnome dug broken roots into the black soil and held tight until the gust subsided.

"Find him," said the voice in the tones of a wooden chime.

A counter-spell I give you to wake him

From the dream lies of men.

They defraud his eyes.

They put forged iron in his hands.

It is the spine of the world

Pulled from the matrix that is its mother,

Heated in the furnace of black stones,

Hammered with the sinews of slaves.

They spit dark spells into his ears.

There they fester into the puss of deceit.

And they live in his head,

Words like worms in wood

That wriggle loose and fall to his own tongue.

And into knots of words they cast their spells

To belie the minds of others,

And conjure falsehoods in their heads.

Which they be-live in a waking dream.

The great tree of the living earth fell silent for a moment. The wood gnome opened one of the eyes it had kept tight shut while listening to its percussive voice. He winced and shut his peeper tight when the voice rose again.

Take this counter-spell with you, Troggle.

We come into you and will go with you

In your searching days.

Find him.

When he has learned the ways of man

And with them he can speak,

He must have something to tell them.

But first he must be freed from all deceit.

We go with you and will show him the way.

He must touch his nature and not be-live

In the world of words that part him from us,

Which make him foreign to the One,

And make false in him the world.

Find him.

Bring us to him.

Huth felt his eyes roll up into their deep sockets as he fell into a trance. He allowed it to happen, felt his will lie down on a carpet of clouds just as a purple twilight ringed the clearing. He felt the sky and earth meet within him as they coursed forward into his body. They flowed like threads of light that pierced his chest. They grasped hands in his heart and pumped the life of life through his veins.

The ghost of nature shared his body, peeked through his eyes and looked upon its own skin, the world beyond, seeing no gnome, no faerie queen, no tree of life, but only the surfaces of rocks and trees, of moss and logs, the appearances that are all men know.

Huth slept.

Rising from the stone alcove where he sat throughout the magical encounter with the breath of earth and then swooned into slumber, Huth climbed down the rocks, emboldened and with new purpose. The great chestnut tree was silent. Simple gnats and dragonflies buzzed in the air. The wood gnome had returned to the place where a broken stump held firmly to the ground. He left the big trees behind, hiking up over a rock-strewn ridge and down into a forest of hickory, maple, oak, spruce, and a thickening underbrush.

By twilight he was mounting the hillside leading to the cave's hidden entrance. The sun had settled below the summit, and he could see the whole ridge silhouetted against a blue-violet cloudless sky. Up over a slide of granite boulders and onto a thick-grown bulge in the side of the hill he clamored. Then he approached the stone face of a steep cliff and pushed aside a curtain of woven wild grape, bindweed and honeysuckle vines.

The cave was dimly lit by the glowing red embers of a fire in the middle of the room. Huth let his eyes adjust to the light, and then saw Tibbs' big form emerge from the shadows, step around the fire pit and come between him and its radiating heat. He felt the air cool momentarily, but then it warmed again as Tibbs embraced Huth with both arms. She pulled him close. "Tibbs wants Huth," she mumbled into his saucer-sized left ear.

He grabbed her close and she kissed his head and caressed his hairy shoulders. They crouched when their knees grew weak with passion, and they tipped over to lay face-to-face on a carpet of straw. They coupled quickly and groaned with pleasure.

Chapter XVIII
Hunting Death

The men secured their horses when the path became overgrown. Thirteen in all made the trip. Their cowled robes dragged and caught in the greenbrier and multiflora rose thorns as they set off up the thickly wooded hillside. They took with them pikes and axes and pitchforks and maces. Some carried green copper daggers and short rusted swords on their belts.

Ospin Tapple led the way for a while, pointing without much reason up the hill toward a scattering of boulders amidst a thinning forest of elm and maple, ironwood and ash. But as the ground rose steeply, he frequently paused to lean one-handed on a tree to catch his breath. Bos Fudlow took the lead, shoving spicebush and honeysuckle aside. Behind him Lathon Urobandis and Milky Prupe noisily bushwhacked a path through the forest understory.

Tapple waited for Cornelius Baldegger and Derrick Deneb to pass him. Then Thad Krebbermoting got out in front. Howe Bistrep and Chetter Flaxton walked past him together, comparing weapons and nerve. Ospin began to walk again when Kreg Jutribackle came up beside him. Burl Oonep, Hopskel Dwil and Pip Skleverly straggled behind.

"Jutribackle. Jutribackle. Your father raised you better than he was, I can tell you that," said Tapple.

"Leave my stinking father out of it," said Kreg out the side of his cowl. He quickened his pace, but Tapple matched it.

"But it's meant as a compliment to you, friend," said Tapple, breathing a little roughly. "Considering how your father died in such disgrace, I see in you a cleansing of the blood and an attempt to return to grace among men. Despite the opinions of others, I think you have promise."

"Bug off," Kreg grumbled without looking at Tapple. "You're as bad as the rest, only worse. I'm here because I think we've got to protect our families. My Shully is no strumpet or a folly-loll for the amusement of these men. I keep and protect my own, and don't give a wink for their stupid talk. They think I'm a coward because I don't gut them belly to tonsils for their disrespect? Well, I've got better things to do, and that means I've got better things to do than listen to you and your empty talk. Now leave me alone."

Tapple spat and quickened his pace to get ahead of Kreg Jutribackle, talking over his shoulder as their separation widened. "Don't be bitter, Jutribackle. It doesn't make you more likeable." Then he was off on a strong jaunt through the marginally cleared brush.

By mid-morning they had cleared the top of the short mountain and crossed the knee-deep stream at the bottom of the next valley. Higher hills were ahead, and the men stopped by the creek to shake out their boots and rest their arses on logs a while.

Milky opened a burlap sack with arm straps sewn onto it. Bottles clattered as he pulled them out and passed them around to the men. "Drink up! I want to lighten this bag a bit."

"I'll save my stash of grog for later." Chetter Flaxton snatched one of the small bottles and pulled the cork with his teeth. It opened with a rich 'thoop' sound. "Oh yeah. That's the way I like to travel. Light in the sack and in the head." He quickly downed its contents and threw the empty bottle into the creek with a dull splash.

Someone else emptied a small brown glass jug and threw it with a crash against the base of an elm tree. Shards of glass flew, and Howe Bistrep yelled, "You wilting idiot!" Then he turned toward a tree near Chetter and unloaded his bottle against a rock around which the tree's roots had grown. A chip flew toward Chetter and caught him on the chin. A bead of blood formed and quivered before dropping from his chin to the ground.

"I knew it was a mistake letting Howe tag along," Chetter yelled. "You coulda blinded me, ya idiot!"

"And you tried to do the same to me!" bellowed Howe Bistrep.

"It wasn't me, you dung beetle. I threw mine in the water!"

"It was me!" someone shouted and as quickly shut up. That was Lathon Urobandis, but he ducked behind the other men.

Howe yelled back, "Coward! Show yourself." But Ospin Tapple intervened. He took Howe by a fistful of his robe and pulled him into breathing range.

"There won't be a lot of second chances," he said. "Save your belligerence for the trolls we're going to slaughter. Do you hear me?"

"Yeah," said Bistrep. He peeled Tapple's fingers free of the cloth. And then he took a deep gulp of ale from another noggin and smashed the empty one on a fern-shrouded rock. An unseen turtle moved under the fronds away from the broken glass and pungent brew. "One less to carry," Bistrep laughed.

When the thirteen gathered their gear and their weapons, they left the streamside wilderness a littered trash heap. Aside from two dozen empty and smashed noggins, they left behind a few piles of feces, a kerchief someone had used to wipe his butt, five broken saplings, and a kitchen cloth with the boney remains of a half pheasant.

They wandered forward loudly, so that they saw not a living creature along the way to the high hills on the other side of the valley.

As the ground rose again, Bos Fudlow held up a hand and the company came to a stop. "Since we didn't bring the dogs, I need you curs to keep your eyes opened and your mouths shut. Look for signs. Notice where the branches are bent in one direction. If you see where something big squatted and unloaded, tell me. We won't see any trolls wandering in the daylight but watch out for boulder piles that could shelter a sleeping cretin. Keep your weapons handy. If one of those creeps bolts out of the trees; you're going to need it."

They moved on more quietly, but though they kept their conversations subdued, the clunk of old swords in ornate scabbards against tree trunks and the cracking of branches under their heavy footfalls followed them through the forest.

As twilight settled on the woods, Huth left the cover of his hidden cave and ventured out over the top of the mountain and down its farther side to find autumn fare under the loose forest soil. He gathered thick tubers and dropped them into a buckskin satchel hung from his waist.

Huth felt the wind rise cool and comforting on his face. The trees whispered on the night air, and the stars sang a harmonious chorale, a fugue of light vibrations that filled him with calm. His otherwise amber eyes were dark with the wide stretched opening of his black pupils. He took in the starlight as we might the light of day reflecting off of everything in the world. Colors we would see as differing hues of gray in the gathering night were vibrant to him. The leaves painted the forest a beautiful mottling of crimson, gold and even cobalt.

He heard a doe munching leaves nearby, but meat was not on his mind. A glowworm flashed its presence, and he gently moved it aside while he dug his fingers through a layer of damp flat leaves down to the black soil underneath. He yanked a ginger root loose, patted it on the palm of his right hand to loosen clinging clods and dropped it into the bag with the assortment of other roots.

Breathing in deep inhalations and long expiring exhalations, Huth felt serenity spread like warm broth through his veins. The spirit that spoke through the great tree still resided in him, ever since his encounter with the gnome and the faerie in the chestnut grove. The ghost of the whole earth reposed inside him as in a hammock. Still, something underneath, a disturbance he did not recognize, felt muffled by the alien calm and was unable to make itself known to him.

He spent some hours wandering through the woodland and at last he stopped by a mountain spring and filled two hefty skins with fresh water. Then he headed homeward.

Bos Fudlow had halted the hunting party below a bulge in the hill above which stood a rock face overgrown with forest grapevines and honeysuckle.

He managed to shush the men and make them crouch low, motionlessly. When he spoke, it was a whisper.

"Up there. There's a light coming from inside the hill. There's got to be a cave, and only a troll would make a fire."

"What do you say we should do?" Ospin Tapple whispered back.

"We're lucky we caught the bastard inside and not out roaming around in the dark. He'd have seen us before we saw him."

"Yes, but what should we do?" Tapple insisted quietly, almost squeakily.

"What we should do is murder it." Bos stared at the shadow he assumed was Ospin Tapple. Then he grabbed Thad Krebbermoting by the shoulder. He knew it was Thad because he was twice as massive as most of the other men. "You! Do you see that rock field to the side of the cave?"

Thad shook his head. Bos said ,"Good. You go up that way and get a good spot just above the entrance. I see a rock the size of a goat that will do the trick. Take Burl with you. We'll draw the troll out of the cave and you two push that block of white rock down on its head. If that doesn't kill it, we'll finish it off with our blades."

Burl Oonep crawled forward on his knees. "How are you going to make it come out?"

"Just get on up there!" Bos seethed. "We'll shove brush and debris in front of the entrance and torch it. The smoke will force the troll to come out. It'll be choking and blinded by the light, but expecting a fight, so make sure you're there and ready."

The rest of the men waited for Thad Krebbermoting and Burl Oonep to sneak up the loose hill of stones and hide behind the limestone boulder seven feet above where firelight glowed from the cave's hollows. Then Hopskel Dwil, Pip Skleverly and Derrick Deneb crept to a pile of brush that the trolls had evidently stacked about twenty feet from the cave. The men grabbed the entwined vines, leaves and sticks and dragged them to the cave entrance. They heard something move inside, and then a loud cackle, so they fled away into the shadows and crouched behind bushes with their backs to the cave. Their eyes squinted shut and their hands wrapped around their heads and ears.

"Damned fools!" Bos Fudlow yelled without trying to be quiet. He ran forward and struck a piece of flint against the hilt of his blade. Sparks flew and some fell on dry filaments of poison ivy vine that smoldered and smoked a moment. Then flames darted out of the pile and the wad of debris suddenly glowed pink and ginger. Big tufts of smoke billowed out of the wadded dry vines and weeds. The wind made sure that it blew straight into the cave. Soon the fire caught the curtain of vines that hid the cave's opening and flames rose toward where Thad and Burl were crouched behind the white clobber stone.

Inside, Tibbs ran madly from room to grotto to gallery. The smoke was thick and choking. Her hearth fire was snuffed out when the fire outside stole all its air. Shadows danced on the walls and the ceiling was lost in a murky gray haze. Tibbs lay on the ground and found a cool current of air, but soon that too was gone. She ran to the shrine and snatched the stone figure with wide eyes, open mouth and huge breasts and held it close to her chest. Her heart was beating so hard she hurt inside. Her lungs felt heavy and dry, and the cave seemed to swirl around her. With nowhere else to go, she turned to the intruding blaze and charged headlong into the flames.

Huth saw the flames from a hundred yards off and ran with all his might toward his home. Men stood bent with anticipation at the entrance, their backs to him. He stooped to grab a fist-sized rock but didn't break his stride. In his other hand he held a carved antler blade as long as his hand was wide. He bounded out of the trees just in time to see Tibbs emerge through the fire and he heard a man shout "Now! Do it now!"

Burl pushed Thad who pushed the limestone boulder loose and let it fall. It rolled through burning vines and took some with it, then bounced off the overarch of the cave's entrance and dropped straight down toward the burning gnarl, where Tibbs stood only long enough to be struck solidly on the top of her head.

Huth heard the crack of her skull, saw the blood fly through the flames, watched her body drop to the earth and lie motionless as he reached ground where men stood with their backs still toward him.

He slit Chetter Flaxton's throat wide open with one swipe from behind. Flaxton fell to his knees gurgling incoherently, then slumped over and lay still. The rock in Huth's right hand cracked Bos Fudlow in the temple and he rose up off his feet and flew through the air, landing unconscious in a patch of red and orange three-leaved weeds.

Huth stood in a hunch. He glanced toward Tibbs, but there was nothing he could do for her. He turned to glare at a man who stood as if frozen, with the dwindling firelight dancing across his soot-smeared face. In his right hand he held Tibbs' severed right ear, a trophy, he'd thought for a moment, until he saw his own death walking out of the darkness to take him.

Huth advanced a step, tilted his head to listen to the man's shallow breathing. Howe Bistrep's chin quavered. He cried out "Pleaaaase!" as he pissed his pants and sobbed.

Huth felt a sharp pain in his right side and then the warm flow of blood gushing from his abdomen from a wound that started next to his spine where the spear point entered. The shaft exited above his waist just to the right of his navel.

Kreg Jutribackle yanked back on the spear with a twist and pulled it from Huth's back. The old troll turned to look over his shoulder at the man who had torn his body so bloodily. He dropped his antler blade and took a stumbling step forward and away from Jutribackle. Then he bolted away from the light of the waning fire, away from the cave that had been his home, away from the body Tibbs' spirit left behind, and into the deep woods where night would conceal him from the eyes of murdering men.

Ospin Tapple got up from the pile of leaves he'd tossed over him to hide. Into the flickering orange light he strode, glancing about at the aftermath of the planned killing. He saw the crumpled heap that was Tibbs. He nodded toward Chetter Flaxton's bloody corpse. When he looked at Howe Bistrep and his stained, dripping pants he shook his head and said, "Behold the hero of the battle of Troll Grotto."

Bos Fudlow was rolling in the poison ivy patch trying to get his legs under him. His head was swollen to twice its natural size on one side. His ear was pinched closed by the swelling and what he could hear out of the other one made no sense to him yet.

"You let the other one get away," Tapple wheezed at Kreg Jutribackle.

Jutribackle mocked Tapple's thin whiny voice and said "Got away! Got away!" Then he spoke in his own rich baritone. "He went off to die, you coward. He faced all of us, trying to defend his home. I'm almost sorry I killed him before he finished off a few more pants pissers like that one." He pointed at Howe Bistrep. "He thought he'd play piss into the wind with a troll." He turned and spit. "He forgot to take his pants off first and let it dribble down his legs. But I give credit where it's due! He did manage to cut an ear off a dead she-troll without cutting his own finger."

Jutribackle spun around on his heel. "And that one," he waved in Bos Fudlow's direction. "He's so single-minded about slaughtering a lone she-troll that he didn't see the big one coming."

Kreg shoved Tapple with a palm to his forehead. "You didn't see a wink of it, lying in the leaves. What a story we'll have to tell when we get back to our homes."

Ospin Tapple let out a loud high-pitched, "You dare!!!"

"I did," said Kreg Jutribackle.

Ospin tried to recover from his humiliation by calling the surviving men together. Cornelius Baldegger and Derrick Deneb came slowly to his side. Lathon Urobandis stepped from behind a tree as inconspicuously as he could. Then Thad Krebbermoting and Burl Oonep clattered down the stony hill trail that ran up atop the cave. Ospin forced an enthusiastic welcome. "The heroes arrive! Troll slayers! Come stand by me!" They got closer but kept a little apart.

Howe Bistrep, Hopskel Dwil and Pip Skleverly joined them soon, and Bos Fudlow came last to the circle, a hand on his head, his eye swollen shut and his hair matted with blood. He tried but couldn't talk. He had bitten his tongue when Huth's rock slammed into the side of his head and now it took up most of the room in his mouth.

"The Brotherhood of Troll Gutters has done its work," said Tapple. Some of the men muttered incoherently. "We've lost Chetter Flaxton to the foul murdering beast. Thad and Burl can count themselves true troll slayers. And Kreg Jutribackle here…" he paused and looked at the big man, who glared at him with loathing, "…he met the he-troll in single combat and gutted him through and through."

Led by Hopskel and Pip, who hadn't seen any of it, for reasons unexplored, the men cheered with as much spirit as they could muster.

Tapple kept talking. "To our families and neighbors, this story will never be known. And so, I propose we tell them what they will understand. A hunting trip turned bloody by a rogue cave bear. It killed our poor friend Chetter. It smashed Bos Fudlow against a boulder with a swipe of its paw. Then, as the rest of you men circled in, Howe Bistrep stood up right in front of him and drew his attention, brave as a man who finds death a plaything. Then this man, Kreg Jutribackle," Ospin placed a hand on his shoulder and Kreg swiveled his body to remove it, "this man slew the great bear where it stood."

Kreg extended his arm and pointed directly at Ospin Tapple. "I'll tell the tale that way if that's the way you all want it. But what about the part where Ospin Tapple hides in the leaves and lets the rest of us face death for him?"

Tapple howled with spite, but nine men laughed, and Bos Fudlow shook a fist in agreement.

A trail of blood led from the cave entrance to an outcrop of glacial boulders three miles down the valley where Huth lay panting. He felt alone. He felt the ghost of the earth prepare to leave him when he fled into the forest away from Tibbs. But he knew it hadn't left him and she hadn't either. Their spirits paused to consecrate the ground as hallowed and commit it to the remembrance of place and time, in eternity. And Huth knew he would never return there, for to do so would be to relive all that had just happened.

He felt his own life teetering between the world of moon and stars and trees and rocks and the world where dreams and the ancestors dwelled. But he could not die yet. There was one more thing to do. First, he must find his son.

Chapter XIX
Stranger in Town

D rowden Erebus arrived in the streets of Irongate inside a plain birch wood carriage with smooth straight lines and scant ornamentation. It was driven by Harry up top. Ogden rode below with Drowden and Argis. The town crier was making his way down the main thoroughfare warning of the impending closing of the ornate forged gates for which the town was known. "Reglars in; rowdies out!" chanted the crier. "Gates is closin'. Gates is closin'."

The sky was still bright, though the sun was tipping over the edge of the world to the west. The brick, stone and clapboard buildings on one side cast shadows on the cobblestones and facades of the opposite facing buildings along the north-south running roads. Meanwhile, columns of bright light sped eastbound through the intersections running east and west. As the carriage crossed these, Drowden shielded his eyes and had difficulty seeing the faces of Ogden and Argis.

The rattling of the metal wheel hoops on the stone matrix jarred everyone inside. But Harry seemed to enjoy the air in his ears as he tapped the whip on Bleacker's brown shoulder for a little more speed. Drowden knocked on the carriage roof with the butt of a walking cane, calling "Slow it down, Harry! We're in no hurry." Harry seemed not to hear, so Drowden tried again to talk with his riding companions. His voice warbled with the washboard ride.

"As we've talked about before, some will be startled; some will be amused; some will be frightened, and some will be openly hostile at the sight of a full-grown troll. Still others will be enchanted, even delighted."

"Aye, an' some will git ther teeth shuffled," Argis added, flourishing a knuckly duke.

Ogden placed a hand over Argis' fist, nearly covering it. "Friends first," he said with a lippy smirk.

Argis smiled back. "Sure, lad. We'll give 'em a chance ta be ladies and gentlemen before I crown 'em wi' glory."

Harry steered them knowingly to their destination: the Tilthinger Inn, where prior arrangements had them expected and welcomed accordingly. Drowden stepped down from the carriage and stretched his arms over his head, then twisted his torso and bent forward to touch his knees, then the ground in front of him groaning with each contortion. Ogden and Argis climbed out behind him. Argis stepped forward to give the stable master instructions. Ogden simply watched Drowden's ritual gymnastics and stood aside as Harry descended from the driver's seat and bowed toward him and Drowden.

"Hopin' yer ride was pleasant, sirs. Regrets fer the rough road. It's Irongate, ya know," he said, and helped lift down the baggage strapped to the rear of the carriage. He lifted a footlocker and a leather satchel free, unstrapped a night bag and a drawstring hempen sack and handed them to the doorman, who loaded them all on a cart and disappeared.

"Let's get some grub," said Drowden, appealing to the vernacular and likely single-minded purpose of his men. Argis said, "Aye." Harry said, "Well said," and Ogden nodded, but said nothing.

They went into the inn and the kitchen was alive with the smell of stews and chowders that wafted into the common room. Drowden settled down into a comfortable maple chair with carved spindles supporting ornate arms. The others likewise settled down at the table and when they were all situated a kitchen wench approached to ask their orders. Argis leaned backward in his chair to look at her upside-down as she approached. Harry shoved an elbow toward Argis and guffawed. "Steady! Steady, man!" He gave back a hard shove.

"Argis," said Drowden. "Manners, please."

Ogden watched as she approached and Drowden nodded politely. "Hello, young lady. We're famished. What's good in the kitchen tonight?"

"Mutton with taters, carrots and cabbage," she said with a curtsey. "We've also got clams and crabs from Deepwater in a broth of taters, carrots and cabbage."

Drowden nodded. "Which do you recommend?"

"Don't eat the mutton," she said quietly. "Seems to keep some up all night with cramps."

"Clams and crabs," he said quickly. The others shook their heads in agreement.

"Me too," said Harry.

"Same 'ere," agreed Argis.

"And for the big fellow?" asked the young woman. "Same for you?" she asked Ogden, looking directly at him.

He shook his head 'no.' "Whatever you ate for supper this evening, can you bring that?" he asked.

The young lady blushed and answered, "Of course. Just cabbage for you?"

"Yes," said Ogden. "Just cabbage."

"Right away," she responded and bowed and was gone.

"Well, Master Troll, I give full credit ta Master Drowden. He's taught ya good manners, he has," said Harry, patting Ogden on the arm. "See how he relates so well wi' the help, sir?" he winked at Drowden. "Lesson learned, I admit it willingways. This here troll is a gentleman."

Drowden smiled approvingly. "Harry, I thank you for this change of heart. It gives me hope not only in the improvability of trolls, but of men."

Argis grumbled something distasteful and waved an empty hand at Harry, but he just smiled broadly and said nothing.

The meal came and disappeared quickly. The dining party disappeared too, up the creaking and winding steps that spilled into the common room toward the rear of Tilthinger Inn's dark interior. On the wide landing at the base of the ornately banistered maple stairs stood a bear-sized figure carved from a single chestnut log. The visitors crept past the gnarled and hunched form almost as if trying to avoid drawing its attention. Its eyes were painted deep red, and they seemed to follow the men and troll as they passed by. Each one drew a different impression of what kind of creature the carving was meant to represent, but none drew the same impression. Ogden shook his head as he passed. A word that was strange to him entered his mind spontaneously. "Ventego," he thought. The sound of the word rolled in his head like rocks being tumbled in a strong flowing stream. It was a familiar sound, but he couldn't remember why.

The worn floral carpet running up the stairs to the next landing was lit weakly by oil lamps set upon stone tables in the corners of the landings. The carpet material was once a rich burgundy embroidered with white and pink dogwood flowers. But now its lighter threads were worn to the surface, and the edges of some of the stairs' coverings were frayed down to the wood. The stairs turned left and ascended to a long hallway, also dimly lit by ceiling hung lamps. They found their rooms — two of them on opposite sides of the hall — and their baggage deposited in the one to the left.

"Ogden, Harry, you take the room across the hall," said Drowden. "I have some business to discuss with Argis tonight. We'll be getting an early start in the morning, so, no roaming in town tonight, Ogden."

Harry grabbed his bag and went across the hall. Ogden picked up his leather satchel and headed for the door.

"Wait a bit," Argis said, halting Ogden with a hand on his shoulder. "Master Erebus, do ya think it's wise ta have Harry bunk wid Ogden? Not too friendly 'as ee been most times."

Drowden indicated Ogden should go with a jerk of his head and a wink. He closed the door as Ogden left. "He's been kind lately. I think it's a good idea. If we can change the hearts of others the way Harry's come around, then I'll be a happy man."

Argis grumbled, "Nobody changes 'at much 'cept they's got a mind ta hide somethin'."

But Drowden would not be swayed. "Let's see those plans again. You've got the supply list?"

"Aye, it's all here," answered Argis.

"Good. A cottage for our troll friend. I've decided to build it up the hill by the tree line. He likes to roam at night. There, he won't wake everyone with his nocturnal roving."

Together they reviewed the drawings and the materials list. Then Argis crawled under a thick checkered quilt while Drowden stretched out across his mattress with his leather-bound journal under his chin. The pages were lit by a nearby lantern. Quill in hand, he scratched away long enough to hear Argis' rough breathing turn to a sonorous rumbling snore. He fell asleep on top of the open pages. The quill dropped to the floor beside the bed. Neither he nor it moved until daybreak.

The sun came through the crocheted curtains as Drowden pulled on his boots and nudged Argis to wake up. Argis snorted mid-snore, coughed, and sat straight up, eyes blinking. His hair was a wild sea storm that curled and twisted in all directions. "I'm up! I'm up!" he blathered unconvincingly. But soon he was dressed and had managed to comb his hair through his fingers so that it pulled back off his forehead in an approximation of order.

Ogden and Harry were already up when Drowden tapped on their door. Harry stuck his head out and said, "Right there! Here we come!" He opened the door and there sat Ogden on his bed. It had not been slept in.

"What? Didn't you sleep, Ogden?" asked Drowden.

"What is this?" He looked at Drowden while patting the unruffled covers.

"It's a feather bed, boy. It's very comfortable. Didn't you even try it?"

Ogden shook his head. "Maybe later?" he said quietly. "It seemed too fine. The bed at Hapstead is…different."

"Yes, it's just a straw bed. But this is town living. Fancy and fine. Come, you need to see it. You'll find many surprises in Irongate. And later, you can take your daytime nap right here on that soft feather bed. But not now. It's time we made off to the lumberman, and the blacksmith, and the slate dealer. I've got a whole other surprise to tell you about. Are you able? Without sleep?"

"Yes," Ogden nodded enthusiastically. "It's time to go out into the light, isn't it?"

And so all four bounded down the wide carpeted steps, past the hulking wooden sculpture on the bottom landing, and through the great hall of Tilthinger Inn. They chose to skip breakfast there and find something "Irongatish" to eat from one of the street vendors.

The sun was bright, and Ogden squinted his eyes down to narrow slits. His protruding brow worked as a sun visor, so he managed the over-bright washed-out look of everything as best he could. Walking two abreast they strode down Kilter Street past the haberdasher, the bank and the land office. A sharp turn on Gilton Road had them walking straight down the middle of the cobblestoned thoroughfare.

As they walked, at twice the speed of casualness, a woman with a toddler in hand on Kilter Street stood aside and remarked "Well, isn't that peculiar?" And a man carrying a rolled carpet on his shoulder stopped in his tracks and yelled "Never seen a troll! Oh my word, they're real!"

Drowden just waved a hand and nodded congenially to each. The others sped on without remark and seemingly without notice. "This way," Drowden pointed to the right and they turned to trudge down a shortcut through Knob's Alley, which was rutted and rocky. They spied the back sides — not the best sides — of stone buildings where wood-framed doorways and sills showed more weathering than the front entrances and windows. But the locally quarried green serpentine stone from which most were built gave them each a certain dignity and unique charm.

Nolan Skels, the baker, took off his cap and scratched his head as they passed. A man with a crude straw broom stopped sweeping a limestone stoop and gawked. Someone shouted from a window above "Cage that filthy animal!" but they kept walking at a good clip and ignored it.

A wagon loaded with iron slag pulled by two large draft horses rolled across the road ahead and stopped. A few pedestrians seemed to hurry unnaturally fast across the intersection with Knob's Alley. Suddenly Bos Fudlow came around the corner of Smelt Road and stood in their path. Fresh from the Brotherhood Hall, he had a small following of men behind him, each carrying a cudgel and each trying to hide his face inside the folds of loose hanging cowls.

Fudlow stood bare-faced before them, menacing as he slapped the knobby head of his club in his palm.

"We're here to protect the folk of this town from wild animals that find their way into our streets. That thing," he pointed toward Ogden with his club, "has got no business roaming though our back alleys."

Drowden stepped forward, pushing Argis behind him. Argis grabbed Ogden's arm and pulled him back. Harry stood next to Ogden and whispered to the side, "Don't worry. They're all talk. All talk."

"We've got business in town, down at the sawmill," said Drowden. "That's all we're here for. Not for trouble; not for anything else. I'm Drowden Erebus. Ask most folk in town; they'll vouch for me."

Fudlow moved closer, looking down on Drowden. He spoke quietly and with menace. "I know who you are. And I don't much care. You brought that wild animal into our town. Doesn't matter who you are. He's not staying."

The men behind Fudlow moved in and formed a half circle, so that the only way open was back the way they had come. But then a shrill voice came from behind them and a girthless arm pushed between two cowled men. They stepped aside and let Ospin Tapple pass. He stood looking up at Drowden, then at Fudlow and back.

"Bos! Bos Fudlow! This is my friend Drowden Erebus. Let's show some respect. What's going on here?"

Fudlow spat, just missing Drowden's left foot. "He's brought his troll. We won't let that vermin walk the streets of Irongate like he's a natural man. Won't happen while I'm here to say."

"Nonsense," said Tapple. "Drowden, I'm so sorry. We'll straighten this out."

He hardly finished his sentence when Harry stepped forward bowing a little and stammering, "Master Tapple, good mornin', sir. Master Erebus, no need ta worry. You and Argis can go on 'bout yer business. I'll take Mister Ogden back to Tilthinger Inn and keep 'im happy a while. Maybe he'd like tha' nap he was talkin' 'bout. That ways we can avoid th' public upset. If tha's agreeable wi' Mister Fudlow an' all."

"Harry, that's good of you," said Drowden with a hand grasping his shoulder appreciatively. "But I wanted to show Ogden the town. He has a right to walk free, just as anyone."

Fudlow put his club on his shoulder and shoved Drowden with three fingers to his chest. "He's seen all he's going to see. Get him off our streets and we'll let you pass. Otherwise…. Not."

Ospin Tapple shrugged at Drowden. "They seem quite determined, my friend," he said. "Perhaps I can reason with them later. For now, perhaps it is best…"

"Alright Harry. You get Ogden safely back to the inn. Argis is with me. We'll return this evening after our business is done." With that, Drowden pushed Fudlow's hand away and glared at him. "He gets safe passage back to our rooms. Agreed?"

"Agreed, of course! Quite reasonable!" Tapple squealed. Fudlow stepped aside and waved toward the street behind him. The wagon that had been sitting in the middle of Smelt Road moved on with a whinny from the horses as a lash came down. The cowled men behind Fudlow turned and fled silently down the same street. He followed them without looking back.

Harry winked at Drowden. "I'll keep 'im safe an' sound. Don't worry." Then he and Ogden turned to retrace their steps back to Tilthinger Inn. Argis and Drowden headed for the sawmill on the banks of the Julian Creek that spilled into the Heatherbloom River.

"That didn't go very well," Drowden muttered under his breath to Argis. They walked the rest of the way in silence.

Harry told Ogden to stay close, and he did. Down Knob's Alley they walked with hardly a hand space between them. They felt eyes on them from above but heard not a word. Turning onto Gilton Road, they saw a boy tossing a ball of knotted rope into the air and catching it ten paces ahead of where he launched it. When he caught sight of Ogden he stopped in his tracks and began to laugh gleefully. Ogden smiled and turned toward him and walked backward, watching him laugh and laugh as he walked past. Then a dog with half a leg gone ran like she didn't miss it right in front of them so that they had to slow down a little.

On Kilter Street, shoppers were out in numbers, passing each other on the walkways, crossing the cobbled street on angled trajectories. Each person they encountered made way for their passage, some nodding in greeting, some scurrying aside with arms raised defensively, and with only a few commenting at all — mostly with surprised exclamations or self-conscious 'hellos.'

At Tilthinger Inn they wasted no time to pause in the great room, where patrons were seated at tables awaiting meals they'd ordered. Up the wide staircase, past the hulking chestnut sculpture, down the hall to the right and into their room. Harry closed the door behind them with a clatter.

"Safe an' sound," he said with a loud exhale.

Ogden sat on his bed and folded his big hands on his lap. "Thank you, Harry," he said, looking at the floor in front of him. "What ghosts haunt them, that they fear a troll?" he asked.

Harry didn't answer. He was going through a drawer, gathering items of clothing and toiletries and placing them in his pack. They didn't speak for some time, until there was a sound. A pebble danced off the window glass and Harry got up to look. He pulled back the curtain and stood motionless for a moment. Then Ogden saw him nod, and he turned and said, "I'll be right back. You stay here. Don't go nowhere."

Ogden nodded, and Harry went out the door and closed it softly behind him.

Harry strode down to the end of the hall and unlatched the lock on the door leading out to the balcony. He stepped out into the daylight and looked over the rail down toward the courtyard. Puckering his lips, he whistled quietly, and a man wearing a green cape and carrying a walking stick with a brass-top in the shape of a wildcat's head stepped out from under the orange leaves of an autumn maple. It was Tucker Scont, one of Ospin Tapple's men.

"What news?" Harry called to him.

Tucker called back, "Hey, Bigworth! Glad you got the message from your brother. Tapple's arranged everything. You just have to play along."

Harry leaned on the rail and answered, "Yeah! Bobbin told me 'bout Tapple's scheme, an' I'm all fer it. But here's th' thing! Whatever he's got planned, he knows Harry's got ta stay clean ov it, right?"

"Sure, sure," said Tucker. "Just meet me at the Bull and Beaver a half past six. Bring the troll. When I say skedaddle, you get up and go. Leave the rest to me and to tomorrow."

With no other word, Tucker Scont was gone. Harry ducked back into the dark hallway and strode back to the room. Ogden was in mid-stretch to lie down on the featherbed mattress for the first time, but bolted back up as Harry came in.

"What news?" he asked Harry.

"Eh, it's nothin'. Just saw a friend who wants ta meet me fer a nip at the Bull an' Beaver. Nice place. Y'ud like it. What say we go there in a couple hours? Maybe supper time."

Ogden said nothing. He got up and paced.

By the time they left for the Bull and Beaver, Ogden was past ready to be free of that little room. Harry gave him a wide brimmed floppy hat to keep his face out of public view, so the five-block walk was uneventful.

Harry led Ogden a winding walk, and they arrived at the Bull and Beaver by quarter 'til six. Ogden asked several times before they left the inn and along the way if they shouldn't have waited for Drowden and Argis to return from their errands, but Harry wouldn't hear of it. "I promised ta meet Tucker Scont at the Bull and Beaver and I mean ta do it 'cause I'm a man 'o me word an'

ya wouldn't want me ta be otherwise," Harry told him at last, pausing under
the hempen awning before they went in.

Tucker Scont was inside, sitting at a plank board table with Millie Truller,
whose face was mostly concealed by a woven hat with a wide brim and a tall,
narrowing top. A loud band of troubadours plucked mandolins, lyres, tam-
bourines and tamburas off to the side. Tucker motioned a waving arm toward
Harry and he and Ogden shuffled past several tables where men sat with elbows in front of them and mugs under their chins. The inelegantly con-
structed maple chairs under each man were adorned with the loose pelts of fox
and raccoon, wolf and muskrat in no particularly regular combination. It was
the same at Tucker's table. Harry sat to Tucker's left on a beaver pelt-covered
chair, so Ogden sat on the fox pelt-draped chair to Harry's left and Millie's
right. Both Millie's and Ogden's hats concealed their faces, lending an air of
mystery to the gathering. Within the noisy envelope of the pub other centers
of activity chirped up.

The bellicose table of six men behind where Tucker sat quieted down from
a boisterous clamor to a subdued hubbub as the barmaid squeezed past them
and asked what Harry would have to drink, then Ogden.

When she was gone, Harry poked his chin at Ogden and said "You can
take yer hat off, Ogden. It draws more attention than yer face." Ogden didn't
respond, so Harry reached over and pulled the floppy sun hat from his head
and tossed it on the floor next to his chair.

Tucker did likewise with Millie, but without the courtesy of inviting her
to remove it herself. He pulled the hat from her head and hung it on the back
of her chair. "That's better. Now we can all see how lovely you are, Millie."

Harry looked across the table at Millie. He stared a long moment, then
grabbed Tucker's arm. "Geez, Tuck! Couldn't ye find a homelier wench? She's
as pretty as a possum with pocks. I think she's got a derned beard comin' in
an' a moostach ye can't stop lookin' at."

Tucker lifted Harry's hand off his arm and twisted the pinky with evident
intention to cause some pain. "She's not with me, you idiot. I thought your
troll friend might like to meet her. Looks his type, doncha think?"

Harry squinted, and he pursed his lips at Tucker, as if wanting to speak but holding his tongue. The men at the table nearby seemed to be in tune with what was going on at the table where Harry and Tucker, Millie and Ogden were sitting. They seemed to lean in, or leer. But it was two men at the bar who barged in with their opinions.

"I never saw a couple of trolls dressed up like people," said the one with a long scraggly beard that stuck out from his cheeks in a cloud of fine orange hair.

"Is that wha' she is? A troll?" said the other at the bar. "Tell th' truth, Patchy. Neither you nor me's ever seen a troll dressed er undressed."

Then a man with a smooth baritone voice called from the table behind Tucker. "I thought it were yer wife, Patchy!"

The man sitting next to Patchy at the bar laughed a loud cackle and slapped Patchy's back. "That's a good one, Pip. Cheers to th' Brotherhood!" and he raised his glass of opaque amber ale toward the six men sitting at the table next to Ogden, Harry, Tucker and Millie.

Ogden looked to his right as Pip Skleverly called back to the bar, "Now hush. She's no troll, just one of those ugly commoners you'll see roving the countryside. Leave 'em alone. They're with my friend Tuck. Just mind your business and I'll buy you a round of ale."

"Aye," Patchy hollered back across the room. "I'll shut me yap if yer buyin' the quiet."

Harry leaned forward to talk over the noise of the musicians and the ambient voices. He looked straight at Tucker. "Friends o' yers?"

Tucker shrugged. "I'll just call them business acquaintances. Never mind 'em. They won't interfere."

Ogden was listening to all of this. He took in the talk of the men around him. Something in their words was false. Their oddity and the way they conflicted with appearances left him confused. Why would so many men come together to try to cast a spell? That's what it was they were trying to do. They were working together to create some deceit for others to live inside of, he thought.

He began to wonder why he was brought here. Some purpose or fate seemed to be guiding events as they unfolded, but whatever scheme they had in mind was hidden from him. Nothing spilling out of the mouths of the men at his table, the bar or the table adjacent to his connected with the sense of foreboding that flooded his senses like the smell of a rotting carcass under a pile of leaves, or the sound of a tree teetering on the verge of collapse in the forest.

He looked at Millie and her eyes immediately fluttered and lowered. Something about her made him shiver. She seemed perfectly normal in a physical sense. Nothing about her appearance told him why she seemed to disgust Harry, the men at the bar, and Pip Skleverly's companions at the next table. He didn't understand why their words expressed revulsion, when their conduct said something else was going on inside them.

Ogden shivered all the same. When he looked at Millie he felt some dread within her, and he felt some menace hovering around her. If he had been asked, he couldn't have conjured words to convey what he knew. It was a truth he perceived in his muscles and veins, but it was not a thought in his head.

But a thought did come. It welled up like a revelation from somewhere inside him. It said: "Thoughts are just words. People put words together and then they see what those words stand for as if they're real." And then he caught himself, knowing that this idea was just more words swirling in his own head. He paused and grew silent within.

Millie's mind was not so quiet. It was full of unknowing fear. Her demeanor reflected none of that inner conflict. She sat immovable, emotionless, showing no concern, for she commanded herself more than the men around her. Her ability to hold within what others would have sputtered out stupidly was something none of them could comprehend.

Ogden stared at her a while. His jaws clenched and suddenly he slammed a fist on the table. "What is going on?" he demanded. "Who is this Tucker, and what does he want?"

Harry leaned in and grabbed Ogden's arm. "Easy. We're jus' havin' a drink an' a chat wi' me friend Tuck. That's all."

Ogden pulled back and dropped his hands to his lap. A tall man wearing high-strapped boots, a knife on his belt, a loose shirt that billowed over his waist and a drawstring bag slung over his shoulder approached and leaned forward to speak quietly in Harry's ear. Ogden looked up at him and saw him wink, and then Harry looked from Ogden to Tucker.

"I've got ta go down the street ta talk wi' the constable. Says it's okay fer us ta be here, bu' wants ta walk us back to the inn when we go."

Ogden stood to go with him, but Harry held up a hand. "No. You stay here. I'll be back real soon."

The barmaid was at his elbow and reached past to place mugs of ale on the table.

"See," said Harry. "Drinks is here. Might just as well stay an' enjoy. Ogden, you drink mine too. I'll get me another un when I get back."

With that, Harry turned on his heel and sped out the front door, leaving Ogden and Millie alone with Tucker Scont.

Tucker leaned in and pointed at Millie. "Don't you think she's a looker?" he said, popping an eye toward Ogden.

Ogden didn't answer. He picked up the mug of ale and drank it down quickly. Tucker pushed the mug at Harry's place toward Ogden. "There you go, lad. Have another. I'll get some more." He turned and waved to the barmaid indicating two more ales by scissoring his fingers over the table.

"Drink up, Millie dear. It's my treat." He took a long swig from his own mug and wiped his mouth with his sleeve. "Let's just get acquainted while we wait for Harry to get back. He's a good enough sort, don't you think? Not smart in the head but means well. What do you think, Ogden?"

Ogden took another mouthful of ale from the second mug. "Think about Harry? Why think about Harry? He's Harry."

"Well, what do you think about Millie, eh? I bet you've got lots of fancy pictures of her dancing around up there," and Tucker poked a finger at Ogden's forehead.

Millie "tutted" audibly. Ogden said nothing. But Tucker kept talking.

"I knew it as soon as you sat down, and I took her hat off. You can't take your eyes off her." He was speaking more loudly. The men at Pip Skleverly's table stopped chattering among themselves. "You know, troll," Tucker said even more loudly, "she came with me, not you. But you've got a mind to have her for yourself, don't you?"

Ogden clanked his mug on the table hard. The barmaid was placing two more in front of him when he said "What game are you playing? Nothing you've said is true. What meaning do you want to weave out of the air when you spit your breath over your tongue and past your teeth?"

Suddenly Tucker jumped to his feet and leaned on the table toward Ogden. "What are you trying to say, troll?" he yelled so loudly that the music stopped this time. "Are you calling me a liar? You're trying to take Millie for your own. Never mind that I brought her here," he continued to bellow. He pointed at Millie with outstretched arm. "Is that what you want? You like this ugly, twisted, unnatural thing more than me? That how it is?"

Mille was voiceless. She didn't understand what was happening. She tried to speak, but no words came out as her chin quivered and her lips moved silently.

Tucker slammed his palm on the top of the table and backed up so fast his chair toppled behind him. "That suits me just fine, you homely ungrateful mockery of a woman. Just as well I find out now how you are."

Tucker stormed out of the Bull and Beaver and Ogden watched as he was swallowed up by the over-bright light of day. The door swung closed behind him. From Pip's table a round of snickering came to a crescendo of loud laughter. The men at the bar joined in, and one of the musicians let out a piercing whistle.

Millie fumbled to pull the buttons of her vest through their buttonholes as she stood and retrieved her hat from the post of her chair. She placed it at an angle on her head and fled out the door. Ogden too stood and then bent over to retrieve the hat Harry had loaned him from the floor where he'd tossed it. He pushed it on his head, pulled it down over his ears, and fled out the door behind Millie.

"Hey, ya bastard!" yelled the barmaid as the door swung closed behind him. "You ain't paid for those drinks!"

Pip Skleverly and his men waved her over to their table. While he talked, Pip held her by the waist and pulled her close to him. "I'll cover those lovebirds. And all that we've had as well." He slapped silver coins on the table. "That ought to cover it." Then he let her go and got up with his companions. They sped out onto the street together and were gone.

Ogden walked with long strides down the street, leaning forward into each step. He glanced around from under the brim of his hat, trying to spy a glimpse of Harry, but didn't see him. He saw Millie walking hurriedly down the other side of the street, but when she turned right onto a crossroad, Ogden went left. After trekking across seven cross streets, the columns and rows of buildings that made up the streets of Irongate yielded to a stretch of fields unblemished by any structure. This was bottomland, apt to flood at least twice each year with the spring rains and the winter thaw.

Ogden saw a grove of willow trees in the distance and walked in that direction. Hardly looking up, he used the hat's brim to shield his eyes from the sun as it approached the western hills beyond which lay Hapstead Manor, a full day's trek from Irongate. Between him and those hills not an eighth of a mile away was the Heatherbloom River. To cross it he turned toward Besom Bridge and the western gate.

At the bridge he stepped aside to let a group of horsemen ride through. A woman stood at mid-bridge and as Ogden approached, she lowered her veil, revealing an aging face heavily encrusted with cosmetic blush, lip paint and eye shadow. She smiled, attempting to conceal her yellowed and broken teeth.

"You're a big fella," she said in a lilting voice. And she stepped forward, blocking Ogden's path. She reached out and tilted his hat's brim back from his face. "Well," she said, looking straight into his eyes, "my name's Petula. I'm game if you are!"

Ogden side-stepped and pulled his hat back over his eyes, saying nothing. He proceeded across the bridge. "You don't know what you're missing," he heard the women call out behind him.

The western gate hung open. No guard tended the bridge, so he finished crossing unharassed. On the far side of the river, he left the road and followed a path along the riverbank toward the south. As he walked, he passed through a makeshift village made of tents and crude wooden shelters. There, the vagabonds who'd lost their traditional lands to the fences and walls of the enclosing laws made their homes.

Here were the dispossessed, the recently evicted, the landless and the field workers who had no work. Ogden heard a baby cry. He heard dogs yapping over scraps. And he smelled discontent and restlessness on the clothes of the beggars, some of whom stumbled by either weak from hunger or from the potato grog that the vendors from town sold them for the little they could pay. The shanty town outside of Irongate had no bonfires, no celebrations, only a palpable sadness.

He walked on and past the last of these makeshift dwellings and didn't pause until the sun was well settled behind him and lights began shining up and down the streets in hundreds of windows across the river in Irongate. He sat down on a grassy hill and watched the town in action as dusk settled in. Then he heard the town crier announce the closing of the town gates. That sonorous voice drifted on the cooling evening air over the rippling sounds of rapidly flowing water.

"Reglars in; rowdies out!" chanted the crier. "Gates is closin'. Gates is closin'."

Ogden made no attempt to hurry back to the bridge or reenter the town before the western gate was secured for the night. He pulled the hat off his head and lay back on the riverbank to watch as the water flowed by. The cerulean, crimson and violet hues in the sky above were reflected a thousand times on the sides of river ripples that tossed a kaleidoscopic vision toward Ogden's eyes. Torchlight from across the river occasionally tipped the dancing, rippling shards of color with sparking chips of white and yellow light.

The trees in the forest behind Ogden were alive with cicada and katydid song. A herd of deer moved through the underbrush nearby and he listened to their breathing, the swish of their tails and the vibration the branches made as they shook and swayed back into place.

He lifted his eyes from the moving surface of the water and looked toward Irongate. As darkness descended over the natural world, the town of men and women pushed back the shadows with candles and lanterns and torches. Ogden heard the clatter of hooves on cobblestone rise between rows of buildings and scatter off on the wind. He heard the muffled speech of men spill out from unlit porches into the darkness surrounding the river. These and other sounds of the town tumbled in his ears.

He turned his attention to the sky where the stars were glinting into view. They broke through the black shroud of night as cold white points, some tinted with the barest ghost of blue, others were orange and twinkling crystals, still others were glassy splinters of sapphire, and a few were yellow like a distant sun.

Tonight, the songs of the stars were different from any he had heard at Hapstead Manor. They began as a buzzing, like a nest of bees agitated by an approaching blaze. They vibrated the air and the spaces between him and everything around him, like static electricity. Instead of the calming peace that holds all things connected to their source and common origin, the star song permeating this place and time rattled Ogden's temples and made his head ache.

Then suddenly a piercing shriek of pain, sorrow and loss intruded. His head rang like he was inside a large brass bell. His whole body shook from within. He felt his hands and fingers quivering uncontrollably. His eyelids fluttered like swift butterflies. His teeth chattered together as he lost command of his jaw muscles. A shadow of grief and longing swept through him like a storm cloud and suddenly tears flowed in streams from his eyes. He held his hands palms up toward the sky and waited for the feeling of dread to pass.

When it did, Ogden could not tell if the scream still lingering in his ears came from the depths of the stars or from the town across the river. Without a word he knew that the disharmony of the singing stars defined this moment in eternity. The discord in the stars and in the lives of the town dwellers across the Heatherbloom River was one and the same.

Ogden watched the colors behind his eyes blend into a swirl of throbbing lights too bright to bear. He held his eyes tightly closed, but it did no good. The stars seemed to twirl like pinwheels overhead and they chittered a faltering song of dissonance upon the elemental filaments connecting them to each other and to every discrete thing that seemed but was not separate.

Ogden felt time expand and bleed into past and future all at once. He watched past and future unreel from an infinite spool of something like light. Then countless chords all made of time unfurled and interwove into an intricate tapestry, erasing the separateness between all things. He understood that this was one of the meanings of the songs of the stars. But there was more he could not yet comprehend.

He had been released from the moment and for a timeless instant he was free of the limitations of being. But, just as timelessly, he was deposited back to the riverbank, where he found himself again listening to the gurgling and slapping waters and the sounds of Irongate across the way.

The sky and earth still thrummed like the strings of a harp that had been stretched and yanked to the point of breaking, but gradually the monstrous noise all around him quieted and was bearable. Scattered clouds moved across the sky, intermittently concealing and revealing stars. An organic and rhythmically tempered symphony of star song returned. Ogden stretched his muscles and regained the feel of his body.

Looking across Heatherbloom River to the streets of Irongate, he watched as drunkards stumbled from taverns. He saw the pantomime of drama from a distance as prostitutes tempted men in the alley behind Tuskers Inn. He thought of the painted woman on the bridge.

Hours passed, punctuated by the clopping of hooves on cobblestone, a shout from a dark alley, the soft paddling of a beaver along the river's edge. These and thousands of other sounds flooded Ogden's senses.

Just before dawn Ogden watched as a butcher rolled his cart down a shallow bank to the river and tilted it to dump its contents into the water. A glopping of cow organs, skin and unusable waste from the slaughter shed tumbled from the cart, slid into the water with gurgling bubbles escaping as the bloody mass floated downstream, a suspended raft of drifting gore that hung between the surface and the stony bottom.

The cart rolled slowly back up the embankment and disappeared down a side street. Ogden saw a man go about the streets from one post to the next extinguishing lamps. He heard the town crier wend his way through the main streets calling sleepers to open their eyes to the new day.

"Gates is openin'; daybreak's comin'. Gates is openin'; daybreak's comin'."

Ogden pushed himself up off the riverbank and brushed off the back of his pants. He slapped the hat on his knee to dislodge a few loose leaves, pushed it down on his head and started walking back the path toward Besom Bridge and the western gate.

He crossed the bridge without incident. A few pedestrians walked past without remark. The gate was open and unattended. He walked through the waking town's streets and alleys, smelled savory meats and breads cooking in ovens and over fires — their scents wafted from homes throughout the town. Eventually he spotted a familiar landmark and turned up the steps and through the door of Tilthinger Inn.

Up the wide steps, past the hulking wooden sculpture, down the hall and to the right he went. And he found Drowden and Argis waiting for him, the door to their room held open by a brick.

"Ogden! You're safe!" cried Drowden with surprise and delight when he looked up from his reading and saw the troll standing in the doorway.

"Yes," he answered. "Safe."

"Where in creation has ya been, lad?" Argis bolted off his bedside and grabbed Ogden by the shoulders. "We figured th' worse. An' where's tha' brig-and Harry?"

"Yes, where's Harry?" Drowden repeated. "And what were you two doing all this time? Was there more trouble?"

Ogden tried to recount the events of last evening, but because it made little sense to him, he only said what he had seen and heard. He told of going to the Bull and Beaver, of Harry being called away by the constable, and of Tucker Scont's very strange behavior. And he told them about Millie, at least what little he could.

"It's stranger in town than expected," he said. "Everything is in disguise. Mostly because people cover everything with words, like they're brushing paint on the whole world. Before you can see the sort of lumber they build their lives with, they've hidden it all under a thick coat of words. They use words that turn you aside from seeing anything straight-away. Most everyone in Irongate uses words to lie. They make it hard to see to the heart of anything."

Drowden watched and listened intently as Ogden tried to explain his encounters in town. He shook his head and smiled, then frowned, but in the end, he said, "I honestly don't know what you mean by all of that, but I'm very glad you've come back no worse for the experience."

"So, where'd ya sleep?" asked Argis.

Ogden told him about his night on the riverbank beyond the gates of town, about the sights and sounds of the town as seen from across Heatherbloom River, leaving out many things he couldn't put into words.

"So ya didn't sleep," Argis concluded.

"And they locked you out when they closed the gates. Well, lesson learned, I hope," said Drowden. "You must be tired, Ogden. You go get some rest before we start off for home."

Ogden's face brightened. "On the featherbed?"

"Yes," laughed Drowden. "Go on. You deserve it. I'll wake you in a few hours when we're packed to go. Harry will likely be back by then."

Chapter XX
No Featherbed

Ogden's head had nearly settled on the pillow when the door of his room burst open with a crash, spewing pieces of broken wood and the metal latch and the porcelain door handle across the floor.

An obese man with a cudgel in his fist stood just inside the doorway glowering at Ogden. He was backed up by a hallway full of men who intermittently hollered one thing or another about trolls and miscreants and dirty, dark and itchy things.

Ogden recognized some of them and as they hollered and bobbled about agitatedly, he noticed how their words and gestures seemed unconnected, like they were rehearsed, and they were actors unsure of their lines or where they ought to be standing on the stage. It was a repetition of the words and gestures they'd displayed when that very morning they had stopped Drowden, Argis, Harry and him where Smelt Road meets Knob's Alley.

Ogden recognized a few others as Pip Skleverly's companions at the Bull and Beaver Tavern from the past evening. His nostrils flared, and he smelled their dread. They were afraid of him, of what he might do. But it was their fear of being wrong about everything they thought they knew about trolls that had them standing there threatening him with bats and rope and chains. That fear smelled more pungent to Ogden than their fear of all the things they thought they did know about trolls.

He gazed at them from the shadow of his brow. They seemed trapped in a kind of collective blindness that let their eyes see, but not comprehend what they saw. He watched them move mechanically as though under command of a puppet master.

"Don't move," said the squat man with a rear-end so large Ogden could see it bulging to either side as he stood glaring at him near the foot of his bed. Constable Glarson Liefson's grimace sculpted deep folds into his pocked face. Ogden sniffed and noticed among other unpleasant scents wafting off the rotund man that he was sweating profusely. His suspenders were yanked up so high that his pants bulged up over his belly and there was a four-inch gap between the button and the buttonhole. The cuffs of his greasy pants rose above his ankles. A metal badge pinned to his leather workman's cap glinted off and on in the backlit gas light as he moved his head from side to side. His cap was pulled down over a head of light brown hair with pinwheel curls. Stubble three days in the growing darkened his face.

The young troll had bolted up when the door crashed in, so that now he was sitting on the edge of the bed looking silently at the constable. His lips quivered. Sweat beaded on his brow as he watched a few of the men press into his room behind the fat man. Others filled the hallway with loud talk. Ogden's heart was racing.

Then he was startled by another commotion in the hall outside his door and as he half rose to see over the heads of the men crowded around him, he glimpsed Drowden and Argis elbowing their way through the men in the hall. Their shadows bulged and shrank and billowed against the far hall wall. Before they could make it past the armed gauntlet, they took more than a few blows from batons and knuckles. Eventually they were seized and held firmly, two men to each of them. Drowden was led into Ogden's room first, an arm twisted up behind his back and an ironwood stick pressed under his chin. Argis got the same treatment and was shoved by darting knees and bulging bellies into the room. Two men forced him to stand next to Drowden by the constable's left side. As Ogden rose fully to confront the men who held them, Drowden yelled, "Stop, Ogden! Don't do anything. Let's find out what this is all about."

Ogden froze between a crouch and a leap. He looked from Drowden to Argis, and then to Constable Liefson. His eyes widened, and the room lit up in his mind.

"What are you doing?" he asked, looking directly and menacingly at Constable Liefson.

Liefson chewed something and smiled. "We're capturing a slaughtering animal," he said. "And we'll arrest anyone who tries to stop us."

"Glarson, you want us to take him down?" a voice in the hall shouted out.

"Wait!" Drowden hollered. "Ogden's done nothing wrong. You can't just take him away without a reason."

Cornelius Baldegger shouted out from behind him. "Reason? Damn you, Drowden Erebus! Damn you for bringing a wild animal into our streets! Poor Millie Truller's been raped and murdered and cut to shreds."

Glarson shook his fat head slowly. "That's right. It's about murthur most vile. It's about witnesses who make plain that this creature is the culprit and it's about me taking your troll out of this room bound and in chains."

Drowden held up his hand in a halting gesture. "Wait! Let's discuss this."

Glarson Liefson spat on the floor. "We just did the discussion part. Now the troll surrenders without a tussle or we'll put him down like a rabid dog right here." He turned to Derrick Deneb, who stood just behind him. "You got a leash for the monster?"

Drowden cried out, "What? No! No leash! You can't do that!"

Glarson yelled over his left shoulder. "Thad, bring the rope and shackles." He eyeballed the troll, clearly intimidated by his size, though Ogden made no menacing moves. He looked at Drowden and Argis, back and forth. "Can you two control your trog...I mean your troll, or do I gotta bring in help?" He pointed backward over his shoulder with a thumb, indicating the eight burly men crowding the door jam.

"Where do you mean to take him?" Drowden choked demandingly. He was still held tightly by Hopskel Dwil, who kept his baton pulled snug against his throat.

"He's goin' to the jailhouse where we're gonna interrogate him and then lock him up until the town master decides what to do — hang him or burn him." He looked down at his hands, and then Glarson said with a nervous yawn, "It's all according to law."

Thad Krebbermoting and Burl Oonep came forward with rope dangling and chains chattering. They stood on either side of Glarson until he nodded, and they approached Ogden cautiously. Ogden watched them impassively and saw no sign from Drowden indicating he should do anything, so he didn't resist. They secured shackles around his ankles, wrists and neck, attached the chains to the shackles, and for good measure Burl wrapped a thick rope around his waist and neck, stretching a length of it between them and connecting that to a lead, the looped end of which he grasped in his hands.

"Ready to go Constable, whenever you are," said Thad.

Nothing in Drowden's past had prepared him for the feeling of loss, devastation and powerlessness that he felt as he watched Ogden being led out of the room. Ogden's eyes did not look up at him, but as he shuffled heavily toward the hall he asked quietly, "So, there'll be no featherbed tonight?"

Argis and Drowden followed the rowdy group of men down the steps, past the giant carved creature on the bottom landing, and out the doors of Tilthinger Inn. A crowd of men and some women stood there and let out a collective cry of loathing and triumph, then fell in behind the mob as it meandered through streets faintly lit by a broadening dawn toward the town jail. Ogden was pulled and shoved in that direction. Loud shouts, curses in fact, echoed against the stone buildings and tumbled over each other on the damp dawn air. The bevy of men and women who had been standing outside Tilthinger Inn moved forward in the procession and encircled Ogden. Half a dozen others broke off to surround Drowden and Argis and block their attempts to advance to Ogden's side.

Howe Bistrep shoved Argis away from the street's walkway and cursed him for loosing a wild troll on the streets of Irongate. Argis and Drowden were shoved onward with punches to their shoulders. A skinny man with a cone-shaped hat followed closely behind Drowden and continually spit on his back as he walked. They lost the sight of Ogden amid shoulders and heads in in the trudging procession ahead of them. Neither Argis nor Drowden could see Ogden, except for an occasional glimpse of his hat above the jostling throng of men.

Drowden could hear the boisterous knot of men and women that brought up the rear exclaiming and shouting in anger. Someone walking behind the line of men policing his movements shouted to a plump woman who was gawking at the parade from her kitchen window.

"That thing is a menace! I saw what it did. I can't get that poor woman's bloody, ruined body out of my mind! There she was, slumped in the alley!"

Drowden turned to see a bandana-wrapped woman's head, stretching her neck as far as she could, her elbows pinned like stilts on the windowsill. She hollered back as the procession flowed by, "Murder? Not again!"

Drowden reeled around and, walking backwards, shouted over the heads of the club-carrying men guarding him. "Did you see Ogden do it? What did you see? You didn't see Ogden at all, did you?"

Kreg Jutribackle was one of the men forming a moving ring around Drowden and Argis as they plodded the cobblestones toward the jail. He smacked his cudgel in the palm of his hand and said "Do yourself a favor and mind where we're going. Turn around. Stay out of trouble."

Drowden opened his mouth to object, but Kreg yelled "do it!" and Drowden complied.

The mobile mob turned down a side street and approached what looked to be a horse stable. Constable Liefson jangled keys and pulled a padlock from the double doors and two men jogged forward to take hold and pull them open. Inside, it was clear that this had once been a horse stable, but each stall had been converted into a cell with iron bars and a straw-packed mattress inside. In the middle of the open space surrounded by stable cells stood a single rough-hewn desk and a rocking chair. That's where Glarson Liefson parked himself as his posse roughly pushed Ogden with shoves of the hand and sticks and cudgels. Ogden stood shackled in front of the desk, ropes and chains held taut from the sides and behind.

Guards lead Drowden and Argis into the room and pushed them aside. They let the men and women who had surrounded the Hapstead men on the way to the jail fill in the space behind Ogden and his handlers. Constable Liefson banged the desk with his baton and called for quiet. Then he yelled out, "Where's Nolan Skels?"

The baker, Nolan Skels, shouted out "Right here!" and he pushed his way forward through the crowd until he stood next to the constable and far enough from Ogden not to shiver in fright as he looked him over head to toe.

"Tell us what ya know," said Glarson, jerking his multiple chins toward Nolan.

"I know that murdering animal killed Millie Truller. I found her mangled and molested body out in Knob's Alley, behind my shop when I went out but two hours ago to fetch some lard from the shed and…"

"Wait!" Drowden cried out. "You found a body in the alley. What's that got to do with Ogden?"

"Shut him up!" yelled Glarson.

"Quiet!" Kreg pushed him back against a clapboard wall with the palm of his large hand. "For your own good, stay quiet!" he growled, eyes widely glaring at Drowden. His teeth were clenched, and the muscles of his jaws rippled.

Ogden lurched toward Drowden but was yanked hard by the shackle around his neck. He nearly toppled backward but righted himself with an extended hand that bounced him erect again.

"Go on, Skels. What else?" yelled Glarson.

Nolan swallowed hard. "Millie…I didn't know her name, but Tucker Scont told it to me when he got there not long after I found her. Millie was laying in her own blood. Her dress was ripped open. I could see her neck was broke. Her head was twisted away unnaturally. So I yelled for help. I yelled my head off. That's when Tuck came running from where I don't know. Then Jeke, my neighbor came running. Then my wife came hustling down the stairs in her robe and came outside. Then…"

Glarson interrupted. "Alright. We get the picture. Lots of people squabbling and panicked. What then?"

"Then somebody sent for you," he said, "and by the time you came around the corner, maybe most of an hour later, we had a big crowd. Matter of fact, most of the folks here showed up. Then we went to grab the troll."

Now Argis cried out. "What's 'at got ta do wid Ogden? Why'd ya decide it was him, ya ignorant pastry pushin' imbecile?"

Kreg Jutribackle turned on Argis, grabbed him by the neck, and held him an inch off the floor against the wall. "I'm telling you to stay quiet. If I've got to take you out of here bound and gagged, I will."

Ogden suddenly yanked at the chain attached to his neck and spun around so quickly that the man holding the other end came off his feet and spun off into the crowd, toppling three men. Other men recoiled momentarily and then lurched toward Ogden. Drowden shouted, "Stop! We're not hurt, Ogden. Stay calm!"

But by then Ogden was buried in a pile of bodies. When he stopped resisting, he found himself held more tightly than before. The men pulled him to his feet and pressed in closer to prevent him from moving freely. At last, when the commotion in the makeshift jail died down, Constable Liefson called out for Tucker Scont and waited as he shuffled from the back of the crowd to stand in front of his desk side. "Scont, tell us what you know," he said.

"Here's what I know," he started. "Drowden Erebus there," he pointed, "his man Harry brought this here creature," and he pointed at Ogden, "to the Bull and Beaver yesterday. I used to work with Harry over in the mine when we were young bucks, before he went off to Hapstead. So, I see him over at Tilthinger Inn and Harry says to me let's have a pint, and I'll bring Drowden's troll for you to meet. I says, 'sure,' and heck if he doesn't bring the troll along with him last evening around supper time."

Scont paused for a reaction and Glarson waved his hand impatiently. "Gwaan!" he said testily.

"So, I'd made the company of Millie Truller earlier on and she was sitting with me when Harry and the troll came into the Bull and Beaver. That one," he darted a finger toward Ogden, "had a hat on, the same one he's wearing now, so he didn't look so out of place, except for how big he is, and that odd way of walking. So, they come in and…"

"Hold on," said Glarson. "Thad, snatch that hat off the troll's head. I wanna see its face. I want everyone to see its awful face."

Thad Krebbermoting reached up and tipped the hat Harry had given Ogden off the back of his head. The room sighed with a mild gasp. Ogden's thick brow ridge concealed his obsidian-dark eyes in the shadows. A drying trickle of blood clung in small rivulets to the side of his face. His thick hair was matted with sweat. Drowden said loudly, but calmly, "It's alright, son. We're going to make this right. Have trust. We'll straighten this out."

"We're going to straighten it out, I promise you that," yelled Pip Skleverly from the middle of the room. He pushed his way forward and stood next to Tucker Scont. "I was there, Constable. Me and my friends in the Brotherhood weren't but six feet away from them when they came in and sat down. Harry and this troll plopped down next to Tucker and Millie, and that trog proceeded to down mug after mug of grog. We saw it with our own eyes, didn't we boys?"

A scattered ascent came from five directions. "Aye, we was there," and "Yep. It's like he says," and "Oh yeah. He was pounding the grog alright."

Patchy, the man who'd been sitting at the bar at the Bull and Beaver, stood at the far end of a semi-circle surrounding Liefson's desk. He shook his head and yelled out, "Wasn't that much grog, an' Harry an' Tuck was pushin' it his way." He said it loudly enough for all to hear, and someone pushed him from behind so that he tripped forward and had to pick himself off the dirt floor.

"Shut your yap, Patchy," said Glarson. "Let sober men talk and you just listen."

Patchy waved his arms in protest but wouldn't be quiet. "I'm tellin' ya, the troll was just decoration at that table. These boys was havin' fun wit him is all."

"That's it!" screamed Thad Krebbermoting. "I'm taking that drunken pile of steaming manure out of here." And he rushed to grab Patchy by the scruff of the neck and dragged him kicking and hollering out a back door.

Tucker put a hand on Pip's shoulder and looked around the room solemnly. He said "What he's saying is the truth. I didn't think it was a good idea to liquor up a troll, but we were having fun. That one," he jerked a hand in Ogden's direction, "couldn't take his eyes off of Millie. Harry got worried after a spell, and he left to find yer honor, the constable. He said to me he thought it wise you escort him and the troll back to their lair at Tilthinger. But before he came back, that troll picked an argument with me over Millie. He said I ought ta not be touching her. Clear as day he wanted her for hisself. No matter what I said he turned it around and I got the clear notion he was winding up for a fight. I admit it. I got scared and got myself out of there." He left off at that point and wiped his mouth with his jacket cuff.

"Then what happened?" Liefson tapped a rolling beat with his fingers on the desktop.

Tucker shrugged. "Got no idea what became of the troll or Millie after that. Not until this morning, when I heard a loud commotion down Knob's Alley. And, oh my sore heart, I couldn't believe what I saw when I got there. It was horrible, just horrible. That's when I told the baker, Nolan Skels and the others, what I knew. Then we waited a good bit for yer honor to show up."

Glarson Liefson popped a wide eye at Tucker. "I got there, didn't I?"

Pip Skeverly held up a hand with an extended finger. "What Tuck didn't stay to see, but me and my men did, was Millie and that troll leaving the Bull and Beaver together. They got up without paying for their drinks and skedaddled out the door, arm in arm."

A rumble of shock and anger rolled through the room like the thunder of a storm brewing over the next hill. Ogden felt the room fall away from him as he sank inward, unable to find anything firm to hold onto. He heard his voice leave his mouth without volition. It came from somewhere beyond time and this place. "You cast a dark spell. It will net you, not this Troggle. Why do you serve this wickedness?"

"Aghhhh!!! Shut him up! Gag him!" cried out Howe Bistrep. "He's conjuring! He's summoning! He'll curse us! Shut him up!"

"Let him speak!" yelled Drowden. "There's no justice here; nor is there sorcery. Let him speak."

Kreg waved his bat in front of Drowden's face. "I've warned you. Stay quiet."

Drowden's face was red with rage. "I can't," he yelled angrily. "Let Ogden tell his side. He wasn't even in Irongate last night when that poor woman was killed. He was outside the gates all night. Tell them Ogden!"

"It's true!" shouted a woman from the rear of the crowd. "I saw him leave just before they shut and locked the gates. He weren't here, lads!"

But by then the men holding Ogden's binding had already slipped a cloth over his mouth and pulled it into a tight knot, so that only guttural mufflings of sound escaped.

"Shut up whore!" someone in the crowd yelled. And there was a struggle near the jail entrance, with loud shouts of a woman's voice, of a man grunting and struggling. And then the door flung open and just as quickly shut. The woman was gone.

"Constable Liefson," Kreg Jutribackle hollered out. "I've had it with these troll lovers too. Let me take them out of here. You can't have a fair hearing of the facts when you're constantly interrupted by nimbiciles and whores. I'll take these two trog fanciers to the edge of town and toss them out. And I'll tell the watch to post a guard at each gate, so they stay out. Drowden Erebus needs to go back to Hapstead and leave the law to us."

"Yeah!" laughed Thad. "Drowden Erebus should go back to Hapstead and leave the law to us."

Glarson got up from his rocking chair and pointed at Argis, then Drowden. "Thad, tie those men up. Jutribackle, can you manage them once they're bound?"

Kreg smiled and shook his head and pulled back the folds of his long coat. He lifted a small crossbow from a brass loop attached inside. "I'll put a dart through the eye of the first one who tries to run. And I'll snap the neck of the other one."

"Good," Glarson croaked. "Then get them out of here."

With that, they were tied and pushed out the stable doors. As they swung closed behind them Drowden shouted over his shoulder, "Be brave, Ogden! I'll be back!" What Argis shouted with spittle flying and neck popping purple snakes of rage is better left unremembered.

Kreg Jutribackle led them out the rear entrance into a courtyard where a pillory stood, decorated with a man's head and hands peeking out from the weathered but solid wooden blocks. Argis grumbled, "Look. It's tha' ole coot Patchy. They didn't waste no time crackin' down on anyone not tellin' th' story th' ways they want it told, did they?"

Jutribackle pushed Argis from behind. "Just keep moving and count yourself lucky. Patchy said the wrong thing. He told the truth."

Argis looked back over his shoulder at Kreg with one eye open and one closed. He couldn't tell if the man was being ironic or cruel.

They trudged down back alleyways and narrow footpaths toward Besom Bridge. Jutribackle told them not to look around or back at him. He had his mechanical bow aimed at one of them, he assured them both. They walked silently on, until he called for them to stop on a path that led straight through the overgrown limestone walls of a crumbling building. Broken timbers from what had been its roof lay in a heap to one side of the hard-packed foot path.

"I've got a plan you might be interested in, Drowden Erebus. Would you like to see your troll free of Irongate's clutches?"

Drowden spun around and looked at the tall man intently. Jutribackle's hands were at his side. He had no weapon in sight. His broad shoulders dropped with a sigh. He spoke again.

"I think I can free Ogden for you. But it's going to come at a price. Interested?"

"Yes, of course I am!" Drowden shouted. "What is it you want?"

"I want to help you. But I can't do it unless you're willing to pay."

"It's a fleecin'!" yelled Argis. "This whole story about a killin' and Ogden carousin' was all made up! They jus wanna blackmail ya, Master Erebus!"

"Hush, Argis. I want to hear what this man has to say." Drowden held up his bound hands, palms out.

Jutribackle reached into his cloak and retrieved a broad knife. He stepped toward Argis, brandishing it, then turned to Drowden, held the knife aloof in the air and with one fast swipe cut the rope loose from his wrists.

"I'm going to free you too," he said to Argis. "And I don't think you'll run, will you?"

Drowden answered for him. "No. He won't go anywhere. I want to know how we can free Ogden."

Argis grunted. "Nope; won't go nowhere. Now whatdya want fer freein' Ogden?"

His rope was sliced free and Jutribackle pointed a finger in his face. "You are right," he said. "The whole story about Ogden killing Millie is a lie. But it doesn't matter. They're going to make sport of killing him unless you stop it."

"How can I do that? Tell me." Drowden held out his hands to either side.

"Leave that to me," Jutribackle said curtly. "But first, you'll need to give me something valuable. Something I can carry in my pocket."

"A bribe." Argis growled and spat. "I saw it comin'."

"That's exactly what it is," Jutribackle shot back. "But without it, nothing can happen."

"I don't have any treasure with me," Drowden said.

"Then you'll need to get it. A handful of jewels or one large enough to cover the palm of my hand should do it. I'll wait and make some arrangements until you have it."

Drowden held up a hand to stop Argis from speaking again, then turned a wary eye toward Jutribackle. "I'll have to go to Hapstead Manor. But I swear I'll get what you want."

"Good. Now get on over the bridge and out of Irongate and don't come back without the treasure. Send someone who's not known in town to find me when you get back with it. Understood?"

Jutribackle didn't wait for an answer but turned on his heel and walked away. Argis and Drowden stood silently for a few minutes to be sure he was leaving. They both had in mind his concealed bow and darts and dared not turn their backs on him until he was at a safe distance.

"Well, that's Irongate for ya," Argis shook his head. "Throw yer friend in chains an' ask treasure ta free 'im. I would no' trust tha' man. Take th' loot an' say he never got it; that's wha' he'll do."

"What else can I do, Argis? They've concocted a case against Ogden and they'll hang him for sure if we don't stop them somehow." Drowden stood quietly a moment, then turned toward Besom Bridge. They heard Heatherbloom River gurgling around submerged boulders as its rushing whitecaps hurried toward the bridge's shadow. They crossed without incident, but as they headed up the far road in the direction of Hapstead Manor Drowden stopped and placed a hand on Argis' shoulder.

"Do you see that shantytown over there?" He pointed toward the collection of makeshift huts, tents and campfires not far from the bridge, huddling in close to the river. Ogden had passed by those same rustic dwellings the night before.

"Yessir, Master Drowden. That's wha' they call Bladicville. It's where th' land-forlorn gather when they lose their farms ta th' bankers and the tax man who comes ta git the money they don' have an' takes their homes and crops instead."

"I want you to go there and blend in. Here: take some coins with you." He fished his fingers inside a sack hanging from his belt. "Make friends. Stay informed about what's going on in town, and especially keep track of Ogden. And try to find out where Harry Bigworth has gone off to. But don't go into Irongate yourself. Pay someone to be your eyes and ears while I go home, gather some things and get help.

"Aye. I'll do it. You gonna bring men ta fight?"

Drowden shook his head no. "I don't think that's wise. But the long walk home will help me clear my thoughts. I might change my mind. Go on now. I'll be back as soon as I can. We'll meet by the bridge in three days, at first light."

Chapter XXI
The Sovereignty of the Heart

Rain came down like an unfurling tapestry. Under the canopy of a wide-stretched emerald hemlock, Drowden Erebus stood. His hair hung in dark strands around his face. Drops drooped at the ends of them and trickled in rivulets around his eyes and nose and mouth. His gaze was full of worry. Something in his gut tightened and made him twist forward with sudden aching.

"By all that's right, none of this should be happening," he yelled at the drenched forest. "I just want to get home and see my Dorina. I just want to understand what I've done. Oh, Ogden! You aren't a monster. I could not have been so wrong about you. But those men — pillars of society, fathers, and husbands like me — how are they able to do what they do? And I delivered you to them."

He had not slept all night, and now he stood among the oldest of trees in the inhabited regions. Cliffs from which some of the biggest of the stone monuments once calved rose back from the road. Concealed in the tree boughs, they defined the shape of the woodland's horizons. It was at the base of these cliffs that Drowden took shelter for the night on his trek toward Hapstead Manor.

Two hours earlier he had been startled by the sound of thunder and a jarring blast of lightning that toppled a white oak tree at the pinnacle of the overhanging cliff that sheltered him. The burst of power from the sky hurtled the tree's flaming trunk down from the precipice above him to just yards from where he slept.

He got no rest after that. Moving as fast as he could through the forest, he took intermittent shelter. Under the outstretched arms of centuries-old trees he found cover, just as numberless others had done over the ages: the spirits of the forest, the creatures of the land and air, the trolls and all their kin, and once, for a heartbeat, the ancestors of common people, the ones who lived here and raised families but were driven out by those who now claimed the land as theirs.

This stand of forest had so far escaped their axes, their fires, their fenced enclosures and their covetous disregard for all things living. Taking advantage of the ancient forest canopy, Drowden waited for a lessening of the deluge, and the sky seemed to brighten ever so slightly. The smell of rich ferns, loamy soil, pine sap and rain-cleansed air filled his senses.

Now daylight teased the clouds. Giant tumbling thunder heads brooded above the forest, still releasing cascades of rain. But off on a distant horizon the sun snuck under the blanket of clouds and shot its rays of light crossways through the rain, hugging the undersides of the clouds and painting a rainbow spectrum of bright colors across the cloud ceiling. Drowden had never seen anything like it. He stared up as he hunched his body down under the cover of another wide-spreading hemlock. He was soaked by another mad dash through the downpour, and he shivered in the cool morning air. The storm seemed determined not to dissipate without wringing the last drop from the fast-rolling clouds. But the sky-spanning palate of cloud-cleaving colors made him catch his breath in awe.

He could see the western road from where he crouched but he stood for a better view. He meant to resume his foot travel on the woodland highway as soon as the rain subsided, even but a little. Anxious as he was to be on his way, the prospect of trudging headlong into a cool wind-blown torrent dampened his resolve. He looked to the sunrise and hoped for a fast-clearing sky. He spoke aloud again, with worry and anger in his voice.

"This whole fiasco must be a scheme of the Secret Brotherhood. It's true I don't know everything about trolls. But I know more than those small-minded men. Sure, it's possible some of the brutish habits they attribute to trolls are true. Possible, yes. But I know Ogden. It isn't possible he's done what they say he's done. But…is it possible I am wrong?"

Drowden's mind wandered off until all thought seemed to vanish and he was left with the sound of the rain and the smell of the leaves, now enhanced by the dampness so that the air seemed to carry the scent of a strong herbal tea to his nose. All his senses heightened in this thoughtless reverie — to the point where he could feel the ground beneath his feet moving ever so slightly.

He felt the soil tremble and half consciously thought the constant pounding of a heavy downpour was its cause. But it was something other than that. The loam was quivering with energy. He could feel a buzzing inside him now, rising through the soles of his feet, through his legs and into his chest, like static electricity, only more physical, more energetic. As he stood absorbing these sensations, he noticed in his peripheral vision that certain old trees appeared to shiver as the ground trembled all around him. Accompanying that subtle quaking wobbliness in the forest came a buzzing in the air like high-pitched invisible bees that were everywhere, but nowhere. Undisturbed, in fact mesmerized by all these impressions, Drowden felt his head open like a flower blossoming in the summer sun. His every sense became aroused, and the weariness of a sleepless night morphed into a kind of unaccustomed receptiveness to the world of subtle conversations between trees and soil, sky and forest, fungus and root that went unnoticed on every other day of his life.

As his tired eyes scanned the ground just outside the umbrella of the big hemlock, he noticed deep pocking splashes in the forest matting of moss. He stared without thought a while longer, and the high splashing divots in the puddling water continued to fascinate him. There was something odd in how they appeared one following another, not randomly, but in an offset line that progressed across the soaked tufts of moss like the footsteps of some invisible little creature. They suddenly appeared and then just as suddenly erased themselves from the smooth wet surface.

The wind picked up unexpectedly and in the wet leaves he heard a coherent sound like a whispered child's voice. It startled him and made the hair on the back of his neck prickle with fright. It seemed to say,

"Could be wrong."

in a singsong mocking tone. His eyes widened. He stood very still and looked around moving only his eyes.

There! Those same tell-tale splashing footsteps in the moss sped through the underbrush just beyond the tips of the hemlock boughs. He saw the lacey tops of wild carrot bob and bow as if brushed by something passing by. The wind blew again, and he felt a shower of cold rain descend on his head and shoulders. But before he could do more than lift his shoulders against the chill, he heard the voice again. It said,

We know what you are.

Drowden shuddered and stammered out a question. "Who are you? Who is 'We'?"

The rain seemed to laugh with the wind. It blew sideways and then a whirl of raindrops, like leaves caught in a spinning gust, stood in front of him, small but turning fast. Again, that child-like voice came out of the little funnel of spiraling wind and rain, and it said,

We see what you don't.

We are what you're not.

The world is a whirl of change.

Your words are stones.

But they cannot hold down the blowing minutes,

The wind of time.

Your mouth defines the dream of the world

Into a nightmare landscape for you to live in.

You cast spells and then accuse

All who would free you from them of sorcery.

Unlike this vision that we share,

This glimpse under the veil that blinds men's eyes,

When We look at you

We know that all you seem to see as real

Is gossamer blown on the breath of your words.

It cannot be;

It will not last;

It has no truth.

Still, it is all you have

And all that will remain

When We are utterly gone from your awareness.

The spout of wind-blown rain collapsed and fled like ordinary rain on a gust. "Wait!" cried Drowden. "Who is 'We'? What do you mean?" He paused for a response.

"What's just happened here?" He waited again. Then he bellowed: "I don't understand!"

But there was no answer. And soon the rain dissipated, and the wind grew calm. Drowden stepped out from under the hemlock, dizzy with fatigue and disoriented. Vertigo took the whole forest and spun it around in his eyes. The great trees, the green moss, and the gray and blue sky circled and gyrated into a blur of color. He stumbled this way and that and then the world tilted and rolled out of his vision and all the colors turned to shadow.

A blue tick hound nudged Drowden's arm with its nose. Clyde was soon joined by Old Duke. Both dogs circled Drowden's crumpled body and poked him with their snouts until a man's voice shouted out. "Clyde! Duke! What've ya got there?" It was Willbee calling from the seat of a weathered hay wagon drawn by the mare Tripply. "Woah-ho!" he shouted again and jumped down from the wagon onto the muddy road.

He ran to where Drowden lay in a gully near a fast-moving brook just off the road's north side. The dogs panted at Willbee's elbows as he stooped next to him. He was just opening his eyes and Willbee was relieved to see half a smile cross his face. "How did I get here?" Drowden said with a groan as he pushed his tall frame to a sitting position and brushed wet leaves and clods of dirt from his arms, knees and shoulders.

"Darndest thing ever," said Willbee. "Chances are I'd've never seen ya 'cept fer Old Duke and Clyde here. Ya alright, Master Erebus?"

Drowden borrowed Willbee's shoulder to push himself to his feet. "Yes. Yes, I seem to be all in one piece. What a long walk I've had from Irongate."

Suddenly memory of what had happened in town flooded back to his mind and he grabbed Willbee's collar a little gruffly. "Listen. We must get back to Hapstead right away. No delays."

Willbee looked him square in the eye. "Sure, an' I will take ya there right fast, sir. Climb up in th' wagon. I'll drive." He supported Drowden to the wagon and gave him a hand up onto its bed. "Hear that, Tripply? We've got ta step fast." He turned back toward Drowden once he was up on the bench. "It'll be fine. Only a couple o' miles an' we'll be there."

Drowden smiled and waved him on. He stayed silent as the wagon rolled noisily through sloshing puddles of water. Clyde and Duke lay panting at his feet, glad for their master's company and content not to be traipsing alongside the wagon down the rain-soaked clay road. The wheels tossed up a torrent of mud; specks of it flecked Drowden's body and the dogs as well, but he paid no attention. The strange night and morning in the forest and the impossible happenings in Irongate consumed his thoughts.

When they rode through the open gate on the road down below the Manor House, Drowden tapped Willbee on the shoulder and pointed. Willbee nodded and turned Tripply directly for the house.

Miranda had spotted the wagon and thought she saw her father riding in its bed, so she ran as quickly as she could from the summer kitchen to greet him. Ian ran out of the house ahead of Dorina and he tried mightily to hoist himself up onto the back of the wagon but succeeded only when Drowden put a hand under his arm and lifted him up. He quickly jumped down with Ian in one arm and the other extended to grasp Dorina's waist.

"You're home early!" She smiled and kissed his smudged face. "And you're a mess! Where's Argis? And Harry? Where's Ogden? Are they bringing the…"

"Shhhh…. shhhh… shhhh." Drowden placed a finger over her lips and kissed her cheek. "I came back alone. I'll explain…"

"Father, where *is* Ogden? Didn't he come back with you?" Miranda was out of breath as she halted her trot and spoke. He touched her chin with a finger and smiled sadly.

"Let's go inside. I have a lot to tell you. And I have important things I must do. There's precious little time."

"Nonsense," said Dorina. "You need to wash up and get comfortable. We can talk later. You look dreadful!"

Drowden kissed her forehead and led her toward the house. "We must talk now," he said. She looked up at him with sudden worry crossing her face. She almost spoke but caught herself. He set Ian down on his feet and the three walked inside and closed the door behind them.

An hour later, the atmosphere in the parlor seemed ripe for a funeral. Bright sunlight poured in through the sheer curtains, but clouds of woe shaded every face.

"It's not true! It's not true!!" Miranda cried. She leaned forward in her chair and held her face in her hands. "Ogden would never hurt anyone. They're lying. We have to free him, Father."

Dorina sat silently on a couch next to Drowden, her lips tight and quivering. She stared at a distant horizon that only her mind could see. Ian sat next to Drowden on the other side, squeezed between him and the high arm of the ornate settee. He clutched his father's hand and whispered, "Daddy, Ogden didn't do it. He'd never do it."

Drowden squeezed back. "I can't do this without support from all of you. My own doubts have filled my heart with so much worry. So many men told stories that I can't challenge. I don't have any proof of Ogden's innocence. He wasn't with me. I didn't see where he went, or what he did. And I don't know where Harry is. He's the last one of us to see him, and he's missing."

There was an uncomfortable silence. At last, Drowden said, "I want to talk with Bobbin. Maybe he knows where his brother Harry is. It's possible he said something about visiting a friend. Maybe he had some other business in Irongate."

Miranda stood up suddenly. "Father! Bobbin's been gone since just after you left for Irongate. Everyone thought it was quite odd. He took his pack, his clothes, and I don't know what all. But he's gone."

Dorina sighed deeply. "I need to be alone, to think, to try to understand. Excuse me." She stood up and brushed past Miranda, heading for the stairs.

As Dorina left the room, Miranda blurted, "Those Bigworth boys can't be trusted, Father. Talk to Odelia. She'll tell you what stinkers they are."

Ian laughed quietly. "Stinkers," he said, and laughed again.

Drowden stood and pulled Ian up onto his feet. "Alright, children, off to your study and chores. I have some studying to do too. I'll be in my library and don't want to be disturbed. Understood?"

"Yes Father," Miranda nodded. She took Ian's hand and Drowden watched them leave by the hallway entrance. He bound up the steps and turned to his library and study. He went directly to the tomes dealing with the more arcane aspects of troll lore. His eyes passed over volumes on the shelves dealing with what was known about troll habits, their diet, their crude homes and dress. His fingers rested at the top of the spine of a book with the title *The Suspicions of Trolls* by Milbrand Pithelwick, the Elder.

Given his current state of mind, it seemed an appropriate place to start. He wanted to alleviate his own suspicions, and discover if, by chance, he had been wrong to think he could teach, let alone trust, a troll to be civilized. He pulled the leather-bound text from a tight squeeze between other books and flapped the cover open on the claw-footed table next to a carved oaken chair. He settled into the chair without looking up and scanned the table of contents, running a finger ahead of his gaze.

"It's all about troll superstitions!" he said with exasperation. "It's not about suspicions; it's about superstitions!"

But as he turned the pages and read what the learned scholar of troll knowledge had written, he began to understand. These were not so much "superstitions" as they were suspicions about how the world is put together, and how trolls fit into the grand scheme. Some of it seemed to be from the troll's perspective. His eyes widened.

Pulling the table closer to the chair, he rested the book there and laid his journal open next to it. He uncapped the ink and dabbed a quill into it and began to take notes as he read.

To the average reader, Drowden mused, much of what Pithelwick had to say would seem like madness, or fantasy. No one living had seen a troll, until Ogden came into their lives. All the old books were presumed to be fanciful elaborations built on sheer imagination. Because such stories were taken for simple entertainment, Drowden's fascination with trolls was long thought to be a mere hobby, and an odd one at that, until Ogden came to Hapstead. Now he had to figure out which of his many books was based on fact, and which on hearsay and bias.

He went on reading Pithelwick with his nose close to the page:

"Trolls, let us understand, are not rude animals. They are in fact people. And whether we accept them as our neighbors or do our worst to see that they never dwell in our environs, simple truths cannot be controverted by avoiding them."

Drowden tapped the page with his forefinger. "Exactly," he said out loud, and continued reading.

"Trolls do not appoint their men as leaders of a clan. They have developed a different wisdom that sees the begetters of life as the center of their communities. In different times, when trolls and men lived in proximity to each other, and some with true curiosity sought to understand the other, we have reports in dusty books in which the most extraordinary observations were recorded. Trolls speak to the dead; they see clearly in pitch darkness; trolls say little but seem to know everything about the natural world. In fact, it is exceedingly difficult to declare in what realm

of knowledge and understanding trolls are not the superior of ordinary men. Except, as it turns out, in the art of lying. Trolls do not know how to lie, and so they never do."

Drowden paused and looked up from the book. "Is that true? Or is Pithelwick engaging in the art of lying himself?"

If true, he thought he must believe Ogden and disbelieve his accusers. But for that to be, he must also believe Pithelwick to be telling the truth, and a dozen men of Irongate to be liars.

He sighed and rubbed his eyes. "I don't know any more now than I did before reading the adept scholars," he moaned. But he read further, to a passage he had read before without much understanding. Now it jogged his mind into unexpected reverie.

"Because trolls understand that deception is the most refined use of words, they distrust them enormously. They speak infrequently, and when they do it is their position that every word is an oath and a promise of veracity. A troll is the embodiment of skepticism when it comes to the words of ordinary men."

He stared without focusing his eyes, his vision impervious to the bookshelves and stacks of books surrounding him. In his mind he re-heard the yammering claims of Ogden's accusers. Listening to those recalled voices, he knew them to be full of lies and that those lies were part of a conspiracy intended to deceive. Then it occurred to him with sudden alarm that Ogden made no attempt to defend himself; that he seemed not to be concerned but looked to him to explain the odd behavior of the men of Irongate. His heart sank at the summoning of that memory.

And then just as suddenly the voice in the forest that materialized out of the vortex of wind and rain came back to him with stinging immediacy. He heard its strange youthful sing-song words. It was as if he'd returned to that moment in the rain-drenched forest, and the sound from the standing funnel of wind and rain was as vivid as if it had followed him into his home.

We see what you don't.

We are what you're not.

The world is a whirl of change.

Your words are stones.

But they cannot hold down the blowing minutes,

The wind of time.

Your mouth defines the dream of the world

Into a nightmare landscape for you to live in.

You cast spells and then accuse

All who would free you from them of sorcery.

When We look at you, we know

That all you seem to see as real

Is gossamer blown on the breath of your words.

It cannot be;

it will not last;

it has no truth.

Still, it is all you have

And all that will remain

When We are gone.

"What is it about human words?" Drowden asked himself under his breath. "We cast spells? We deceive? Is that all we do? Are all the books and all the songs and all the conversations just elaborate conjurations that keep us living in a world of word-spun delusions?" He shook his head. "How can I make sense of this?" he mused.

He turned to other volumes, looking for accounts of trolls displaying violence toward women. But in every text that he trusted, the consensus was that trolls revere women of their own kind and presumably women in general. Still, there were worrisome tales in the more sensational books — just salacious hearsay — about male trolls molesting human women. Landry Felphs was one of those authors. This is what Drowden found in his book titled *Fury in the Forest*, one of the few obviously biased volumes on trolls that he had purchased:

"Trogs go berserk in the presence of women. None was ever known to be able to control its lust."

Not much to go on considering the author was a known "Troll Gutter," as the once militant but presumably defunct organization was named. He was less than credible. Even his use of the disdainful term "trog," a word never used in gentle company, tainted the reliability of anything he wrote.

With Felphs in mind, Drowden turned to one of Troutner's books. He flipped the pages to one of the later chapters, a chapter on the Troll Gutters. The author had nothing good to say about them.

"They accuse trolls of many barbarities of which they, it must be said, are the guilty ones. They have been known to use trolls for sport and have taken troll concubines for their slaves. They have even fathered children with these sad creatures and made more sadness for the world than ever a troll has brought."

Drowden scribbled furiously in his notebook as he read. He meant to make a case. He meant to argue for Ogden if he had to. But he wasn't sure who he was trying to convince — himself or everyone else. If it was the men of Irongate, he knew that his research was a waste of time. And so he concluded it was for his own peace of mind that he searched for proof of Ogden's innocence amidst the pages and pages of ink that his eyes and mind transformed into the voices of those many now dead authors.

He turned to other books, hoping that something he'd overlooked would finally settle his thoughts.

Cleaton Elbridge's tome called *We Troggles* was the most difficult to read. Drowden found Elbridge's erudition on troll thinking and language to be all but impenetrable. But he did learn from him that trolls call themselves collectively "Troggles," the probable origin of the human expletive "Trog." Curiously, Elbridge claimed that trolls never refer to themselves the way humans do — as "I" or "me."

When a troll speaks of itself, the referent is not the individual but the clan, the 'we.' No troll sees itself as separate from its family, its clan, or even apart from all of nature. A troll sometimes refers to its own name, but only to speak of part of the group, not to invoke an identity separate from the group.

Drowden paused at this and tried to remember any time when Ogden used the word "I" or "me." He poked at the page with his forefinger, his nose only inches from the print. "It's true," he muttered. "I've never heard him refer to himself as himself. Only in relation to what was happening around him."

He closed his eyes and rubbed his temples. "How can I argue for Ogden's sake if Ogden won't stand for himself? If he doesn't see himself ...?" he asked the empty room. But it was not empty. Dorina stepped up behind him and placed a hand gently on his shoulder.

"We know he is innocent," she said, startling Drowden from his reverie. "There isn't any way to prove it with evidence and arguments. There won't be any answers in your books, my love. What we know in our hearts is all that matters. And none of the lies matter."

Drowden turned to look over his shoulder. He smiled and placed a hand on hers. "They matter only insofar as they might lift the arms and voices of others against him. The words of those liars are like a curse — they threaten Ogden with a death sentence."

Dorina brushed her hand though his thick black hair. "I think they are afraid of him. I don't know why. So much fear makes liars of cowards, and maybe heroes of the courageous. As for you and me, we aren't open to their fabrications. Neither of us believes that Ogden killed that women or did any of the horrible things they say he did." She paused a moment, and then said: "We can't let those men hurt Ogden. How can they be so heartless? If women ruled the world, things would be very different."

Drowden stood up and faced her. He took her hands in his and held them behind his back. He leaned his chest against hers and kissed her gently. "Something astonishing happened to me in the forest as I made my way back home to you. I don't know how to talk about it. I can't seem to contain it in words, other than to say that it opened me. It spoke to my heart, not my mind. And for all my trying to find answers in my many books, none could tell me what my head has a hard time understanding, but my heart knows to be absolutely true."

Dorina looked at him quizzically. She scanned his eyes but said nothing.

"I've come to a decision," he said, "if you will support me in it. But I have a very big favor to ask of you."

She pulled her head back. "What do you want me to do?"

"Your grandmother's jewels: I need to take them, to pay a bribe to free Ogden." He looked down, ashamed.

Dorina gasped lightly. But then she shook her head yes. "Of course. I'll get them from the locker and bring them to you. What else?"

Drowden smiled with love. "Let me go back to Irongate to do whatever I can to free him. There can't be any delay. I'll take some of the men in case…"

She looked at him with tears trembling in her eyes. "Husband, do whatever you must. So long as you save our Ogden. But you must come home safely."

He pulled her close and held her tight. He whispered in her ear, "You are right to say that the world would be better if women ruled."

She whispered back, "Unlike so many men, we understand that it is love that must govern. But I think you are an exception to the rule, sweet man."

Drowden pulled away and looked at her face. He gave a bittersweet smile. "My books were no help, but I am so used to seeking their counsel. I kept hoping to find answers there that would provoke me to do the right thing. But I should have turned to you first, the sovereign of my heart."

Dorina returned his smile. "You did come to me first, but we are creatures of habit. Knowing you to be the man you are, it is no surprise to me that we came to the same conclusion: that the heart and not the head must be our sovereign."

He held her tightly and smiled broadly over her shoulder. "Then, let me pledge loyalty to the sovereignty of the heart."

The rest of the day was filled with preparations for a return to Irongate. Drowden called all his workers together to let them know what accusations had been made against Ogden and to ask if any of them had second thoughts about staying on at Hapstead Manor. To the last of them, they expressed shock and anger at Ogden's treatment and vowed to support whatever he decided to do.

That night the family quietly shared memories of Ogden's rapid growth and occasional clumsiness. They made a list of all his extraordinary qualities. Miranda told about his stories of listening to the singing of the stars, and how he described the interplay of their overlapping spectrum of energies as not only influencing our lives and everything in the world, but that the web of those converging forces is actually what we are made of. By then Ian was breathing deeply in a dream. Dorina and Drowden listened quietly, keeping their own thoughts to themselves. They retired for the night, full of the warmth of family love and heightened determination to rescue the one who had been taken from them.

The next morning was bright and warm for early October. The sun sent shadows of men, wagons, dogs and horses across the lane. Drowden had rounded up Hector, Bill Macatee, Willbee, Fred and Tom. They loaded the wagons with their own gear, and slid scythes, pitchforks, pikes and machetes under a tarp in one of the wagons.

The dogs, Clyde, and Jocko, Barkiller, and Grisswold, and even Old Duke circled round the wagons, tails wagging and tongues salivating. They sensed some adventure was in the works.

Piscote, the old farm hand, sauntered to Drowden's side with hands in his pockets and head down. He looked up to peer into Drowden's eyes, and boldly put a hand on his shoulder. "Ya knows, sir, I would no' have ya parting for this task without me. I'll ask ya agin. Will ya let me come along wi' ya?"

Drowden patted his arm and shook his head. "No, old friend. I don't know what we might have to do, and I wouldn't sleep another night if something were to happen to you."

"Oh?" said Piscote. "Then I suppose you'll sleep just fine if somethin' were ta happen ta Tom? An' he's near my age! Dang it all, yer even takin' ol' Duke wi' ya. That dog is my granddaddy's age!"

Drowden smiled. "He's still a good tracker. As for Tom? Shh...don't tell him, but he's not much good around here, and I need you to keep up with the hay field. Will you do that for me until I get back?"

Piscote waved his palm in front of Drowden's face and spat over his shoulder. "Ah, be gone wi' ya then. I'll tend yer fields. Might even eat yer vittles while yer out adventurin' since ya won't be missin' 'em anyway."

He trudged off muttering to himself and Drowden climbed up on the lead wagon. He tucked a bag containing clean clothes, his journal, and a charcoal pencil behind the seat and called out, "Let's go men!"

There was a flurry of action and soon the wagons were loaded with the riders and drivers. But before Drowden could loosen the brake on his buckboard, Miranda came breathlessly running to his side.

"Father, wait!" He turned and jumped down from the bench.

"What is it, Miranda?"

She stood in front of him and reached behind her neck to unfasten the clasp of a silver chained necklace with a carved bear tooth pendant in the shape of a broad oak tree. It hung from her hand as she extended her arm toward him.

"Please, give this to Ogden. No matter what happens, tell him I send it with my love."

Drowden frowned. "Your love, is it?"

"Oh Father!" she blurted. "You know what I mean. He is loved. I know you love him. And so does Mother, even if she would never say so."

"Oh, but I do," said Dorina as she approached the wagons with Ian in hand. "So does Ian." She nodded toward the necklace, still hanging from Miranda's hand, and let her eyes speak privately to Drowden. "It's alright. I think it is a kind gesture."

Drowden nodded back almost imperceptibly, took the necklace from Miranda's hand with a quick smile and deposited it in his vest pocket. "There. I'll see that Ogden gets both the gift and the sentiment that goes with it." Then he paused and sighed. "Now, we have got to be off. No more words." And he smiled at each of them, one after the other, turned on his heels and mounted his wagon. With a flick of his wrist, he slapped the reins down and coaxed the horse into motion.

Looking back as the other wagons began to roll, he yelled to his wife and children, "I am the most fortunate man in the world!"

Chapter XXII
Illusive Truths

The three wagons made good time throughout the day and paused for only a few hours to rest the horses, dogs and men at twilight before continuing in darkness on toward Irongate. The half-moon lit the road most of the night, so there was no need for lanterns until just before first sunlight. Laurel and sassafras huddled along the perimeter of the dark forest, watching the passage of the wagons silently, but for a little breeze that occasionally wagged their leaves like tell-tale tongues in the wee hours of the morning.

The dogs had tired of tracking alongside the little caravan and now slept soundly in the bed of the wagon driven by Hector. The men were quiet. They rocked to the rhythm of the road as it rolled out under the wheels and their minds sped off from the creaking of the wagons and the clacking of horse hooves into reveries full of apprehension and imagined bravery. Each envisioned the rescue of Ogden differently. None foresaw the truth of how events would unfold.

Miles meandered behind them. Night birds ruffled in the bushes. A badger gagged a gravelly growl and stopped just as it was about to come out of the understory onto the sandy road. They were getting close to Heatherbloom River. Drowden could smell its musty waters.

Dead silence hung like morning mist, but for the steady sound of horses and wagons, until a patch of bats blasted out of a forest grotto and swarmed past, just in front of Drowden's mare. It was that rush of bats that startled him out of his introspection, but the sudden appearance of a man with a broad axe slung over his shoulder and standing in the way of his passage is what made him grab the reins and pull back. He heard the men behind him "ho-ho" their horses to a halt. And he heard Hector yell out: "Master Erebus, look about!"

Drowden caught movement in his peripheral vision and glanced to the right. A phalanx of men and women armed with farm and woodworking tools emerged like shadows with lives of their own from the dark of the woods. And to the left, another cohort of armed commoners shed the blanket of forest darkness for the open road. He twisted his torso to look to the rear. Behind the third wagon that was driven by Willbee, a host of ten or more men and women closed in, some carrying improvised weapons, some seemingly unarmed.

When Drowden brought himself around to look forward, the lone man on the road in front of him jerked his chin toward him. He spoke in an even tone, without raising his voice. "Are you the troll-lovers?"

Drowden stroked his jaw and pondered how to answer. He figured the truth would cut through to the rest of the truth, so he said, "Yes. We are troll-lovers. And who are you?"

The man hefted the broadaxe off his shoulder and onto the palm of his right hand. He held the butt of it in his left. "I'm Doltun of Bladicville. And you're Drowden Erebus of Hapstead. Come to get Ogden, isn't that so?"

Drowden nodded his head 'yes.' "Do you mean to stop us?" he asked. And he stood up tall on the wagon and gestured behind him with a flap of his fingers onto his hand to Bill Macatee to flip the tarp on the wagon floor and hand him a weapon. He shouted out to him and the other wagons, "Men, get ready." And to Doltun of Bladicville he said, "We mean to cross Besom Bridge and enter Irongate. We won't be stopped."

Doltun smiled a toothy grin and spat. "Don't think you'll be goin' into Irongate. Nope. Not now if ever."

Bill handed Drowden a pitchfork and then he took up a scythe. Tom grabbed a pike and leaned on it to pull himself up from a squat in the back. Men in the other wagons were jumping down onto the road with bladed instruments in hand.

"Stay where ya are!" a familiar voice rang out. "These ruffians is friends." It was Argis. He trotted up from behind, laughing and slapping men on the shoulders as he passed them. "Willbee! Fred! Hector! Aye! Good men! Glad ta sees all of yas."

He came astride Drowden's wagon and looked up at him. "Ya arsked me ta befriend th' folk in Bladicville, an' wouldn't ya know it, they friended me first! These are good people! Right Doltun?"

Doltun strode over to Argis' side and draped an arm over his shoulder. He too looked up at Drowden and said, "You are welcome in our little shanty-town. Friends of trolls and foes of chain-makers are friends of ours. Take the rough road through the woods just up ahead on your right. It's a quarter mile before the bridge. We'll go on ahead. When you get there, we'll tend to your animals and hide the wagons."

He didn't wait for a reply but waved the broadaxe high over his head with one muscular arm. The phalanx from Bladicville disappeared into the shadows as quickly and silently as they had appeared. Argis stayed behind.

"Slide over," he said to Drowden. "I'll take th' reins an' steer us th' right ways."

So off they rode as the first spears of sunlight lanced through a cloud bank hugging the horizon.

Hector and Willbee took charge of settling the horses in a rough-hewn corral. Two men brought hay and water for them. The rest of the men were shown to a good-sized tent where blankets had been rolled out for them to rest. A homely woman came in with a basket of food, including bread, wild berries, starchy tubers and a delicious tea brewed from roots and bark.

In a nearby tent, Drowden and Argis sat on straw-stuffed cushions beside a pit fire, talking quietly. Argis took some time to tell Drowden all that had happened while he was away at Hapstead.

"It's bad business we're up agin. Treachery an' betrayal. I dunno if I should believe him or no, bu' that Kreg Jutribackle fella came by th' other day an' told me some bothersome news."

Drowden squeezed his shoulder. "What has he to say? Will he still take a bribe to free Ogden?"

"Oh, aye. There's no doubt he'll take what ya brought, but I'm deviled with mistrust of 'im."

"So what did he tell you?" Drowden insisted.

"First," Argis waved an index finger, "he says he's a part o' the Brotherhood. But he tells me it's no' some club fer bored men to play at moonlight shenanigans. No. He tells me it's been the Brotherhood o' Troll Gutters all along. An' they mean ta kill every las' one o' Ogden's kind an' Ogden inta th' mix."

Drowden pondered on that a moment. "I had some suspicions. But if Jutribackle is part of that crowd, why would he help us?"

"Aye. Why indeed? Tha's why I don' trust 'im." Argis shrugged and held his hands up as he spoke. "But he tol' me even more. Now get this! He says Harry is wid th' Brotherhood. Saw him there just night before last and guess who was wif him?"

"Bobbin," Drowden answered quickly.

Argis cackled. "Ya knew because he weren't at Hapstead, right?"

"You've got it." Drowden smiled a little. "So, the Bigworth boys have shown their colors. I never thought them capable of this kind of treachery."

"Yuv got no idea how bad. Turns out Harry is in th' thick of th' plot ta take Ogden in chains. These are violent men able ta do horrible things wid out a blush," he said, but fell suddenly silent as the tent's flap flew open and Doltun poked his head inside.

"Will you two come with me?" he said.

Without a word Argis and Drowden stood off their haunches and followed Doltun down a winding path around the lean-tos and little huts, then across a wide common area where a fire that had blazed high throughout the night now languished in the sunlight on a bed of white-hot glowing coals. He led them to the larger of the shacks facing the fire ring and pushed the rickety door open. He entered first and waved them in before closing the door behind them.

Inside was a long table with benches on either side. Candles lit the interior. The windows were heavily shaded. He indicated they should sit at the table, and then went to a corner where a long curtain hung, cordoning off what passed for a private room in this room of limited space. He pulled the curtain back and out stepped a woman neither of them had seen before. She was short, big-bodied, and dressed in ragged clothes that had once been rather fine.

"This is Petula," said Doltun. "She's going to strip away some lies for you." Turning to Petula he said, "Come on and sit. Don't worry. I'll stay right here."

She smiled and patted his chest as she moved into the room. "Thanks, Doltun honey. I'm fine. You don't has to protect me from these gentlemen." She walked with short steps and sat down on the bench right next to Drowden, in fact, very close to him. She put her hand on the back of his hand where it rested on the table, and she looked him in the eye, her nose two inches from his. He could smell the wild garlic on her breath and the musky scent of her body. Drowden smiled softly at her.

"So, you have some truth that you want to share with me?" he said gently. Despite his impatience to hear news of Ogden, he felt a gentle wave of calm flow through him when she placed her hand on his.

"More like what Doltun said," she smiled back. "I've got some lies to expose. For one thing, your own man, that Harry fella, is untrue to you. Harry is hiding, with help from the ring leaders. And he's been telling every blabbermouth in the Brotherhood how he helped snare a troll, how he betrayed you and caught up your Ogden in a spell of lies upon lies. No, Ogden never touched poor Millie. He never harmed her even a little. It was all the doin' of the Brotherhood."

Drowden nodded. "I know that. He wouldn't. So, who would hurt her so cruelly and then murder her?"

Petula shook her head sadly. "I'm going to tell you what I know. Those Brotherhood knuckle draggers came here a week ago and baited Millie away from our little pit of poverty with promises of good food and maybe a man to see after her. They knew what they was doing. They got Harry to bring Ogden and Millie together in a public place. They played a trick on Ogden — Harry and that despicable Tucker Scont. And the rest o' those Brotherhood bastards at the Bull and Beaver that day were in on it."

Drowden placed his free hand on hers. "Do you mean the whole thing was plotted in advance? But how? Doesn't that mean that one of them killed Millie?"

Petula grinned. Her teeth were dark and irregular. "You're a smart one. Sure, that's what it means. It was the Brotherhood who killed Millie. And they did it all to trap Ogden in a lie that they conjured up. And everybody fell for it. What do they care — she's just a Trog wench to them. They had it in their minds to rape and murder her all along. An' that's what they did. Behind it all is Ospin Tapple, that lying pissant of a troll-gutter. Him and his Brotherhood of boot-licking followers."

There was a brief silence. Argis cleared his throat after choking back a shout of anger. "It's monstrous..." he finally muttered.

"But how do you know all of this?" asked Drowden. "I need to understand."

Petula stood up and walked to the middle of the room. She turned quickly toward them and her loose dress spun to catch up with her twisting turn. "Look at me," she said. "Not much by most men's reckoning. But when those heartless men across the water," and she pointed in the direction of the river, "when they get lonely 'cause their wives are sick o' their shallowness, they come lookin' for me and my ladies here in Bladicville. An' I know what they want. An' I give it to 'em. An' they talk to me about all sorts of things you'd be surprised to know. Why? Because they think I'm stupid, just a Trog wench with nothing going on behind these eyes. An' I let 'em think that."

Drowden looked up without raising his head, across his eyebrows, at Argis. He said "Very clever. But I am sorry you give so much just for information."

Doltun stepped forward and squatted down so he was at eye level with Drowden. He put a hand on his shoulder and Drowden turned his head to look at him directly. "Master Erebus, this woman, Petula, is my wife. Believe me, we know what price we pay just to stay ahead of what's barreling down on us because of those selfish, feckless people."

Drowden caught his breath. Argis groaned almost inaudibly.

"Now tell the rest, my pet," Doltun said, squeezing Petula's leg.

She nodded and batted Drowden's chin gently with the side of her index finger. "I know you be-live that Ogden is innocent, whether or no you believe all I said about the Brotherhood's cutthroat ways. It's a good sign of your character. But I can swear that he wasn't even in Irongate when poor Millie was violated and murdered. I know, because I met him on Besom Bridge leaving town just before they closed and locked the gates. Oh, aye. I offered him my company figuring I might learn something new from the troll."

"But," Drowden stammered. "Ogden?"

"Ha-ha!" Petula cackled. "It's not like that! He didn't even know what I was offerin', and he went on his way, up the river, to muse all night on the banks of the Heatherbloom. I know. We watched him. Ain't much escapes our attention, Master Erebus. He didn't go back 'cross the bridge until after daylight when they opened up the town again. Take our word as truth, not trickery."

"Yes, I do," Drowden said quietly. "And now it occurs to me that your testimony might go far in proving Ogden's innocence."

"Ha-ha!!" Petula blurted out a mocking laugh. "Them take the word of a Trog? Never."

"Them's idiots." Argis pounded the table with his fist. "Yer as fair and honest as they come. Why wouldna they believe you?"

"I thank you, sir," said Doltun to Argis. "No finer woman do I know. But around these people, where Trogs are loathed, they wouldn't know a diamond from a pebble in their shoe."

Drowden looked at Doltun sharply. "Why do you call your own wife such a name? I am sure she is a fine woman, and yet you've called her by that accursed name — a 'Trog' — more than once. Why is that?"

Petula answered for him. "It's because that's what I am, like many among us poor and rejected folk. I am part common man, part Troggle, or 'troll' as you might put it. That's why the Brotherhood hates us. That's why they could treat Millie like she was nothing to them. Because she was."

"What? Part troll? Is that it? That's what they mean when they slander with 'Trog?' But…how is it I don't know anything about this?" Drowden stammered for more words but couldn't put them together in a sentence. He blabbered a bit but wasn't making any sense.

Petula patted his shoulder. "You're a good man, Drowden Erebus, but not one who knows the world too well outside of your books and what others may tell you."

Drowden hung his head for a silent moment, then at last he spoke. "So framing Ogden for a hideous crime that they committed serves only one purpose — to justify their hatred of trolls and the children of trolls. It's to give their hatred a sheen of fairness. Is that what you're telling me?"

"Worse," said Doltun. "There are some who are so shamed by the troll blood in their veins they'd kill every troll, and then every Trog who reminds them too much of what they never want to admit is the truth. As if killing could silence the past — the enslavement of trolls and the lechery of men: it can't. So, they invent lies upon lies to keep everyone hating the Trogs, hating us poor commoners. It lets them sleep at night though they've plundered our lives and taken what we work for. It gives them what they call 'meaning,' and it steals away their own hearts and twists their souls."

Drowden stood up and put his hands on Petula's shoulders. He gave them a light squeeze, and then offered his hand to Doltun. "I've got a lot to think about," he said. "I hope you'll pardon me if I go now."

Doltun took his hand and looked him in the eye. "There's not a thing to think about, friend. None of it gets better by piling on another spell of words. Just feel it, act on it, know it for what it is in your heart. That's what sees us through."

Drowden squeezed his hand firmly and left. Argis did likewise and departed, saying to them both, "Blessings on yer home an' all who come ina it."

It was late afternoon and the sun made the air in the tent warm as a heavy blanket, though out in the encampment a slight chill blew through the maze of paths between the huts and tents. Drowden was sleeping when he was startled by a hard press to his right shoulder. Argis was stooped over him, so when he turned to open his eyes, he caught a strong scent of onions on his breath.

"What, Argis?" he mumbled.

"Got a visitor," said Argis. "Think we oughta talk to 'im."

Drowden got up to his feet as Argis pulled back the tent flap. A guard armed with a machete entered first, then Kreg Jutribackle, followed by another guard hefting an iron-headed sledgehammer on an arm's length pole. "He's unarmed," said the first guard.

"Thanks. No need for you to stay," said Drowden.

"Then we'll wait outside," the guard answered, and he and his companion ducked out the tent opening.

Jutribackle strode in and stood confidently looking Drowden in the eye. He hooked his thumbs on his belt and spoke. "I see you've made some new friends. Your man Argis has a sweet tongue when he puts his mind to it."

Argis growled in his throat. "Just hafta treat people like ya wanna get treated," he said to Kreg's back. Drowden held up a hand for him to remain silent. He eyeballed Jutribackle closely.

"You still willing to take payment to release Ogden?" he asked pointedly.

"Don't trust 'im, Drowden." Argis couldn't stop himself. "Remember he's one o' those Brotherhood cutthroats."

Jutribackle turned on his heels and shoved a finger at Argis. "You're right, Master Argis. I'm no lover of trolls. I'm one of those cutthroats you hear whispers about. And the last thing I'd want to do is fall out of favor with those other cutthroats in the Brotherhood. So the only way this is going to work is with enough treasure to change the odds."

"Aye, an' it's pitiful. Getting mixed up in this business ya could risk yer poor wife's life. We know they'd no' stop at killin' an innocent woman. What'll they do when they learn ya been double-dealin'?"

Kreg poked Argis in the shoulder with two stiff fingers. "Leave my Sully out of it. I'd never put her in any danger, I can promise you that."

"Argis, stand aside if you don't mind," said Drowden. "We have no choice but to trust this man. He's agreed to payment for his help. It's none of our business where he stands with the Brotherhood, and surely not with his wife, though I wish no harm to come to her."

"I thank you for that," said Jutribackle. "But you're right. It's my business and I'll decide what's best for me and mine."

"As will I," said Drowden. "And so, let's talk about what you will do to free Ogden, in exchange for something of value that belongs to one I hold dear. She gave it willingly for Ogden's liberty."

Kreg nodded slightly. "If you hand over the treasure, then you and Ogden will be reunited. So, do you have it?"

Drowden shook his head 'no.' "I need to know that he's alive and safe before I'll give you my wife's precious heirlooms."

"That's wise," said Argis with a little laugh. "Why should ya get nothin' for somethin'? Is he safe? Are ya sure ya can free 'im?"

Kreg sighed deeply and held onto a tent pole as he leaned toward Argis. "It's a bad idea for either of you to be seen in Irongate. I don't think you want to be reunited with Ogden on the Brotherhood's terms."

Drowden grabbed his arm and spun him back toward him. "No. We'll do it on my terms. That's final."

Kreg shoved his arm away and shouted, "Don't be an idiot! You can't just stroll into the Panopticon and take him."

Drowden fumed at that. His eyes were wide, and his nostrils flared. He bellowed. "What? He's not at the jail? What's he doing at the Panopticon? That place is a circus arena, a place for public spectacles and low entertainment."

Kreg shook his head gravely. "That's right. And that's where he is. There's nothing in this town someone won't try to get rich off of. They're charging people thirty copper coins to go in and see a live troll. They have him parading almost naked, like the wild creature they think he is. Believe me; you don't want to go there. If you want him freed, you're going to have to trust me."

"I'm going to Irongate with or without you, and that's the end of it," yelled Drowden.

Kreg yelled back. "You've got to stay away from that place, or you'll interfere with my plan."

Drowden screamed inarticulately. He seethed in anger and grabbed Kreg by the collar. They struggled, with Kreg grasping Drowden by the neck and Drowden elbowing Kreg solidly in the ear, causing his head to rock hard to the side. Argis clutched Kreg from behind, wrapping his strong arm around his neck and grasping his wrist with the other hand, then pulling tight. He heard Kreg Jutribackle choke for air, but suddenly Argis was up off his toes and flying across the tent's interior. He hit the ground with a thud and rolled over, trying to get up, but the wind had been knocked out of him. He saw Drowden and Kreg dive at each other, both howling in rage.

The guards came running. The men of Hapstead came blasting out of their tent, led by Willbee and Hector. The dogs barreled out with them, darting between their legs and almost tripping up the men as they ran. They heard more shouting and cursing — and then Argis stuck his bleeding head out of the tent, yelling "Stay back! We've got this in hand. Jus' keep clear!" Then he disappeared inside the tent again.

The ruckus inside was just shouting and cursing now, but no brawling or flying bodies. Soon even the loud voices died down and the growing crowd outside could hear whispering and muttering and hissing. A few more loud shouts, what sounded like a hard slap to a face or a back, and Kreg Jutribackle bolted out in a big hurry. He ran, shoving people aside, and leapt onto the back of his horse, then rode off hard in the direction of the Heatherbloom River and back over Besom Bridge.

Hector and Willbee ran into the tent and emerged a minute later, with Argis and Drowden behind them. Bill and Tom ran up to see if they were alright. Doltun was next to come to their sides. "We'll round up some men and bring him back," he said, but Drowden waved him of.

"Let him go. We've finished our business with him. Lies and deception: that's the law in Irongate."

"What happened?" Hector asked.

"He took the jewels I brought for a bribe, and we have nothing to show for it but a lot of talk."

"Then we've got to go after him!" growled Bill Macatee.

"Don't bother," said Drowden in a throaty, phlegm-filled voice. "I promised him we're going to free Ogden." Then he spit a mouthful of blood into a patch of grass. He looked toward the sky and in a loud voice he proclaimed to the men and women who surrounded him, "Tomorrow, we're going to take what I paid for. We're going to free Ogden!"

The crowd had grown to more than twenty souls, and they all cheered in unison. Then Willbee started to yell "Ogden! Ogden! Ogden!" and the chant was taken up by the crowd.

Argis turned to Drowden and spoke quietly. "It'll be a good day tomorrow, sir… if ya know what yer doin."

That night, Drowden and Argis gathered the men of Hapstead around them for a private meeting in the hut where Doltun and Petula made their home. Only the men of Hapstead attended, but no one else. Even their hosts made themselves scarce, appearing only to greet the men as they arrived, and to serve them with water poured from large ceramic jugs, and bread torn from long loaves. When these modest amenities had been served, they left their dwelling to join others around the communal fire, where soft songs and storytelling were shared around the circle of these neighbors of necessity.

The men of Hapstead were not long in their deliberations. Before the midnight hour they departed the cobbled hut and returned to their tents for a few hours of sleep. At daybreak, there would be an early commotion and quiet departures.

Chapter XXIII

Mirage

The Panopticon was once a large icehouse, where blocks of the frozen Heatherbloom River were sawed with two-man blades and hauled in by wagon to be packed in hay and stored over for spring and summer use. This, the tallest structure in the town, was built of thick planks of wood on a round stone foundation, taller than five stories with its pointed cone roof. A tall lightning rod topped that spire. There were no windows to let sunlight in.

But inside, the Panopticon's rounded walls were lined at ten-foot intervals from ground level with enclosed mezzanines, and every two feet along each mezzanine enclosure a glassless window looked inward. There the many spectators would stand, looking down into the Well where, at ground level, many an entertaining spectacle of athletic prowess, comedy and drama, musical talent, public oration, natural oddities, and blood sport were staged for the pleasure of the paying people of Irongate.

To the west side of the structure, attached like a barnacle to a conch, the Panopticon's proprietors had raised a rectangular building with windows on the outside on three sides and interior doorways on each floor leading into one of the mezzanines. This now ageing addition to the overall structure was known as the Spire, and it housed offices on each floor off its interior stairway landings for various important town leaders and businesses. From those same landings, spectators gained access to the Panopticon's mezzanines and a view of its exhibitions.

Admittance to one of the mezzanines granted the spectator either exclusive occupancy at a chair looking out into the interior Well, where all the action took place, or for a more modest fee, one could share a window seat with one or more other spectators. The number increased as the cost of admission decreased. There were, of course, tables at each peep window, which hung on loose chains and could be raised to close off the view. A few larger windows, with correspondingly larger tables, were available on the lower level for guests seeking a novel close-up experience and a good meal supplied by the Panopticon's kitchen staff.

On the north side of the Panopticon, at ground level, a single-story building that had become known as the Priory was attached. Through it on their way to the Well passed the entertainers, the animals, the politicians, the clowns, the orators alike. And the first person each of them met before entering was an armed guard.

But today, and all week, the spectacle inside was unique, and so was the contingent guarding the entrance to the Well. The Constable's entire platoon of guards packed the Priory with their loud chatter, clinking bottles of grog and rattling blades in their scabbards. Noteworthy of these guards, to a man they were dressed in the robes of the Brotherhood.

When Kreg Jutribackle arrived at the door of the Priory, he too wore the hooded robe. It covered his head and concealed his face in shadow. The cowls of his two Brotherhood companions covered theirs as well. He knocked at the guardhouse door and waited a moment for it to open. The guard — it was Thad Krebbermoting — pulled the door halfway and looked out.

"That you Kreg? Whatya want?"

Jutribackle answered from inside the folds of his cowl. "Yeah, it's me. And I've got the Bigworth boys, Harry and Bobbin, with me. We need to talk with Constable Liefson."

"The Bigworth boys are already with the Constable," said Thad with a laugh. "They're over in the Spire catching an earful for wandering the streets and not staying hid at the Brotherhood house."

"Hmph," said Kreg. "You're an idiot. The Bigworth boys are right here. Glarson booted them out before they could talk with him." He pointed to indicate the Bigworths, who stood behind him to either side, and then at Thad. "I still need to talk with him. In person. Very important."

"I'm sure it can wait," Thad said. "He's already seen the Bigworths and I doubt he'll want to see them again," and he started to close the door. Kreg shoved his foot in the way and grabbed Thad's robe, pulling him out the door head and shoulders first.

"I told you it's important. Me and the boys will wait here. You go send someone to fetch him. Tell him I've got word that Drowden Erebus and his men are planning to charge in force against the Panopticon fully armed and raring to free the troll. Now, you think he might not want to be interrupted over a little thing like that?"

Thad's eyes widened. He loosened Kreg's grip and opened the door wide. "Come in," he said. "Go inside and sit at the Mole Window. They're feeding the troll now, I think. They're going to make him fight with wolves over a goat carcass. Once the wolves chew him up a bit, I hear they'll set lose a few wild tusker boars just to see how they get along. And later tonight they plan to set the bear on him. Says so on the sign out on the old barn on Kilter Street. I think that'll be the end of him. He's big, but not that big. Even a troll's got limits. Jorgy should be happy 'cause it's bringin' in the coppers, but like Tapple says, he's too stupid to realize that all that ends once the bear kills the troll."

Kreg shoved past Thad and headed for the Mole Window. Harry and Bobbin's hoods followed behind him and they sat on tall stools near the table that dropped in front of the opening with a clear view of the Panopticon's Well. Kreg twisted his neck backward to look at Thad Krebbermoting.

"Are you going to fetch Larson, or do you plan on talking until Drowden and his men get here?"

"On my way," said Thad. He ran out the door and closed it with a clatter.

Kreg Jutribackle and his companions pulled up benches aside the dropdown table in front of the Mole Window and put elbows on it. They looked inward, at Ogden, and the tableau the promoters of the Panopticon spectacle invented for the diversion of their patrons.

"What are you three doin' here?" Milky Prupe broke off from a game of dice with Burl Oonep, Howe Bistrep and Hopskel Dwil. He was losing, so it was predictable he'd find some other amusement. "I thought you Bigworth boys were hiding from Drowden Erebus down at the Brotherhood house," he cackled. "You two find something to swagger other than your tongues?"

Kreg grabbed Milky's robe at the shoulder and shoved him backward. "Go back to your game. Spare me your small talk. Leave us in peace."

Milky's face went...milky. He held up quivering hands in front of him and turned away, talking loudly over his shoulder as he peddled his feet the other way. "It's no wonder nobody likes to be around you, Jutribackle. Fine! Keep to yourself. Didn't want to talk with you anyway, ya big goat."

When Kreg looked back toward the window, he could see his companions were absorbed in the spectacle. In the center of the Well of the Panopticon, Ogden stood tall, alert and observing. He was naked, but for a plume of wildly colored feathers hanging down his back from a wide rope torque tied around his neck. His body had been painted in streaks and handprints with ochre. His hands were tied in front of him with a braided cord, and he held them casually.

Crouched only a few feet away directly in front of him was a very large gray and black wolf. Behind Ogden another wolf, mostly white with a dark tail and paw markings, mangy and rib-bone thin, inched closer on its haunches. Both animals had blood dripping from their teeth. But Ogden appeared unscathed. The wolves had only minutes ago torn apart what little meat clung to a goat's spine. Men had run out with it from the Priory, dropped it, and ran back for cover just ten minutes ago. The wolves cracked bones and chewed a little while, but now they turned their attention on fresh troll flesh.

"It's barbaric," said one of the Bigworth boys in the privacy of his cowled hood. Then he pounded the table, as did dozens of other spectators who were goading the wolves to strike. "Get him!" he said under his breath. "Finish him!" he said.

Up from behind Kreg Jutribackle and the Bigworth boys came a loud shout. "Look who it is! Troll-gutter Jutribackle hisself!"

It was Bos Fudlow, the burly leader of the Brotherhood's Troll Patrol. He was brasher than the rest of the guard that now stumbled and pranced around the Priory like it was a club for clandestine drunks. Kreg turned away from the spectacle again. When he saw who it was he grumbled: "Look who it is: the great killer of she-trolls and troll-bludgeoned grass napper. Bos, what do you know about anything?"

"Everything I taught you and more, turtle fart."

Kreg threw a crude gesture his way and said, "I faced the buck troll. You're a turf kissing blow-hard. Go bugger yourself."

Fudlow shoved Kreg down the bench with his hip to make room to sit. He stabbed his big index finger toward the window. "That troll might best those wolves," he said dryly. "But wait 'til he sees the tusker boars that come next. And then, tomorrow, a ripping starved cave bear. I think we can collect troll bones once that giant Ursus meets what's left of the Trog after today."

Kreg said, "He's a full troll, not a Trog."

Bos pulled a knife from his ankle strap and slammed it into the tabletop. "I don't be-live in trolls!" he yelled. "All we've got is ugly Trogs who need to go off somewhere and die. Trolls? They're fairy tales. If ya be-live in that kinda nonsense; you're a right ravin' moron."

The taller of Kreg's companions shook his head and said quietly, in a shrill voice, "I doubt a whole sloth of bears could take the troll."

Bos spat on the table right in front of him. A spatter or two must have splashed that cowled face. "You're an idiot," Bos growled. "Think I'll go talk to some brothers with brains. This company smells false to me." He slid back off the bench, pushed his large body up with two hands on the table, turned and strode off.

"Shut up," said Kreg to his two companions. "Just shut up. You're not helping."

In the Well of the Panopticon, Ogden did something none of the spectators expected. As the two wolves moved in, he knelt down and placed his
bound hands on the ground in front of him. Then he lifted his head up,
arched his back so slightly, and he let out a heart-piercing howl.

A chill ran along the spine of everyone watching from every window on
every mezzanine. In the hallways the kitchen staff froze. Down the entryways
and stairways of the Spire, where no one could see but everyone could still
hear the sounds coming from the Well, the wailing voice of Ogden calling to
the hearts of the wolves thrilled the nerves and minds of everyone who could
hear it with a lonesome longing.

And then the wolves trotted forward and nuzzled Ogden like tame dogs.

An audible collective sigh poured out from the spectators hiding within
the mezzanine windows. In the Well of the Panopticon Ogden looked up as
he stroked the backs of the wolves who huddled close to him, one under each
arm.

Kreg and the Bigworth boys were as enthralled by the spectacle as all the
spectators hidden behind mezzanine windows up along the interior perimeter
of the Well. They didn't notice Constable Glarson Liefson walking into the
Priory past the gate guard and shoving his way through a knot of men in robes
of the Brotherhood. Until they heard a commotion behind them, they
watched Ogden and the wolves. Kreg turned and jumped to his feet. The
other two stayed put and kept looking in toward the Well. Kreg bolted toward
Glarson and grabbed him by the collar.

"We've got to talk," he said, an inch from his face.

Glarson shoved back with a palm to Kreg's chest. Kreg's body didn't move,
so Glarson did. He took a step backward. "I'm here since there's talk o' battle
and blood. What's this about Drowden Erebus? He's got no fighters. Yer
talkin' out yer arse, Jutribackle. As usual."

Kreg took a step forward and grabbed Glarson's robe. He jerked him to
the side, away from the other men, and then he grabbed the loose black hairs
curling over the chest of his shirt's open collar and yanked him close. Glarson's
eyes got big, and his mouth opened for a shout of surprise and pain, but Kreg

tapped the end of Glarson's nose with his forefinger and pointed down at the palm of his other hand. There, in a tumble and glittering light, lay Dorina's heirloom jewels. Kreg rolled them across his fingers.

"You want these?" he asked, before the cry rose to audible.

Glarson looked down as his mouth snapped shut, then his eyes jerked up at Kreg, then down again at the precious stones again. "Yes," he said simply.

"Good," said Kreg. "Then tell your men to bring the troll to me. Me and the Bigworth boys are taking the troll out of here for safekeeping. We'll keep him hidden until Erebus and his men try their stunt to spring him loose. You can catch them and be the hero. And you'll have these for your trouble. Agreed?"

Glarson looked at Kreg for half a minute without saying anything. Then he shook his head doubtfully and gave a mocking smile. "Who told you to bring Harry and Bobbin here? You stinking, sun-bloated dead gopher belly! They're to be kept incognito, secret, and invisible until this troll business is done with. What don't you understand about that part of the plan, you possum-witted goat burp! I just wasted an hour telling them two ta stay off the streets and out o' the taverns. And now you mean to tell me those Bigworth boys followed me down from the Spire to take that troll out o' here with you? What's your game, Jutribackle? You usin' those two morons for spies against me?"

Kreg started putting the gems in his pocket. He smiled at Glarson and said, "I thought we understood each other. When you bought your way into the Constableship, you beat me out of it fair and square. Now you get to reap the rewards, but if that's not what you had in mind, I guess I was wrong about you. My mistake. Alright then. My business is done. I expect Drowden Erebus will put up more of a fight than me."

"No, wait. Yes! Agreed!" Glarson whined under his breath. "Just give me those stones and we'll get this thing done."

"Good. Tell them. Bring the troll. Do it now." Kreg shoved Glarson's shoulder, and the Constable turned and waddled toward the gate door. He grabbed Thad and yelled something in his ear. Thad trotted off and mustered

294 Ben G. Price

half a dozen men, and they all headed through a thick oak door that they first
unbolted and then disappeared into the Well.

"No!! No!!" suddenly Kreg heard shouts throughout the Panopticon, and
horrible beastly sounds, loud whining and barking, howls of pain. He ran to
the window and gazed through to the Well's pit as men with pikes and arrows
slaughtered the wolves and grabbed Ogden to drag him away. The Bigworths
were on their feet, clearly agitated. They were growling and snarling and spitting, but Kreg grabbed each by the shoulder and shook them hard.

"Shut up. Keep still. We'll be out of here soon if you can hold your
tongues," he snarled demandingly but still under his breath, leaning in between them.

The Well door flew open. Ogden staggered in ahead of the men of the
Brotherhood. They shoved him forward. Thad yelled commands and the troll
was instantly surrounded by a phalanx of guards. "Those Hapstead men will
learn a thing or two if they come for the troll!" he shouted.

"Wait!" cried Kreg. "The troll is leaving with us. We've got a safe place to
hide him until the fighting is done."

"We're better off here, idiots," yelled Bos Fudlow. "Advantage is ours. Let
those pansies come!"

Glarson spat and wiped his lips with the back of his hand. "Stand aside,"
he shouted. The men encircling Ogden made an opening for him to come
forward. "This troll is going with Jutribackle and the Bigworth boys. Let
Drowden and his mob think the monster's still here."

Kreg picked up the discarded feather headdress and tossed it at Fudlow,
who caught it instinctively. "Bos, take those feathers and that loin cloth from
the troll and put them on. Then get in there and play the decoy. Constable
Liefson and the rest of the men will capture the Hapstead renegades when
they show up. You'll be the bait in our trap, and they'll be all too ready to
walk into it. Does everyone understand? Let's put an end to this troll-loving
madness."

"Wha'?" said Bos. "I ain't..."

"Do it!" yelled Kreg Jutribackle. "We know what we're doing here. It's a plan the Constable put together, and I agree with him."

Glarson stammered half a word, but Kreg slapped him hard on the back and knocked the rest of it back down his windpipe.

"You're a genius, Constable," Kreg laughed. "Tell this pissy pants coward to do what he's told."

Glarson put a fist over his mouth and gagged a phlegmy cough. "Don't be stupid, Fudlow. Just get those feathers on yer head and somebody grab the ochre and smear him up good once he's got stripped out of his robe."

Bos protested all the while a press of men coaxed him to don the headdress. They tried not to but laughed under their breaths. Meanwhile, Kreg threw a large set of pants, a shirt and a straw hat at Ogden. "Put those on, boy. We need to make you a lot less conspicuous."

Ogden held out his hands and one of the men cut the bindings on his wrists. He dressed quickly, while Bos Fudlow was helped into the costume that the Panopticon's promoters had imagined would titillate the crowd and have them believing that all trolls dressed so colorfully.

Finally, the thick oak door was opened, and Bos Fudlow trod into the Well to loud cheers from the mezzanines. The spectators suspected nothing. Fudlow's large muscular frame, the ochre skin paint, and the wild plumage dangling from his head were enough to divert their attention from the fact that there was no troll in the Well.

Kreg Jutribackle and the Bigworth brothers took hold of ropes newly tied to Ogden's hands and feet, and they headed for the Priory door. The guard opened it for them, with Constable Liefson looking on.

"Don't play me false," he said to Kreg as they passed him.

Jutribackle glanced over his shoulder at the rotund lawman. "You've got what you want. I have what I want. All is well." And with that he gave Ogden a shove out the door and the three men in the robes of the Brotherhood, plus one troll, were gone.

Pouring out from inside the Panopticon, the four could hear laughter, then shouts and hollered expressions of surprise. The wild tusked boars had been loosed, and Bos Fudlow was running hard, sweating profusely, and giving the spectators what they'd come for.

Kreg Jutribackle stopped a moment. He bent over like he was going to be sick, his cowl completely hiding his head and face. The two other men stopped next to him, holding the ropes that bound Ogden. Suddenly an enormous, explosive horselaugh blasted out of Kreg's hood and he fell to one knee and pounded the grass by the roadside with his fist. The other two broke into guffaws and chortles and slapped each other hard. Then Ogden joined in with a blustering belly laugh that set the others off into bouts of hilarity they could not control.

When he caught his breath, Ogden held out both his hands, palm up, and exclaimed, "Father! Thank you and Argis, and this man who laughs so strangely."

The supposed Bigworth brothers stood tall, and each pulled back their hoods to reveal their faces. Drowden and Argis smiled broadly at Ogden, who extended one of his hands and helped Kreg Jutribackle to his feet.

"We're glad to do it, lad," said Kreg. "I have to admit I've been no lover of trolls. But liars and cheats and murderers are worse. They make talking plainly and tending to family matters impossible."

Drowden rushed to Ogden and hugged him close. "I've been worried. Really worried, son."

Argis placed a hand on Ogden's shoulder. "Thanks ta Kreg, we've got a chance ta git outta Irongate an' away from these bloodthirsty nincompoops."

Kreg pointed a finger at Ogden. "You may be a full-blown Troggle, but you're family to these men and their kin. I can see that. So, before those leeches in the Panopticon guess they've been played for fools, let's tend to family and make for the gate."

The four travelled through the back alleys and fallow fields around Irongate. When they reached the middle of town, walking through the milling crowds seemed too risky, so they slipped into a dilapidated building of crooked boards with a skylight hole in the roof through which birds occasionally ventured. The place smelled of old hay and dung, and flies pestered them the whole while they stayed, waiting for sunset and the cover of night.

They spoke quietly about the escape they'd just contrived. Argis apologized to Kreg for mistrusting him. Kreg muttered something Argis couldn't hear. Then he said cryptically, "What we did was foolish in all the right ways." And he turned to Argis as they sat on a rustic bench well inside. "You didn't think I'd help you get the troll loose, did you?"

"Never did," said Argis. "Didn't see how it could been done. They was watching Ogden every minute from every peep hole. What could ever get 'im free? That's wha' I kept askin' myself."

Kreg looked Argis hard in the eyes and as Drowden put a hand on his shoulder he heard him say, "The truth. It's the only thing that would do it."

Drowden talked directly into Kreg's left ear. "The truth is the only thing they can never hear," he said.

"Exactly." Kreg twisted to look directly at Drowden. He smiled. "That's exactly right. I told them you were coming to free the troll, and they handed over the troll to you."

Drowden waved Ogden to come closer, and he did. He nodded toward him and said to Kreg, "Friend, I'd like you to meet Ogden. He's not just a troll. He has a name. And now and then he'll even talk with you, if he's in the mood."

Kreg looked up and into the shadows that concealed Ogden's eyes. Then he held out a hand, and Ogden took it in his. "The truth made you free," Kreg said.

Drowden waved a hand at Ogden. "I almost forgot. Miranda gave me something for you, and I promised I'd make sure you got it." He reached into his inner pocket and retrieved the silver chain and the carved bear tooth necklace his daughter had entrusted him to deliver. "Here," he said, and he leaned forward and put the chain around Ogden's neck, clasping it in the rear. "Let this chain be a reminder of your freedom, not your captivity," he said with a smile.

Kreg clucked his tongue in his mouth. "Rather a personal present from a young lady," he said acerbically, "to a troll."

Drowden nodded but said nothing. He looked again at Ogden and at the broad pendant in the shape of an ivory oak tree. "You have friends. You have people who care about you. We aren't all like those robed men of the Brotherhood."

Ogden felt the cool metal of the silver chain and the carved likeness of an oak tree against his chest and said nothing. But inside he wondered what the words 'having friends' and 'having people' could mean in this world full of words. What is 'having?' he wondered.

"It's getting dark," said Kreg. "Let's be on our way."

Argis extended his arm to block Kreg's way, but he smiled to show it was a friendly move. "Th' good people o' Bladicville says they'll take us in an' keep us hid a while. How'd you like ta join us?"

Drowden nodded. "You're welcome to come with us tonight. We can have Doltun send someone to fetch your wife, Sully. I'm worried the Brotherhood might make trouble for her once they realize you helped Ogden get free."

"Aye," said Argis. "They's gonna want ta kill ya an' leave her a widder. But if they can't do that, then no tellin' what they might do ta yer dear one."

Kreg's eyes dropped, and he shook his head sadly. "Too late friend. I'm already a widower. My Sully died trying to birth our first-born, now two months past. I lost both of them. There's nothing for me in this stinking nest of liars and backstabbers. Thanks for your kind invitation, but I've still got business in Irongate."

"Oh, so sorry. I did no' know," said Argis with an embarrassed shrug. "It's terrible news. Jus' awful. Wife an' child lost! It can't be imagined! Still, what kind o' business can ya have in Irongate after tonight?"

Kreg puffed up his chest and blew the words out like he was trying to stoke a fire with them. "The thing is, I don't mean to let your man Harry and his worthless brother Bobbin spend the blood money they got for handing over yon troll, I mean Ogden, to those Brotherhood shadow-creepers."

Drowden turned in a circle as he walked and listened. "You're a good man," he finally said. "And getting revenge from those two isn't worth risking your life. The Brotherhood will be looking for you and Ogden, we can be sure of that. But remember, they're going to be after the Bigworth boys too. As far as they know, they were in on Ogden's escape. Let's let the Brotherhood make them answer for being traitors. That's what they are, and it would be perfect irony. And even though it's funny in a way we should not laugh at, they should meet their fate at the hands of their fellow murderers. The truth is going to catch up with them. Now, you come with us. We'll make for Bladicville, then for Hapstead. Kreg, come with us to Hapstead. "

Kreg bowed slightly toward Drowden. "I thank you for that."

Drowden winked. "You're a very good man. I don't want you to throw away what your good wife saw in you for the sake of punishing that ruthless pair of scoundrels."

Ogden chimed in, "Not for this troll."

Kreg stared out into the empty streets of Irongate and said nothing more, but momentarily started out at a fast pace toward Besom Bridge and away from Irongate. The others followed closely behind.

Heatherbloom River flowed quietly. Cicadas filled the night air with their raspy songs and a gentle breeze ruffled the men's robes. The tall iron gate that blocked passage across the bridge was closed and locked. They could see orange light flickering among the trees across the river from the scattered campfires of Bladicville.

"We need to get across," Drowden said quietly. "Can we break the gate lock?"

"No. Too noisy," said Kreg. "There's a path down to the river. We can swim it."

Argis groaned. "Not me. Go on, the three of yas. I can't swim. Not gonna get drownded."

Ogden looked at the gate and suddenly ran full speed directly toward it. Without slowing down, he leapt from the ground and grasped the topmost spires, arranged like a row of spears along the top of the gate. With the palms of his hands cupping the points of the spires and with toes pointed to the stars, Ogden did a backward handstand and broke into an upside-down smile at the three men as he tilted back and tumbled down the other side of the gate. He landed flat-footed, and then pressed his face through the bars and said, "step here, then here," as he held his two hands low through the bars.

Argis went first, using Ogden's hands, one after the other, as steps. To help Argis climb higher, Ogden pushed his legs through the gate's vertical rods and shimmied up, using only his legs to climb. As he ascended, he offered his palms as steps for Argis, one after the other, higher and higher, until he reached the top. There, Argis paused, twenty feet in the air. Ogden said, "Step over the top and hold on!" Then he pushed away from the fence and dropped down to the ground, flat on his feet again. Looking up, he whispered to Argis. "Jump!"

"Wha'?" Argis whispered incredulously.

"Jump!" Ogden repeated. And Argis did, almost before he took another breath.

Ogden stood like a deep-rooted tree and caught him in both arms, without bending his back as the flailing man landed.

"You go next," Kreg said to Drowden. "Help Drowden over the gate, Mister Ogden," he said. So, Ogden repeated the operation and soon Drowden Erebus was on the outside of Irongate, looking in.

"Your turn, Kreg," said Drowden through the bars. But Kreg shook his head and turned to walk away.

"Wait!" yelled Argis. "Don't be a fool! They'll be lookin' fer ya!"

Kreg turned back toward the gate, but continued to walk backward, away from it. "I've been a fool all my life, Argis. No point changing now," he said. And then he was swallowed up in the darkness of the night, for all but Ogden who saw him wave before he turned away and disappeared in shadows too deep even for a troll's eyes.

Chapter XXIV
Coming Apart

The encampment that was Bladicville woke slowly. Here and there a dog barked. Squirrels ran from tree to tree along the branches overhead, and some chipmunks sniffed cautiously around the perimeters of the fire circles for morsels lost in the dark.

Drowden and Argis were sleeping in a tattered but often repaired cloth tent. The rest of the Hapstead men were stirring. When they went looking, Ogden was nowhere to be found. He had gotten up hours before dawn, as was his habit, to roam in the night woods. But this time he did not mean to come back and go to sleep among waking people while the sun bounced up off the horizon. Instead, as his feet carried him further into the forest and up into the surrounding hills covered with old oaks and chestnuts, when he looked back at the shantytown where his friends slept, and then across the river to Irongate, where lights burned throughout the dark hours, he said to himself in a low voice, "This is not a place for trolls." And he strode on.

The encampment at Bladicville was astir with news of Ogden's rescue, and now his disappearance. Drowden gathered his men together, and they were in agreement. They would gather enough food and gear for a fast hike into the forest. They hoped to find Ogden quickly and bring him back to Hapstead Manor. To a man they expressed concern that he was in danger of being hunted down by the Brotherhood.

As they made their final preparations news came that justified those fears. Petula and Doltun arrived at the hut where the Hapstead men were gathered to review plans to search for Ogden. Hector stood watch at the door and escorted them in. The men all stood out of respect. Willbee bowed at the hips and took off his cap. Drowden stood up from his seat at a table where Tom had been drawing a rudimentary map of the surrounding wilderness from memory. He had lived among the Bladicville folk before taking work at Hapstead.

"What have you heard?" asked Drowden as Doltun and Petula approached.

"It's not good," said Doltun. "Tell them, Pet."

Petula sat on the end of the table and the men gathered around her. "I spent the night in Irongate, reckoning you'd want to know what went on after you left the Panopticon. For one thing, Bos Fudlow got pelted good when the gawkers there figured out he wasn't a troll."

A rumble of subdued laughter rolled through the men who crowded in to hear her.

"Did Glarson give us away?" asked Drowden.

"No. By the time everyone decided you weren't going to show up with your men to free Ogden, he threw up his hands and let out a long poem in vulgarity. He kept saying he was going to find Jutribackle and the Bigworths and make sure they got what was coming to them. But he figured it was no use doing anything 'til morning, so he told the men of the Brotherhood to rest and then meet at their clubhouse first thing in the morning."

Drowden asked, "Did they meet? What are they going to do?"

"Let 'er finish," said Doltun. "Here comes the rest of it."

"Yep," said Petula. "There's a bolt more to the story. Here. I'll roll it out all at once and you can stitch together what you want from it."

"Alright. Go on," Drowden agreed.

Petula began. "So, before they could even meet, the whole town was starting to buzz about last night's marauding."

"What marauding?" asked Hector.

"Shhhhhhh," said Drowden.

"So in the morning, people started meeting on the street, down at the market and at the Plough Blade Inn just like they always do, except this time there were odd stories circulating. At first it seemed like an isolated story here and there. In the Tilthinger Inn somebody was tellin' of a goat slaughtered by some large animal during the night. Then word came that the market storehouse was broken into, and a goodly amount of produce, furs and smoking weed is missing."

Petula paused to look around at the faces of the men. "Then there was what the blacksmith, Chicky Niddion, had to say," she went on. "He barged into the Plough Blade Inn where I was stayin' and he announces all out of breath that he found the oak slatted door of his shop torn apart and inside a pile of tools and wood and furniture all thrown into a mess. So far as he could say, it seems his digging tools — a pick, a shovel, a long iron pry bar, and maybe one of the hardened pikes with a sharp spear end to it were gone."

Drowden held up a hand to interrupt. "I'm sorry, but what has any of this to do with us?"

"Tell him, Pet," said Doltun. "Now listen close, Drowden," he said.

Petula shrugged. "Here's the thing. No one connected all this mischief. They figured some bandits were on the prowl at first. Except for the goat. But then Ospin Tapple — he was at the Plough Blade Inn too…" and she paused slightly, glancing over at Doltun. She lowered her eyes and continued, "He says that 'I bet it's that vile Ogden troll, come back to stock up, and maybe be ready to do who knows what with that pike and those iron tools.' Funny how fast everybody latched onto that and be-lived it for the truth."

"Do you really think it was Ogden?" Willbee blurted.

"Not for a minute," shouted Drowden. "I won't be-live it."

"Well it's not all that happened," Petula said loudly. "The Panopticon got trespassed and destroyed inside. Some people I wouldn't be-live if they said water's wet said they saw a wild giant troll come crashing out the Priory door, leaving it hangin' in splinters."

Petula went on to tell how the men of the Brotherhood rushed to their meeting house. She even told some details about what went on in that meeting but wouldn't say how she knew. "Here's all I'm going to say," she said. "They've gathered a posse, the Brotherhood has. They're gettin' ready to hunt him down."

"One more thing — no, two," she added. "Harry and Bobbin Bigworth were dragged out of hiding from the old mill down on Julian Creek. They swear they don't know where Kreg Jutribackle is, and they say they had nothing to do with Ogden's escape. That didn't save them."

"Ya mean they killed 'em?" Argis said somberly. "Had it comin' I guess, but it ain't right."

"Hung them from the rafters is what they did," said Petula. "Left them swinging while they had their little meeting. And the other thing is this — they don't think Drowden Erebus had anything to do with it. They're putting all the blame on Jutribackle. They burned his house with torches. It's still burning right now."

"How can that be?" Drowden asked. "They couldn't have had time. Kreg's farm is on the far side of Irongate. You said the Brotherhood met early this morning. No doubt those cutthroats were busy with all the news of marauding. They must've wasted two hours arguing over whether Ogden is a rabid animal or a murdering rapist. I need to know: did you see the Brotherhood burn the Jutribackle farm?"

"Why do ya want to know? Who else would have burned him out?"

Drowden's eyes narrowed. Tears trembled in them. He said, "Kreg lost all he loved. He risked his life to save Ogden, even though he was one of the Brotherhood. He said he did it because family is more important than anything. So I want to know. Did you or anyone see them burn down Kreg's farm?"

Petula shook her head once. "No. I just figured it had to be them."

Drowden stroked his chin and looked off into the mid-ground. If the Brotherhood didn't burn Kreg's home, then......his thoughts meandered into a thicket of depressing possibilities. A daydream danced in his eyes and tightened like a steel band around his heart. He saw Kreg Jutribackle run from barn to house with a lit torch. He saw him close the door behind him as he entered the front door, and he never came out. A scream coiled up in Drowden's chest, but he held his breath a moment and kept his thoughts to himself.

Argis stepped forward from the huddle of men encircling Petula. "I got somethin' ta say. It's this. Kreg Jutribackle is a man o' his word. Weren't fer him, Ogden might be dead. If that band o' bullyin' cowards burned down his home, we've gotta help him somehow."

Drowden held up a hand to halt the chatter of agreement spreading through the knot of men. "No use," he said over the din. "I'm sorry to say it, but I don't think there's anything more we can do for Kreg Jutribackle than remember him as he was."

"Was?" said Willbee with ascending pitch to the word.

Drowden simply shook his head. Gasps, obscenities, and curses erupted wherever men grasped the meaning in Drowden's downcast eyes. Doltun took Petula's hand, and she stood up next to him.

"He'd already lost everything that mattered to him," she said. "I thought maybe I'd spare you, but I see that Drowden's sniffed out the truth. It's true. Jutribackle's gone."

Drowden cleared his throat. "And so's Ogden if we dawdle any longer. He's gone, but not out of reach of the Brotherhood." Suddenly he grabbed one of the men's shoulders and pushed him toward the door. "Hector, gather the dogs." Then he wheeled around and poked a finger right in Willbee's face and said, "Grab any of our men still dilly-dallying over their gruel and bring them to the fire ring. We'll leave within the hour." Then with a scattering motion of his arms he said to the others, "no excuses. Be at the fire ring with your gear before I get there. Anyone who doesn't want to go into the wild can go back to Hapstead. We won't wait for you, so decide quickly."

Ospin Tapple was gathering his select mob at the same time that Drowden's company set off to find Ogden. But Tapple's men of the Brotherhood would not depart their secretive meeting until hours after the Hapstead men took to the woods. In fact, the sun was diving toward the horizon when they finally made their way down the root and rock-strewn path to the woven rope bridge that crossed the Heatherbloom River and bypassed the town gate.

With a three-fingered tap on the shoulder, Tapple personally had chosen his men. Each of the chosen ones quietly snuck away to collect their weapons, robes and packs. Each one of them unfurled the sashes of the Secret Brotherhood and slung them over their shoulders as they made off for the rope bridge, torches in hand. Some wore necklaces of bones and teeth taken from looted troll burial mounds. All seemed in a somber mood.

At sunset Ogden stood high above Irongate on the northeastern slope of Sentry Mountain, a steep incline that formed the eastern wall of the Heatherbloom River Valley. Ogden had slept a goodly part of the day in the shade of a cedar tree that had been cracked by lightning. Now, as he hurried across the exposed clearing of a mountain meadow, he could clearly see the town in the valley below. From the streets of Irongate he heard men and horses and dogs yammering, whinnying and barking. The sounds rose to the heights like smoke from an untended fire. They sent a chill up his back, and a sudden pooling of moisture in his eyes made the light from the lanterns and torches below blur into dancing halos of orange and yellow.

The forest was alive with smells and sounds. As the day's light faded, sounds carried crisply on the cooling air and Ogden could hear the men from Hapstead traipsing up the same footpath that he had followed. They were not too far behind, but they were being slowed by the fading of the path into little more than a fox's lane in the thick wood. He could hear the dogs yapping as they ran between and around trees where he'd been. They knew his scent. He hastened his steps.

As he mounted the steepest slope of Sentry Mountain Ogden knew that over the past few hours another troll had passed this way. The disturbed dry ground and the pungent scent of rotting meat suggested a carcass was being dragged along for food. But Ogden sensed that something wasn't right and though his intent was to travel south, he decided to follow the trail he'd picked up toward the north. He knew that Drowden and his men as well as a posse of Brotherhood cutthroats were on his trail, and he knew that meant they'd be following two trolls. He decided to slow down as he approached the mountain's ridge. He had to do something to divert the men and allow more time for him to disappear into the wild.

Before he reached the summit, Ogden heard the dogs fast approaching. He hunkered down in a stony depression overgrown along its rim with burdock bushes chock full of clinging burrs. In the center of the little crater grew a low canopy of multiflora rose brambles, and all of it was laced with a dense knot of thorny greenbrier vines. He could not have found a less hospitable place to hide, and he thought perhaps the dogs might be discouraged from venturing into the thicket after him.

He was wrong.

Old Duke and Grisswold found him first. They came bounding up the hill, their tongues dripping and their tails wagging. Grisswold's barking was constant. Duke howled his hound alarm intermittently as both circled the thorny pit in opposite directions. Soon Clyde and Joko joined them, and they began probing under the overgrowth of vines, yapping excitedly.

Ogden didn't move for a little while, but finally he emerged, pushing pricking tendrils away from his face. They clung to his clothes but did no damage to his sun-toughened skin. When the dogs saw him pull free of the shroud of green, they rushed to him, licking his hands and, when he bent over to pet them, they slathered his face, then kept circling around his knees and rubbing up close.

Ogden let this go on for a few minutes, but then he hunkered down, and the dogs gathered around him. The three mutts sat and panted happily while he stroked them and patted their chests. He said not a word, but looked into each of their eyes, taking time with each one, sharing an unutterable message that, by all appearances, they understood and gave their full attention.

With no more delay, Ogden stood and patted each of their heads. Then he turned and walked north, following the trail of a troll that not even Clyde, Duke, or Grisswold had yet detected. And they stayed where he left them, content to lie on the cooling ground as the sun dipped behind a nearby hill.

Ogden crossed the ridge and reentered the thick forest that spread out further than sight or sound. Down a rock-strewn slope grown thick with pin oaks, red maples and shag bark hickories, then up another less steep hill after crossing a narrow mountain brook, Ogden took in the aroma of leaves turning bright colors — their scents creating a rainbow of odors more brilliant and distinctive than their blazing hues in bright daylight.

Stars flickered among the tree limbs, poking through open patches of sky that intermingled with the night canopy of the forest. When he looked up, the silhouettes of a million leaves pressed a deep gray stencil of their undulating shapes against the heavens. Ogden felt the solemn notes of stars' etheric song playing among the living and breathing giants of the wood. He could feel their music on his skin like the gossamer of spider webs that now and then netted his nose or clung to his ginger hair.

As he mounted the top of the next ridge he turned to listen. The stars' subtle harmonies gave way to the coarser sounds that echoed between the hummocks. Across the valley he'd just traversed, up on the hill he recently descended, he could hear the dogs barking and the men grunting and cussing as they pushed through the dark that now surrounded them. With nothing but oil lanterns that did little more than cast menacing shadows all around them, they trusted the dogs to show them the way. The lamps served one useful purpose — to give them away to anyone or thing paying attention. Although they too were on the prowl in the night wood, Ogden saw no sign of the Brotherhood's band of vigilantes. But he felt their presence through the trees when he held a hand against their living bark, and when he touched the soil with his fingertips.

Over the next ridge he continued, ever led by signs in the undergrowth, a scuff in the dirt, a vine pushed back and hooked on a branch, a turned pebble still moist on top, where it would have been dry had it been undisturbed. But easier to track was the faint but constant odor of pungent, rotting flesh that clung to the wilting leaves of spice bushes, the wispy needles of struggling pine saplings, and the broad green leaves of squat mountain laurels.

He turned and followed that trail toward the dawn's mantle of orange clouds in the far hills. Before descending into the shadows of a steep gorge he decided he would soon take his rest.

Ogden's sharp ears pricked at the smallest sound: a deer fly's wings, a gray jay walloping through the branches after an unguarded sparrow's nest, a squirrel romping through leaves in the distance, and a lynx spraying its scent over the scat of a competitor. But he hadn't heard the men or the dogs of Hapstead since crossing into the wildwood men called the Spathe Valley. He wondered if he dared rest. Soon the sun would sweep away night's shadows the way it lifts morning mist. But he did not decide. Weariness decided, and he paused by a marshy bog and found a tuft of soft green moss that rose above the standing water, surrounded and retained by thick-barked elm trees. He stretched out upon it and, using his left arm for a pillow, fell into sleep.

What we would call dreams came to him. But they were not foreign, not strange, only different from waking. His lips smiled. Until…

A large millipede that had made its home under the soft carpet of moss emerged into the open air. It lifted its front end, its forward legs scrambling for purchase, until they fell upon Ogden's sideburn hair and began to climb. Up, up, and up further the millipede climbed. At Ogden's right temple, it splayed its thistle-thorn legs and walked onward, up and further up onto his forehead.

Ogden snorted, still asleep, and his right hand came up instinctively. "Squeeesh!" The millipede writhed. Its back end squiggled independent of its severed front end. A soft splash of gooey bug gut oozed a little down Ogden's brow. His eyes opened suddenly; his mind spun free of star song and moon rumbles. The sun was up. He wiped his forehead and apologized to the millipede. Then he heard the dogs. They were close by.

He heard Willbee yelling, and Hector bellowing. "C'mon, Joko! Joko!!!" That was Hector.

Willbee's shout was as clear and high-pitched as a chicken protesting an egg culling. "Duke! Good boy! Find Ogden!! Find him Duke!"

Ogden stood straight up. His heart pounded. He was ready to run. But then he heard another sound. It was loud and horrible. Off to his right, to the south, harsh noises, artificial and metallic, screamed through the trees. The gibberish of random noise clanged and boinged. It tingged and warbled. There seemed to be no pattern. Ogden knew that there was intent behind it. For a moment he froze.

A strong sense of loss and longing washed over him. He looked back over his shoulder toward where the dogs were fast approaching. He wanted to wait for them to catch up, but the loud metallic clanging up above a large outcrop of lichen-covered boulders persisted. He understood someone was trying to drive him forward in fear. It was the way he'd seen men force deer into a trap.

Sure enough, not fifty yards away, he spotted saplings all bent over unnaturally. Suddenly he stopped running. Just as suddenly he saw the saplings spring up among the surrounding underbrush. They slapped bushes and tore vines as they sprang erect out of nowhere, then they swayed a moment and stopped. A rope net tangled among the meadow flowers and settled to the ground.

Ogden sniffed the air like he was asking a question, and what he smelled made him tremble. Fear and decay concealed themselves among the rocks above. Whoever he'd been following had saved him from the trap by intentionally setting it off. But there was blood on the leaves leading up the hill and he was reluctant to charge on up to see who it was. Suddenly the choice was no longer his.

Five dogs bolted out of the brush below him. Joko, Barkiller, Grisswold, Clyde and Old Duke came blasting out of the bushes at a full run. Ogden saw them erupt from the cover of low mountain laurel, but rather than stop to claim him as their prize, all five barreled past him and sprinted up the forested hill toward the rock outcrop, in the direction of the loud screeching, grating and gonging noises that suddenly ceased. On they scrambled at full speed toward its source, past the place where the bent saplings had suddenly shot up from the ground and cast the empty net over the ground.

From down the hill at some distance Ogden could hear Drowden's voice amidst the clumsy bushwhacking progress of the other Hapstead men. He paused only a moment then glanced back up the hill and sprinted off in the direction of the dogs and away from the men.

He pranced back and forth from rock to rock on either side of a gurgling mountain stream. The dogs' commotion filled the trees with whelping and howling and barking. He couldn't see them behind the giant boulders just ahead, but that's where the hullabaloo was coming from.

Ogden clamored straight for the giant gray stone near the center of the outcrop. From the highest flat top rock below it he leapt with all his might and clung to its side. Then he shimmied to the top and peeked over, down into a grotto that surrounded a crystal-clear pool of water at least twenty feet deep at its center.

Ogden could see the ragged rocks lining the deeps of the transparent water, but the submerged side just below the promontory where he lay in hiding was dark and impenetrable to the eye. He kept looking to see if whoever he'd been following would come back up for air. He'd heard a splash and knew without seeing that someone had jumped from high up where he now hid, down into the depths.

Around the pool stood a host of robed men. Some were busily gathering in a large net that floated across the surface of the water. Another trap, prematurely sprung.

As they reeled it in, they gathered the rope network in a crescent pile surrounding the edge of the crystal well. Among the men were Burl Oonep, Pip Skleverly, and Tucker Scont. Three others stood with their backs to the pool as they fended off the Hapstead dogs with pikes and scythes: Milky Prupe, Thad Krebbermoting, and Cornelius Baldegger. Baldegger cracked a whip and stung Joko on the nose. Bos Fudlow stood atop a large rock barking at the others.

"That's Drowden Erebus' bitches. Means he can't be far behind. You boys ready for a fight?"

Thad turned to him and shouted up loudly enough, so Ogden could hear his words plainly. "There's nothing to fight over. We don't have his troll."

Bos shook a pointed finger at Thad. "You boys are trigger-happy. That scum for a mother Trog never came back up! Our trap was supposed to catch him, not drown him, ya doltish cretin! Who set the springs, so the net would come down over the tarn? Wasn't me!"

The dogs were still barking and snapping at the men of the Brotherhood. Bos Fudlow bellowed over them. "There'll be no trophies! The Trog's probably stuck on a rock way down under that overhang. And I ain't goin' in after his sorry carcass. Anyone want to go for a swim?"

Ogden stayed concealed on top of the boulder that formed the back wall of the mountain pond. He listened as the Brotherhood men talked, and he gathered that they had chased a troll into the hills and that they had set a trap, a net triggered by the release of bent trees. But their plans had not gone as intended.

He watched without moving. The dogs stayed at a safe distance, but they kept the men cornered in the grotto. Then something disturbing caught his eye. It was a bloody mass of flesh laying in a heap near the pool. As much as the dogs wanted to harass the cowled men, they wanted to have at that haunch of meat even more. It lay in high grass and was now swarmed with flies. But though it delivered the unmistakable reek of blood and flesh to his nose, it was a different scent than he had picked up back in the forest. This was a relatively fresh kill.

The men had retrieved their net. The dogs seemed content to lay close to the ground and snarl when one of the men tried to approach. Fudlow slid down from his perch and Ogden listened as he talked to his men.

"Erebus will be here soon with his farm hands. Let's take the high ground and surprise them."

"What about the dogs?" Baldegger asked in his booming voice. "They'll give us away!"

"Kill the mutts!" Bos shouted back at him. "We need to surprise them. We'll attack when they're looking over their dead pets and not paying attention."

That's when Ogden jumped to his feet and shouted. "You men are looking for a troll? Well, here's a troll! Catch him if you can!"

"Wha'??" yelled Bos Fudlow.

Burl screamed. "There he is!!"

Milky Prupe grabbed his pike and tried to run into the forest, but Grisswold leapt toward him and latched his teeth onto the hem of his robe. Milky tried to pull away, but his head jerked back, and he fell flat on the ground.

Ogden stood up tall. He waved his arms and shouted a loud indecipherable cry of distress, warning, threat and anger all in one yodeling wail. Then suddenly Drowden's voice cried out from behind him. He was scrambling up the forest-hidden boulder field toward where Ogden had leapt to the giant lichen-papered sarsen stone.

"Stay there, Ogden! Don't run! We're coming!" yelled Drowden.

And from the other side of the outcrop, below in the grotto, Bos Fudlow was screaming, "I'll kill you, damned Trog! I'm coming to cut your throat and eat your liver!" And he dashed to the rock wall, followed by three of the Brotherhood men.

They scrambled up the rock wall toward Ogden, who watched their quick progress, then glanced back to see Hector, followed by Willbee, followed by Drowden as they clamored over the strewn boulders up and up toward him. He looked down at the men of the Brotherhood once more. They were nearly within arm's reach.

Ogden stepped toward them. Bos Fudlow reached out to grab his ankle. Then Ogden jumped.

His arms waved madly as he plummeted down. Then there was a loud splash as he descended into the crystalline waters of the mountain tarn. Immediately the shouting of the men and the barking of the dogs were muffled and dissolved in the ascending bubbles that raced up past his body as he sank. He saw daylight fade. He saw shadows under the rock overhang. And then he didn't see anything.

Chapter XXV
Reunion

The dogs had run forward to the edge of the crystal pool when they saw Ogden drop from high above and disappear into its waters. They now had the seven men of the Brotherhood trapped inside the grotto. Soon, Drowden and the Hapstead men appeared from behind the wall of boulders. They joined Barkiller and Clyde, Joko, Grisswold and Old Duke. From his perch above the tarn, Bos Fudlow screamed crudely at them. Hector yelled back at him, but Drowden raised a hand to tell him to hush.

"Where is Ogden?" he hollered up.

"He's gone," Thad Krebbermoting hollered back. "Drowned, if you ask me."

Fudlow spat through his teeth. "The Trog jumped in the water and hasn't come up since. He probably smashed his head on one of those rocks on the way down."

"There's no blood," Drowden said to the side where Willbee stood. "Can you have a look for me? See if you can spot anything in the water."

Willbee slapped Drowden on the shoulder and hurried to the pool's edge. He pulled off his shirt and kicked his shoes to the side. Before bending to dive, he jerked his head to the left and pointed. "It ain't our Ogden's blood, bu' look ye over there! Sompthin' got kilt."

Drowden spotted the goat's shank in the high grass off away from the pool, and the swarm of flies that made a gray moving cloud around it. His heart sank. He wondered if Ogden was responsible after all for the marauding in Irongate. He remembered that Petula had told him about the butchered goat, along with the other mischief. He shook off those thoughts and turned his attention to the crystal pool.

Willbee dove and he went deep.

He seemed to be down there a dangerous length of time. Drowden and the others watched as Willbee pulled himself deeper by grabbing the irregular rock wall and thrusting himself downward. Then he disappeared for a while. Drowden squeezed Hector's shoulder. "I don't want to lose Willbee too," he said quietly.

Meanwhile the Brotherhood men came down off the rocks after Drowden had his men pull the dogs back and he promised them not to attack while they searched for signs of Ogden.

Willbee emerged from the clear water with a sputter. He shook his head and gasped for breath. "Nothin' down there!" he choked out. "I couldn't tell fer sure, but maybe there's a cave in under the big rocks. I stuck me head up inta a hole and caught a lung o' fresh air."

"Did you see anything in there?" yelled Drowden.

Willbee yelled back. "Nah! It was black. Maybe jus' a pocket o' air."

Ogden sat in a dark gallery that would have been entirely black, but for a few pinholes of light that penetrated the thick mossy cover above ground, and the luminescent moss that lined the ceiling and walls and gave off a ghostly green glow. The glimmer from this moss, called goblin gold by some, was just enough light for his eyes to make out the contours of the cavern and to see that off to his left the cave extended down a corridor weathered by the ages. He panted for air as the water dripped off his body to the stone floor. He could hear the splash of the water lapping against the rim of the granite hole in the cavern floor out of which he'd just pulled himself. At the top of the mountain tarn, just under the ledge of the overhanging rock, the shadows hid the entrance to the cave that was only accessible from underwater.

Ogden waited because he wasn't sure what to do. His body shook, but it wasn't the cold air gusting up from the Earth's guts that raised gooseflesh on his arms. He felt the pressure of being squeezed, literally, between two worlds as he sat hidden in the dark sarcophagus of the Earth.

Flanked by the caring and kind Drowden Erebus and the men and women who shared his goodwill, and the murderous and conniving Ospin Tapple and his men of the Brotherhood of Troll-Gutters — he knew he provoked in them two different sentiments, and he brought them together as blood enemies. Without him in the mix, there would be no strife between them.

As he sat, eyes blank, submerged in feelings of confusion and a growing realization that he had embarked on a permanent departure from the company of men and women, he fidgeted with the pendant of the necklace that lay on his damp chest. He felt with his left pointing finger the irregular contours of the ivory-like tree amulet, and he remembered Miranda's face. The hungry emptiness of melancholy filled his stomach. He sat quietly, motionlessly for what seemed a long time.

But suddenly his reverie was broken as a human head bopped up out of the water that filled the round stone hole in the cavern floor from which he'd just pulled himself. It was Willbee. Ogden didn't move by as much as a twitch. Willbee's eyes were wide open as he blew water out his mouth and nose and gasped in a breath of air.

"Ahhhhh.......!" he blustered from deep in his chest. His eyes looked around. He stared straight at Ogden with what seemed like surprised recognition, and Ogden thought he was about to say something to him. But Willbee saw only darkness in every direction. With a loud and deep inhale, he lifted his chin and tilted his head backward. The water rolled in little eddies into the space where his eye sockets were as his face submerged down below floor level. He was gone.

Ogden blinked. Then he burst into laughter.

Although he felt the need for rest, Ogden stood and stretched his muscles, pulling his arms behind him and holding his right wrist with his left hand, then swiveling on his hips. He glanced back at the watery hole in the cave floor, then, turning away, he headed down a descending stone corridor toward an unknown destination.

The luminescent moss that grew in irregular patches along the cavern walls and ceiling lit his way a little less brightly than starlight as he walked the uneven path but, thanks to this goblin gold, his eyes saw well enough. He could see the general shape and direction of the passageways. Above, the rock ceiling was arched. The walls bulged inward here and there, and in other places disappeared into shadow, where there may have been other corridors leading to other places. He followed the dimly illuminated path rather than descend into utter darkness down other trails. As he went, he heard the trickle and drip of water. He slid precariously down a steep slab of limestone, and then crept slowly down an even steeper scarp of granite. Near the bottom he bent over to walk under a crystal-encrusted rafter supported on either end by two massive blocks of rounded stone. When he stood straight up on the other side, the glow of goblin gold revealed that the cavern widened dramatically, its farthest reaches lost in the gradually encroaching darkness at either end.

It was only a little way for him to scramble down an embankment of crumbled rock that a constant flaking from the scarp face had piled up over long ages. When he reached the bottom, he felt wet stone and squishy mud under his bare feet. The air was cooler. The ceiling now was far above and out of sight in the gloom. But stalactites as big around as the trunks of oaks hung down like an inverted forest of stone. Goblin gold shimmered along the lengths of many of them but not others, so that the silhouettes of hundreds of those rock pillars seemed to float in mid-air, unattached to anything solid.

The cool air here in the depths of Earth was without the scents of flowers or grass. There was, to his nose, a dull smell of stone in the air, mixed with a slight mildewy odor that burped off the walls.

No bird called in the distance. No breeze rushed through wavering leaves to make them chatter. Only the unseen drip of water here and there made his ears twitch. As he climbed over a pile of rock debris he noticed that its sediment of coarse sand had been disturbed, shoved by a large hand not too long before. Ogden's eyes widened. Down in a broad depression in the cavern floor he saw a perfectly smooth pond with an oval perimeter that was lit by the jade glow of foxfire. That luminescent fungus grew densely on sections of rotting logs that appeared to have been dragged to the spot and placed evenly around the mirror pond. They had been there a long time.

He stepped slowly toward the still pool, then stooped at its edge. The surface of the water was perfectly smooth. On the far side about thirty yards away, beyond the smooth rock that formed its edge, the ceiling of the cavern plunged down to become a low roof overhanging a dark shelf of rock. Ogden felt a slight cooling of the air fleeing like invisible bats from those shadows and brushing against his cheeks.

He looked down and saw the water's surface tremble a little. Reflected there he could see the chamber's many jagged stalactites. So clear and un-distorted were those images that they seemed to jut up out of a deep depression in the floor. Suspended above those seemingly submerged spires, his own face looked back at him. He furrowed his thick brows and noted the deep shadows made by the concave recess of his eye sockets. The reflection of the nostrils of his prominent nose flared, and when he sighed the water wobbled a little.

The surface grew still again. Ogden stared at his face in reverse until his eyes watered and he thought he heard a child's sing-song voice well up from the reflecting mere — not here or there, but from everywhere. It seemed to say,

Come ask away; come seek a way.
Find him, search for Ever.
And ever will your fate fulfil
The way is closing — never.

Over the shoulder of his reflected image he saw another face, gnarled and knotted with age, leering at him. It startled him so that he looked back to see who was standing behind him. But there was no one there, and when he looked at the water again whatever he had seen in the reflection was gone.

He stared. He was sure he had seen something and that he heard that gentle chant. Far above, in the darkness of the cavern's ceiling, roots and cilia that drooped down from under the forest floor silently rained a fine dust into the subterranean world. As he sat motionless, and gradually mindless, he felt the chill air that seeped from the narrow crawl space across the water. It touched his senses with crisp freshness. But then from above he caught a hint of a whiff of mildew. It was a scent that only a troll would have noticed. Then it grew strong and pungent, like decaying vegetation.

Ogden's ears pricked at sounds that were undetected before but suddenly he heard them clearly. A small rivulet gurgled under a rock ten yards away and then disappeared. Some small creature that would not reveal itself lurked amid the rock and sand off to his right. He felt pebbles roll down a mound of stones as if they were bouncing down his chest. To his surprise he could taste the pale green light that seemed to be evaporating like a mist off of the ancient logs surrounding the still pond. The emerald haze had a rich curry flavor.

And then the child-like voice returned in a whisper.

What are you? Are you a who?

If so then how are you — you?

Why are you here?

What do you bring?

Speak not an answer;

We know you're no man, sir.

A boy

A lad

A Troggle

Looking for him whose will is spectacular.

Listening for him whose mouth is oracular.

Feeling for him whose heart is so splendid.

Thinking of them with whom your time's ended.

Tasting the water of life as a tree.

Smelling the potion, the air wafts to thee.
Look, listen, feel, think, taste, smell...
Which of these senses from grace fell?
Breathe in the mindful memes.
Drink down the waking dreams.

And then the voice fell silent. Ogden sat in a trance as he heaved-in deep breaths of air that smelled to him like rich, loamy soil filled with the spores of mushrooms. The invisible smoky dust tickled the back of his throat. He leaned forward and dipped his hand in the glass-smooth pool to take a drink.

With the cupped palm of his hand, he scooped up a good swallow of the crystalline water and brought it to his lips. After a tentative inhaling sip, he drank the rest of the fresh cool draught without hesitation. Then he closed his eyes a moment. And again, that child-like voice returned. It talked sweetly. It spoke softly. It only breathed its words. It said simply:

Look again.
Stop thinking.
Just know.

Ogden's eyes widened. When he gazed into the mirror-still water, he saw again the tips of stalactites jutting up out of pitch darkness. His face was like a stranger's that he tried to memorize by noticing the bulge of cheek bones, the strong protruding brow, the wide and prominent nose, lips concealing firm straight teeth that were revealed when he reached up to stroke his round chin and he smiled at the ruddy hair that formed a wild halo around his head.

But then his stomach tightened. His face seemed to melt like heated wax as a cool breeze from the crawl space across the way disturbed the water. When the surface grew still, he saw superimposed on his own face the face of Ospin Tapple. There was something eerily similar in those eyes, that brow, those cheek bones. Tapple was smaller than Ogden and the sharp features of his face seemed less prominent, but unmistakably troll-like.

Ogden shook his head from side to side and the vision in the pool evaporated, only to be replaced by another phantasm.

Emerging out of the dark depths of the water, all along the lengths of the stalactites, the thorny ceiling mirrored in the depths of the water appeared to writhe and wiggle with inner life. One and two, then more holes widened along the lengths of the stony cones. Then figures at first unrecognizable seemed to climb up out of the opening pores and cling to the spires of the reflected stalactites.

The hair on Ogden's arms tingled and he could feel the moisture prickling from his body as distinct droplets on his skin. As the first of the fleshy grubs crawled out of the stalactite, it crawled to what in the reflection looked like the uppermost tip of the mirrored cone of stone. The maggot lifted its indiscrete head as if looking up at him. But if it was really there, it was above him, not in the image reflected in the cavern pool. And if it was really there, it was looking down at him from above.

Suddenly the shape-shifting gray blob reached up at him out of the pool with an outstretched arm. Ogden shivered and gooseflesh spread all over him. The face looking up from the pond — or down from the rocky rafters — was Traunton, Nathan Bladic's foreman. That face had the same look of rage as when Ogden had angered him for assuming he was a troll.

Traunton's face loomed menacingly, his muscular arm stretching toward Ogden, his thick fingers and massive hand twitching into a fist, then opening wide, then tightening again. He turned his menacing reach to grasp another form emerging from another wriggling pore in the living rock. He plucked and dragged the lifeless form of Millie from the guts of the stalactite. Her limp body moved with macabre life in the pools reflecting image. Was it really dangling from Traunton's fist, above him? Ogden did not want to look up to find out.

Then below Traunton in the pool's mirrored image more squiggling grubs were birthed. They squirmed out of the pores of animate stone. Out of each bursting orifice emerged a gray maggot that transformed into a hooded man. Each one scurried 'up' a shaft of stone and clung precariously to the pointed tip.

In the pond's reflection they seemed to stand on their hands and kick into the air, as if trying to break the surface of the water with their feet.

Ogden wanted to look up, to see if they were really dangling above, preparing to drop down from the stony rafters. But suddenly the whole gallery was saturated with the echoing sound of a woeful dirge.

The compulsion to look up to see if men of the Brotherhood of Troll-Gutters really hung from the stalactites above was overwhelming. But Ogden couldn't pull his eyes away from the conjuring waters. He dared not chance breaking the spell that reverberated in the air. The sound of the heart-wrenching lamentation seemed to billow out from the chests of the men who seemed to be standing on their hands in an upward fall.

A blink was enough to temporarily break the spell. When his eyes opened, the vision was gone. Ogden sighed heavily and looked around the gallery. The requiem of doleful voices had fallen silent.

He heard a loose rock scamper down a long incline, brightening the air with light clattering noises as it bounced and rolled. There was no one there; no sign of Traunton and no sign of the mournful men of the Brotherhood.

He turned his eyes back to the water and his hair bristled with fright. Again, there looking over his shoulder was the reflection of an old, gnarled face atop a knobby diminutive body. The contorted figure smirked a toothy smile. Red eyes squinted as Ogden watched breathlessly. He spun around fast to look directly at the odd creature. And though he wasn't fast enough to see it fully, he glimpsed something scuttling away across a pile of rocks. It disappeared into the dark crawlspace on the pond's far side. Then came that childlike voice again. It taunted him from the shadows.

Troggle lad, our common mother greets you.
Now bring your body back into her womb.

Here will rest long years the missing clue
Your bones point at from deep within your tomb.

A sense of dread filled Ogden, but he got up to follow. He rose to his feet from a squat and stepped into the cool water. The reflecting pool was shallow. It cooled and refreshed him. But whatever spell the musty cavern air and the mesmerizing waters had cast over him was far from finished. As he walked, the wide gallery brightened in intensity. The ripples and wavelets that his legs made as he progressed through the water sparked like metal on flint and he winced to protect his eyes. The ground seemed to tilt away from him the further he walked, although the pool didn't spill its bank in that direction. He felt queasy. The damp walls of the cavern undulated as if mocking the way his stomach was rolling with nausea.

He splashed through to the other side and stepped over one of the ancient, glowing logs as he approached the far wall of the chamber. There gaped an opening as wide as three men laid head to toe and as tall as a child. It was knee-high above the level of the floor. Ogden bent to look inside but it was too dark to see anything. He went back to the log he'd stepped over and grasped an irregularly shaped chunk of loose wood. It broke free without much effort, and he carried it back to the shelf-like crawlspace and shoved the foxfire-coated log chip into the darkness.

The luminescent fungus that covered the chunk of wood lit the way as he ducked into the crevice and stretched out to pull himself forward through the opening with his elbows and knees. Oddly, he didn't feel the cool air breathe over him as it had done when he was sitting by the pond. Now the air was warm and damp, with the organic smell of rich loamy dirt. He continued to pull his body through the fissure, and it closed in on both sides to the width of his outstretched arms. Then the ceiling dropped low, so that he could feel it scrape against his back as he progressed forward.

For what seemed an eternity he lowered his head all the way to the ground and turned his face to the side in order to fit through the narrowing cleft in the earth. Under his chest, legs, and arms he felt smooth damp clay that allowed him to slide forward. But he was fretful the tight squeeze would tear the ivory tree pendant from his neck and that he would never find it again.

He came to a place where the cranny narrowed so much that he had to exhale hard and clench in his breath until he pressed past to a space where the boulders above him hung a little higher and let him breathe again. Reaching under his chest, he was relieved to feel the clay-caked form of the necklace and pendant Miranda had sent him as a gift.

With great effort he forced himself to steady his mind and with three strong pulls with his arms and tearing pain in his fingers he was free from the narrow crawlway. But now he was teetering on the rounded crest of a boulder clad in red wet clay. Down the other side, in the light of the cool ember of wood he could see nothing but pitch black. Careful to avoid a treacherous head-first fall into that unknown abyss, Ogden slowly brought his legs up and under him. He sat for a while, motionless in mind and body. At last, he looked around. Above was only rock. Behind was the slim crevice through which he'd dragged himself in pursuit of something he wasn't even sure existed. Ahead was another endless barrier of rock. And below, over the boulder's slick humpback, was unknown darkness.

He saw no sign of the creature that had goaded him into this crypt-like recess of Earth. He felt his stomach tighten and looked back, for a moment considering a return through the constricted crevice he'd just crawled out. Then he turned and looked down into the gloom.

Ogden dared to stretch his legs out in front of him and felt his heels drop down to rest on the rounding surface of the clay-glazed boulder. There was no foothold ahead. The bottom of the chamber turned downward so precipitously that he hesitated to pull himself forward any further. He thought of returning the way he came, but the uncomfortable feeling of having tons of rock perched on his back and hard packed clay under his belly inspired him to take the risk of plunging ahead. It was a perilous gamble.

Without a further thought Ogden shook his head and clenched the splinter of luminescent wood in his teeth. He dug his fingernails into the mudpack on either side of him. The smell of wet clay and his own sweat filled his nose. Leaning back, he pointed his toes downward. Tipping back further, he felt his bottom slide along the slick clay and then his whole body lurched into freefall.

He plunged with accelerating speed. In the faint foxfire light, he watched the walls and top of the sluice begin to heave and contract in an undulating blur. The jagged ceiling dropped lower and lower until he could feel it brushing his eyebrows.

Nauseating claustrophobia grabbed his throat and constricted his breathing like choking hands. A sense of spinning vertigo threatened to overwhelm him. He closed his eyes, but that didn't lessen the stupefying sense of disorientation.

His right heel was suddenly twisted aside, and his high-speed slide shoved his leg under him forcefully. Somehow, he managed to straighten his leg before gravity spilled him over a ledge and dropped him twenty feet to the floor of a cavern gallery.

He was coated with red clay. His back was scraped from shoulder to shoulder and all the way down. His hair was damp from mud and blood and his forehead was swollen and bruised.

He lay on his side, eyes closed in the dark. He was breathing heavily. Something was poking him in the ribs, so he rolled onto his back and opened his eyes. Suddenly Ogden could see the crystalline walls and domed ceiling of the room-sized grotto where he had landed. He'd been lying on the foxfire encrusted log splinter. Now its light revealed the smallness of the sarcophagus into which he'd been spilled.

He plucked the glowing chip of wood off the ground with his left hand and held it up. He leaned his head on his right hand and his red hair hung loose and damp. His eyes scanned the concave ceiling. There he saw the ghosts of large animals undulating in the dim light. Life-like drawings of bison and elk and giraffes and unicorns, great bears and maned lions festooned the smooth limestone. He was not the first one to come to this place. He sat up and looked around. The chamber was a mere fifteen feet wide and nearly circular. He saw no passageway anywhere except for the opening high up on the wall behind him. That's where he had been spit out onto the hard rock floor.

There, situated about two feet from the edge of the wall base on his left and reaching across the ground to the same distance from the wall on his right, stretched a black patch in the shape of a canoe, about three feet wide in the center of the room and narrowing in both directions. 'Maybe a coal seam?' he thought. But it reflected no light at all. Ogden crept forward on hands and knees; the foxfire light again clenched in his teeth. He put his face close to the patch of dark, but the light revealed nothing. Then he felt an eddy of warm air on his cheeks and realized it was a pitch-dark hole in the floor of the room of rock. He was leaning into an abyss. and was lucky not to have plummeted into its depths when the smooth clay walls above spit him onto his tenuous ledge of existence.

The foxfire light could not penetrate the depths of the darkness. Ogden probed around the full length of the fissure, but wherever its bottom lay, it was too far for the dim green light to make it out. He sat back, crouching beside the pitch pit. His muscles told him it was time to rest. After some sleep he would decide what to do next. So, he lay on his back, with his feet only inches from the black void. He closed dark eyes and fell into a deep sleep.

Some sound startled him, and he opened his eyes. Again, he heard the child-like voice of the gnome that had tempted him into this subterranean trap. His whole body shook as he listened and heard once more the words:

Here will rest long years the missing clue
Your bones point at from deep within your tomb.

But there was more:

Below rest many kinsmen from before.
The ones who made these images you see.
Leave your mark; the future to implore,
Then through the crack, let falling set you free.

Ogden noticed that he was sitting in the middle of the floor. Some vague presentiment that things weren't right came over him. Then he realized that the crack in the ground wasn't there anymore. He was sitting on solid ground, but that couldn't be right. Although he hadn't noticed that it was gone, now the absence of that deep fissure convinced him he was not awake but lost in a dream. He rested easier, closed his dreaming eyes and ignored the foreboding words of that maddening gnome.

His rest was short-lived. Now he heard throaty voices coming from overhead and he felt the rumble of the feet of large animals reverberating on his chest. He opened his eyes and looked up at the ceiling. The charcoal images of buffalo seemed to rumble across a broad grass plain, tossing beige clouds of dust behind them. Gazelles loped and sprang in alarm; a herd of one-horned beasts moved in chaotic patterns across the apex of the vault.

Then Ogden heard the voices of kinsmen like him shouting to each other, and he saw their images drawn on the rock above, mixed in with the moving forms of those large animals. Some of those two-legged beasts hefted long lances. Some held bows with notched arrows. And he knew in his entrails, and especially in his heart, that these were his ancestors. They were the ones of whom the gnome had spoken.

The sounds of shouting voices; the rumble of hooves and the taste of dust in his throat filled Ogden's senses. He pulled himself close to the wall of the room of rock and closed his eyes again, exhausted and confused. A dreamless sleep crept over him and there he rested for a while.

But dreams came again into Ogden's mind. The commotion of his heartbeat thrummed like a signal drum. He clearly heard the message. It said,

"The time is come, rock dweller".

Ogden looked around on the pebble-strewn floor for the foxfire encrusted shingle of wood, but he realized suddenly that the surrounding walls of stone shone with their own light.

The rock walls were embedded with thousands of crystals of varying size. They radiated an iridescent glow; each created a rainbow display made up of hues as unique as their individual multifaceted geometry.

To Ogden's surprise, that ephemeral light seemed to sing, like the song of the stars, although with a weightier air. Each crystal produced a gentle note.

Then something other than the faint crystalline sounds seeping from the shimmering walls caused Ogden's ears to prick up. It was a sound coming from far off and getting closer.

A great wind rose abruptly up from nowhere and a chilling blast of cold air wrapped his body like a blanket doused in freezing water. In the center of the solid rock floor a deepening sinkhole opened. The rock seemed to crumble to sand. Dust slid down and disappeared in shadow. Ogden lurched back against the wall but leaned forward to peer down into the widening maw. Shapes like a multitude of stretched blanched bodies whirled in the gyre. Some had fiery eyes that glowed like embers. Some had eyes the color of amber and in their wild gaze there seemed to be trapped ghastly scenes of terror.

Now from their mouths a chorus of horrific voices called out in lamentation from the depths. They cried out with desperate woe. They yammered a jumbled warning. They chided and tempted and begged him to jump into the maelstrom.

Ogden covered his ears and shivered with fright. He clung to the dimly glowing wall but could not hear the song of the crystals above the deafening din of the whirling cyclone below. "Is this another dream?" he cried out.

And he heard the familiar child-like voice call out in reply:

Your short life is a dream.
And all lives are stories
That rise like rain turned to steam
In the warmth of nature's glories.

"Who are you, gnome?" Ogden yelled to the rocks and stones. "Why do you conjure these visions? What do you want?" Then the child-like voice called back, tying its voice to his echo:

I've seen the future; I've known the past.

All is but one thing always the same.

Nothing is separate; everything lasts.

Only the wind in your mind gives them names.

Your skull is a conch in which you can hear

The roar of life's ocean; the sense and the feel

Of things you think different - the far and the near.

By name I am Agamond, a gnome of this Earth

For whom I have guarded your steps since your birth.

Ogden felt sure he no longer slept. Stinging chips of flint and quartz zipped from the roiling pit and nicked his cheeks and chest. He shielded his eyes and peered into the brilliant light blasting out of the pit.

Suddenly a long thin arm reached out of those depths and groped at his leg. He bolted back, but it stretched toward him. The cyclone of light and fear expanded once again, gulping in more solid ground into its hungry mouth. And the grasping glowing claw at the end of a stretching arm of blue hot fire lurched after him again.

Ogden ran in panic around the narrowing ledge along the room's periphery. He ran closer and closer to the wall as the whirlwind widened, threatening to engulf every inch of solid ground. The voices in the throat of the cyclone cried out again for him to jump into the jaws of death. Ogden covered his ears and yelled back at the shouting chasm, not knowing exactly why these words came to him. He shouted with all his might: "The one you're looking for isn't here!"

Ogden opened his eyes. He was startled out of his visions, his fear and his confusion, and all memory of Agamond evaporated from his mind. His head jerked and he felt a pain in his neck. He was lying on his back. He felt the sudden sting of dirt and sharp pebbles biting into his back's scraped skin. He reached out and grabbed the foxfire-coated wood chip in his clenched right hand. Its light had gone out.

It should have been pitch dark, but as he lay prone, looking up, he could still see the creatures and people drawn in charcoal relief up on the ceiling. Their images were subdued, no longer stampeding or hectically wandering the way they had before. But they still seemed to flicker and dance in place, and he wondered how he could see them at all.

The explanation came immediately when he turned his head to look for the dark fissure in the floor. No longer dark, it emanated an orange-red aura of light. That light tickled the crystalline walls of the room and they shimmered and laughed in reds and blues. But then there was a laugh that was much deeper, cruder and loud enough to drown out the star songs that Ogden heard just before.

He didn't move. His muscles tensed; his eyes widened; his ears twitched, and his nostrils flared. He smelled a fire's smoke. He heard foot stamping, someone talking, and another odd laugh pour up out of the chasm in the floor.

The foot stamping went on and the loud hollering came intermittently. Ogden couldn't understand the words — they were lost and distorted in the echoes and muffling of the boulders. He wanted to see who was making all the racket, so he rolled on his side and looked over the edge of the crevice in the floor.

The floor below was at least thirty feet down. He could see bones and sticks and rock debris strewn haphazardly. Through an eye-watering updraft of smoke he saw the trembling glow of a fire and the long shadow of someone prancing around it. He heard gravel-crunching footfalls, and chest-deep huffing and puffing. And then he heard the voice call out. It was a booming voice that flew like bats up through the fissure and crashed against the painted ceiling. It said:

"We know yer here! The fire tells us. The quiet tells us. Yer smelly bloody carcass tells us. Yer hiding up there in the ancestors' vault. Musta come the long way. Yer stars are still singin' yer song, or else yer fat body woulda gotten caught up in the narrow guts of the mountain. But yer alive, not dead. Yer chin and yer legs and yer ribs and yer conch ain't been washed down here ta join this here pile o' bones."

And with that, Ogden heard the hollow wooden sound of bones being kicked about. He leaned far over the ledge of the of the long narrow fissure, hanging his head down and straddling the mouth of the opening. He was holding onto the far ledge with one foot. His head dangled under his torso. He held onto the side opposite his foothold with his left arm and extended his right arm down past his upside-down face. He waved it fast.

"You're right!" he hollered down loudly. "A tight spot. Glad to be free of it. Now tell me: who are you and how did you get down there?"

There was a long silence. Then a gravelly voice muttered "By not doin' what yer doin', fool." Then a massive figure strode away from the blazing fire that Ogden could see at the far end of a large stone gallery. The back of the creature's burly torso and broad shoulders were draped with long graying reddish hair, but its face was in full shadow. It walked with an awkward gait, bent somewhat forward. Ogden heard it groan with each step. With a turn on its heel, the firelight danced on his barrel-chested form. His face was large with big cheekbones. His protruding brow hid his eyes in shadow. It was a massive troll, one that had seen its share of seasons. He stood directly under Ogden. Then he looked up. Ogden's face blushed red in the fire's glow when he heard the old troll call up to him: "Who am I? Well, if ye have any respect fer life-givin' ya'd call me 'Poppa.'"

Chapter XXVI
Earth and Fire

Huth strained his neck to look up. His arms were crossed in front of his chest and his eyes squinted. Ogden dangled from the crystal-lined fissure in the ceiling like a spider in the center of a web. His red hair draggled lower than his head and his face grimaced, showing Huth his clenched teeth. Ogden's shoulders quivered as he strained to see who was glaring up at him.

"Are ya comin' out?" Huth shouted loudly enough to make the cavern rumble with echoes.

Ogden gulped air and tried to answer. "Going to fall," is all he managed to get out of his mouth.

Huth clucked with his tongue. "Fall? Don't fall, moron. Jump! More decent."

Ogden shifted weight from one arm to the other because he felt the fingers of his right hand slipping their grip on the lip of stone. He spoke quietly. "You should stand aside. You could get hurt by the fall…. ehhh…jump."

"Still yappin'." Huth shook his head. "Jump, boy. Huth'll catch ya."

Ogden grimaced and his muscles shook. His voice came out with a warble. "Huth is it? Well, Huth, here comes the jump. Get out of the way. Don't try to break the fall. It's more likely to break you."

Huth unfolded his arms and extended them in front of him. Still looking up, he yelled, "Shut yer yapper. Tired of listenin'. Come outta that hole. Huth seen ya do it once. Be-live it again. Let's see ya jump!"

As soon as Huth said 'jump!' Ogden lost his grip. A short yelp blew out of his mouth. His arms and legs flailed as he fell. At the bottom there was another gasp and groan, this time from the huge old troll. His arms held like iron as Ogden landed and was cradled by them, but his back buckled, and he went to his knees. He had stopped Ogden from hitting the ground, but now *he* was on the ground.

Ogden rolled out of Huth's arms onto a floor strewn with bone fragments, crumbly pebbles, and whole rib and leg bones. He scrambled to his feet. Huth fell backward with his legs bent under him. He bellowed in agony and grabbed his left side. A stream of tears flowed down his temples and his face contorted into a cringe of throbbing pain.

"Why did you do that?" Ogden called out in distress. Then, seeing how grizzly Huth's hurt was, he said more gently, "What's wrong?" But Huth could not and did not answer. He writhed and squirmed, rolled onto his side and clenched as nearly into a ball as he could; drawing his legs up; tucking his knees under his chin. His hands pressed on his side, and they shook.

Ogden saw wet fluid glimmer on Huth's hands in the light of the fire. He bent to look closer. It seemed the old troll was clasping a wound that seeped and oozed. He didn't wait another second, but scooped Huth up off the graveled ground and carried him close to the fire. There he found a cloth blanket spread out near the circle of rocks enclosing the flames. He dropped to a knee and gently settled Huth on the blanket. Then he looked around for binding for Huth's wound.

What he found was a stash of digging tools, a long iron pry bar, and a hemp bag with cabbage, carrots, and rutabagas in it. Ogden knew immediately that it was Huth who had burglarized Irongate the night after Millie was murdered. He emptied the bag, set the vegetables on a shin-high rock, and ripped the seams out of the bag with his teeth.

When he pulled Huth's hands from the wound, Ogden pursed his lips and groaned quietly. The old troll's side below his ribs was puffy with infection. A gray crust ringed the dried blood-brown divot of a three-inch wide wound. There was new blood pooling in the indent in Huth's side. The swollen skin all around it was red and warm to the touch, surrounded by a yellow and purple halo of wrinkled troll hide.

Ogden found a nearly empty buck hide water bag behind a stack of firewood piled against a limestone slab that Huth had used as a bed. He untangled its leather strap and dribbled a stream of water over the wound. Then he tore the vegetable sack into long strands and wrapped the cloth around Huth's waist, covering the wound as best he could. He tied it tightly. Throughout, Huth moaned unconsciously, but stayed motionless.

While the old troll slept, Ogden grabbed the water bag, slung it over his shoulder, and searched the parameter of the cave as far as the fire illuminated the cold stone. He could hear water running somewhere behind the rock walls but there was no way to get to it. As he felt in the shadows he cast on the wall, searching for dampness, his fingers touched something fibrous and hairy, so he went back to the fire and pulled a burning stick out to use as a torch. It turned out to be a crudely woven lattice of sticks, vines and evergreen boughs all held together by a cord of sinew still attached to squirrel fur. It was a gate that concealed a small archway. Ogden knelt and pushed the gate aside. Holding the burning stick in front of him, he pulled forward on his elbows.

The wall was about three feet thick. On the other side, Ogden picked up his head to look around, then pulled himself all the way through and stood up straight. Moonlight from a surface opening not far off coated the walls with a silvery glow. To his right, that light flickered on an animated surface of water that pooled on a broad rock ledge. He heard it gurgling down a helix-shaped stone that had been eroded by the ages. High above the shelved pond came a bubbling gush out of the wall that kept the receptacle full.

Ogden immersed the water bag and filled it quickly, then returned to where Huth lay, careful to replace the camouflaged gate in front of the floor-level threshold. He revisited Huth's wound and cleared dry scabby flesh with his fingernails as he dribbled fresh water over Huth's side. When he had done all he knew to do, he covered the wound again, tightened the binding around his waist, and left the ends of the old troll's ragged shirt hiked up around his barrel chest.

"I think it needs air, not musk to heal," Ogden said to himself before throwing a log on the fire.

He drank a little water that was left in the skin and then slumped down to the floor, leaning his back against the raised limestone slab. Overcome with exhaustion from his subterranean scuttle, he closed his eyes — and immediately awoke in the real world.

Someone was speaking to him. The voice kept repeating, "Leave the world of dreams and nightmares. Leave the world where nothing is real." It was a child-like voice, pleasant in its way. But it carried the weight of great age.

Ogden felt peculiar. He was lying against the limestone slab. The flesh just below his chest seemed soft and permeable to his probing hands, as if it had dissolved and there was nothing keeping the inside of him from mingling with the outside of him. He could feel pin-thin strings of light tickling his fingertips. Those narrow threads of intense brilliance emanated from deep inside him, but also arrived from beyond. They reached outward and inward and mingled inside him like interlaced fingers of light that somehow, he *felt* touching each other, as if they were as much a part of him as the fingers on his hands.

The sensation made him feel mildly nauseous. He felt everything around him shooting shafts of light into his heart, and at the same time his heart emitted lines of light to touch them back. Every crystal in the cave wall, in the ceiling and floor, pierced him, not with pain, but with some preternatural joy as subtle as an eyelash flutter.

The fire, its blazing embers, and the warm rocks that surrounded it all reached out and delighted the core of him with threads of light that were infused with rays of warming energy.

He felt other shafts of light piercing straight through the mountain of rock from every direction and instantly knew that it was the radiant song of the stars. Those notes of light played in new ways upon his open heart. They were richer, intertwined and harmonious in ways that the star songs he listened to on every clear night he could remember never were. They radiated feelings and understandings that pulsed within Ogden.

Images from other worlds and visceral sensations he could not name filled his mind and body. Out from the cavern walls, down from the stone ceiling and up out of the floor through his feet and legs, the threads of light penetrated the earth and made his heart their focal point.

And then he felt another source of energy. It was coming from a creature that stood over him looking down and speaking in the voice of an ageless child. Ogden looked up, forcing clarity upon his spinning mind and said, "You seem familiar."

The wide thin lips of the dark misshapen gnome turned upwards at their corners in what might have been a smile. His red eyes glowed like embers snatched from the fire ring. "Of course I do," he said. "I'm Agamond, elemental spirit of the earth, and your guardian companion since you stumbled through the forest on your birthday."

"Guardian?" Ogden stuttered the word. His head swirled with vertigo.

"Oh sure! We've met many times before. But every time we do you fall back to sleep. Then you wake up in your make-be-live world where men and women whisper spells in your ears."

"What do you mean?" Ogden asked with a twisted brow as he pushed himself up straight from his slump.

Agamond's sharp features sharpened more as he bent down over Ogden and pointed a long, crooked finger at him.

"You always go back to be with the ones who took you out of the forest and into their home. You seem to like it there. I've tried to wake you up, and sometimes you start to listen. Like when you hear the stars and feel them mixing with the earth. It almost brings you out of your trance. But those Youmans — they enchant your heart with spells that make you forget we exist."

Ogden shivered. Shimmering threads of light kept swirling all around. They mingled with the spiral of light that wrapped around Agamond and Ogden heard himself ask wordlessly, "What 'we' is forgotten?"

"What we? I mean all of us — the one that is us with many faces," said Agamond. "You'll understand, the more you wake up. You're still groggy. Living under an avalanche of spells can do that to you."

Ogden still felt oddly out of focus, and he had difficulty making his thoughts solidify into words. The narrow ribbons of light streamed into and out of him without interruption. He waved a hand in the air, and it passed through them as they passed through his hand.

"Is this vision real? Is it a dream?" Ogden asked. "Familiar things seem real. My poppa. The cave. Men. All of that. All of this, even you, are part of a dream. You should feel dreamy. But you don't."

Agamond hooted a high-pitched laugh "I'm no dream, troll. I'm as real as that shiny bauble lying on your chest."

Ogden grabbed for Miranda's pendant and when his fingers touched it, he was flooded with relief. "It was a gift," he said as though apologizing.

Suddenly he was blasted by a pulse of joyous energy that leapt from the ivory ornament. It joined the knotted threads of light entering his body.

"Enchanting," said Agamond. "How rare. That's no ordinary necklace. It's a thread of life. It connects you to the dream world of men. There's magic in it. I'll bet if you tugged on it from your heart you'd be right back there, spellbound by the force of the word 'love.' That's powerful magic."

Ogden glanced down at his chest and at the carved pendant. The glow of light hovering above his solar plexus drew his attention. It appeared to his eyes as a delicate nebula of light. The narrowest wisp of cloudy brilliance wavered and flowed on an unseen current from the amulet and swirled into the cloud of light hovering above his heart. He looked up at Agamond.

The gnome shook his head, understanding. "Nothing to be concerned about. It's just the world creating you and you creating the world. Everyone you've ever known and everything you've ever seen and not seen breathes the same air you just breathed out, sees the outside of you while you see the outside of them — except...time is a dream. The light *comes* from your eyes. The light comes *from* theirs. You *see each other* into being. You be-live in the pres-ence of everything you know. It happens to everybody all the time, know it or not."

Ogden shuffled to his feet and stood, towering over Agamond. He looked down on the bald spot on the top of his head. "Why would things need to keep being made?" he asked.

Agamond smacked his knobby knee with his right hand and cackled from his throat. For a while he laughed so hard that tears puddled in his eyes. He wiped one then the other with the back of his hands and stood up straight. He sucked in his cheeks, narrowed his eyes, and let his sharp, long nose extend like a compass needle to point at Ogden. "That's a very good question. I'm going to answer it," Agamond said, shaking a loose hand in the air like he was patting the head of an unseen pet. A little dust devil spun away from him across the floor of the cave.

"Shhhh...You'll get your turn," he whispered under his breath and looked up at Ogden sheepishly. Ogden frowned down at Agamond.

"Who are you talking to?" he asked.

"You'll find out soon enough. She's a little impatient to have her say. I'll take my turn first. The others will wait their turn, if you don't mind. So, here we go."

"Begin." Ogden nodded.

Agamond leapt from the bone-strewn floor onto the flat stone slab so that he stood eye-to-eye with the troll.

"Good. I speak for the earth elementals. You asked why everything has to keep creating everything else after things are already made. Once you under-stand, I think you're going to laugh at yourself for asking."

Ogden shrugged doubtfully.

"It's really so simple," Agamond continued. "You have to learn to fly along the strings of light to be anywhen you want."

"Anyone?" Ogden stopped Agamond by holding up his hand.

"Any-when, not anyone," corrected Agamond. "But yes, anyone as well." He popped a red eye toward Ogden and smiled a toothy grin. "Let me put it this way. If you were really stuck in the present moment in time.... I mean...as many mortals think they are, then nothing would change. You wouldn't feel time carrying you along like you were a stick in a river. But we know that's not how it is. If you're alive, time seems to move from now to later. If time stopped, your life would be over. The rest of creation wouldn't keep making you by interacting with that part of you that was free to move in time, from past to future. You wouldn't know you were alive since nothing would happen. And you wouldn't keep doing your part to make all the rest of creation you encounter what they are, partly because of you. But things do happen, so we know that's not how it works. The world is alive."

Agamond stopped himself with a rapid fluttering of his eyes. "Wait. Look. You're wondering how it's possible to move along those threads of light, to be any-when in eternity you like. Let me ask this: if you can move in time from the past to the future, why can't you move from the present moment to any time in eternity and look at creation from every angle? What's stopping you from sampling the 'every-when' I've been talking about?"

"Who can say?" Ogden answered hesitantly.

Agamond nodded. "I can, that's who. And so can you. You already know how to glide along your own thread of time. You cross paths with people and things and spirits like me. You notice those meetings with everything else in big and small ways. That noticing is what changes you, and it changes everything else in subtle ways. We keep remaking each other in the dream of time. Understand?"

"No," said Ogden.

The gnome growled a little when he said, "Look at what I mean, not at what I say. Feel it!" But then he smiled.

Ogden stared at the gnome intently. "You said time is a dream. But you said this right here — this right now — isn't. You said the world of men is a dream. This isn't. That's what you said."

Agamond shook his 'no.' "Time is a dream all its own," he said, "and you're still sleeping inside of it. We elementals aren't trapped in time quite as fully as you are. But you, young troll, have been given a magnificent present. The nature of all things gave us leave to teach you another way to live in time. It is our task to help you become what you are meant to be."

"Wait," Ogden said. "You said this world right now is real and the place where men live is a dream. But if time is a dream, then how can this be real?"

Agamond grumbled something incoherent as he looked over his right shoulder and then looked back at Ogden. "You are more awake than them," he said. "This isn't the real everything. It's just more real than the dreams where men live their lives. When you learn to fly along the strings of light free from time, then you will be all the way awake."

Ogden looked to where Huth lay, breathing shallow breaths. "You say time is a dream. He will take time to die," he said, lowering his eyes. "That's real. Nothing is more real."

Agamond bowed his head and rubbed his chin. "Time is not against us, no matter what you think. Time lets us be in the world together, but only for a time."

Ogden looked at Agamond from the shelter of his brow. "You aren't helping," he said evenly.

"I'm muddling it up pretty good, aren't I?" Agamond smirked and shrugged. "Alright, let's let the tongue fire of creation talk with you for a time. It might crack through your noggin."

Ogden turned his body toward the fire pit as Agamond hopped down from the limestone slab and walked not toward the fire, but toward Huth. Agamond beckoned Ogden with a wave of his hand. Ogden's feet clattered through scattered bones until he stood looking down at the old troll. Huth's face was twisted into a dream-driven grimace. His hand was buried under him, cushioning his wound. The dusty mat was damp with blood. He breathed roughly and trembled.

"What are you doing?" asked Ogden. "You said the fire will talk. The fire is there," he said, pointing toward the burning logs.

Agamond crossed his lips with a finger and shushed him. "The fire of nature is there, in your poppa's heart. The ghost of nature holds fire, and water, and air, and even me," Agamond nodded toward Huth. "He brought us here for you. You've got to accept his gift. Then you'll hear the voice of the flames, and of the air, and the waters. They'll become present to you. You were born a troll, so you are already in touch with the gift of earth wisdom. That's why we can talk."

A rush of light, like a wind from nowhere, erupted from Huth's chest and shoved Ogden backward three steps. His eyes popped wide, and his jaw dropped as a scream flew out his broad lips. He fell to his knees and the wind of light blasted into him, drowning out the feeling of sweet brilliance that inundated his body and mind. The song of the stars and stones bowed and withdrew reverently. The spirit of nature came as a voice of voices, a multitude that crowded his soul, seeming to say wordlessly and powerfully "We are with you!"

Ogden knelt, transfixed as a thousand and then millions of minds shaped his thoughts like they were sand dunes shifting in many directions in the path of a mystical maelstrom. Huth's memories flew into him and became his own past with that gush of light. Ogden lived the odyssey of Huth's wanderings, became imprinted by the memories stowed in every place his poppa's feet had ever trod in life.

Then phantoms from beings living and long dead, from near and far, entered and possessed him, but he could still see the gnarled face and form of Agamond. And then his appearance changed and transformed as Ogden watched silently. From a diminutive brownie to a sprite, then an elf, and a wood nymph, then a gob, a dyad, and at last, after assuming all the many forms of earth elementals Agamond returned to his familiar form.

Ogden felt like he was stuck in a spider's web. A net of intersecting threads of light held him immobile. Cords of light flowed into him like they were weaving a nest in his heart. But gradually the overwhelming sense of being everywhere and nowhere all at once dissipated. He felt himself freed from the all-permeating cloud of creation.

Ogden was centered in his own space and not stretched. The muscles in his abdomen relaxed and joyful contentment overwhelmed him. He breathed the cavern air like it was his first breath.

"He is sleeping," Ogden said to Agamond with one eye on Huth.

"And his promise is kept," said Agamond. He smiled and nodded up and down. Then he reached up and patted Ogden's chest just over his heart. "You'll need to tap deep down inside, plumb the depths of this gift to raise the voice of the flame and tap its wisdom. Remember, we were going to consult the fire?"

Ogden leaned down to look directly into Agamond's red eyes. "What about 'time?'" he asked. "You said the fire knows what it is."

Agamond held his hands next to each other, palms pointing upward, and then he spread his arms slowly until they were spread wide to either side. "The answer to the riddle of time is right here," he said.

Dropping his arms, he bounced as he walked Ogden closer to the fire ring. He spoke quickly, in short bursts. "Come close. Watch the fire. Look closely, but not just with your eyes. He should come to you now."

Ogden stared at the ring of stones. The glowing halo of heat surrounding the orange embers burned atop a pillow of puffy gray ashes. Flames licked up and around the underside of a fire-gnawed log.

He kept watching intently and then noticed something small but quick move around the stones that formed the lower wall of the fire pit. It was a horned and winged salamander that scurried in between and back out of the rounded stones. Its flesh was all bright orange-red, with narrow black shading along the creases of its folded wings. Then suddenly it spread those wings and took flight.

Ogden took a step backward when the salamander buzzed at his face, but it quickly turned and circled the fire, closer and closer to the flames and burning logs.

Agamond grinned at Ogden. "You've seen this before," he said. "Only, you mistook the little fire dragons for moths when you looked at them with your dreaming eyes."

Ogden said nothing. He watched the winged salamander tighten its circular flight and then lurch down suicidally into the shimmering embers. At once, large flames erupted out of the red glowing coals and danced rapidly all around the immolated creature. The flames roared with power, and they rolled up into the shape of a grimacing dragon's face, with eyes as fiery as Agamond's own.

"Startle not, troll," spoke the flaming dragon's head from its perch above the blazing log. "Fire elementals shape-shift; that is what we do."

"Why?" asked Ogden.

Something in the fire hissed, bubbled and steamed. Agamond fanned his hands in front of his face in warning from across the fire. "Ogden, meet Pyreft. Our mother sent him to you. He'll speak for the element of fire and all it commands and serves. You should listen."

Ogden nodded and refocused his eyes on the mid-ground between him and Agamond. The flames reconstituted themselves in the form of a salamander with outspread wings suspended on the updraft created by the heat rising from the fire.

"We greet you, troll. You have a gift given freely of nature. It is the freedom to move through all of time, down every connecting pathway, into any heart or mind. Don't puff up importantly. You're different, but not more special than the slightest glint of light or the merest droplet of dew, nor the lowest clod of earth or the faintest wind. The elements of creation and every being we come together to create can cross eternity in no-time and gaze at the world through other eyes, if they but wake from the dream that tells them they can't."

Ogden nodded and listened.

"Our ever-present origin bids us awaken you and make a passage for you down the silver threads of time. We will try."

"Why?" asked Ogden.

The flames gushed upward. Sparks flew in swirling billows of smoke. The cavern walls glowed with new brilliance and the voice of Pyreft, the fire, echoed against them and came back in waves of repeating sound.

"You have slept long enough in the dreaming world of men. You are their familiar. You know their talk. You could, if it is fated, fashion a counter-spell and awaken them before they wander down into a darkness of spirit from which there is no escape. You must try. It's their last chance."

Ogden sighed. He felt he understood what Pyreft meant. He had suspected something was very wrong about the way people live. It worried him ever since he grasped human speech. There was something false in it. Now he wanted to know what he could do to save them. "What if they won't stir from their nightmare?" he asked. "It doesn't seem possible that more words will convince them to change."

"Then they are doomed. They need a counter-spell more than anything in the world." The booming voice of the flaming salamander rumbled around contours of the ceiling. Loose stones clattered down from the unseen rafters.

Ogden cried out. "What if they won't listen? Do you see a wizard standing before you? You think a troll can scatter the spell men have woven around themselves? There must be another way to save them!"

The fire settled lower and hovered just above the shimmering embers. The dragon-headed flame collapsed down into a rising cloud of gray smoke. The winged salamander crawled out of the scalding embers onto the ring of rocks and perched atop the tallest one. There it crouched and spoke again.

"To touch their souls and free them from lies, you will have to end the distance between them and you. Traverse the threads of light. Cross the chasm they are building between themselves and the rest of creation."

"Will they listen?" asked Ogden somberly.

"We don't know. We doubt it. But you've got to try," hissed the flames.

Ogden considered this a moment. "That is a hard thing for you to ask," he finally said. "How can it be done?"

Pyreft flapped wings once. "You will glide along the strands of light, the threads of time, to touch the souls of men," he said. "Know that you can do it and it will be done."

Ogden said, "If that is what must be done for men to hear the voice of nature, a troll has to learn. So, teach."

"Well said," Pyreft answered.

"Fine," said Ogden. "Then, say it again. Is time the space between things?"

The winged salamander coughed a gray plume of smoke. "You have it a little backwards," he said. "Distance is what time looks like to someone who is bound to the ever-changing present. To overcome the illusion of distance and unite everything into the all, you will have to move faster than the soul of fire."

Ogden was puzzled. "How? And, what's the soul of fire?"

"Light, boy; it's light," Pyreft answered. "It's as fast as a thought. We salamanders are messengers that crisscross the universe, and even the smallest space. We bridge the chasm between a book and its reader. We are the messengers who call you from dreams and we can call you back to them too. We're the light of illumination and the fire of inspiration."

"This isn't easy," Ogden said, shaking his head and holding his temples with the palms of his hands.

Pyreft flapped his wings and rose into the air, coming nose to nose with Ogden. "It's not meant to be easy. Are you giving up?"

"No! Of course not!" Ogden cried out, and the stones echoed his words.

"Then listen," Pyreft said. "We salamanders are the light. We bring the fire of creation to the world. Without us, you wouldn't know anything."

"You said you want a troll to walk on threads of light?" Ogden's voice rose in frustration. "How?"

Pyreft said, "Find the essence of fire within you. Like everything else, your body is made of that light. It's anchored in eternity by all the filaments of being that connect you with everything else. Everything is attached to everything else at the ever-present origin. That's why it's possible for you to traverse the threads of light and commune directly with every other being. You can undo the otherness. It's the gift you've been given."

Pyreft seemed to pause for a breath. "I know it's complicated, but it'll come to you. Well, no; I mean, it won't come to you. It's already there, right there!" Pyreft shot a bolt of fiery light and gently touched Ogden's chest.

Ogden's dark eyes glowed in the flame's light. "One pure light holds all those colors and strands together, outside of time," Ogden said as though in a trance.

"Of course," Pyreft answered. "That one light is the source and origin of everything. It's the fountain from which time gushes in floods of light. The threads weave and intersect to make the fabric of our being."

Ogden spun on his right foot to look away, then turned back and said, "Men and women don't talk about this. Likely, they can't think of it because they don't know how to say it."

Pyreft alighted on the limestone slab six feet from where Ogden stood. He moved slowly back and forth, conveying a mood of impatience. Turning to the young troll with an outstretched left fore-claw he yelled in a hissing voice, "If men's brains worked better, time would seem very different. They only hold onto the tidbits that amuse them."

"Men don't hear the songs of stars," Ogden said. "It's strange. They talk words but never listen to the stars."

Pyreft took flight again and hovered just above the hot coals. "Too bad," he said. "They want to create a world of their own, but don't want the world that creates them. It makes no difference. Everything is connected and always has been. You and me — we are tied together for eternity. But they choose to disconnect, to part ways from you and me. We might have to let them."

"The room is spinning!" Ogden yelled, holding his head in both hands. "This talk is dizzying!" He sat down on a rock and leaned forward, his head between his knees. "You're right. We move each other, and you have moved me — from the inside out."

The fire crackled and spat with the voice of Pyreft. "The life force you radiate is part of what makes them real. We create each other. Every being is essential. Remove one, and we all change. We are all less. That's why men have gone so far wrong in thinking they can learn the essence of a thing by removing it from nature. Or worse, by disassembling it and torturing it for its secrets. All that can be learned that way is tricks; not truths."

Ogden sat up straight. "That's what the stars were trying to say."

"Yes," Pyreft said, and was silent.

"That's a great gift," Ogden said quietly. "So is time. No one could know the joy of living without it."

"If not for time," Pyreft laughed, "everything would happen all at once in the same place. What a mess that would be."

"Rather crowded," Ogden said with a hint of a smirk.

The salamander's head turned slowly to one side and then came back to look at him critically. "Yes."

Suddenly Ogden felt the umbilical cord of light at his solar plexus awaken with energy. The words of the winged salamander took on a different form, no longer words but threads of silver light that braided into a rope and tugged him forward, up and out of himself. He felt a rush of vertigo as his presence fled out of his body and into the world around him. He heard Pyreft's voice all around him. It said: "Even my kin, the elemental spirits of nature, doze in a dream of particulars and separation — a little less than men and other slow beings. We know the swiftness of light and how to shorten the illusion of space. But even we, all the denizens of fire, can't do away with distance and separation. We can only skein the threads of light and shorten the separation between all things that live in the forest of time."

Pyreft launched into the air above the smoldering embers. "The ghost of nature is inside you now. You can outstrip the sound of my voice and reach the stars even before their songs leave to meet you where you are. You can touch the soul of all things. You can know the marvel of creation all at once. It's time to try out your new wings."

Suddenly Ogden felt himself lift out of his body and expand in all directions. He was touching everything he encountered with his soul. He roamed within the hearts of men and women and peered through the eyes of creatures large and small. All of creation poured in through those countless eyes. Through innumerable hands and fins and toes he felt the world. He was aware of the inner lives of trees and gnats, stones and bubbling springs. And from a million gurgling fountains he heard a voice call out to him.

Ogden shouted in his mind, and he felt a jolt shudder throughout his body. "No!" he screamed. With a sharp and brilliant light shocking him from inside and blasting out his pores, he snapped back into full awareness of his body, and he felt the world again through his accustomed senses. He suddenly bolted up and sat with eyes blinking.

He felt with his hands and touched the big rock where he was sitting. His eyes began to focus, and he looked around in every direction until vision coalesced into a sense of reality 'out there.' Finally, when he had gathered his composure and oriented himself to his surroundings, Ogden spoke. Neither Pyreft nor Agamond were anywhere to be seen.

"It felt like buzzing bees," he said. "Everywhere. Just a humming rumble underneath everything. Everything was real and present all at once. It was like drinking water. You don't have to argue that water is wet. You don't have to tell yourself any of it. It's just there. It just is, and you know it."

A laugh blew out of the fire ring and the winged salamander, Pyreft, scrambled out of the gray ashes at the outer edge. Then Agamond emerged from the dust on the floor like a shadow that gained depth and dimension.

The materialized gnome strode into the firelight and walked closer to the troll. His laughter braided in echoes with the fire spirit's crackling laugh. Pyreft leapt from the flames and took form. "Ha, ha, ha! No, you don't argue with water. You'll find that out soon enough."

Ogden didn't want to, but he forced himself to talk. "The whole world was nothing but doors. Lots of them hung open. But others were shut tight. They seemed to say, 'stay away.' Doing that seemed best."

Agamond stepped forward and stood on his toes looking up at Ogden. "You thought it would be trespass. Well, we will let *her* tell you about boundaries," he said with a smirk.

"Who are you talking about?" Ogden's voice rose quizzically.

"Over there," Pyreft pointed with an extended wing. "In the pool of clear water behind that wall. That's where Aguaqui waits for you."

Chapter XXVII
A Spinning Compass

Drowden gazed at the crystal pool's still surface. There was silence in the air, all but the occasional squeak of a leather scabbard or clink of a blade on a rock. The men of the Brotherhood stood on high ground. His men were scattered around him, unprepared for a confrontation. He looked up with water trembling in his eyes.

"Would you agree Ogden is gone?" he shouted up the rocks, meaning for Ospin Tapple to answer. But Bos Fudlow responded.

"We don't know. Could be a trick. If it's drowned, we ain't seen the corpse. We gotta be sure the Trog is dead."

"Hold your tongue!" Tapple shouted down to Fudlow. Then he pointed at Drowden. "Our business is our business, Drowden Erebus. We'll fight for this ground if that's what you decide. But we'll let you go unscathed if you leave now. What will it be?"

Drowden looked around at his men. He was desperate not to have them bludgeoned by the armed men standing on the rocks and boulders above. But whatever Ogden's fate, he couldn't leave him to the Brotherhood. He'd neither surrender Ogden's life nor his lifeless body. Anger welled in his chest, and he yelled back: "If we go, you have to go too. I'll protect Ogden, whatever's left, with every bit of fight I've got in me, and so will these men!"

He glanced around him and saw Argis raise his weapon and shake it. Willbee did too, and all the others brandished pikes, pitchforks, machetes and scythes.

"We'll steal your last breath!" shouted Bos Fudlow.

"Don't be rash!" Ospin Tapple's voice yelled down the rocks like skittering pebbles. "I told you this is our business now." And then he caught himself and turned to his side toward Thad Krebbermoting. "These hills are laced with caves, am I right?" he said too quietly for the men of Hapstead to hear.

"They are," answered Thad. "Honeycombed. What are you thinking?"

"Quiet," spat Tapple. "We're not done troll hunting."

Then he lifted his chin and called down to Drowden. "Alright. We can be reasonable. Withdraw your boys and we'll come down. You have my word we'll leave this grotto and be on our way. No need for us to kill you if you go. But go *now*."

Drowden felt a cool wind blow down from the hills. Across his face it flowed like he'd been doused with water. His collar flecked against his chin. "I'll hold you to that," he yelled back at Tapple. "Leave this place when we're gone." Then he glanced around at his men and darted his head backward and turned to climb down the tumble of stones.

The Hapstead men followed Drowden without a word. They soon disappeared among the trees of the forest. Ospin Tapple held up a hand when a cheer rang out from the men of the Brotherhood. The noise petered out quickly and they looked to Bos Fudlow, who was the only one to keep yelling epithets at the retreating Hapstead band.

"We're going that way," Tapple shouted, and he pointed up the boulder field in the opposite direction from Drowden Erebus and his men.

Fudlow turned back to look at him. "Let's send somebody down to find the entrance," he growled. "Down under the water. Got to be a cave. He's in there. I can smell him from here."

"He's not coming back that way," Tapple shouted in his nasally voice. "There's a tunnel in the ground that winds all through these hills. You'd get lost and never come out."

Thad Krebbermoting stepped down from a boulder above Tapple. "Ogden's going to get away!" he shouted. "These hills are drilled with openings into the caverns."

"Are you talking about that wild animal?" Tapple scowled at Thad. "I don't name the beasts I plan to slaughter. He's not going to escape death easily."

"Gotta catch 'im first," Bos laughed. "Could be anywhere. Might even be more of 'em Troggs down every hole."

Tapple scowled in horror. "You're wrong." His lips sputtered spittle and they quivered like he wanted to say more but couldn't. His eyes glazed and his vision went inward. He saw dark entrances into the hollow ground strewn across a field of boulders. From each one emerged a gnarled hand, a misshapen head, until a legion of trolls stood all around him, newly resurrected from the earth.

Hopskel Dwil clapped him on the shoulder, snapping him from his daylight nightmare. "Where do ya think he went?" asked Dwil.

Tapple's eyes blinked, and he sneered at the man. "I think I know." Then he pointed up the hill and yelled "That way!"

Soon a clatter of metal and the grunts of climbing men filled the grotto, then faded away into the birch trees above.

The Hapstead clan was not far off. Drowden stopped his men and had them sit in silence soon after descending into the forest from the grotto of the crystal pool. Then they circled around the base of the hill and stopped again. They listened to every sound. They heard muffled human voices among the sounds of birds and insects. Bill Macatee crept up the stony woodland slope and near the meadowed top he crawled out from the trees to spy on the Brotherhood. When he saw them at last clamor over the rocky peak and disappear behind the ridge he scuttled down to report.

Drowden listened and nodded. "They're going deep into the hills," he said. "Up where the big stones have been moved and arranged. They say by trolls long gone, but I don't know for sure."

Argis eyed him with doubt but kept quiet. The other men looked on, waiting to hear what Drowden planned to do. Hector broke the momentary silence. "There's more of them than us," he said. "What you wanna do?"

"We're goin' ta follow 'em," growled Argis. "We're goin' ta do what we gotta," and he spat out the side of his mouth. "More o' them is just easier ta track."

Drowden stood up. He looked from man to man. "Alright. We can keep to the hollow going west, then up the ravine over there," he pointed. "That should keep us close enough but not too close."

All the rest of the day the men of Hapstead Manor trudged through the underbrush. They stayed in the shadows and kept out of sight of the Brotherhood, but never far from them.

Twilight turned the forest into a cool damp place full of owl hoots, snapping branches, curling mist. The Brotherhood found a grassy hillock exposed to the night sky where they lay down and snored.

Drowden's men stayed in a rough thicket of greenbrier matted over knobs of rock. They slept uncomfortably but deeply. Drowden sat up, leaning against a sassafras sapling. His thoughts rambled. "If I've lost Ogden," said his mind, "maybe I'll lose some of these men too. Which ones?" He caught himself and felt ashamed. "What's the difference? How can I live with myself after that?"

The night dark grew rigid, and the forest went silent. For a long time Drowden sat, occasionally clicking a fingernail on his tooth. He wanted to wake his men and tell them to go home. Then he thought "What if Ogden is alive? What if the Brotherhood finds him?" And then he thought, "We'd have to fight. No way around it."

A chill went through him, and he shivered. A sudden certainty overtook his reverie. Any doubt he had that Ogden was alive evaporated. He could feel him nearby. He sensed the young troll's eyes upon him. He glanced from one side to the other and he felt the hair prickle on the back of his neck.

In a while he was alone again with his thoughts. Drowden's mind raced. "If Ospin Tapple were to disappear, the Brotherhood would give up their search. They'd go home and leave Ogden to the forest and rocks." That thought spun in his head until his eyes closed, and he nodded down, his chin on his chest.

Drowden awoke with a jolt. He saw Ospin Tapple standing in front of him, smiling a nasty grin. He almost jumped to his feet, but immediately realized it was the remnants of a dream. The apparition disappeared, but a deep loathing for Tapple remained.

Drowden's temples pounded, and he could hear his heart drubbing in his ears. He got to his feet and looked around. The faintest edge of dawn dusted the hill. He knew what he had to do.

Quietly he lifted a machete from the ground next to where Bill Macatee was sleeping and then crept off into the shadows. Drowden fumbled up the rocky hill grabbing tree trunks for balance. Morning light gradually brightened the way, and he could see more than feel his way. The higher up the hill he went, the stronger grew his rage.

"Tapple!" he said under his breath and clenched the machete in his hand. "Tapple!" he said again and clenched his jaws and ground his teeth together.

He broke from the tree cover and emerged on the grassy glade where the Brotherhood had stopped for the night. A shock went through him. "Gone!" he half yelled. All that remained was flattened patches of grass where men had slept, as though a herd of deer had rested there. His heart sank, but the seething hatred for Ospin Tapple festered like a wound. He'd lost his chance to end this ordeal on his own. Now he had no choice but to take his men deeper into the wilderness and into danger.

He turned back down the hill and entered the forest. Halfway down to where his men had bivouacked, he was met by Argis and Hector. Argis extended an arm and touched Drowden's chest with the back edge of a scythe blade. "Where was ya off too? On yer own, I mean?"

"They're gone!" panted Drowden. "Gone!"

"Ya didn't answer," growled Argis.

Bill Macatee arrived from below. He looked Drowden in the eye and shook his head, then leaned down and took the machete from Drowden's hand. "I'm gonna need that, Master Erebus," he said.

Chapter XXVIII
Water and Air

Agamond reached up and touched Ogden's wrist. "You should go. The lady of the water is waiting."

Pyreft, the spirit of the flames added, "Go now," and Ogden took a lurching step in the direction of the passage Huth had concealed with the woven door of vines and squirrel skin. But suddenly the winged salamander exploded into an orange-yellow fireball that cried out, "Stay with me when you go. I will keep your body warm."

Ogden turned back to look at the newly blazing fire. He hitched his hands onto his waist. "Stay *and* go?"

"Sit down," Agamond said gently. "Close your eyes. It will work better that way."

"But," Ogden protested, "It's a short walk…"

"It's even a shorter reach for your heart," Agamond said. "Now sit."

Ogden sat cross-legged on the stone slab and closed his eyes. In a moment he felt the bundle of luminous threads gathering at his chest, and next he felt himself dissolve into a point of radiance that tested one, then another of the narrow silver ribbons. Looking inside and down along the length of several of them not with eyes, but with some new sense, he saw that each was a conduit leading to some being's living spirit.

"There are so many beings of light!" he cried out from his heart. But observing the world through the eyes of countless others was not helping him find the water elemental who waited for him in the underground chamber next door.

"Which one?" Ogden called out from where he sat.

Agamond answered. His youthful voice sang out, "Listen for her calling to you. You will hear her and there won't be any mistaking it. Find her voice. Pick it out and hold onto it. She will show you the way."

Ogden's inner eye gazed down at a million silver threads, felt the rhythmic waves of star glow and tree prayers yammering as a swarm of dancing vibrations on a cord of silver light. He knew creatures wild and magnificent and all their secret feelings. And then he heard from among the multitude of songs the song of water babbling and bubbling through a stone wall. Behind the wall of rock that parted like insubstantial gossamer she called to him, laughing.

"This way, young troll. Here I am. Here is Aguaqui. Follow your heart. I am waiting."

Ogden felt his heart being pulled along a current, a river of light. His mind sailed a spaceless distance, and in no time at all he stood beside a sink of water that pooled below an underground spring. It was a lake to him now, not the bowl-sized dent in the rocks where he had filled Huth's waterskin. Now he stood miniscule, small as a mouse, beside the shuddering surface of the clear water.

"Welcome, troll brother," said a pleasant female voice from nowhere he could tell. How he could not help but pity this suddenly apparent diminutive being known to covet his powers was disorienting. As he looked around the outer cavern where the spring gurgled out of the rock wall and into the rippling lake before him, the immensity of the space above yawned and seemed to recede away. Ogden looked around in all directions. Then he noticed a shifting mist floating just above the undulating surface of the pooled water.

"Is that you?" His thought projected the question like an arrow lightly plucked into flight.

The soft fluid voice of Aguaqui rose from the vapor hovering over the water. "The mist? The ripples? Am I the ripples? Am I the mist? Am I the star song that sings them into being? Am I the thought that is the Aguaqui that you notice in this moment? Where are my boundaries? Where is Aguaqui? Who will decide? Is it you or is it me?"

"Who can say?" Ogden's soul asked.

"You seem to know many things, different people, kinds of trees, shapes of stones and tasty foods. All these many things you know, but what makes them stand apart and not seem a part of each other? Is the world made of chunks and clods, or is it fluid and blending and merging, one thing sharing its being with another, like water from a spring flowing into a pond?"

The mist hovering over the rippling water extended two long wisps of vapor that lightly touched the surface. Above those stalky cloudlets formed a body, arms and a head. Aguaqui appeared as a spritely young girl draped in a gauzy fog.

Ogden answered hesitantly. "No one can say."

The nymph laughed. "Of course, it can't be said! But can it be known? Tell me: am I the mist? Am I the water's smooth skin? Am I what lies beneath the surface? Am I the spring flowing down from the rocks, or the raindrops splashing on the ground above us? Or am I the cloud showering rain upon the earth? If I am Aguaqui, the spirit of the waters of the world, am I one of these or all of them or none of these at all? Tell me troll."

"Who can say?" asked Ogden again.

The apparition of the nymph grew more substantial. Ogden watched her dance across the surface of the water, kneel and dip her hand to form a cup and sip from the edge of her palm. "You are thirsty to understand. That's good and bad. I'll tell you this: don't mistake Aguaqui for the spirit of the waters of the world."

"But," Ogden objected, "you just said that you are!"

"No," said the nymph. "Aguaqui is my name. The word is not my essence."

"That was a rude trick," Ogden said with annoyance.

"Oh, don't be so sensitive," Aguaqui laughed. "It was an innocent trick of words, that's all. But you're right to be cautious. Many such tricks can rip out your soul if you let them."

"Please, don't do that," Ogden pleaded gently.

"Please don't let me," Aguaqui laughed. "You need to protect yourself from deceit. Don't let anyone misuse you."

"How?" asked Ogden. "Build walls and fences?"

"Never!" Aguaqui billowed and grew tall, so that she was looking down upon Ogden. "Boundaries are all false and unreal. They serve no one but Ventego."

"That name seems familiar," Ogden said haltingly. "Who is Ventego?"

Aguaqui's misty outline wavered and jittered as if disturbed by a subtle wind. "It is the name we call the divider of souls, the one who keeps us apart, the one who watches for ways to separate all from the all. It is the one who tempts your favorites, thee Hyumans, toward greed, the love of owning what possesses them. It is the thing that sets them against each other and also the haughtiness that keeps them from joining in community with nature. It is the opposite of love, and the creator of time. Some say it is the father of sorrow."

"It's hard to understand why anyone would listen to it." Ogden felt a shadow cross the silver thread connecting him to his body and a wave of panic surged in his heart. "I did not know that evil is real."

"Don't be afraid," said the gentle voice of Aguaqui. "Ventego is a very good liar. With stories wrapped in fear he mocks trust as foolishness. The ones who fall under his spell part ways with their own kin. What once was for all to share they take as properly theirs alone. What in their greed seems proper for them to hoard, they defend as property. They build walls and fences to keep others out and to lock away what grace they once had. Do you know what a boundary is?"

"A border, I suppose," Ogden thought, and it was as though he spoke.

"Is a border real or imaginary?" Aguaqui asked.

Ogden felt a damp mesh of cloud brush past him and knew it was Aguaqui's hand touching his face. "Men say borders are real," he answered. "They act like they're real. The towns have walls, and it's said that countries have boundaries too."

"The walls are real enough," she said, "but not the boundaries. Where there are fences and walls there is Ventego. Minds bewitched by a fear of sharing write laws and gather armies to protect borders that can't be seen. Around those boundaries sometimes they build walls to make them visible."

"Even without walls," Ogden said, "they be-live boundaries are real, and they act like they are real."

"If they're really real, then show me one," Aguaqui giggled. "Where is the boundary between two kingdoms?" The nymph slumped down into the water and seemed to float half submerged, like a swimmer.

"Where they meet to fight," Ogden said. "Where they say what is theirs begins and end."

"Let's look. Are the borders really there?" laughed Aguaqui. And suddenly Ogden felt himself taken by an insubstantial hand and whisked up through the ceiling rock, out above the hills that hid the caverns below the ground and high over the clouds in the unseen sky. Through breaks in the clouds below he could see green land, a march of hills and then a jagged row of white-tipped mountains. And to the west a great sea shone blue as a huckleberry.

"Are they there?" the water nymph asked again. "Can you see the borders anywhere?"

Ogden blinked against the bright sun. "There are no lines," he said. "No boundaries to be seen anywhere."

Aguaqui giggled. She hovered nearby, a little wisp of vapor that swirled and tumbled upon itself. "Then where are they?"

Ogden paused. He couldn't answer right away. And then he felt for the answer with his heart and he smiled. "On paper," he said. "They're just ink on paper."

"Yes," Aguaqui cried happily. "On maps, in human minds: that's where boundaries live. But somewhere else! Think! Where else can we find those lines, those borders, those maps and laws?"

Ogden again quieted his thoughts and searched his heart for the answer. Without knowing how, he found himself back in the depths of the earth, standing next to a gurgling pool of water, the diaphanous mist of the elemental spirit of water undulating just above the rippling pool. In no time he said, "Boundaries live in the waking dreams of those who be-live in spells cast by ink on paper."

"And nowhere else," the nymph whispered. "Only on paper and in the minds of those deceived by the spell of words. Weak brains are etched with the predatory scribblings of cowards and tyrants."

Ogden's heart felt momentarily heavy. "That feels true," he said sadly.

"Building walls and hiding behind them won't protect you from deception or from the changes happening all around us."

Ogden felt time flowing past him like a cool stream, and finally asked, "Then what will?"

Aguaqui paused a moment as if considering what to say and then said, "Don't try to change the world outside you. It isn't yours. You are just a little part of it. Instead, become true to your nature and grow with the world around you. You and it are creating each other."

Ogden nodded silently and Aguaqui continued. "The spirit of the waters change constantly. In the cold of winter, we are ice. In the pleasant spring air, we are rain and brooks and creeks and immense surging oceans. And in the warmth of the sun, we are mists, steam and vapors. In changing ourselves, we change the world and in return it changes us. And so, life proceeds."

"That feels true," said Ogden.

"Ice, river, and cloud — our spirit is in them all and we are all one, though we seem to be different," whispered Aguaqui. "That is how we adjust to the whims of time. Not by separating ourselves from nature, but by finding within ourselves our own nature."

In his left ear Ogden heard Agamond's voice. It interrupted Aguaqui's lesson, and though he still stood in his diminutive form by the edge of the rippling sink of water, he was also sitting on the limestone pad near the simmering fire, just feet away from Huth's reposing form.

Agamond stood right next to him, leaning in to speak quietly. But Aguaqui hovered just above the rippling water almost within reach of his shrunken self. Ogden experienced both in the same instant and noticed that the ribbon of light on which he moved had tangled around two others.

"The spirit that sees and hears the two of us at once is more than one," Agamond said evenly.

"It's odd to be here and there at the same time," said Ogden with his heart, but also with his lips.

Agamond laughed his childish laugh and called to Pyreft. The winged salamander lurched from the orange embers of the fire to hover just in front of Ogden's coal-black eyes.

Ogden focused on the fire spirit for a moment, but then Aguaqui pulled his attention through the wall of rock and into the outer cavern. "There are no boundaries. We are all one being," she said to his heart.

Ogden heard Agamond calling him from the inner cave. His voice was muffled by the wall of rock between them. It also came into his ears, clear and strong. Suddenly Ogden was looking at the gnome through his eyes.

"He hasn't heard from Waft," Pyreft's tongue lashed the air and his voice sizzled.

"He will!" Agamond yelled triumphantly. "She's next."

Aguaqui's voice gurgled through the porous rocks and echoed from the stone rafters. "She'll tell the troll all about how dark magic works."

"Good," the winged salamander flared.

"Who is Waft?" Ogden asked.

"Eh, in this dream that's the name we give the spirit of the air," answered Agamond. "She's all around us. You'll hear from her when she's ready."

Suddenly a gust of wind roared through the cave, tossing up a storm of dust and debris that stung the flesh and eyes. "She is ready!" blew a voice as loud as a thunderclap. The haze in the air hung and remained suspended. A vortex as tall as a walking stick rose from the floor and stood in front of Ogden and Agamond.

"As promised," Agamond said, "meet Waft."

Ogden got up off his haunches and stood atop the slab, then jumped down to stand right next to the twirling maelstrom of orange-brown dust. The whirlwind rose in stature and fell again as it inched closer. Ogden stood firm and let the whizzing wind brush his eyelashes. He heard a breathy voice whisper in his right ear.

"I'll tell you about your favorites. Those people," it said.

Agamond laughed. "Waft, elemental Diva of the air. Whether she comes as a gentle breeze or skin-blasting wind, she's hard to ignore."

"And invisible, unless I kick up some dust!" the air around Waft roared with power.

Agamond bowed to the vortex. "The dust is happy to oblige, my lady."

Waft's voice blew out from the twisting funnel of dust. "I am here to commune with the troll. Ogden!" yelled a yowling squall. "Humans are changing."

Ogden opened his mouth to speak, but it was impossible. The whirling funnel stood directly in front of his face. When he opened his mouth, the whizzing gust pulled the air out of his lungs and held him tied to the whirlwind from the inside. Then he heard that fluting voice again. It seemed to be inside him.

"They forget we are one. They forget I am the breath in their chests. They forget I am the smell of roses, of bread, of autumn in their noses. They forget I am the life they inhale every moment. They are changing, and not in good ways. They are parting from us and from each other."

Even though he could not speak, the vacuum created by the spinning funnel of air seemed to suck words right out of Ogden's body, unspoken by his lips. He heard his voice swirl up from down inside him, spin from his chest, narrow in his throat, and fly out from his open mouth. He heard his words swirl around with accelerating speed until they were absorbed by the maelstrom.

Though he seemed not to breathe, with his mouth wide open and the wind flailing visibly in front of his eyes, Ogden felt no distress. He was content to let the air breathe for him. He felt himself connected to the whole of the world through the air that filled his lungs and yet extended out beyond him, into the farthest reaches of the earth.

Waft said, "They used to live with us in peace. No more. They want to take everything for themselves."

"And so, you judge them?" Ogden's question was voiced by the wind.

Waft blurted out, "We can't stop them! The thread connecting people and nature is being cut — by men. They don't hear the song of the stars anymore."

"What do they hear?" Ogden heard his voice ask.

"The loneliness of their own words. That's all." The spinning wind seemed to slow a little. "They are very clever. But then they named all that is. And then they saw only the names and not the world anymore. Their words separated them from everything they named. Nowadays they can't become. They can't renew. They won't let the world create them and they insist on remaking the world the way they want it to be."

"How can they do that?" Ogden's voice blew out of him uncontrollably.

"They save their words in binders and feed them to their children like candy. But they are never used up; there's an endless supply. They hand them down through generations. They make everyone be-live in those words instead of in the world. Words; not world. Words; not world. Now most of them forget that their eyes are meant to see beauty, not to read more words. Their ears are meant to hear music, not commands. Their hands are for touching the world and each other, not for making and taking. Their noses are best for roses, and their tongues…let them taste the sweet water…"

From beyond a wall of rock they heard Aguaqui giggle. Ogden felt his chest swell with air and blow out like a bellows. "Are words bad? Are they evil?"

Waft's windy voice came as a sigh. "Only when they disperse instead of gather," she whispered. "When they make distances, boundaries, mine and thine, that is when words possess and own us."

"Is this the dark magic you have come to teach?" asked Ogden on the wind.

"I will not teach it!" Waft bellowed. Then calming, "It is a warning that I share. It is the reason for our judgment of men. The evil is not in the words, but in the separation they cause. Living beings move through time. Words rip life from things and lock them in place. De-finite them. Make living waves into dead pebbles. Binding the world to time is not the purpose of life."

Ogden felt his head nod. "The purpose is being in a story together," he said.

"And becoming, together," said Waft. "It's sad when beings stop becoming and just wait for the wind to blow them away. Trust me; I'll do it!"

Ogden paused to reflect, and then said, "All those things they take as theirs are made of earth and air, fire and water. You, elementals, are enslaved by all of it."

Agamond stood off to the side. He held up a hand and looked skyward when he said, "I wish we were free of them! Maybe soon we will be, when you have made your judgement. We aren't to blame for the things they use us for. They treat us as badly as they treat each other. By chaining themselves to things they cherish more than life, they bind themselves in time. By binding themselves in time they strip the world of becoming, of life. By enslaving the elements, they put themselves in bondage. They are at war with the very elements of being, yes. But they aren't just at war with the world and all of time. They are at war with each other. Because of this, they've left no place for their children in the days to come. Sadly, they never will be at peace nor ever be content."

Ogden's eyes dropped and his shoulders slumped. Waft withdrew her whirlwind and stood off a way, in the cave's shadows. Ogden said, "I do not want to make this choice."

Agamond sighed and Waft tossed dust into the space between them. "Men rip the elementals out of eternity's embrace," he said. "They shape us into dead things: gears, rods, wheels and cogs. They make machines they think free them from toil, but that's a plain lie."

Waft interrupted by raising the velocity and volume of her whirling gusts. "Listen young troll and try not to forget when you wake in the dream world of men. It's the wind in their mouths that gets spun into the confusion that besets the world. They write down their words and remember everything, while they learn nothing, all the while telling themselves they are improving the world that gives them life and breath and joy."

"It conjures deep grief," Ogden grumbled loudly.

Suddenly Pyreft piped up. "And they think they're very bright. They tell their children they 'know' things. But to 'know' what is separate from becoming is to be ensnared."

"True," Aguaqui's voice bibbled up like bubbles roiling out of a swamp. Ogden looked with his eyes but could not see her. Then he felt with his heart and knew just where she was.

"Their spells don't offer wisdom," she said. "The time is coming when people will study only their own creations. They'll stay locked in the world made by their own minds. They'll be-live only in their inherited jibber-jabber."

The light in the cavern brightened and Pyreft's thoughts penetrated the silent dark. "They are tearing their own children away from the ever-present origin and their natural connection to it. Their stories pretend that the spirits of nature are the creatures of magic, but it's them, those clever sorcerers, who cast spells that lie, day and night. They cast spells to gain advantage. They cast spells to take possession of what's not theirs and should be no one's. They cast spells to discredit what everyone's eyes can see. They cast spells to send fear into the souls of many — to control them. The worst of them cast spells to convince their neighbors that they are wise though they are not. They cast spells mostly to deceive, and they snuff out the inner life of all who be-live in their enchantments. They don't experience the being of all as miraculous. But miracles are not magical; they are the real character of being. The magic of men, the power of their spells, denatures the miraculous and defines all things by how the dead hulks of their form can be used to build mausoleums to the astonishing stupidity of their power."

Agamond paced between Ogden and Waft. He patted a stone and asked Ogden to sit. He threw a log on the fire and Pyreft sighed like a parched man drinking from a fountain. Agamond sat on the ground next to Ogden's perch.

As Ogden looked down at Agamond, waiting for him to speak, the gnome bowed from the waist and suddenly vanished. But Ogden heard his childish voice reverberating in his chest. "Earth bids you seek us out as need arises. Hold every element near your heart and listen to our advice. We are the voices of the spirit of the world. Trust us when we speak our wordless wisdom. You will hear us in the silences, in the moments between your breaths."

Ogden's head swirled with vertigo, and he caught himself from falling backward off the hip-high boulder. "What's happening?" he asked the shadows, and he heard Waft's voice answer, though he heard and felt no wind.

"We're taking away your words."

Pyreft's thoughts touched Ogden's next. "Since leaving the forest of dreams you have learned a lot. Now leave words and thoughts behind, and let your heart show you the way."

"Sleep now, troll," said Aguaqui. "You know what has to happen."

Agamond's voice was next. "Feel earth beneath you. See sky above you. Sense all in motion."

Ogden felt, as his eyes closed, the presence of the air around him. He knew it in hidden pockets and voids in the ground, in his lungs and veins and every corpuscle of his being. And he felt the fire of life zapping messages between the nerves within him — tiny beings who lived their own lives and made his possible. He knew his kinship with nature and all its elements.

The voice of Agamond returned and spoke to Ogden's shaking heart. It said, "Take to your dreams this tale of the end of Hyumunkind. I have seen it. It is not yet to happen; it has already happened. Time is a wheel. Men have placed the whole of creation upon that wheel, to break it, to torture their mother for her secrets. Here is the tale as it will unfold."

And then he began to chant the lamentation of humanity's end. And each of the other elementals added its voice:

Out of the barbarous valley of strife

Stewing in murder and toying with life.

Out of the path of crude death by sharp shafts,

Tempered blades, cold steel, and the ominous crafts,

Agamond stepped lightly, retreating in haste,

With a scourge on his lips and a scowl on his face.

'Men are berserkers; men are now lost

Beyond the salvation of nature — the cost!

They trammel the mountain and trample the earth,

Offending the hillside and cursing with mirth.

The time is arising; the land will rebel

And bury the wretches and send them to hell!'

The gnome gave a signal no mortal could hear,

While the fate of the warriors was sealed with a cheer.

'No more shall the elements of nature give aid

In the struggles of men or the way they behave!

The gnomes are all with us, the nymphs of the sea,

The dragons of fire and sylphs of the breeze!

They band as a power and make their demands:

No slaves to the madness and death at men's hands.'

The form of the gnome melded in with the stone

As though soil his flesh and pebble his bone.

Then the mountain cried out and dark clouds ringed 'round

And fire spat out with a hideous sound

To send molten hate flying into the sky
While the whole earth emitted a hideous sigh.

Nymphs leapt and chanted out from the sea.
Gnomes rolled boulders and watched them fly free.
Salamanders lapped and lashed with their tails,
Listening to men give out their death wails.

The valley was littered with armor and limbs
As mortals bowed down to start chanting their hymns.
But their gods were not with them, and all was aswirl
With sylphs in the steam that could choke them and curl,
And with nymphs in the river that flooded and hissed
With the sound of the lava that rolled like a fist.
Gnomes shook the tree trunks and woke the wood folk
Who added their strength and put on the yoke,
And aided the movement of earth against men,
Since that was their purpose and that was their yen.

The kings of the warriors cried out in awe,
Yet surrendered no power, since they were the law.
But the sylphs all hissed in a wispy, thin voice
Of sulfuric vapor, explaining their choice:

'For we have borne arrow and spear to the heart
Of men — we're the wind — but now we depart.'

The gnomes of the earth yelled as a crowd,

Angry, surly, and gutturally loud:

'We've borne the hooves of your steeds on our spine
'cross the fields of your warfare and each battle line;
No more will we help you to kill off your friend,
And this is our answer: Forever and End!'

The voice of the salamander, the dragon's word
Snapped in a flame that could almost be heard:

'Eyes we have given you; warmth we have fed,
But you make us vultures to consume your dead.
This is enough — we crackle and sway.
Last, we shall bear all your souls far away!'

And the nymphs cried in turn:

'Though salamanders burn,
We've carried your war ships from harbor to coast.
Protection we gave you as borders and moats.
But now it is time, for the sake of the sea
To drown out the demons and set ourselves free!'

And so was the curse of each element fulfilled
'til the last of the mortals had somehow been killed
And dominion returned to the spirits at hand,
And silence and peace were restored to the land.
The fire subsided; the lava was cooled.

The boulders had toppled; the waters were pooled,
And the wind gave a sigh with the end of the strife,
Proclaiming its joy and the promise of life.

Then all was silent.

'Was it a dream?' Ogden pondered, but immediately knew the answer. Exhausted, he lay on his back upon the alabaster slab. He tucked his hands behind his head. As he slipped into mindlessness, he felt a myriad of threads of light tugging at his heart and exploding out into the universe. He knew himself to be a callow seed rooting itself to the soil of creation. From the place below his chest where that bundle of knotted light emerged to grasp the universe, he felt those same ribbons of luminescence return to enter and lightly wrap his heart. They wrapped and then they slightly unraveled and blew in a breeze of care. Their loose ends flapped like tent straps before a breaking storm.

Suddenly his whole body vibrated and buzzed with excitement. He twisted and writhed. He felt his muscles lose control. He punched the stone bed and his back arched up. His eyes shot open and rolled up into his head. He felt his toes clench. His fingers stretched and his neck convulsed. His mouth opened wide, and he laughed loud and hard.

Chapter XXIX
Troggle's End

Ogden's body quivered and trembled. His hands clenched into tight fists and his spine flexed in waves from neck to pelvis. His chest yelled for air to return. He squinched his eyes hard and clenched his jaw tight. And in between all of this he was shrieking.

Ogden awoke to thick fingers poking at his chest, then his armpits, then his sides below and behind his ribs. He jumped uncontrollably when a hand grasped his leg just above his knee, the big thumb on the inside of the leg, four fingers on the outside, and they squeezed. Jittery muscle tremors gave that leg a life of its own. It shot straight out, then recoiled and straightened again and again.

He reacted automatically. His arms swung high over his head with tight-clenched fists. They came down hard. He swung and bashed repeatedly while his slowly focusing eyes sharpened and at last, he saw that it was Huth he was pounding with all his might.

Immediately he held his arms rigid at his side. Huth stumbled back and fell sitting on the floor. Ogden bolted up and braced himself with his hands behind him.

"What are you doing?" he yelled. "Why are you doing it?"

Huth gasped for breath and tried to talk. He swallowed hard and dry, but he was smiling. Ogden jumped up to grab the water skin. He pulled the stopper out of the top, shoved the neck into Huth's mouth and squeezed.

The old troll gulped and belched and gulped again through heavy breaths that heaved his chest up and down. With his head down and wheezing breaths rattling in his chest, his jaundiced eyes peeked out from under his bony brow to gaze solemnly at Ogden. The young buck of a troll stood over him, looking down.

"I was tickling you, ya fidgetin' fool," Huth said on the back of a gasp. "I figgered that's what Poppas do to their sons, so I did it."

"Tickling?" Ogden said incredulously. "Felt more like skinning and boning," and he laughed involuntarily. He reached a brawny arm out toward the old troll, offering to help him to his feet, but Huth shook his head with revulsion at the gesture. He placed his knuckles on the cave floor and with a guttural groan and the popping of stiffened bones in his spine, he stood, but not quite erect. His back was bent. He recovered slowly from Ogden's barrage of blows, but not from the overwhelming pain in his guts. He leaned forward and looked Ogden in the eye.

"They give ya a name?" Huth said through one side of his lips.

Ogden opened his mouth to speak, but Huth interrupted. "Never mind. I already give ya a name an' that's what I'm gonna call ya."

Ogden stooped down and balanced his weight on the knuckles of his right hand. "What name did you give, and when was that?"

Huth grabbed the chain of the necklace hanging from Ogden's neck and pulled him forward to whisper in his ear. When he was done, he pushed Ogden back and sat down again. The young troll plopped down to sit in front of his father. He blinked and said nothing.

"Don'tcha like it? I told the Old Uns whiles you were getting' borned half in and half outta this world what yer name'd be." Huth stopped and coughed hard. He held his side while his eyes squeezed tightly, and his face turned red.

"But, that name . . . that's the name Drowden chose. How could you know it? How could he know it? How could that be?"

Huth held up a finger and shook it at Ogden. "Cause it's yer name!" he choked through a continuing cough. "Ya couldn'ta got a different one."

Ogden nodded. He knew the old troll was right. His name existed before he was born. He didn't know why, but he knew it was true. And here was a troll who knew his name and claimed to be his father. Was it a trick? Was it true? He wanted to know more, especially about how he came to be abandoned. But he began by asking about Huth's injuries. "What happened to you?" Ogden asked with true concern.

The old troll shifted, stretching to lift pressure from his wound. He grimaced and moaned. "Crappy damned bums o' th' Brotherhood done this ta me. But I got worse ta tell ya. Sit down — aw yer sittin'. Okay," he gritted his teeth and held a hand over his side. "They was the Brotherhood o' Troggle-Gutters come out lookin' fer blood. An' they foun' yer momma, Tibbs an' me. Boy, they kilt her quick. I couldna saved her, but I fought 'em off best I could. One o' th' long-coat lankers snuck up behind an' 'schlippy-gob!' I was poked through an' bleedin' bad. Yer momma was already gone ta th' old un's house. So, I snuck off."

Ogden's face showed sorrow and worry. He looked down at Huth's seeping wound. "Are you in a hurry to join her? How long have you let this wound fester?" he asked with alarm. "It's horrible and rank."

Huth snorted out his nose and his nostrils flared wide. "Been a while," he answered. "Had a coupla things ta do. Been lookin' fer ya everywhere. Had a message from the old un's fer ya, but now I can't thinka what it was."

He began coughing and shaking all over. Huth bent over and clutched his side while bloody spittle bubbled from his lips. Ogden moved closer and wrapped his arms around him and the old troll didn't resist. His shivering was harsh and deep, and he felt cold to the touch, except anywhere near the seeping gash where the flesh was hot.

"What would help?" Ogden asked.

"Nothin'," said Huth between gagging and spitting off to the side. "I'm dyin'. No way ta stop it. Just gonna be a sore long crawl inta shadows."

"Not yet," Ogden whispered.

Huth gurgled phlegm and spat out the side of his mouth. "You growed up fast, like the old 'uns said. An' I'm glad ta meet ya like a man so soon before I'm dead. Wouldn'ta been the same if ya were still a little squirt. Worries me some, though. You got big fast, an' turned a man in a season. Hope that don't mean yer gonna get old real fast. Well, least I'm not gonna see it, but it's a rotten deal fer you."

Ogden smiled and looked off into the distance. He didn't say anything, so Huth continued.

"I came lookin' fer ya an' switcheroo! Ya found me," he grumbled and spat. "How'd you do that?"

Ogden patted Huth's shoulder. "There was help," he said. "You need to get closer to the fire."

Ogden clasped Huth's left hand with his and put his right hand behind the old troll's elbow to steady and raise him to his feet. But Huth had no balance, so Ogden pushed his body into Huth's shoulder and steadied him as they shuffled over to the blanket near the fire pit. When he had lowered him gently, Ogden placed a rolled rag under Huth's head for a pillow. Then he sat cross-legged next to him for a long time and occasionally got up to add wood to the fire.

He thought Huth was sleeping and was mildly startled when his father said, "When they came huntin' us the time before they kilt Tibbs, they murdered so many it took me an' your momma an' the little 'uns all o' three nights ta drag carcasses ta th' henge pit an' bury 'em."

Ogden looked at his father's sun-dried and wind carved face. He barely opened his eyes, but those amber gems looked unerringly at him. "Children helped?" he asked.

"Naw," groaned Huth. "They kilt the kids. Was th' little 'uns, the folk o' the forest that helped us ta do th' burryin'."

"How long ago?" Ogden asked, and then, "Is the graveyard nearby?"

Huth coughed hard three times and turned away to spit. Red-brown blood puddled next to him. "Seventeen winters now," he finally said. He squinted an eye and looked up into the cave rafters to reckon. "Musta been more 'n 'at. I dunno. But ain't no graveyard. A circle o' stones is fer th' good ole gals ta call down th' moon an' take 'em back up inta her momma belly. It's right up there." Huth pointed directly overhead.

"The moon?" asked Ogden.

Huth hacked again and spat. "No! Ya fog-addled oaf! Th' standin' stones. Right atop us. Up!" he pointed again with a jab of his finger, but his arm quickly fell limp to his side.

Ogden put his hand in Huth's and raised it to his chin. "Do you hate those men?" he asked.

Huth squeezed Ogden's hand but didn't answer directly. "They's after ya, not jest me. Wantin' ta kill ya. Just like th' last time — they wanna bury all o' us. Like as not they're still huntin' ya …. Ogden. When I'm dead, don'tchu let 'em find ya."

Ogden blushed to hear Huth use his name. It was the first time, and it sent a thrill through him. He said, "They won't quit. What can be done? Confront them; beat them? No. There's no good in that."

Huth tried to roll toward Ogden, but the pain in his side forced him to fall back and lie flat. He groaned and said, "A lot o' yer words are jest fancy man-talk. Here's what I know. Trolls don't wanna kill men, but those Brotherhood pups want all trolls dead. We doesn't hate 'em. Never did. Well, maybe when we was slaves and they took our women fer fun." He grimaced and gritted his teeth hard. "Never mind that crap," he growled through foaming lips. "They got cursed fer it all. Their day's comin'. But those kids they spawned? — No love in th' world fer 'em."

Ogden stood up quickly. Gravel crunched under his feet. He let out a long sigh as he paced a short distance and came back. "Slaves?" he said in a voice deeper than had ever come out of him. "Trolls were slaves?"

Huth pushed himself up on an elbow and looked sternly at his son. "It was long ago. We don't hafta talk about it," he said with his voice trailing off.

"Men owned trolls?" Ogden insisted.

"Yup, they did," is all Huth offered.

Images of Hapstead Manor flitted through Ogden's mind. The outbuildings where field workers and household servants lived, the plainness of those homely homes in the valley, nestled up against Northemberly Creek, sharply contrasted with the opulence of the Manor House. He shook his head. "Did many men kept trolls as slaves?" he asked.

"Jus' th' rich 'uns," Huth responded, then spit to the side and gagged a little. "They kept poor men and women too. Still do, far as I know."

"And no trolls now?" Ogden stooped next to his father and touched his face. "Say the truth," he said, looking sternly into Huth's eyes.

"We fought an' got away," Huth said. "Long ago. Before I was borned. Then we hid, way up in the mountains ta th' north. An' when they found us wanderin' too close, they kilt us."

"Why?" Ogden's voice rose in pitch with an edge of despair. "Are trolls so worthless? Are men so evil? Is life so cheap?"

"Yup," said Huth. "Same things wander through my head sometimes. Don't we look like men? Don't we got two arms, two legs, a face an' a voice tha' we use when we gotta. Sure, we're smarter. Those lanky loafs o' skin are always talkin' out their faces. Always blabbin' out their faces; hardly never out their hearts."

Ogden shifted and rested on one knee in front of Huth. "You should lie down," he said quietly. "Your face is wet with sweat."

Huth responded by dropping his head to the rustic pillow and wrapping his arm around his chest. "I'm sweatin' bu' I'm cold," he said.

Ogden got up and put two good-sized logs on the fire. Orange sparks flew into the air and swirled on an eddy of air until the glow died out of them and they spun and settled as gray ash on the cave floor.

"Men thinks us stupid," Huth said into the cave's ceiling. "They don't belive we know nothin', not even tha' th' world is a circle o' circles and every one of them circles is a dream."

Huth eyed Ogden curiously. "Tell me if yu've heard this stuff before." He sniffed and went on. "What they doesn't know is how ta wake up when it's time."

"Why do you suppose they don't?" Ogden asked, snapping back into the moment.

Huth rolled his head from side to side on his rag pillow. Moist trickles seeped from the corners of his eyes. "I told ya. It's that hobgoblin 'greed.' It takes over 'em. They can't move on an' leave anything behind. They wants ta take it all wif 'em."

"What makes them do that?" Ogden asked.

"There's a bad name fer that devil. It's called 'Ventego.' We doesn't wanna talk 'bout it."

Ogden held his breath with a question on his tongue. He almost didn't ask, but then said, "Do they worship this demon?"

Huth clenched his jaw tightly and gritted out some words. "They must," he said. Then he turned his eyes away.

Ogden changed the topic. "Manners were very important to Drowden and Miss Dorina," he said as cheerfully as he could.

"An' you prolly think your man dad was smart 'bout lots o' things." Huth sighed deeply. "But if ya'da held tight on yer birfday 'steda wandrin' aways, ya coulda lernt lotsa things from yer real poppa. Time's short an' I gotta waste my breath tellin' 'stead o' showin'. I want ya ta be my Wielder an' not be worthless."

Leaning forward from his cross-legged position, Ogden said to Huth, "Worthless?"

Huth grumbled quietly. Then with more volume, "I didnah want ya ta turn out like them!"

Ogden was silent for a time, until he said, "Poppa. They don't mean any harm. They don't think they're doing wrong."

Huth spat a huge wad of phlegm and it slid down the side of a stone off to his left. "They don't think? They think too much!" His eyes bulged out of their sockets. His nose crinkled up toward his thick brow and his lips squeezed wide to expose his broad white teeth. "I'm sick o' talkin'," he seethed, and fell silent.

Huth held his side and looked at the oozing puss when he pulled his hand away. He said, "Take me out o' here one las' time afore I gotta stay in th' ground fer good. I wanna see the sky, the stars, the moon and sun. I wanna see the woods an' hills. Take me outta here son."

Ogden pushed himself up and stood over his father. "Okay. Let's go." He went about gathering two long poles and six shorter branches from the wood pile. With long tears from a burlap bag that once held potatoes he lashed the sticks crossways to join the poles and fashion a litter on which to place Huth. Laying this rough lattice next to his father, he knelt on the other side of him and slid his arms beneath Huth's body to lift him and slide him on top of the cross members. Then he retrieved the blanket from the ground, shook the dust out of it, and laid it over Huth, tucking it in under his knees and shoulders.

Ogden put more wood on the fire and then returned to grasp the pole ends in his hands. He stood between them like a horse between wagon shafts and dragged his father to the lattice gate covering the entrance to the inner cave. He pushed that aside and pulled the litter through to the outer gallery where the spring gurgled out of the rock wall and pooled in a concave depression above the cavern floor. He saw light pouring in from an opening that was mostly hidden by vines and shrubs. It was the moon, high in the sky, approaching full. He could see it as he pushed aside brambles and tangle weed to make a passageway out.

When he emerged from the ground into the crisp open air, he was startled by two huge hulking forms to the left and right of the cave entrance. But they were motionless. The moonlight grazed off the smooth skin of giant standing stones.

Looking further afield he saw there were more of these irregularly shaped pillars. They formed a circle in a depression in the ground. The cave opening was a hole in the east side of that earthen basin.

Ogden yanked Huth and the litter free of the tangle wood with some difficulty, and then he stood breathing heavily, puffing billows of condensing breath into the chill autumn air.

"Drag me over there, boy," Huth said in a weak voice. "Let me hear the sky. Prop this sledge up on tha' far wall o' earth."

Ogden did as Huth asked. The berm stood back from the ring of stones, a dirt and rock slope topped with dry grass that sizzled in the wind.

"You hear the song of the stars too?" Ogden asked when he had secured Huth's makeshift stretcher and retucked the blanket around him.

"It's not jus' th' stars, boy," Huth answered after gazing upward a minute. "It's everythin'. Can't ya hear them stones? Sure ya can hear the grass whisperin' but can ya hear th' whole Earth in that little song?"

Ogden stood near Huth and didn't answer. He just listened with his whole heart.

Huth continued. "Witout us they're not the same. Witout them, we're not us. It's all one thing, little Ogden." Huth smiled and winked at his son. "Not so little, are ya?"

"It is a happy thing to listen to creation with you, Poppa," Ogden smiled, and a light laugh passed his lips.

Huth shivered and his voice came out choppy and uneven. "Those people who got yer head full o' fancy words coulda parted ya from everything that matters. That's what they do best. I'm glad ya can hear th' stars."

"In dreams," Ogden whispered, "the stones and crystals in the bowels of the earth have spoken. The wind and water and fire spoke and. . . ."

"Stop thinkin'," Huth interrupted.

"It wasn't this dream," Ogden answered. "It was the dream that dreams this dream. I don't hear the stars with my ears. It's my soul that hears them."

Huth raised a brow toward Ogden. He looked at him suspiciously.

Ogden shook his head. "None of this is new, Poppa."

"Damn it!" Huth yelled suddenly and coughed hard afterward. "You know everythin'.... damnable brat always thinks he's smarter than this ole troll..."

Ogden yelled back, "All of it came from you! While you've been sleeping, you brought a message from the great tree of life. The ghost of nature spoke through you. It was a gift that you brought to me and shared. You didn't keep any of it to yourself! But you already know so much! Tell the truth! You've conspired with powers beyond my ken. And always, I have been the toy of the fate you spelled out for me. Who are you to scream hot breath at me?"

Huth tried to hide a wry smile and said, "Talkin' in me sleep again, eh? Trolls are odd like that. We got more dreamin' than wakin' time." He paused. He felt a brilliance of light that he could feel with his skin and taste on his tongue flood into him. "Take me back inside if I die," he said to Ogden.

As Ogden readied to pull the litter back into the cave, Huth reached out from under the blanket and held his son's forearm in a strong grip. "Wait! Ain't dead yet. See that stone?" he asked breathlessly with an extended forefinger.

Ogden looked up. A massive monolith lay on its side and rested atop two upright columns. Something about it seemed out of place. "Yes," he said. "It seems ready to topple."

"When I stop talkin'," Huth said, waving that finger in the air, "put me in th' cave an' shove that big rock's bottom into th' hole in th' ground ta cover up me bones."

Ogden looked again and smiled doubtfully. The chiseled monolith was massive. If it could be tipped just so, then it's narrow end could be made to slide directly into the cave's opening, concealing it forever and completing the circle of stone monuments. But he couldn't imagine how he could make it budge. Ignoring the problem, he asked, "Are these other stones the ones you raised over the dead?"

Huth coughed and laughed in reply. "I told ya there was helpers." After a short and painful coughing fit he fell silent and Ogden leaned back against the berm to gaze upward. He would need helpers to move that monolith, for sure, he thought. And so, he thought to himself, it would never happen.

After watching the moon creep slowly through the branches of a dead, leafless elm tree, Huth turned to Ogden and said, "Wish I could be here ta teach ya what I learned from me own pappy an' his. Do ya even know 'bout th' moon? An' th' wanderin' stars?"

Ogden stood upright and leaned in to whisper to Huth. "Don't go. Stay. You can teach me what they taught you if you stay."

Huth growled angrily and spit. "Ain't enough time fer me ta tell ya," he said. "The magic o' th' ancestors gets weaker an' weaker, cause there's no one to pass it on."

There was a short pause as the wind kicked up and blew the breath out of Huth's mouth. When he could, he spoke again.

"When th' line from th' ancestors ta gran'maws and gran'pappys is broked, th' livin' young get chopped off from th' tree o' wisdom that's got roots all th' way down inta th' beginning o' everything."

Ogden held onto the sides of the stretcher and leaned in over Huth to shield him from the blowing chill. "The men in their settlements don't seem to have any Old Ones to teach them. They save the old memories in books that they read. Some love the books. Some hate them. Drowden Erebus would spend hours late at night reading, looking for old wisdom. Others thought it hateful. Drowden seemed filled with internal fire sometimes."

"An' wha' did he find?" Huth grumbled disapprovingly. "He found tha' he's cut off from old wisdom like a finger from a clumsy axe swinger, and it ain't wisdom, jus' dead words kept like keepsakes. They don't mean nothin'."

Ogden whispered earnestly, "But there is very much knowledge locked up in those books. You can bring them to life if you know what letters spell what words and what those words save inside them like memories."

Huth moaned and shifted uncomfortably. "It's poison, not medicine," he mumbled under his breath. "Knowing where th' broken shards of a clay pot fell won't help ya carry any water."

The dome of the sky kept turning overhead. The moon slid earthward and approached the western horizon. The rising sun was heralded by a brightening in the east just over their shoulders. To the south the low mountain ridge came into view. Its slopes were quilted with the colors of autumn. Reds, oranges, yellows, browns and deep purples mottled the far hill. The trolls heard crows cawing from the tops of a tall spruce tree. They lay on the hillside quietly watching cloud shadows roll over the mountain.

Then a sheet of white cloud came up behind the crest of that broad hill and the bottoms of the clouds, which stretched the length of the summit from the west to the east, just brushed the ridge and hung there unmoving for a long time.

Ogden nodded toward them. "See that, Poppa? It looks like Mother Nature is dragging the hem of her gown along the top of the mountain."

Huth opened his eyes and looked up a while without talking. The sky hung a drape of clouds that lingered along the very ridge of the hill, but then it lifted itself up over the summit and rolled down into the valley fast toward Ogden and Huth.

Huth groaned and chuckled all at once. "An' now she's gonna straddle over us, lift 'er skirt, an' piss on our heads!"

Within three minutes it began to mist; then it drizzled, and soon it was raining steadily. Ogden got Huth back inside the cave just as the sky let loose with a heavy downpour.

Back inside, with the mesh gate pushed back across the inner archway, Ogden stacked wood he had gathered and lashed to the sledge. Soon the fire was burning high and hot. But Huth was soaked and cold. He shivered. His strong straight teeth clattered, and he groaned intermittently. Ogden watched helplessly as Huth's whole body shook. He pulled logs from the fire and brought them close, and soon he had encircled his father with little fires that he coaxed into modest blazes.

"Please don't die," Ogden said quietly as he stepped inside the ellipse of flame surrounding Huth. The old troll turned his nervously jolting head to look at his son with sad shining eyes.

"What's to lose?" he said with a forced smile. "Dyin' don't mean nothin'. Ya oughta know that. When ya die, only thing that goes away is your words."

"Your words are kind and welcome, Poppa," Ogden said. His dark eyes shimmered in the firelight.

Huth crawled his fingers over to Ogden's hand and Ogden clasped his father's firmly. "What good did talk ever do me?" the old troll's quivering voice asked. "Witout words I'm still gonna be here forever. Right here, under the ground with the old 'uns whose bones're scattered all 'round. Don't worry, boy. You can find me again any time ya like. An' don't you try tellin' me you'll be-live it when ya see it."

Ogden squeezed a little harder and said, "More like see it when it's be-lived." A wry look crossed his face. "But Poppa, before you go answer this: are all words lies?"

Huth smiled weakly. "Yer jus' tryin' ta keep me talkin', aren't ya? Well, that's fine. I feel there's enough wind in me lungs ta tell ya one or two more stories. Then it's lights out. No arguments, understood?"

"Understood," Ogden nodded and dropped his eyes to look at his father's hand in his.

Huth pulled his index finger free and pointed at Ogden with it. "Lots o' beasts talk, boy. But mostly not to lie. Eh, how can I tell ya? Ever hear about how th' owls learned ta talk?"

"Owls?" said Ogden. He shrugged.

"Yeah. Owls. Ever listen to owls? Them big horned ones, they say 'hooo—hoot—huuh—hooo—hoooooooewww.' Do ya know why? Do ya know how they learned ta say that?"

"No. Who can say?"

"I can say; that's hooo!" Huth cracked half a smile.

"So say it," Ogden said.

"I just did," Huth shot back. "'Hoo' means 'I can say.' Th' rest o' th' owl's call tells a story."

Ogden rolled his eyes. "Will you tell the story?" he said with feigned exasperation.

Huth smiled on one side again. "Listen, then. Th' first owl was hatched from a puff ball that a raccoon pounced on at jus' th' right time. The owl flit up inta the woods an' sat there quiet in a tree he came ta love. He sat there fer a measure o' time alone in that tree. And alone in that tree is jus' wha' he wanted ta be. 'Cept one day what comes flittin' up onta a branch o' his special tree but another owl cock. It made him hop from branch ta branch. It made him circle and dive close ta the new owl. It made him want that new owl ta go away an' leave his tree. And so the first owl tried yelling at the new owl. He said 'hooo—hoot—huuh—hooo.' That means, 'I can say, this tree is mine alone.' But no matter how many times he said it, th' new owl didn't budge. Didn't even seem ta notice. In the end, the old owl got wise and tried somethin' new. He weren't nasty, but he figured there was nothin' else left. So he started ta swoopin' down on the new owl an' stretchin' out his talons. Sometimes he'd scratch at the new owl as he came in close. Sometime's he'd get just so close and whip back up inta th' sky. But every time he dove he showed those talons and he'd screech 'hoooooooewww!!!!!' Now whadya think that did?"

"Scared the new owl?" Ogden asked obviously.

"Course it did!" Huth said with as much force as his weakened voice could tolerate. "What else?"

Ogden blinked without response.

"It made th' new owl know that anytime he heard 'hoooooooewww' that there could be talons reaching out ta tear at him. So, everytime he heard 'hooo—hoot—huuh—hooo—hoooooooewww' he knew it meant 'I can say, this tree is mine alone, and I got talons ta back it up.'"

"Did the new owl leave the old owl's tree?" Ogden asked innocently.

"Sure did," Huth cackled wetly. "An th' old owl never had ta show them talons again, 'cept to some foolish owls that came later an never learned th' owlish word for 'I'm here with my talons' from their mommas. But th' old owl didn't mind helpin' 'em learn."

"What's the lesson?" Ogden asked.

Huth's eyes were still on the cave ceiling. "Suppose th' story's gotta have somethin' ta learn from it, so here it is: Every critter but them men says words that mean sometin' true. That's the diff'rence among how them men and how owls talk. Yon owl tells the other cocks he's got talons. An' he means it. An' he don't haveta use 'em."

Ogden smiled and asked, "What does he tell the lady owls?"

Huth laughed. "Yer dumber'n a dog chasin' a skunk, boy. He tells them hens he's got a magic wand and likes ta use it!"

Ogden laughed a while, but soon the only sound was hot snapping wood on fire. Huth dozed off and after a short respite his loud snoring joined the echoing sound of the popping fires. And then Ogden dozed off, for just a minute.

"Ever hear th' story o' the monkeys an' th' foxcat?" he heard someone say as he swam to the surface of consciousness. It was of course Huth.

Ogden picked his chin off his chest and looked at his father. "What are monkeys? What is a foxcat?" he asked, trying to be alert.

"Doesn't matter," Huth said. "Th' story matters."

"Then tell your story." Ogden shifted his weight off his legs and stretched them out in front of him. He noticed that the old troll had stopped shaking. His eyes seemed calm, and his face was relaxed. He seemed like a troll who had come to a decision after a long time of worrying.

"It's like this," Huth started. "On an island in th' middle o' the wavy flood lived a band o' monkeys high up in the treetops. The trees they really liked was full o' fruit. So, most days they'd move from one tree ta th' next, whatever direction was loaded wi' fruit."

As he spoke, Huth lay still on his blanket, looking up into the high shadows of the cave. His amber eyes glimmered in the reflected firelight. His mouth moved slowly as he spoke. Ogden leaned in close to hear him, since his voice was unusually quiet and smooth and even.

"Then there was th' foxcat," Huth continued. "All yas gotta know is that foxcats like th' taste o' monkey meat. An' there was a foxcat that prowled around them fruit trees just waitin' for a monkey to come down low ta th' ground. The foxcat could claw his way up on th' bark o' th' tree a little an' snatch a monkey's life away."

"Horrible," Ogden whispered. And he reached out to touch Huth's head. He felt the cool, oily texture of his wiry hair and played his fingers through it gently. Huth's eyes closed a moment, then opened again and he continued.

"Th' monkeys were wary an' 'fraid o' th' foxcat, so they put a sentry on guard who always kept lookin' in case trouble came in th' skin of a foxcat. Th' monkeys' look-out would yell 'CABLAHHH!' whenever a foxcat came 'round those fruit trees. It was a warning call. When th' other monkeys heard it, they knew that th' foxcat was near. And every time they heard 'CABLAHHH!' it was like each o' the monkeys saw th' foxcat with its own eyes. They heard the word, an' a picture of the foxcat popped up in their heads an' they ran fer cover."

"Smart monkeys," Ogden sighed. "Taking care of their friends."

"We'll see about that," Huth chuckled quietly. "Jus' listen. . . One day the look-out monkey noticed he was keepin' alert fer danger while th' other 'uns got their bellys full o' fruit, an' it made his noggin sizzle. So, guess wha' he did then?"

Ogden shrugged. "Did he quit?" he asked.

"Naw," Huth laughed lightly, but that made him cough hard. When he caught his breath, Huth said, "Th' look-out monkey pretended he saw a foxcat. He yells "CABLAHHH! CABLAHHH!" an' all th' other monkeys scattered off into a hundred other treetops, away from th' fruit and danger. Meanwhile, that lyin' ole look-out monkey? Yep, he swoops in an' has a good ole time eatin' up as much fruit as he can shove in his gut. All th' best pieces. An' no waitin' his turn."

"Well," said Ogden, "Didn't the other monkeys catch on? Didn't they stop listening when the look-out yelled 'CABLAHHH!?'"

Huth patted Ogden's knee. "Oh sure. Some did. An' lots who didn't listen ta th' warnin' was eaten by th' foxcat. So now it's gone on fer long ages an' whole families o' look-out monkeys teach their young'uns ta lie ta feed that inbred hob o' greed. Every one o' them bums an' their brats is fat an' happy. Yep, they still call out when there's a real foxcat nearby — an' that's enough fer 'em ta make th' other monkeys listen an' run when they yell out. So, some o' th' foxcats are real. An' some o' th' foxcats are empty air they blow outta their face holes ta hide th' truth that they been stealin' from th' rest since rememberin' got buried wi' th' old 'uns."

"So, what are you saying?" asked Ogden. "What's the lesson of the story? Drowden always had a lesson to the stories he told me."

Huth poked Ogden in the thigh hard with his finger. "Maybe he's one o' them Yoomuns that has some common sense. So, what does I mean? Ya wanna know?" Then he lay back flat and sighed hard. There was a long pause, and Ogden jolted forward to see if Huth was still breathing.

Suddenly the old troll gasped loudly, and his mouth opened wide. He stared sharply into the high shadows of the cave. "Ahhhhh," he exhaled. "Stand aside, Ventego! I don't fear ya!" he yelled. Then his eyes turned to Ogden. "Them men. Sad case," he whispered. "Just monkeys conjurin' foxcats."

Huth's eyes popped wide open and he lurched up off the ground. But then he fell back and puffed air out his nose.

And then he lay still.

Ogden lay down next to him and brushed Huth's hair with his fingers and palm. "Oh, Poppa," he muttered with tears trembling in his eyes. Ogden spoke quietly, like he was talking to himself. "You kept the company of owls, buried children before their time, listened to the ancient ones when they told you what had to be done. The ghost of the world rode curled up in your chest and came to this place to tell me all you would've shown if you had time. Thank you, Poppa."

Ogden rose to one knee and looked down on Huth's peaceful face. "Good night, Poppa," he said, and tears dripped down from his cheek to his father's.

Then Ogden spoke two words — "my" and "I" — that he had never said before. He spoke from his heart, so those words came naturally, honestly to his lips. Peering down intently on Huth's still form he said, "Dream softly, Poppa. You are in my heart, and I'm in yours. Dream softly. We share the same dream and needn't wake each other to explain."

Chapter XXX
Henge Night

The storm had blown over the far ridges, then down the mountain slopes, across the valley, and up the opposite hills. The rain tore most of the brightly colored tapestry of leaves from their branches, leaving behind a smoky grayness to mark the bare heights of the forest. Behind the rain's retreat came a nip in the air to herald the changing season. In the cool sun of the following day, glinting droplets clung to foliage on trees that fought off sleep. The leaf-covered loamy floor of the woods chattered in a gentle wind and tumbled autumn leaves the color of cinnamon, saffron, ginger, and curry around and between the big standing stones.

Suspended between two monumental blocks of chiseled granite, an alabaster column teetered over the eastern arch of the henge. The twenty-foot-long translucent stone changed colors throughout the day, then captured late afternoon sunshine, pouring that pure white light through its crystalline fingers, and scattering a glimmering array of primary colors like seeds across the landscape.

The enormous alabaster gem was balanced like a compass needle, with one end pointing to the cave entrance in the eastern wall of the henge, and the other pointing westward, toward the hill over which had rolled last night's torrential storm. Beyond those hills, clamoring up the far side, an armed band of the Brotherhood of Troll-Gutters came. Directly behind them, close enough to shout insults to each other, followed Drowden Erebus and his men.

While they scrambled their way through the forest, in a cavern beneath the circle of standing stones lay Ogden, weary from his vigil with Huth. Nearby, atop the limestone slab that rose from the cavern floor like a bed, his father's body lay. His face was cleaner, less contorted, and more youthful. He had left behind his words; let them go silently into the past, there to live forever. His body remained among the huge boulders, the little crystals embedded in the walls, the small stones and the bone shards scattered on the cave floor. These bones had been washed over the ages down from above, through the guts of the earth.

The rains had soaked the ground above and now bled rivulets of mineral-saturated water from cracks and crevices along the base of the cavern walls. From high up in the cave's ceiling, big drops trembled in the dark, shivered down along spines of time-built stone, and then tumbled to splash in growing puddles all around.

Time entered the present and fled to the past. In the depths of the cave all was shadow. Ogden remained in that darkness, pondering, Outside, above ground, the cool autumn air sharpened its edge on rocks and tree bark as the sun slid out of the slippery sky toward a horizon pinkening in layered streaks of rosy light. The tips of the far hills were ablaze with the last touch of the day's brightness, while lower on their slopes, shadows deepened and turned to black in the valley below. But there were specks of light, hand-held torches that jostled about and moved and danced toward the plateau upon which stood the circle of stones.

Beneath the ground Ogden stirred from the dream of the earth. He felt the approaching footfalls of men as though on his chest. The flickering light of their torches reflected on his coal-black eyes and burned there with a heat that drew beads of sweat to his brow.

"Come," he said to the near pitch dark in the cave. But his eyes saw in the darkness. He approached his father's body one last time and kissed his forehead. Then he pulled the silver chain from off his neck and lifted Huth's head to pull it down around his neck. Ogden tugged at the carved bear tooth and arranged its oak tree likeness on his father's bare chest.

"Rest here," he intoned. "Inside the earth and across the ages, among the spirits who make the world real. Friends, "he felt the world lean in to hear him, hold this Troggle in your hands."

Down in the valley below the western hills Drowden Erebus squatted among his men. They formed a circle around him. Their torches flew like tattered banners in a variable wind. Their scythes and machetes, pikes and pitchforks occasionally clinked together or scraped on stone as they came to rest. Willbee wrapped his arms around the shaft of his spear and leaned in to hear Drowden's quiet words. Argis stood next to Drowden and placed a hand on his shoulder as he spoke.

Bill Macatee coughed and patted Old Duke's short-haired head and scrambled his chewed-up ears in his rustling fingers, while Nith Piegel shook nervously in the cold air. Hector answered Drowden's whispered question. "Yep. Just up over that rise. Bos Fudlow's taken the lead. Tapple is in charge, but Fudlow's the one's got the nerve for blood sport."

Drowden held up a hand to silence him. He looked around the circle of men and met each eye to eye. "Let's not allow him to play that game if we can avoid it," he said. "We'll wait until they move on and we'll follow them no closer than this."

Argis squeezed Drowden's shoulder as the younger man stood up tall and then asked, "We know where they're headin' to?"

Drowden nodded. "I think so. The hills are laced with caverns and caves, but up there, just four miles or so, is an old circle of stones. The Brotherhood knows something about hunting trolls, so they've got a purpose in mind by heading in this direction."

Just above where Drowden and his men parlayed, the band of troll hunters had paused on the uphill trek at Ospin Tapple's command. Though he said he was waiting "to smell troll" before plodding on, he was, in fact, winded and needed a rest.

Bos Fudlow paced anxiously. Milky Prupe smacked a short-bladed sword in his palm while Tucker Scont chewed on dried meat he had shoved in his pocket before setting out to hunt what Tapple swore would be "the last of the stinking trolls." The other hooded men sat scattered in a patch of dry brown ferns which only two weeks before had been emerald green.

In the depths of the cavern below the standing stones, Ogden piled a bonfire of cedar trunks and oak boughs high and wider than the fire pit, stacking and stuffing it with old bandages and rags for tinder. He lit the pyre using dry spruce needles for kindling. As the flames roared up, smoke billowed out between the logs and filled the cave with the aromatic scent of the burning red wood.

When the cavern was too filled with the incense of cedar to breathe, Ogden left Huth's body behind, found his way to the outer gallery and washed his face and hands in the overflowing font. Pushing his way through the tangle of vines at the cave's entrance, he emerged into the circular henge. He walked to level ground and there he stood with hands extended to either side, looking up at the alabaster megalith that seemed ready to topple from the shoulders of the tall stones.

The sun had abandoned the sky. In the west, a ghostly light painted the blackness of space with silver. The moon would be rising within an hour and Ogden prepared himself for what was to come. He felt the presence of approaching men in his chest. But he felt another presence tugging at his heart. And then he heard a familiar childish voice call out from the tree line above the henge berm.

"Ogden, my boy, can we lend you a hand?" It was Agamond, the earth gnome. He was accompanied by a host of pixies, brownies, elves and sprites as he emerged ahead of them from the forest.

"What a welcome sight!" Ogden exclaimed. The smile on his face was wide and toothful. "Yes, I could use some help. These muscles won't do the job on their own."

"Looks like you need a gravity assist," Agamond laughed. "Our brother, your father and our friend, Huth, has earned our respect and love." Then he turned to the column of little beings who had left their homes in the forest to come to Ogden's aid. "Earth spirits, I implore you. Don't wait to lend your weight." Then he turned to Ogden and shrugged. "Where would you like them, troll friend?"

Ogden fell to one knee to speak to the lead elf, a diminutive fellow of not quite three feet with barely an ounce of meat on his bones. He doubted there'd be enough mass to tip the stone, until more than twenty others scurried forward and crowded in to listen. Ogden whispered, "Can you climb up and jump on this end of the crystal stone?" He pointed to the eastern end of the balanced column and then called out to Agamond, "Not if every one of them lends their bulk to the task will they tip that giant!"

Agamond pointed to an ever-growing column of little beings as they scurried out of the shadows of the forest, into the moon bright understory. Each one ran to the henge and shimmied up one or the other of the two standing stones that balanced the alabaster obelisk. Then they ran out to the end hanging eastward over the cave entrance. They leapt upon each other's backs and shoulders until there was a high stack of pants, shirts and hoods stuffed with tiny folk. "Not enough?" shouted Agamond.

He bound down the henge berm and without warning leapt up onto Ogden's shoulders, and then sprang onto the opaque crystalline column to add his weight. He laughed as a bevy of arms and hands reached out from the stacked pile of sprites, pixies, brownies and elves to steady him.

The milky lith budged and its far end tipped upward, leaving a two-foot gap between it and the second stone that had held it securely balanced. It teetered on one pivot point but remained aloft.

"Many hands make easy work!" Agamond yelled from above.

Ogden leapt from the tips of his toes, grasped the sharp crystalline rock and wrapped himself as far around as he could with his arms and legs. His added weight finished the job of tilting it upright. With a raucous grating and rasping scream of granite against alabaster, the monolith slid off its temporary perch. The broader end plummeted to the ground and buried itself deep into the hard-packed soil, filling the hole that lead to the caverns below and sealing Huth's crypt for the ages.

"That was wonderful!" Ogden exclaimed, standing back as a billow of dust rose and curled. He admired the perfectly vertical stance taken by this final addition to the circle of standing stones. The alabaster menhir completed the ring of monoliths, adding an ethereal spirit of light to the earthiness of the carved boulders.

The moon sat on the ridge of the western hills, enormous, silver and brilliant. Ogden watched silently as its light filled the sparkling megalith throughout its crystal lattice, revealing its concealed depths as it shone with inner life. He wanted to say something about the beauty that had been revealed and looked around for his helpers, but there was no sign of the woodland spirits. They had vanished. He didn't see Agamond either. But then he heard his voice call out from well within the forest. "You should have been here when we helped Huth get that rock out of the ground and up on those pillars!" he laughed. "We had to ask Waft and Aguaqui for extra help."

"What about Pyreft?" Ogden yelled out to the woods.

"He was with us then. He is here now. It could be no other way. Let's just leave it at that," Agamond answered. And then he was silent and gone.

The smell of aromatic leaves invaded Ogden's senses. The newly erected alabaster lith took in the moonlight and transformed it into a halo of brilliance that rose steadily and glowed uncannily across the henge. The wind grew gentle.

Ogden walked from one point of the circle to the other and became familiar with the maze of dolmens, menhirs, capstones and great monoliths that rose above this height of land overseeing valleys on all sides. As he walked, he felt the rhythm of the world thrum in his heart. The stars, dimmed by the dominant light of the moon, still hummed a song of creation. The tall stones, much closer and smaller than the stars, buzzed a lyrical chant that lifted his heels faster from the loam and made him dance. He pranced about the megaliths, spun with arms spread wide. He fell to one knee then rose to a jump, then fell to the other and slapped the ground with the palm of his hand. Then he rose to his height and stretched out his arms to the stars and the moon. He yelled "Ogden!" as loudly as his big lungs could. But then he fell to the ground, panting, holding himself up with both arms behind him, and tears fled his eyes.

"Who is this Ogden?" he yelled amid sobs. "What is an Ogden?" he cried with the sorrow of one lost in despair. He saw what was coming.

Through the ground beneath him he felt a rumbling. From the earth around him he smelled the musky loam. In his mouth he tasted the dust of ages past and the breeze of days to come. His ears prickled to the sound of leaves cackling in the wind, and the flute-like panning of a breeze in the needles high in the pines. Then his nostrils flared with the smell of hate that seeped into the air like poison into a well. He felt the friction of conflict chafe his skin like a rash that, if he scratched it, would spread and itch all the more.

"Who carries this hate," he said out loud. "Who brings such loathing to this sacred ground?"

He feared what was to come but told himself it was not yet time. There was an eternity between this moment and that one. So, he stood upright and breathed the clean clear air deep into his lungs. His chest swelled and he held it.

Ogden lay back down and stretched out on the ground. He let the autumn of the world embrace him. The moon rose higher. The alabaster megalith rumbled with inner power, and the light that burst from its lattice of linear crystals escaped in a rush, more brilliant, like a dying prisoner suddenly freed from material bonds.

He felt eternity rise up beneath him like a tide, and his body rose with the buoyancy of cork on a swelling sea. Then he was tossed up and sprayed out of the surf of existence as it crashed on the shore of forever.

He stood apart from his resting body, saw it drift above the earth. Suddenly he found himself counting his heartbeats. Time collapsed upon him again. The air in his lungs exploded outward in a mighty gasp as the forest to the west erupted into a chaos of men and steel shoving forward into the ring of stones.

Bos Fudlow screamed a foul epithet and bound into the circle. Behind him came a scuffle of hooded men wielding weapons and shouting anger and hate. Only Fudlow had blustered into the circle of standing stones. The others paused at the sight of the moon engendered glow emanating from the alabaster column. One other extraordinary sight held their gaze as all came to a sudden stop.

They stood back, growing silent in the silver light. Bos Fudlow laughed nervously. So did Ospin Tapple from beneath a bush in a shadow where none could see him. From there he shouted, "Seed of demons! Mask of deceit! Spellcaster! Untrue being! Filth and falseness! We come to sever you from creation."

There, in the middle of the ring of stones, lit by the light of the moon and the inner glow of the great obelisk, the men saw Ogden. He lay there sleeping. Not upon the ground, not as a natural man might stretch out on soft grass. No, Ogden's body floated above the ground, casting a moon shadow below him on the patch of earth over which he hovered. The men of the Brotherhood saw this and all were amazed.

Yet Ogden stood right in front of them at the edge of the circle of standing stones. He looked to where the gaze of the men was fixed and smiled to see his dreaming self, insubstantial, unreal, but visible. He held his hands high in the air and heard himself shout with the voice of nature.

"Welcome troll-gutters! Step deeper into the orb of thought so that I may look on the masks that pass for the faces of those I dream into being."

The men heard nothing. Not a word from outside their world of thought touched their ears. For them, the troll seemed suspended in sleep between the earth and stars. Ospin Tapple crawled out from under the spicebush where he'd been hiding. He brushed off his legs, chest, and buttocks as he strode forward with growing confidence. A sleeping troll seemed to pose no threat, not even a sleeping troll hanging in midair.

Cornelius Baldegger walked up the embankment and into the henge circle alongside Tapple. He turned back to look into the shadow of the trees and jerked his hand to signal Howe Bistrep, Hopskel Dwill, Lathan Urobandis.

and Pip Skleverly to move in. Then he turned to Ospin Tapple and spoke much too loudly for the moonlight.

"What kind of magic is this?" he almost yelled.

Bos Fudlow turned around slowly, breaking his gaze from Ogden's suspended body for the first time. "Shut yer mouth!" he spat angrily. But Baldegger kept chattering.

"It's some kind of spell!" he said a little more quietly. "Careful. We don't know what we're getting into here."

Ospin Tapple reached out to his side and shoved Baldegger hard, so that he stumbled rightward and almost fell. Tapple walked past him until he stood next to Fudlow.

"Who's got a bow and quiver of arrows?" he said, leaning his head leftward to look up at the big man's face.

Bos Fudlow looked down. Then he yelled over his shoulder. "Skleverly! Bring me that crossbow and some darts!"

As Pip jogged forward and handed Fudlow the bow and quiver, Ogden stepped closer and stood between him and Ospin Tapple. They could not see him, be-living him to be drifting above the ground at the center of the circle of stones, sleeping and unaware of their presence. But it was all otherwise.

Ogden said to the two men, "In your heart, the one I dream to be, do you feel the evil in what you do? Will you stand against nature and your own?"

Bos Fudlow notched an arrow and drew back the string. He braced the crossbow stock against his shoulder, took aim and let fly. The short arrow struck with an audible 'thrump!' and pierced deep into the sleeping Ogden's side. The men watched for some movement but there was none. Their eyes and thoughts deceived them.

Ogden trembled but stood taller. He stood among the men who now gathered around him, not seeing him, but seeing his dreaming form at the center of the henge. He called out to the moonlit dark as Fudlow notched another feathered arrow, "Why do you fashion your hate into arrows? Isn't there enough sorrow in the world? Is this the path you choose?"

Cornelius Baldegger ran fast, right through him, and hefted a pike onto his shoulder, pulled his arm back ready to throw it as he got closer and closer to Ogden's dreaming form. But as he ran a hatchet thrown by Hector of Hapstead spun through the air and caught him in the back of his neck. Blood spurted up like a deep red fountain and he fell flat on his face, his arms and legs squirming mindlessly.

A loud cry went up from Drowden's men and the Brotherhood of Troll-Gutters reeled to face them. Hector was still running forward with a drawn butchering knife when Bos Fudlow came about and pulled the crossbow trigger meant for Ogden. The arrow shot out with a twang from the string. It hit Hector at close range and drove through a gap in his ribs, ripped the side of his heart and exited under his shoulder. The dart clattered against the bark of an oak tree and fell blood slicked to the ground.

Hector cried out in pain, ran three more steps, and fell dying at Fudlow's feet. But as he sprawled forward and took his last breath, he managed to plant the sharp end of his knife deeply into Fudlow's left foot so that it was momentarily pinned to the ground.

The big man screamed in rage and pain. He pulled his foot free and clasped the knife, yanked with force, and after kicking Hector's body aside he dove into the growing fray.

The dogs were yapping and snarling madly and spinning among the men, who fought with makeshift weapons from the farm. Clyde clamped his strong jaws around Thad Krebbermoting's calf. His teeth cut through his trousers and sunk deep into flesh and muscle. Thad whirled around and caught Clyde across his left shoulder with the edge of his blade and the dog released his grip with a yelp of pain.

Joko, Barkiller, Grisswold and Old Duke had picked out their marks and were snarling, lunging, dodging blades and pikes. The uproar they made echoed among the stones.

Bill Macatee grabbed Milky Prupe from behind, jerked his head back by grabbing a handful of his flying blond hair, and slit his throat. Howe Bistrep ran crying from the melee into a stand of silver birch trees that glowed in the moonlight. Tom, the old quarryman from Hapstead, chased after him. In a few moments, screams flew like alarmed crows from the forest.

Drowden Erebus was running hard up the embankment west of the standing stones. He sped with a pounding heart and a throat tight with fear and sadness toward the place where he saw Ogden's dreaming form floating in midair, his side pierced by an arrow revealed only by protruding feathers.

"I am not there," Ogden said as Drowden rushed by him, unseeing. "It is a dream."

But before he could reach the apparition, Drowden's way was blocked. Bos Fudlow stood panting in front of him, a long pike held firm between his hands. Those hands were dripping blood. Willbee lay gasping and thirsty outside the ring of stones; a knife plunged deep into his chest. He cried out sorrowfully, "Don't lemme die! Aw, please! I promise to be good!"

"I killed that one with the knife your boy Hector poked in my foot," Fudlow bellowed. "I'm going to kill you with the spear he carried up the hill for me."

That didn't happen. Argis ran fast and he crouched low just as he closed in on Bos Fudlow. His right arm was stretched behind his back with a sharp sickle clutched in his fist. He brought it forward low and hard. The curved blade cut deep into the back of Fudlow's knees. The big man's calves came loose, cut free from his thighs, and they tumbled about like two sides of a split log. Fudlow bellowed in agony. His wailing pierced the night air as the top of him fell hard to the ground and he lay on his back crying.

Drowden looked about in horror at the carnage. Cries of pain, loud weeping, pleading for help, all rang upon the air like the bells of a demonic church where death and loathing are adored. Tears rolled from his eyes so that through the quavering veil of light he wasn't sure who it was he saw emerging behind him from the forest. It was Bill Macatee. He was poking a machete tight into the back of Ospin Tapple. He held Tapple firmly by the collar and shoved him up the grassy hillock toward Drowden and Argis. "Look who I found running for the hills!" Bill yelled.

Suddenly the blood rose to Drowden's face. He screamed until his lungs ached. Rage pounded in his temples as he looked around at the dead and dying that littered the sacred ground. He saw the insubstantial form of Ogden, pierced by an arrow, motionless in mid-air and he tasted blood in his mouth.

He screamed an oath that caused the hemlocks to shiver. An owl went silent in the night. Ogden's heart sank at the self-cursing words, and they burned with rage as they left Drowden's lips. "If it means my life is doomed, I'll have yours Tapple!!" he screamed.

With no thought of home, Dorina, the children or his reputation, Drowden turned to grab the sickle from Argis' bloody hand and wheeled back around. He broke into a fevered run straight at the unarmed captive, Ospin Tapple.

Drowden's heart was pounding in his ears. His eyes were wide and wet and red with rage. Tears flew from his face like diamonds filled with starlight as he ran. His legs felt as though they were running ahead of him while he flew down the embankment and closed on Tapple. Drowden raised the dripping curved blade high over his head and bore down.

Ospin Tapple felt the blade held by Bill Macatee poking his ribs low in the back. He saw Drowden Erebus snatch the large sickle from Argis and bolt down the grassy hill toward him at a full run. He opened his mouth to scream but nothing came out. His eyes popped wide in terror, and he raised both arms in front of his face as Drowden reached him and swung the blade with all his strength down at Tapple's head.

Time ceased its illusion of motion from minute to minute. Drowden Erebus stood suspended, his feet inches off the ground, his right arm stretched in the air in front of him, the sickle less than a foot from Ospin Tapple's skull. Drowden's face appeared flooded by a maelstrom of rage piped up from the deeps of his soul, and that expression was frozen in eternity.

In that same eternal and static moment, Ospin Tapple's face projected terror through eyes brimming with tears. His cheeks bunched into mounds of flesh pushed aside by his wide grinning mouth, an unnatural smile that sang anguish, surprise and fear.

Behind Tapple stood Bill Macatee. He was immobile, yet with a tension memorized by the muscles of his right wrist. The blade held in that hand and pressed against Tapple's ribs seemed inclined to withdraw. Bill's left hand held Tapple's collar and the loose cowl that spilled around his neck was shoved to the left. Tapple's head tilted slightly to the right, as if being pushed out of the path of Drowden's descending weapon.

Beyond the perimeter of the circular henge, Willbee lay sprawled on the ground. His head was tilted awkwardly, and a thick stream of bloody spittle hung from the corner of his mouth to the still green grass. Sorrow welled and froze in his eyes. His chest was gouged and torn and red.

Bos Fudlow's prostrate, legless body was stretched, arms spread wide, his chest caught in mid heave of agony. Wrinkled, strained eyelids hid eyeballs that, in the prior moments, had rolled wildly, bloodshot and crazed.

Ogden stood, now returned to his ethereal body, suspended above the ground. His eyes too were closed. Behind him, the alabaster pole of light warmed and burned and began to melt, like a candle. It shimmered like the sun's heat on a slate roof.

Ogden felt the tug of many strands of pure white light intersect in his heart. Wordlessly he sensed the place where each thread terminated in him, and how each projected outward, connecting him to each of these men. Time-lessly, without sequence, all at once, Ogden let his awareness glide along each ribbon of light. He visited each man of Hapstead and the Brotherhood who still lived in that frozen moment. They each heard his voice, though it was the voice of nature's spirit speaking through him. It spoke to all of them individually, with separate messages and simultaneously.

Drowden Erebus' mind was a burning cinder of murderous loathing, suspended in the moment, trapped by eternity, never to be erased even if he wished it forever and regretted it without end.

Ogden spoke to Drowden, as he now did to each of the men. He spoke simultaneously to every one of them, even to the poor dogs who'd fought so fiercely. If one were to tell even a part of what he said, it would have to be done one at a time. So here, for the time-bound, is that part.

To Drowden Erebus, as best as can be told in words, he said, "You disappoint just now. You have let down everyone. I had hoped never to live this moment, but it has come. And it will live forever here among these standing stones, desecrating the sacred ground you trod upon. This moment of self-inflicted damnation will remain in the memory of the Earth without end."

Ogden appeared suspended above Drowden Erebus and spoke in his ear so that the man stirred from his prison in sequential time and listened with the ears of eternity. It was not Ogden's voice, but the voice of all creation. It spoke to him as if in a dream. "We will it that though the whole Earth will never forget, that you will forget this day and this moment of loathing."

Then Drowden heard Ogden's own voice encroach upon his mind as if from every-where and every-when. "You have been my protector in this life. Like a good and fair father, you taught me what you thought to be important. Now I see it was childish wisdom you shared. Things everyone should know. But here in this moment of horror even the simplest courtesy is occult to you."

Ogden felt the soul of Drowden swell timelessly with sorrow and he knew the words Drowden might say if he were allowed a moment more to speak. He would argue that not all men are evil and not all things they do are foul. And even good men sometimes descend to wickedness. Ogden nodded and answered this way:

"You are mistaken. Men build upon past evil and smile on their creations as though good can come from rotted seeds. Even your wholesome home was built, all of it, upon the murder of my kin. The land, the wealth, the hope in your children's eyes — all of it was ripped from the backs of those who men thought their lesser. Everything you gained through marriage to your wife's family was stolen from the ones who once lived in peace upon the ground that sprouts your crops. Never did you use your words to conjure the thought that their blood nourished your every meal. Memories of those murderous days are lost far upstream in time from where you've lived your privileged life. Their

bones filtered the water you drank. The whipped and tortured bodies of Troggles — and men too — stand frozen in time, in moments of agony and sorrow,
just as you now stand here, frozen in your loathing race toward slaughter in
this sacred place."

As these words seeped into Drowden's unbeating heart, Ogden knew the
sadness that they brought. He knew the things Drowden would say in his
defense. "But I have been a good man. I never take what isn't mine. And I
have loved the world…"

Ogden's voice showered into Drowden's heart from all sides in response.
"Words weave a web of deceit."

Drowden's heart cried out, "In what have I lied?" and it was answered.

"You say you do no harm, and that you share the land of Hapstead Manor
with all who work it. But you are their master. They are not their own. You
say you have the rightful claim to enjoy the bounty they bring to you. I tell
you now, it isn't yours. Before you married, and before Dorina's family came
to claim it, the land belonged to no one. It was taken through bloodshed from
those who lived there long before you. Your law, those spells your kind cast to
control all things, says the land is yours and too the labor of all you claim to
share it with, but your law protects wrongs from restitution. None of it was
yours to inherit. The world belongs to no one. We all belong to it."

Drowden's mind was amazed at this, and his words were silent. Then he
heard Ogden's voice again and his heart withered in the heat of its truth.

"Drowden, you have seen the machines that Nathan Bladic erected at Ironwood. Those black rock-burning monsters are rising across the land and in
time they will engulf the Earth with their poisonous breath. And yet more
with the passing years will you inflict on the living world. Your kind rip the
rocks from the ground, then fill the holes with waste, or leave them as hollow
unhealed wounds. Your people have chosen the path of dark magic.

"Even worse, you, Drowden Erebus, you have deceived in silence your own
kin, as well as the workers and servants who depend on you. You've kept hidden your plan to make of Hapstead a home for manufactories and smoking,

soot-machines. In Irongate you bought materials to build a lowly troll's cottage. But secretly you ordered — unknown to Dorina, your children or anyone else — the makings of a workshop animated by coal, steam, and iron. I am but a Troggle and would not have guessed you could be so deceived by aspirations of power. But the soul of nature has always known, and that is the voice that speaks through me now."

Drowden's spirit withered, exposed to the crosscurrents of eternity. Nothing he could say would dissipate the truth now laid bare.

"I speak in words borrowed from you and your kith," Ogden's voice resumed. "The burden is mine to judge the value of man, and to deliver to the spirit of life a dire verdict. Will you join the living world, or will it have no choice but to sever your branch from the tree of life? I must choose. That is why I came to you and lived among your kind. I was preparing for this very moment in the days we shared before.

"Drowden Erebus, I speak in words you taught me so that your heart will understand in days to come. But your mind will not recall any of it. It is in the power of the spirit of *this* earth, *that* wind, *these* fires, *those* torrents, to summon forth a great counter-spell to all the spells and conjurations that you and men before you cast upon the world. *The knot of lies must be untied. Hear then the spell of release.*"

The voice that then filled Drowden's heart was a chorus of multitudes. It came on a whirlwind that tossed moments of time like branches snapped from a bending tree.

"— We bid you eternal rest in an endless dream of separation from nature. It is the land of extinction into which we mercifully send all our failures.

"— We release the dreaming of Earth from the nightmare of mankind. We set you, the living spirit of the human world, free as you have always wanted.

"— We release you to dart and dance and battle and seek contentment among the mirages you summon from the air that your mouths have warmed and chiseled into words."

Then there was a long silence.

Ogden felt another question rise in Drowden's heart, felt it form into words. "Was it all for nothing?"

He answered from the thread of light that joined their hearts together. "What good is in your legacy enriches the ages. But the path you take into this false future is cold and soulless. Your kindred are doomed to abandon too much of your humanity on this false journey. First to go will be sympathy, then kindness, then honor. Next you will shed truth and responsibility. The further down this barren road you go, the less your heart will seem worth carrying along the way."

Ogden felt the question in Drowden's aching chest and answered. "I will unremember all the words you taught me, Drowden. They are not real things to cling to in the stream of life. They are anchors forbidding a voyage beyond their depth, forbidding life itself.

"Drowden, you will unremember me and our paths that crossed in time will be uncrossed. You will be swept into a different future, down a different branch of the river of time. When you look back, the bend in the river will conceal me from you."

"I will remember you," Drowden's heart sang out.

"What you remembered of me today will be forgotten tomorrow. What this troll touched in your yesterday will be untouched by memory tomorrow."

"I want to remember you. I will never forget you!" Ogden felt Drowden plead.

Ogden sighed in body and heart. "If you do remember me, you will be called 'mad' in the eyes of other men. They will not remember, and they will not believe there were such things as trolls. The one who remembers what others can't will be an outcast. You don't want that."

Then Ogden spoke sadly. "There are so many people without joy. No one is permitted joy without bowing to those who guard the spell of words against the truth. But that is not true joy. Joy comes from seeing what is and telling the truth. When that is the voice you follow, life is real."

Drowden's heart cried out, "Let me be mad! Let me be a brigand, a thief, a beggar. I beg *you* not to erase my memory of you. Leave something of you with me!"

Ogden said, "That would be unwise."

"Can love be taken from memory?" cried Drowden's heart.

Ogden was silent. Time inhaled and held its breath. Then he spoke again. "I will not leave you without something touching me, and I you. I will leave you a trace remembrance. Your own words, in a notebook that you carry even now. In it will be words you have written, but they will be without power to conjure this troll or this world again. The crossroads of time that once joined our worlds cannot be opened to each other again once they are closed."

There was what seemed an eternal silence. At last and finally, Ogden mumbled, "Here in this eternal place, and in every moment that went before, we will always be together, though memory be lost."

Drowden's heart cried out again, "What future do you send me to?"

The voice of creation replied through Ogden again. "The one you chose for yourself. Whether or not your fate can change is in your hands. But it seems even honest men like you cannot resist the temptations of Ventego."

Ogden could feel the shame rise from Drowden's heart. It danced like static on his scalp. If it were possible, he would have wept.

"Don't grieve, Drowden. We part as friends. But we part because we must. Your children will forget the magic of sod, flames, wind, and waves. They'll live in a make-believe world apart from the water, away from the forests, out of the rain and snow and hiding from the fire that burns in them. They won't know where food comes from but will eat what they are served. They will be enchanted by new words that have no connection to real things — nor will their thoughts about them. They will not see what we have seen of life and the world that is alive. They will be separated from all that. They will do everything in their power to feed Ventego. That is the path you have chosen to lead them down."

Ogden's voice paused, but only for an eternity. Then it spoke again.

"Your children will learn, from one generation to the next, a tangled web of deceit, and they will be deprived of the comfort and joy of a nurturing life. They will know the echo of the voice of the dead — not as Troggles know the dead, as wisdom holders who live among us and change with the days of our lives. Yours will remain dead, captured in their best moments between the pages of books both great and minor."

Ogden knew Drowden's desperate heart and understood his despondent unspoken question. He would have said, "But we don't worship our ancestors."

And Ogden answered, "No, your people belittle old wisdom, while they obey dead tyrants. Their commands live on in lawful lies, not life. But more wisdom stands at the grave's edge looking in than all the quoted thoughts of judges and lawyers now looking out."

Then the voice in Drowden's head was quiet, as if considering what to say next, weighing and deciding whether to talk or cease. Eternity enveloped the moment like a sea surrounding a reef of living stone. The next time Ogden's voice was heard, it spoke prophetically.

"Drowden, I have this fate to tell. Your kindred have been granted eternal freedom to pursue their folly. It is not our wish. It is the demand of your own souls. We have opposed you mightily in all of it, but we cannot halt the will of creation to grant you freedom even in idiocy."

The voice paused again but briefly and resumed. "Your kin enter upon a time of great undoing. Children will mock their parents as naïve, unclued about the world that cunning, self-serving men are creating, beyond your control. Their parents will not share the sayings of the Old Ones with the young. Wisdom will die and cleverness will reign.

"Your people will learn ever more witty ways to chain the elements of earth to their desires. They will save memory of each new technique for enslaving nature in spells bound in books and in other devices of shadow magic. Each generation will combine and recombine these enchantments.

"From every iteration they will build new devices, thinking they will make the days easier, but they will toil endlessly to purchase these mechanical slaves with their time and sweat, and from them they will have no contentment.

"Always they will be-live they are at the vanguard of creation and each new great thought conjured by their alchemists and philosophers will in time be proven wrong. But each grand idea will be held in reverence during the age of its ascendancy. And each will as surely be discarded in favor a newer one.

"They will cobble from the Earth amusements made of all its metals and they will take its burning waters to make carts that run from place to place without a beast to pull them. One for every man and woman they will make so that byways are full and crowded and walking might be quicker and more pleasant.

"They will surrender the hearts and minds of their children to charlatans and hucksters and allow the young to gaze long hours unrestrained into charmed crystals that speak and teach them things both false and devious. They will be artless.

"They will wreak devastation in the forests and mountains and pour poisons upon the ground and into the very water they drink and the air they breathe.

"They will forget the wisdom of their ancestors and the hopes of their children. In short, they will continue to sleep in the hazy twilight of a word-worked trance. And the world will descend into misery.

"They will… they will… they will all these things to be."

Ogden fell silent. He felt pain rising in Drowden's heart. It sang a discordant lament that reverberated along the silver cord of light that joined them.

"Whatever doom is ours for all our evil acts," cried Drowden's soul. "I don't want my children to forget what is good and what is to be cherished. And I do not want to forget you, Ogden."

Ogden replied, his voice bold and commanding. "I bring to you a great anamnesis — a remembering of things that never were — a whole new past and a world you will be emerging from when next you wake. We grant you a merciful forgetting of things that once were true to men, though men were untrue to them. Because love cannot be unremembered, and love cannot be utterly parted from our hearts, we must grant you this justice:

"Your heart will always know something precious has been lost even though nothing is ever truly lost. From this night until forever you will not remember that the troll, Ogden, was ever in your life."

Ogden paused and took a deep breath of cool autumn air. Then he said quietly, "There is one chance, one road that could undo this fate. It is this..."

Drowden's spirit leapt above the gravity that weighed it tombward, and it cried out a song of hope: "Yes! What must I do?"

Spoke the words of the troll: "When all has come to pass; when memory of me is gone and all the past is different than the one you have forgotten, then, in a different life, you must find and befriend the one and only someone who remembers this troll very well. That someone is the very one you would have killed in this frozen moment. And you must befriend him not from necessity but from a caring heart. Then there is a chance we will share the world together again."

"Yes, I will! I swear it! I will!" cried the essence of Drowden's being.

"Then, if you do," the voice in Drowden's mind replied, "you and some like you will once again be embraced by the family of life. But both you and he whom you befriend must first convince the larger part of your spell-bound species to return to the fold of the living. And you must teach your young to carry this mission onward, through generations. For it will be for some long years that the spirit of Nature withdraws its breath from you, awaiting the final days wherein what you call 'reason' leads you to doom, if you do not succeed. You and those you teach have until that last moment in your story to amend its outcome. Do you understand?"

As these last words from Ogden to Drowden Erebus were being delivered, in that same timeless instant Ogden was speaking to Ospin Tapple.

Ogden seemed to hover in the air above a smallish body suspended in mid-hop in the air. Looking down at the moment Tapple's high, squeaky voice was expelling a banshee-like caterwaul of terror, Ogden was whispering to him, and his voice filled Ospin Tapple's awareness from every direction.

"Our children are among you," said Ogden. "The children of men and trolls walk your streets, plow your fields, sit at table and dine with you."

Some part of Ospin Tapple looked with fear upon memories of wide-browed cousins and playmates from childhood, those who used their left hands to write, offspring of respected families who became poets and artists, the shunned ones who quietly left, not to be heard from again. Somewhere in Ospin's head he heard himself cry out "Liar!" But Ogden's voice returned with even tones.

"You hate what you are and hunt all remnants of that you wish to hide from yourself. From us nothing is hidden. That is why you want to kill us."

An aching shaft of remorse pieced Tapple's heart. Ogden knew it to be a jumble of sorrow and self-pity. He said, "Though you do not deserve forgiveness from us, we grant you the grace of being able to forgive yourself.

"That cannot be while we remain. And so, I depart in peace. Your life will be more brittle. It will be harder than you have ever known. All things are more difficult when the truth is traded for cozy falsehoods. And yet you long for the comfort of a guiltless heart above all else, and this we grant you. But the price will be the loss of all other comforts. Through this trial your peace will come."

Terror upon terror descended on Tapple's heart. The curved blade in Drowden's hand suspended in time above his head, and the fate with which Ogden now anointed his remaining days — they shocked him to his soul. He had eternity, but only the briefest moment in it to decide. In the end it was up to Tapple.

"Ospin Tapple!" Ogden's voice intoned. "It's you who have so fully deceived others to see not what's real but what you want to be real. Lies have been your poetry, your religion and your oath. Our place in this world is coming to an end. I am the last of the Troggles upon this good earth, and no man will remember me once I am gone.

"But this will be your curse, for you deserve it: Only you will be spared the forgetting of this world and the remembering of a false past. Only you will remember these days, this night, and all the days and nights that went before.

"Try as you might, you will not forget the smallest part. Try as you will, it will be impossible to persuade any others that the truth you know and remember is not a lie. You will say that trolls once lived in your midst, and no one will be-live in your words. Your utter aloneness in your memory of the truth will be more than you can bear. I fate to you a life of be-living what no one else be-lives, since from your lips have come such lies that have stolen the breath of life from so many."

"Is there no escaping this fate?" Tapple's heart cried out.

"Only one," came Ogden's answer. "Make a good man be-live in your truth. Trust him who your heart has feared and hated. Give him reason to trust you." He said no more.

Miles away in the Manor House at Ironwood, Nathan Bladic stared mindlessly as he lay on his back in his soft bed. No thought touched his mind. To him, time had stopped, and nothing moved. The stars he knew hung above, frozen like ice crystals on a celestial pond. He saw them through his bedroom ceiling and thought it funny he could see them. He didn't know why.

The echoes of the forest, the clack and squeal of widow-maker boughs about to fall, the wind in the leaves of birch trees, the late autumn crickets, all fell silent.

Despite the darkness and the sense of nothingness that touched Nathan Bladic, there was a presence that seemed to stand not a distance off, but instead within his own body, in his head, an unknown doppelganger, an intimate companion who strained at his own muscles, saw through his own eyes, felt his own heartbeat and his own shaking knees and tightening abdomen. He was not alone. No. Not at all.

A voice foreign and yet familiar whispered in his right ear:

"You fear what you hate and hate what you fear. You want whatever isn't yours as protection against what you fear. Want to know where you went wrong?"

Nathan's spirit seemed almost more eager than Drowden's to reveal itself. "I didn't like me," his words said. "That's the truth of it. Do I have to tell you why?"

"Tomorrow will fix everything for you," Ogden said. "Be-live it."

To the side Ogden said in a quiet way, "I erase me and we remove ourselves from the nightmare you embrace."

The ghost of nature that inhabited Ogden reached like plant roots through the loam of time and touched more than many; it touched us all.

In a rough cottage several hundred yards down the road from the Iron-wood Manor House, a hulking figure, half human, half Troggle, stood trans-fixed, listening to the same voice that spoke inside Nathan Bladic's head.

It said different but similar things, and then departed, leaving no memory of having made this visitation, but changing utterly the fate that would befall Traunton, Bladic's foreman.

Simultaneously, in the far hills east of Irongate, on the plateau that rose out of a valley between them, on the periphery of an ancient ring of stones, Argis stood frozen in time, in a place where a bloody battle had just been fought. An expression of resolve was chiseled on his unmoving face. Then he heard that same voice others were hearing at the same time, and he listened.

"Earth and sky and mind are one. We the Troggles feel this truth each day. Time is an endless wheel, not a line as some imagine."

He spoke some kindly words to Argis, but then departed, leaving him like all the others without memory of him, and recalling a different and never be-fore remembered past.

Hector, Bill, Tom and all the other surviving men of Hapstead simultane-ously heard Ogden's voice conveying personal messages to each of them, but none could see him, and none would remember him in the days to follow.

Thad Krebbermoting, Cornelius Baldegger, and the living men of the Brotherhood heard that same voice and each received a message that spoke individually to their hearts. Some tried to respond, but heard their responses interrupted by a loud voice that intruded like the wind and echoed in their ears. "Glance at me!" it said. "Let your heart see me." And they did. And they listened. And they forgot.

Ogden nodded and said to each one, in various ways, "It is hard to bear the tears we've caused. We release you from that pain."

Once he was done having these discussions he lay down and rejoined his dreaming body. A great bolt of light and a peal of thunder descended from the sky, piercing through the crown of his head and enveloping the soles of his feet.

Ogden was consumed by the cloud that formed around his body. A glow-ing outline of his form burned images into the eyes of everyone who witnessed this vision.

As quickly, that after-image flashed into shadow. The light that had illu-minated the henge was extinguished and the forest dark swept in like a rushing tide.

Ogden's thoughts rolled heavily, instantaneously, discretely and inde-pendently, into the mind of every person who in life he had touched. His words settled like a warm wet fog, creating a torpor that snuffed out every sense. Memories ended and were replaced. And then the spell dissipated and was dispersed.

Ogden was gone.

Chapter XXXI
The Presence Of The Past

Ospin Tapple walked in a daze. As he crossed Besom Bridge and entered Irongate pedestrians stepped aside and let him walk against the steady flow of foot traffic. He was in shock after encountering one after another denizen of Bladicville and demanding to know if they had seen a troll lurking about. Had they seen Drowden Erebus and his men returning all bloodied, with the bodies of their fallen? Had they not heard about the magic and mayhem in the mountains? They reacted with surprise, sometimes alarm. He heard a woman mutter "poor man," as she veered away from him, shaking her head.

Many hours before, Tapple had awakened at the periphery of the henge, surrounded by immense standing stones. He had searched everywhere for signs of the battle. There were no fallen men of the Brotherhood or of Hapstead littering the ground. He was alone in the wilderness, shivering with fright. And so, he had turned for home, for Irongate.

As he walked, he felt in in his veins — the world around him had turned to shadows. Nothing was real. Everything was completely different, though no one seemed to notice.

He hurried down the streets and alleys to the meeting place of the Brotherhood of Troll-Gutters. He approached the big storage building with hesitant steps. A sign above the massive oak doors read "Tapple Industries," but he didn't remember putting it there.

He spotted Burl Oonep and ran toward him, grabbed his shoulder and battered him with questions. Where was the Brotherhood? Did they finish the job? Did they bury Bos Fudlow and Milky Prupe and whoever else had died at the henge? How did he escape?

Burl kept looking at Tapple with wide eyes. His mouth hung half open. At last he sputtered, "Mister Tapple, I don't understand a bit of what you're talking about!"

Tapple fell to one knee and his head lolled madly. Burl Oonep spun away quickly and glanced over his shoulder, saying unctuously that he had to go.

Tapple thought about the last words Ogden had said to him. He'd be the only one to remember any of what had happened. If he tried to remind even those intimately involved in the troll business, no one would believe him. With growing shock and horror and a terrifying sense of being completely alone with the truth, Tapple wept bitterly into his hands. For everyone else, the present was disconnected from once familiar memories. Their memories had been grafted to a different history. But Tapple remembered everything. He couldn't help remembering.

The real past, he thought, had been replaced. He understood many things that once were far beyond him. He knew that Ogden had set him apart from everyone else. Not as a punishment, but as the natural outcome of everything he had ever done and felt and thought.

And now he knew too much to bear. He knew that nature had consigned humanity to extinction. He knew that only a few more generations would live, and they would do so in a waking dream of odd normality. But there was nothing normal in it. He knew from what he learned from Ogden that not be-living in their place in nature had mortally imperiled humanity.

He thought, "Who knows? Maybe there's time." And then he thought, "But what if all the world's a dream and humanity is hopelessly enchanted and can't wake up?"

Tapple spoke to himself out loud. "I have to warn them. They have to believe me. They simply must take my word as the truth!"

Drowden Erebus felt himself falling up, as always happened when he was emerging out of dreams and into wakefulness. He heard someone talking to him, from above, and he chased after those words like a swimmer submerged in deep water, pushing against an enveloping fluid he could not see toward the impression of light above.

Drowden felt overwhelmed and giddy. His eyes rolled up into his head and he spoke one word.

"Ogden…" though he didn't know what it meant.

He awoke with a snort and unconsciously grabbed toward the nightstand for his dream journal. Trying not to think, to introduce language into his day just yet, he flipped the leather cover open, grabbed with blurred vision for the quill sitting on the table next to the book. Allowing words to rise from inside him from the receding tide of dreams, he wrote quickly.

Even as he wrote he was forgetting. He wrote of the henge, of the battle. He vaguely recalled with horror the blood lust that overtook him, but he couldn't recall the object of his hate. He wrote feverishly, with a sense of terror tightening his throat. And then the rest disappeared from memory. He lay staring into space, nothing left of his dream to retrieve. It was gone.

Drowden slipped quietly out of bed, careful not to disturb Dorina, and walked down the hall to his library. There he stood, surrounded by books that, in the new morning light, seemed strange and unfamiliar.

Gilded spines and titles in gold leaf shone dully in the dawn light with words that, at first, Drowden could barely comprehend. He approached the shelves slowly and ran his fingertips across the inlaid titles.

Gradually, a newborn consciousness swept over him like a wave from out of the sea of time. His eyes cleared themselves of their drowsy haze. An odd sense of loss sharpened in his wits. He felt like weeping and didn't know why.

Placing the fingers of each hand into the corners of his eyes, he pulled them down his cheeks, then crossed his arms and looked more closely at the first shelf of books. He focused on the gold leaf letters and squinted to read them. He didn't recognize the titles. As he flipped through one then another, he found they had nothing to do with living beings, but catalogued intriguing fossils and bones found in the local environs.

"Curious," he said out loud. "I seem to still have a foot in my dream. All of this seems foreign."

As he read page after page the words evoked memories in him that were at first unfamiliar, but as quickly as they were evoked, memory returned. He paged through one book, then another and seemed to reconstruct the memory — a life of anthropological study — as he turned each page.

The words in black and white assembled an unfamiliar world in his mind that, once read, seemed suddenly familiar and normal. Several books spoke of "Neanderthals" and Neolithic cultures long dead. There were whole texts with dozens of line drawings depicting skulls and anatomical bits and pieces that, as Drowden scanned them, left an imprint that created a cascade of memories he assumed to be personal experiences from his own life and work. He was once and was becoming anew a gentleman scholar obsessed with reconstructing the past.

Turning to his desk, he saw a stack of papers under an ink blotter, a quill and ink well next to them, and most prominently, sitting on the raised back of the walnut roll-top, a tawny skull with thick, broad brows, strong teeth, and a large, oval shaped cranium. He walked over to pick it up. Holding it in his hand, he turned the ancient bone to gaze at the eye sockets that were large and deep.

A sense of abysmal loss inexplicably overtook him. After exploring with his fingers, the place where ancient eyes once gazed upon the world, he placed the skull back on the desk and returned to his bed, where he sat on the edge and reached for his dream journal again. Reading its scribbled, disjointed entries had the odd effect of calming him, so he flipped toward the earliest entries and read from there.

He read notes that seemed to chronicle the capture of a young feral child. There were long entries about the nurturing of that child of the forest, his rapid growth and acquisition of speech. Drowden shook his head. "I don't remember writing any of this," he said quietly to himself.

He noticed that Dorina was no longer in bed. He shrugged and tossed the journal on top of the quilt, saying to himself as he got up, "Dreams effervesce like steam from a teacup."

He looked around the room, not knowing what for. He thought to himself, "Maybe my books are the inspiration for the strange dreams I've been having. I think imagination compels me to dream of a time when men lived with their primitive cousins. And here I've saved those dreams in a stream of ink."

Compelled he was, in fact, he was afraid that he might lose his mind if he didn't save those cloudy memories of dreams in his journal. A sense of emptiness roused in him a now remembered feeling that, each morning when he left those dreams behind, it was as if memories of cherished loved ones were being extinguished when he awoke. And always there was one word, one name that stood out as somehow real among the many fantastic words in his dream narrative. It was 'Ogden.'

He picked up the journal from the bed and resumed reading his own words. When he considered his other books, rich as they were in facts and theories, he knew they lacked whatever his journal conjured. The words evoked wonder. But in his library there were books that resurrected only curiosity and questions from the grave of his heart, where dreams of another life hovered like ghosts on the verge of fleeing.

Drowden stood up quickly and slapped the journal closed. He reached his right arm into the empty space in front of him like he wanted to touch something that he knew was there but couldn't see. He stood there a long time, staring and feeling very alone until Dorina entered the room and said his name. This trance would engulf him again and again in the days to come and it worried her, but nothing else seemed out of place for a while.

Elsewhere in Hapstead Manor the day had its new beginning and proceeded into the remaining years unremarkably. Argis awoke like on any other day he remembered. He had to round up the workers to get them busy building the new cottages they'd be living in up on the hill above the creek. They had to make room for the new manufactory Drowden had long planned to erect.

Many years later Argis would sit in a room of shadows in the poor section of Irongate and remember back to this day and hear himself thinking out loud "Things are gonna change."

When they did, the changes did not come from the erection of a temple of industry on the grounds of Hapstead Manor. It never happened. On that day, less than a year into the future, Argis would find himself rocking in his chair, feeling pains and nagging aches of mysterious origin. He would remember being 'let go' by Lady Dorina about a year after the day he woke up remembering a different past than he had lived. "Almost a year after Drowden Erebus mysteriously disappeared," he would recall. "That's when I noticed the big changes."

At the time, everyone blamed Drowden's sudden departure on melancholy. People couldn't help but notice his odd behavior, his disquieting habit of standing in a trance and looking into a distant place no one else could see. Some thought he simply wandered off, lost, mindless, a sad case. There were rumors that made others suspect he'd fallen in with a madman just before he went missing.

But that was all in the yet to be. Today was the day Argis woke up and everything seemed normal and quite familiar, though nothing was.

Nothing much changed for Odelia and the kitchen staff. She made meals as regularly as ever. And no one talked about Willbee or anyone else no one remembered. It was a mercy of the new times, perhaps, that no one remembered those who died at the battle of the henge. Or maybe it was just the cruelty of a certain reality. Some things and some people were not real anymore.

Out in the barn, Bill Macatee stretched on a straw-filled mattress and shook his head clear of the wild dream that seemed to have caused him to kick over the lamp from the three-legged table nearby. He was thankful it had not been lit, or he might have burned down the barn and him in it.

Safe in his bed in a many-gabled house on his Ironwood estate, Nathan Bladic emerged from troubled sleep. When he was fully awake, he had strange momentary doubts about his surroundings, the odd feel of his wife Hattie's big rump pressed against him. There was no recollection of a night of magic and mystery except for the receding tide of sleep and dreams that exposed him to the chill air of a room made familiar by forgetfulness. He moved slowly to drape his right arm over Hattie's shoulder.

Back at Hapstead Manor, Miranda opened her eyes and let inexplicable tears roll down along both temples onto her pillow. She wept quietly, not knowing why. Dorina sat on the side of her bed and took her hand. "My sweet child, whatever troubles you will pass when today is yesterday, and tomorrow is filled with promises. Think of the happy life you'll share with your fiancé when you are married."

These words caused Miranda to weep with swelling sadness. Her shoulders quavered with distress. In her dreams she had known a boy, a silly lad named Willbee. He seemed so real, but when she woke, she knew that she had lost him. All she could think was that she wanted her life to be more like her dreams.

A sound outside Drowden's window, down in the yard behind the Manor House, broke his reverie as he again stood next to his bed holding his journal and staring into space. He set it down on the nightstand and pulled back a curtain. He saw horses pulling heavily laden wagons up the road toward the yard. Quickly he sped to his wardrobe and pulled down a warm robe. He pulled that over his shoulders, tugged his arms through the sleeves, then tied the cloth belt with a knot and bow in front as he bounded down the stairs and out onto the back porch.

Drowden watched as a train of wagons kicked up dust rolling along the road into Hapstead. They proceeded through the yard and onward to the valley where the servants' quarters nestled up against Northemberly Creek.

The wagons were weighted down to their metal leaf suspension by loads of cast iron machinery, sheet metal, and solid beams that hung off the backs of the tailgates precariously. Drowden's plan was to move the worker's hovels up onto the hill nearby and then construct a hydro-mill and manufactory in place of them, taking advantage of the creek's decent down the overlooking hill.

"That way," Drowden had said when he first asked his business acquaintances to throw in with him, "my workers can run down the hill in the morning toward their work full of energy for the job at hand."

Drowden smiled to himself and thought, "When my dream is finally a reality and the machinery is up and running, I'll have time to go up north and roll up my sleeves at that new fossil excavation in the caves."

He walked across the yard and talked to the foreman for a while, then stopped by the smithy's shack to send him down the road and take an inventory of everything that came in on the wagons. Workers were assembling around the carts and horses, ready to help unload them. Finally, Drowden walked back to the house. From the porch, he stood watching the swirl of activity until he was again lost in reverie.

Suddenly he was startled by the sound of Dorina's voice calling his name not a foot away. He felt the skin on his scalp shiver. He smiled instinctively before turning around and, when he did, he clutched Dorina's shoulders and said sweetly, "Good morning my love!"

"Drowden!! Where have you been? I've been looking for you everywhere. We've got to leave within the hour and you're not dressed for the ride. Miranda's in a tizzy about something and I've been busy with her. I can't keep track of you as well. Hurry! The cart is loaded, and we'll all be waiting!"

Drowden sped past his wife with a "Yes, m' love" and into the Manor House. He dressed quickly and soon climbed into the coach, where Dorina and the children were, indeed, waiting. The driver snapped a short whip and the cart lurched forward.

Then came the long journey down the miles to Irongate. He held Dorina's hand and nodded at her anti-profundities. They slept intermittently and spoke occasionally — of Ian's impending departure to the Deepwater Boarding School, of plans for Miranda to at last meet her betrothed, Pip Skleverly, and of other things.

When at last they arrived, the coachmen unloaded their baggage at the Tilthinger Inn. Dorina, Miranda, and Ian followed Drowden through the massive doors and past the room for dining, then up the banistered staircase to their rooms.

At the lowest landing of those stairs Drowden stopped to tilt his hat to the hulking manikin statue carved of ancient chestnut wood that had stood there or somewhere in the town for as long as anyone could remember. "Ventego," he said, wondering momentarily about the origin of the cursed name associated with this disturbing apparition. Then up the stairs to their rooms they went, and soon to sleep again.

In the morning Drowden awoke and instinctively reached out for his journal, which he had placed on a table nearby. But this morning he had nothing to write. There were no remnants of dreams to recall and record. So, he rose, dressed and ate breakfast with his wife and children, and then he parted them with rehearsed pleasantries.

He met with academic colleagues in town to discuss a promising site where shards of bear bone worked with flint blades had been found. "Jewelry, that's what we think it is," a man with porkchop sideburns and a handlebar mustache shook his head. They spoke for about an hour and then parted with handshakes.

Then he was off to another gathering, this time with investors in his new industrial enterprise. They had lots of plans not worth recounting, but consequential in the ephemeral production of profit. The wide flat-top desk in the office of attorney Dradly Keepier was strewn with papers he'd spread out for the six nattily dressed men to review and sign. The sunlight pouring through

the big storefront picture window warmed the air and cast a shadow of the
gold leaf lettering across the floor in front of the desk. "Keepier, Charnow,
and Gotherd, Law Office" read the darkness surrounded by light.

"Gentlemen, that finalizes the paperwork. Congratulations: you are now
partners in contract," Dradly said and extended a hand to each of them in
turn.

"Excellent," Drowden replied. He slapped Burl Oonep on the back and
nodded to the other men. "Shall we celebrate?"

"Why not?" Corny Baldegger said too loudly. "Let's walk over to the Oil
Pump Pub on Kilter Street."

"Amen to that," Tucker Scont laughed. "They've got a brown lager with a
head bigger than Pip's."

Pip Skleverly gave a friendly shove to Tucker's shoulder as they pushed
through the lawyer's door and onto Besom Street. They walked past the hab-
erdashery, the cobbler, and the dry goods store, then turned left on Kilter
Street.

On the far corner of Besom and Kilter, by a lamp post, on a wooden crate
stood a man shouting loudly in a high-pitched, whiny voice. A small crowd
had gathered around him, and the gathering was growing by the minute as
pedestrians crossed the street to get a closer look and to listen to what the
scrawny man with disheveled clothes was saying.

His voice rose in pitch and then fell to lower tones, as did its volume. Here
and there in the milling press of men and women that surrounded him, a
laugh exploded and was answered from the other side by a shushing, answered
by another loud guffaw from the crowd, and then a shouted word, and then
another.

"What's all that racket?" Drowden asked as his cadre of business partners
stopped and turned to look from across the street.

"That," said Thad Krebbermoting, "is our own town madman. Come on.
Let's listen a little while. You'll find this entertaining," he said and pushed
Drowden by the elbow toward the throng of people.

The six men crossed the cobblestones and stood below the curb behind a wall of bodies. It was impossible to see past them or to catch a glimpse of the man speaking, but they could at last understand what he was saying. The shrill voice filled the air.

"Hear me, men and women of Irongate! It's all a dream. Look left and right. The man next to you imagines the woman next to him and you imagine both of them. Each of you listening to me hears a different voice, and each hears his own message, and every one of you believes something different from the same evidence. But nothing is impossible when everything is only a dream. Am I the only one who remembers? Don't you remember? What about you? You look like a bright boy!"

Burl rolled his eyes at Cornelius. "Raving lunatic," he laughed. And Pip chuckled in reply. They heard the madman's voice squeal on.

"This is what's real — what I'm telling you, and you have to believe me. Everything else is a dream. Everything you think is dead serious is just warm air, words, and chatter in your head. You're all guilty of casting spells on each other. And you? You're ensorcelled by your own children and kin with all your talk. Your mommies and daddies cast spells on you as children and now you can't even touch the world and know it on your own terms, free of the spell that cloaks the truth. Your eyes lie to you! Your ears hear whispered fibs. Why can't you remember yesterday? Why can't you admit that a troll lived nearby and came to this town, and that you caged him, mocked him, and he escaped? A talking troll! Why won't you remember?"

At this, Drowden's ears prickled. What the madman was saying made sense to him for some reason. But Tucker Scont snapped him out of a blank-stared trance, grabbing him by the arm and, leaning into his ear to be heard above the squeaky orator and the rowdy crowd, said, "C'mon. Let's go get that pint of lager and let this clown have his say without us."

"Alright." Drowden nodded blankly. "Let's get out of here."

The two men turned to walk away, and the others followed their lead. But Drowden walked slowly, pretending not to listen, but listening to the diatribe that continued without interruption. The lunatic jabbered on and on.

"Some of you here today want desperately to reach beyond the veil of dreams. You secretly pray for a counter-spell that will free you from this prison of inescapable lies. In future days, people everywhere will rue the day we made a slave of the waters and fire and fed the forests to our cauldrons of iron. Your children will curse you and wish you had turned away from the precipice toward which you all fly. They'll pray to the darkness that surrounds them, but no answer will come. They'll wonder why those who once listened to prayers have abandoned them."

Drowden quickened his pace to keep up with his companions, but he could still hear the disturbing diatribe ringing from the far street corner. Then the crowd seemed to have had its fill. The circle of people broke apart and meandered away. "Who is he?" Drowden asked Burl.

"Name's Ospin Tapple," he answered. "Sad case. He's been ranting in public since nobody knows when. Used to have a pile of money. Inherited more than anyone knew, but he lost it all donating to poor people. They say he went mad. Gets by on handouts. Sometimes the constable lets him sleep in the jail."

"Come back!" yelled Tapple to the dissipating crowd. "Come back! I've got so much more I want to tell you. Things that are hard to believe, but true anyway. Listen! Hear what the last of the trolls told me."

Drowden stopped in his tracks. He said aloud, without regard for his companions, "That's the dream I've been having. How does he know about it?"

Tapple called out to the street, "Ogden, they called him. Ogden, the troll. The weed that grows wild in the garden of life. Pluck it! That's all I was doing. Weeding the garden path. I was a gardener. I pruned the human shrub. Now look at me. Look at me! Am I the only one cursed with memory? Am I the only sane man in the world?"

Suddenly Drowden spun around on his heels. His face was red. Sweat broke out on his forehead and he glared intently at Ospin Tapple, who looked up with a jerk as Drowden ran toward him with loudly clacking soles on the cobblestones. He froze and stood immobilized in the middle of the street, staring directly at Ospin Tapple, with waking dreams dancing in his eyes.

Drowden took a step forward, and then he yelled out, "Ogden? Do you know Ogden?"

The air turned to ice.

Ospin Tapple's expression went from dumb surprise to abject fear. The near-death last encounter he had with Drowden Erebus on the field of battle flooded his mind. He tripped coming off the wooden crate he'd been using as his dais and he pushed off the lamp post next to it, launching into a panicked run away from Drowden along Kilter Street.

Drowden acted on impulse. He didn't know what possessed him. As fast as he could, he ran, feeling the muscles in his legs strain. His slick soled shoes slid on the cobblestones, and he almost twisted his ankle. He gritted his teeth and sprinted, hard on the heels of Ospin Tapple, with no thought for his business associates. He left them behind to scratch their scalps, rub their chins and shake their heads.

Tapple scrambled down another block, slowly losing ground to Drowden Erebus, until he reached Gilton Road, where his feet skittered on loose gravel as he made a quick turn. He ran half a block to Knob's Alley, heard Drowden skid to slow down and make the quick turn. He heard those determined feet keep running. They were catching up.

Ospin Tapple made a wide turn at full speed into a dead-end alley. He stopped and spun around to look backward. Terror filled his eyes. He looked in horror down the alley from where he'd just come. Drowden Erebus was scrambling toward him at full speed, shoes slapping the cobblestones and yelling full-throated after him.

"Tapple! Tapple! Wait! Can you remember? We have to re-member!! The land does not forget! Tapple!! Tapple!! Stop! A word!! A word!!

What more can be said must wait for another time. What once upon a time was -- has been lost in a great forgetting. This story is unfinished. Its sequel can be read in the clouds, it can be heard on the wind; it is visible in the diminishing forests, the discolored waters. It can be felt in the pit of your stomach. Who will finish this story? You will; we will. Everyone.

End

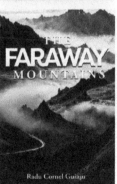